MARINER
BOOKS

Dear Reader,

Angela Flournoy published her first novel, *The Turner House*, in 2015, to rave reviews and prize attention. She was thirty years old.

Ten years later, on the cusp of publishing her fantastic new novel, *The Wilderness*, Angela has entered the next decade of her life. She is on the other side of the exhilarating, heady, beginning days of adulthood, where new freedoms, the right soundtrack, and perhaps strong espresso fueled all kinds of fun and (mostly) innocent menace. Where figuring out how to be a grown-up—with all the good, bad, and ugly that comes with it—made for tricky terrain.

For Angela, that included writing for Hollywood; getting married; losing close friends and family members, including her mother, and becoming a mother herself; moving across the country to Los Angeles and back to New York; and now, gearing up for her second novel. Writing about the wilderness period for the five unforgettable characters in these pages sustained Angela for years, as she traversed it herself. Readers will relate, either because they are in their own wilderness stage right now or remember it well . . . with a sly smile and a slow shake of the head.

And that's what makes this read irresistible. The relationships Angela writes about feel lush, joyous, sexy, complex, cozy, sometimes a mess. In a word: *real*. She *shows* us *to* us, in ways unexpected and eventually chest-clenching. She thinks deeply about both the personal and the political, with a sure hand and plenty of tenderness. It's what only the very finest novels are able to accomplish.

If you want to do this all the way right, queue up *Channel Orange* by Frank Ocean, *A Seat at the Table* by Solange, some Sampha or early Adele, a few amapiano mixes, and maybe even André 3000's flute album. Then settle in for the big ideas and feelings that Angela beautifully conjures. It's rare to see superb literary craft so poignantly embody a whole generational experience. But here it is.

Happy reading!

Rakia Clark

Rakia Clark
Executive Editor

PRAISE FOR

THE TURNER HOUSE

"An engrossing and remarkably mature first novel. . . . Flournoy's prose is artful without being showy. She takes the time to flesh out the world. . . . In her accretion of resonant details, Flournoy recounts the history of Detroit with more sensitivity than any textbook could. . . . Flournoy gets at the universal through the patient observation of one family's particulars. In this assured and memorable novel, she provides the feeling of knowing a family from the inside out, as we would wish to know our own."

—*NEW YORK TIMES BOOK REVIEW* EDITORS' CHOICE

"*The Turner House* speeds along like a page-turner. Flournoy's richly wrought prose and intimate, vivid dialogue make this novel feel like settling deeply into the family armchair. A–."

—*ENTERTAINMENT WEEKLY*

"Flournoy's knockout debut is one of those books that should, by rights, be described as the Great American Novel. . . . The book tells the story of the thirteen adult children of Francis and Viola Turner, who must decide what to do with their family house. The characters are fascinating and funny, and anyone who has played a role in the ecosystem of his family life will recognize the joys and challenges that plague the Turners. But perhaps the strongest character is Detroit itself, as it morphs from bustling modern metropolis to a potent symbol of post-industrial decline."

—NPR

"Flournoy has written an epic that feels deeply personal. . . . Flournoy's finely tuned empathy infuses her characters with a radiant humanity."

—*O, THE OPRAH MAGAZINE*

"An elegant and assured debut."

—*WASHINGTON POST*

"Poignant and timely."

—*SAN FRANCISCO CHRONICLE*

The Wilderness

Desiree, Danielle, January, Monique, and Nakia are in their early twenties and at the beginning: of their careers, of marriage, of motherhood, and of big-city lives in New York and Los Angeles. Together, they are finding their way through the *wilderness*, that period of life when the reality of contemporary adulthood—overwhelming, mysterious, and full of freedom and consequences—swoops in and stays.

Desiree and Danielle, sisters whose shared history has done little to prevent their estrangement, nurse bitter family wounds in different ways. January has a relationship with a "good" man she feels ambivalent about, even after her surprise pregnancy. Monique, a librarian and aspiring blogger, finds unexpected online fame after calling out the university where she works for its plans to whitewash fraught history. And Nakia is trying to get her restaurant off the ground without relying on the largesse of her upper-middle-class family, who wonder aloud if she should be doing something better with her life.

As the women move from the late 2000s into the late 2020s, from young adults to grown women, they must figure out what they mean to one another—amid political upheaval, economic and environmental instability, and the increasing volatility of modern American life.

The Wilderness is Angela Flournoy's masterful and kaleidoscopic follow-up to her critically acclaimed debut *The Turner House*. A generational talent, she captures with disarming wit and electric language how the most profound connections over a lifetime can lie in the tangled, uncertain thicket of friendship.

The Wilderness

ALSO BY ANGELA FLOURNOY

The Turner House

The Wilderness

A NOVEL

ANGELA FLOURNOY

MARINER
BOOKS

New York Boston

Credit lines TK

This is a work of fiction. Names, characters, places, and incidents are products of the author's imagination or are used fictitiously and are not to be construed as real. Any resemblance to actual events, locales, organizations, or persons, living or dead, is entirely coincidental.

HarperCollins books may be purchased for educational, business, or sales promotional use. For information, please email the Special Markets Department at SPsales@harpercollins.com.

FIRST EDITION

Library of Congress Cataloging-in-Publication Data has been applied for.

ISBN 978-0-06-331877-9

$PrintCode

For Candice, Latonia, and Angie.

And in memory of Renée.

I am blessed within my selves
who are come to make our shattered faces
whole.

—Audre Lorde, "Outside"

PART ONE

our high-pitched laughter was young, heartless & disrespected authority. we could be heard for miles in the night

—Wanda Coleman, "In That Other Fantasy Where We Live Forever"

2008

You Can't Pronounce It

Some descents thrill more than others. Landing at Charles de Gaulle is not thrilling, as it's one of those major metropolitan airports tucked away from the city in a way that prevents worthwhile aerial views. In Cairo, depending on your point of origin, if you sit on the lucky side of the plane you might see the pyramids at Giza brushing up against desert on one side and high-rises on the other, as if the pyramids were digitally superimposed instead of the oldest structures there. Arriving at LAX, if you're traveling west, from New York, say, you might have to wrap your head around snow-capped mountain ranges, smog-blanketed valleys, and the glinting Pacific before touching down. When the pilot announced their descent into Charles de Gaulle, Desiree looked out the window, expecting to see what? The Eiffel Tower, maybe. She saw nothing so spectacular. Deep browns and greens, the blank gray of cement apartment buildings.

They had taken a red-eye from Los Angeles. The cabin was quiet, and most shades were drawn. Nolan slumped a row ahead. His arm had drooped over the aisle-seat armrest for most of the ride, liver-spotted knuckles grazing the tube of light on the floor. Desiree had hardly slept, and when she did she felt guilty, jolting upright and peeking between the seats to check on him.

Now, at landing, her grandfather coughed. An uncomfortable cough, because it made others uncomfortable, reminded them of mortality. Anyone within earshot felt culpable. Should they pat him on the back? Call for help? Offer water? A wheezing, hacking, full-bodied affair that prompted a biological anxiety, like riding an elevator with a very pregnant woman. An awareness that something, some type of above-and-beyond compassion or physical contact might be required of a stranger toward another stranger. He brought his handkerchief to his mouth, and Desiree watched it come away dry. She decided to break an unspoken rule about how he liked to be treated in public: she handed him her half-full water bottle. He put the bottle in an unsteady grip, fingers curled tight around the cap, and drank with unsteady hands.

"I missed the little breakfast?"

He lifted the inflight menu up to his face. Still mostly smooth, save for the hairs that sprouted from the flesh-colored mole on his right cheek. His nose, beakish, kissed the cardstock.

"Like half an hour ago."

"Mm. Shoulda woke me up."

A week of firsts: first trip with just her and Nolan, first time sitting in business class, with its obscene amount of space for each seat, seats that reclined flat into little cots, and attendants plying her with food throughout. By the time she'd relented and booked their tickets, it was either business or a later flight, and Nolan wouldn't hear about any more delays, so here they were, on his dime. Her first time, and she was the only brown face on this side of the curtain. She suspected others thought her to be some sort of nurse escorting Nolan, who appeared to be an elderly white man. She was sort of a nurse, kind of. In any case, there were free cocktails, as many as she wanted, and a comforter softer than the one she used at home.

Every morning, beginning two years ago, she'd rub alcohol on his lower abdomen, secure a piece of butter-colored flesh between her forefinger and thumb, and try to be quick and neat with the needle. It marked the beginning of a new kind of intimacy for the two of them. When his weight dropped, she moved to the flap of his withered biceps, where the blue veins showed through, and finally to the underside of his thigh, where the skin was pale and pliant as biscuit dough. Six months ago, as she helped him put on his socks, she saw a black patch of skin just beneath his heel. No bigger than a kumquat. She reached for it, palm upward, and Nolan jerked his foot away, curled his long toes into something like a fist. His eyes were vacant, but his mouth trembled. Desiree, who had not cried in at least five years, sat back on the floor and wept.

Prior to him needing help with insulin injections, they had lived together like a couple who'd long ago stopped touching each other but had never bothered to separate. They said good morning and good night when the occasion arose, sometimes ate meals in the same room, and discussed unavoidable household matters, such as needed repairs. Nolan would not admit he needed help. He treated Desiree's return home like an imposition, refusing to hire someone to clear a space for her among the old wiffle ball bats, pool noodles, and a Ping-Pong table in the back house. She spent the first month back home covered in cobwebs and dust from making space for herself. Three years later and he was still acting surprised and a bit shy to see her at the breakfast table in the morning, as if he anticipated her leaving any day, as if he hadn't come to depend on her for meals packed away from the restaurant where she worked, as if he even kept a datebook anymore and could keep track of his own doctor's appointments.

Another airport observation: if the surrounding city has a decent black population, then a good number of them will be working at the airport. A dark-skinned, long-limbed young man whose nametag read "Ade" met them at the gate to push Nolan's wheelchair. They'd packed light, one duffel bag between the two of them, which Desiree carried, plus Nolan's portable dialysis machine, which Desiree rolled. This was supposed to be a quick trip, and he would not allow her to bring anything that required checking. It was the first time in her life she felt excited at the thought of her grandfather's musky, menthol-and-sage smell seeping into her clothes. Two shirts, three pairs of socks, and one pair of jeans. Desiree had rolled up five pairs of panties tight and tucked them into her messenger bag.

Ade parked the wheelchair on the passenger-pickup curb, and Nolan cleared his throat, which was Desiree's cue to tip the man. But he'd insisted she wear a traveler's money belt under her shirt, so the cash was strapped tight around her torso like a girdle. The seconds that passed as she fumbled for the money were too awkward for Ade to bear. He smiled big, ducked his head a little, and took a step toward the sliding doors.

"Merci, merci," Nolan called to him. "Désolé, we're sorry."

Ade put a hand in the air, brushing away the apology, and turned back to the terminal. Nolan's gravelly, outdated Louisiana French was bad. Cartoon skunk bad. Desiree couldn't even speak French and she could discern that much.

"Already acting like tacky Americans," Desiree said. Her grandfather didn't hear. She'd said it in that special register—loud enough to be heard by most, but not loud enough for Nolan—that she used when he was embarrassing her in public.

Their driver pulled up, hustled out of the van to help Nolan out of his wheelchair. A chubby, balding white man too cheerful for so early in the morning. Nolan held a file folder with all the papers for their itinerary and a few maps from the Triple-A office off Adams back home. For more than a decade he had not made a single plan, not even dinner plans. He delegated when necessary, but he would not organize an event. Birthdays and holidays came, he blew out candles and thanked Desiree, her sister Danielle, and the neighbors for coming, but not once did he request a gathering, propose an outing. What others planned for him, he enjoyed. Now Nolan was Mr. Plans. He sat up front in the van, chitchatted with the driver in his rudimentary French, spread his map on the dashboard.

The driver merged onto an expressway. Its cement walls bloomed with graffiti. Words—some French, some English—juxtaposed with names and images. The name Farouq bubbled out in a harsh burgundy at a forty-five-degree angle. A buxom, black-haired woman planted one orange stiletto on the nipple of a pink pacifier. A wide swath of gray paint bisected the image, someone's vain attempt to impose order on the wall. Or perhaps the artist desired a clean slate but ran out of time to finish the job. Desiree would lose herself in this jumble of shapes and messages if possible. She would wait for the van to slow down, pull back her door, and step into traffic. Jackrabbit her way to the thin shoulder. Disappear. There hadn't been time to prepare for what she was doing here. She hadn't thought about how hard it would be to do alone. But private as her grandfather was, she'd known better than to try to invite anyone else. He hadn't even invited Danielle.

"I wanna go to the Tuileries," Nolan said. His voice was a croak.

"Say that again?"

"The Tuileries, the garden, Desi. I said I want to go to the Tuileries. Today."

"You want to go to a garden. Today?"

"That's what I said."

"For what?"

"To have a look at it. God-lee."

"Alright. I'll figure out where it is when we get to the hotel."

Nolan rapped on the map on the dashboard.

"I know that already. Can't miss it. Ain't that right, Michel?" He put a hand on the driver's shoulder.

"Yes," the driver said. He kept his eyes on the road. "Ask anybody at your hotel."

Desiree wasn't sure if the driver's name was really Michel, or if that was the name her grandfather had created for him, some less objectionable albeit still inappropriate form of "garçon." He liked feigning familiarity with strangers, a completely new approach to being in the world that he'd picked up in old age. She couldn't recall him being so chummy with folks he barely knew when she was growing up. Back then Nolan lived by a steadfast "never wear out one's welcome" philosophy, which extended far beyond the usual sorts of wearing out a kid might undertake—too many sleepover requests, say—to include speaking too much to acquaintances in general. It was as if he feared he'd bore everyone to death, and therefore opted to say very little. He'd encouraged Desiree and her sister to do the same.

He liked to be alone back then, to drive alone. He hoarded Thomas Guides. He would buy a new one each year even though the particulars of his usual routes were rarely updated. The outdated editions crowded the trunk of his car, an ancient diesel Mercedes that smelled like cigarettes and cracked leather. He would pick Desiree and Danielle up from the airport and make one of them navigate through Inglewood back to Leimert Park. The flight from Oakland to LA was short, not even an hour, but the flight attendants always called Desiree and her sister brave for doing it on their own. Desiree spent a lot of time back then regarding her grandfather, trying to decide whether he liked her or not, whether she and her sister were summertime burdens getting in the way of his golf and zydeco parties. Then they came to live with him for good, when she was nine and Danielle was almost fourteen, and it didn't matter if they were burdens or that his golf clubs grew a caul of spiderwebs in their corner of the garage, because Desiree and Danielle had nowhere else to go.

Nolan planned to kill himself in Switzerland. He'd paid over seven thousand dollars, not to mention nearly five thousand dollars on flights and accommodations, to do it this way. With dignity, he said. He was still young in Desiree's eyes, but it turned out that he was old enough and sick enough to elect to die. He would not lose an entire foot, having already lost two toes and that black portion of his heel last spring. He would not breathe through a tube, he would not have others bathe him, and he would not wear a diaper. He was too old for a new kidney. He had no interest in watching himself waste away any more. And now he seemed determined to have a grander death than he'd ever had a life. Desiree thought this made him similar to his sisters back in Louisiana. Auntie Lena and Auntie Jo had wanted white-and-gold caskets and expensive jazz funerals with horse-drawn carriages when they bit the dust, one after the other during Desiree's late teenage years. Their deaths had been the biggest parties ever thrown in their names.

Desiree and Nolan would take a train to Zurich in the morning and settle into a studio apartment in the city. A physician would come over, take a quick look at him, and make sure he was close enough to death's door to die. Then Desiree's grandfather would leave this world via a painless injection. She'd have a few days alone in Europe after that, and she had promised him she'd do something nice with his ashes on the continent, but she had not even thought ahead to where she'd sleep the night after he was gone.

"I have the papers from the doctors with me now," Nolan yelled into his cell phone, an expensive international kind he'd had Desiree hunt down back in LA.

He was speaking with his Journey Guide from Eternus, the assisted suicide organization. A dumb name, Desiree thought. It sounded like "eternal," but also "internal," with a macabre sprinkling of "interred" and a communal "us" tacked on the end—or was the "us" supposed to make it sound like Latin? On its website, Eternus promised a "dignified transition into death for the terminally suffering." That sentence alone would have made Danielle tsk and giggle, Desiree knew. Danielle would say she'd seen death plenty of times on rotation. "Death ain't dignified, and if it is, that lasts for about ten minutes," she'd say. "Then it starts to get nasty."

Danielle had been the one to find their mother, Sherelle, dead in her own bed from a heart attack at the age of forty-two. A nonsensical, gruesome death. Danielle had known that Desiree, four and a half years younger than her and scared of everything, an easy crier, shouldn't see their mother that way. She called 911 from the bedside table and sat on the floor against the door, blocking Desiree from coming in. Desiree screamed and kicked and screamed on the other side.

What did her sister look at for the twelve long minutes it took the ambulance to arrive, when it was just her and the bedframe and their mother, close by and getting cold? Where had she decided to focus her eyes? Desiree wondered. "I don't know. The floor," her sister always claimed. "You know Mommy always kept the floors real clean, even under the bed. I probably just looked at my own reflection." After they moved south to LA, Danielle announced she wanted to be a doctor when she grew up, and Nolan, who made it a habit to never appear surprised by them, had said, "Well, how bout that, then?" and now she was.

The receptionist at the hotel check-in asked them if they'd been to Paris before, and Nolan launched into a story about being stationed there during the war and a little after. How he'd been a company clerk, keeping inventory of things—"They wouldn't let too many of us fight back then, but clerking got me on the accountant's path"—then a supply-truck driver.

The lobby was small, just a counter roughly Desiree's wingspan, and two armchairs wedged near the front window. Nolan leaned against the counter, flirting for no clear reason.

"Spent my time mostly in the fifth and sixth," he said. The receptionist nodded. Fifth and sixth were the troop numbers or the arrondissements? she wanted to know.

"Arrondissements. Right around here. Had me a girlfriend and everything," he said. "Couple girlfriends." His eyes went a little glossy, the way they did when he got worked up telling a story.

Had Desiree ever heard this story before? She couldn't remember. She knew he was in the war in Europe and Africa; she'd seen his enlistment and discharge papers, which confirmed that he'd been honorable and the military confused (someone at some point had decided he was Hawaiian before deciding he was Colored). She expected to one day soon get an American flag folded into a triangle delivered to her from whoever took care of that sort of thing.

"My granddaughter here, she's still figuring out what she wants to do," Nolan was saying. "Nowadays in America the young folks gotta take their time."

Nolan wanted a jelly doughnut. And a box of Lorna Doones. And a box of Parliaments. And steak picado. The cigarettes were easy enough, but the rest of the list sent Desiree running all over the Latin Quarter while he sat hooked up to the portable dialysis machine. What she found was a currant-filled profiterole, a box of Petit Écolier, and steak and frites. She brought all of this with them to the Tuileries, which was not the prettiest nor the greenest garden in Paris, the receptionist mentioned on their way out, but Nolan either didn't hear her or didn't want to hear.

Desiree found a spot under a tree and not too far from the sidewalk to park the wheelchair so that they could eat. The garden had wide promenades and prim lines of sculpted shrubbery. The bushes reminded Desiree of the sculpted hairstyles women in the south used to wear—a pile of pom-poms, a cylinder with its top sliced off at an angle. Like the Bronner Bros. hair competitions, or that movie *B.A.P.S.*

Nolan directed Desiree to stand directly in the middle of the park, between two fountains, in line with the pyramid of the Louvre, and then to slowly turn around. She did what he said, saw how an obelisk lined up with an arch, which lined up with her own body and the pyramid. "All that symmetry," he said. "Very French." He nodded to himself, as if that explained everything.

The park was nice enough, not too crowded with tourists. The sand on the walkways smelled a little like kitty litter, but no one could deny the beauty of the park's design. The rows of trees stood rigid and regal. Desiree couldn't look at Nolan while he ate, so she looked at two kids pushing paper boats in a fountain. It had been years since she'd been so complicit in his bad eating. Back when she first moved in, after she'd dropped out of culinary school, she hadn't known the extent of his sugar problem—no one had, not even Danielle, who made it her business to be in other folks' business. Desiree had picked up the things he asked for when she went out, thinking nothing much of it until she found him collapsed on the kitchen floor one morning, cruller in hand. There hadn't been a grain of processed sugar in the house since.

"You don't have to scowl," he said. "This is my last meal. My first last meal."

"Who's scowling?" Desiree swiveled her head around. "Nobody's scowling."

He held out a french fry until it was right under her nose, trembling. She snatched it and put it in her mouth. She hadn't eaten since they landed.

"Mmm-mmm. Desi don't do sweets, but Desi sho love taters," he said in a voice much more country than his own.

She laughed, and allowed herself to face him a little more. Her lawn chair was lower than his wheelchair by a few inches; her eyes met his trembling chin. She ate some more fries. Across the way, at the fountain, the mother of the two boys was holding the smaller one by the waist as he leaned over the water for his boat. A corner of her pink hijab got wet and turned dark.

"You should have let me bring Danielle," Desiree said. "She should be here too. Imagine me alone tomorrow, after."

Nolan stopped trying to unwrap the box of cookies with his teeth. He said nothing for a while. Then he said: "This is the kinda date I always wanted to have with one of them French gals way back when. Just a good time sitting in the park. But I was scared for no reason. Thought somebody might have said something to us. You heard about colored fellas getting caught up like that over here, lynched even, but that was more in the countryside. Still, I never risked being in public."

The mother had sat back down and was staring at nothing in particular as her boys, boats forgotten, chased each other and kicked up dust. Nolan got the box open and bit down on a cookie, eyes closed. There was a time when Desiree would have rolled her eyes at Nolan, reminded him that nobody would have even known he was not white had he gone on a date in public, but there was no point in doing that now. Maybe there never was. It was about what he believed, and where he was from. And who knows what others had seen when they looked at him back then.

"Danielle woulda been better at talking to all the Eternus people than me, you know," she said instead. "She coulda helped."

"Mmm," he said. "I shoulda tried to stay here longer. But I met your mother's mother soon as I got back, so that wouldn't have worked out, huh?"

After the park, he just wanted to drive around. He had a list of places, some no more than residential street corners he thought he remembered, others landmarks everyone wants to see: Eiffel Tower, Sacré Coeur, Notre Dame, Panthéon. They passed them all in an accessible van, the cost of such extravagant transportation, Desiree tried to forget about. In Montparnasse, Nolan told the driver to pull over near a corner, in front of what looked like an apartment building with a big red door. He was next to Desiree in the back seat this time, and she saw him sit up straighter, as if he was going to move. His eyes misted up, and his mouth opened, but then he changed his mind and they were off again.

They sat in traffic, their high perch in the van making the Smart Cars look like toys. He turned to her, said, "You know, you're not gonna get all the money you should on account of me doing it this way."

This man is determined to make this miserable for me, she thought.

"Nobody wants your money, Granddaddy."

He laughed.

"Hell, I want my money, but I heard it's not worth a lot where I'm going."

Where was he going? Heaven? Hell? Desiree's hell would be what she imagined as his heaven: a golf course in the sky.

"I'm just trying to—what do you call it? Manage expectations." He pulled out the last Petit Écolier from his pocket and ate it, then dabbed at the crumbs sprinkled on his shirt and ate those too.

They drove through an area crammed with African hair-braiding shops and African restaurants. Huge signs hawked international calling cards and what she took to be skin-bleaching creams. Brands like Fair & White couldn't feasibly be anything else. Crenshaw on steroids, Desiree thought. She missed home, and then regretted even thinking about home. Nothing in Los Angeles would feel the same after he was gone, not even things that had little to do with him, like her job. How could she go back to setting down plates, rolling silverware, and counting out cash after this? It might be better to move to Cleveland and be near Danielle, but Danielle would not likely stay in Cleveland after her residency. Desiree had never felt this unmoored before, not even as a child after her mother died. There'd never been a question about where they'd live back then, Nolan being more of a father to them than their biological father, a man who had left Sherelle when Desiree was not yet born, remarried within the year, and moved to North Carolina by the time she was four. That man, Terry Joyner, with his new wife and new children, had long been a stranger, was a stranger while Desiree was yet in the womb, such that her mother did not give her his last name. Danielle Joyner, after Terry, and Desiree Richard, after Nolan. Sisters with surnames that spoke to their mother's heartbreak, her anger.

She'd seen Terry fleetingly when her mother was alive and exactly twice since her funeral. Each time, Danielle had been cold to him, and Desiree had dutifully followed suit. Their grandfather rarely brought Terry up, unless one counted the moments when he'd be upset about the cost of something—a school dance, maybe—and remind them that he was the only provider they had. This bothered Danielle more than it ever bothered Desiree. He was right, Desiree always thought. They didn't belong to Terry Joyner, but Granddaddy Nolan belonged to them.

Back in the hotel, alone on the bathroom toilet, Desiree tried to think of a good reason to stop Nolan from doing what he planned on doing. The bathroom was tiny, just like the room itself, and she could rest her head against the side of the sink. She wasn't religious like Danielle, who'd recently abandoned the Catholicism they grew up with for Baptism and would have given all of the obvious reasons. It being the gravest sin, the will being God's, etcetera. More than anyone, Desiree knew how small her grandfather's life had become. He dressed everyday with her help like he was going to golf someplace. He ate a little, pretended to watch TV a little, then sat on the front porch and watched cars drive by until lunch. He was in constant pain. After lunch he usually took a nap. Then he woke up and waited for Desiree to return with dinner. That was all.

"Michel said there's a good place for crepes around here," he called now through the door. "Said all the students love it."

"Uh-huh," she said.

Through the crack where the door met the floor Desiree could see the light shifting in the room. He was shuffling around, too anxious to sit still.

"Or we could just drive around some more. I got more places on my list."

She said nothing. He had a short coughing fit but got through it alone, so she stayed where she was.

"I know you're tired but you can nap when I'm dead. Heh-heh."

Mr. Plans, Mr. Fucked-Up Jokes. He was somebody else now. One of

Nolan's favorite retorts when Desiree was trying to get him to understand why he needed to do a thing, like stay away from churros, or wear those extra-tight blue medical socks, was "I don't have to do nothing in this life but stay black, pay taxes and die." She hadn't thought that he meant the death part was elective.

"Come on out now, Desi, gotdammit. This is all already bought and paid for. If your sister wanted to be here, she would be here. If she ever wanted to be here, she would gotdamn be here."

Desiree wiped, flushed, washed her hands. When he got very angry, or worried, Nolan tried to curse. It never sounded right.

What would it feel like? She imagined the brain, knowing what was to come, giving itself one last run-through, flipping through memories like a deck of cards. The synapses on fire. Or, maybe not on fire at all; maybe the brain would be calm and death a velvety tongue taking its time, whisking in and out of the folds of gray matter, smoothing over patches of regret, and alleviating fear. The Journey Guide—she still could not believe this is what they called themselves—had assured them via email that Nolan would go to sleep, like any other aide-induced sleep, but this time never wake up. Desiree knew sleep could be restless, even when it appeared to be the opposite. Plenty of times after she got off from a long shift at the restaurant, she lay still in her bed but tossed and turned in her mind, her anxiety about some stupid mistake she'd made manifesting in her dreams. And what if Nolan dreamed? Would that dream, recurring, become the theme of his afterlife, if that's what happened next? She couldn't remember a dream, not even a pleasant one, that she'd like to take with her to whatever came next. Well, maybe one: The dream where her mother lives. Lives to walk with her on the beach, to wander grocery aisles, lives to do anything with her at all, maybe just sit side by side. That dream still felt good enough, old as Desiree was and long-dead as her mother had been. Maybe Nolan had a dream like that, too. Maybe it was the same one, with the same woman at the center of it.

She opened the door and reached out her hand.

"You can't do it without telling her," she said.

Nolan sighed. He handed her the phone. She punched in the only number she knew by heart. Her sister's.

She could hear someone announcing something over a PA in the background. It was six a.m. in Cleveland, and Danielle was already at work.

"What? I can't talk right now. Why are y'all just hanging out at three in the morning? Go to sleep."

"No, we're not in LA. We're in France. He's . . . I'ma let him talk."

She held out the phone. Nolan looked at it, then held his hands up and shook his head. He turned, shuffled away.

"He can't talk right now. Sorry for calling."

"What? Wait!"

A two-toned chime, either from an elevator or a door with a sensor, on Danielle's end.

"Alright, I'm on break. Don't hang up. What are you talking about? Where are you?"

Four years shouldn't have been enough of an age advantage to establish complete authority over a sibling, but Danielle had established it, even before their mother died. She was born bossy, and Desiree born compliant. She could avoid her sister for months, but she couldn't lie to her.

"He's gonna kill himself tomorrow. Or actually somebody else is gonna do it but he's gonna die. In Switzerland. He already paid for it all."

"Desiree . . ."

"He's a grown man and he's old and he's in pain, so—"

"Is he of sound mind?"

"At his age and with his health there's people who will do this for him. There's even some people in America, but that's not what he wanted."

"Desiree . . ."

"He wanted this big adventure and how could I tell him no, huh? He's grown! And he never goes anywhere, and planning this has meant a lot to him."

"Desiree, listen to me."

"I'm listening." Her head hurt. She'd said everything in a whisper.

"I'm asking you if he's of sound mind, Desiree. Can you answer that affirmatively?"

Why was she talking like this?

"He's the same as always. Don't do him like he just stepped into the ER from the street. You know him. He's sharp."

Another muffled announcement over the PA.

"You can be sharp and demented at the same time, especially in the early stages."

"Demented?" She closed the bathroom door again. "What the fuck, Dan?"

"Don't curse at me. I'm saying that he could be suffering from dementia and you could be aiding and abetting him when you shoulda been getting him care."

Desiree sat on the edge of the tub. What did dementia even look like? He knew who he was, where he lived.

"So now I'm a criminal? Jesus Christ. See, this is why he didn't wanna tell you—he was of sound enough mind to know how you'd react."

A long, exasperated breath on the other end.

"This is my area of expertise. If it was taxes or golf or food plating or whatever, I'd defer to y'all."

Desiree had wanted her to be here, but why? It had nothing to do with the actual elements Danielle would add to the situation and everything to do with an attempt to assuage future guilt for leaving her out. There would be no assuaging.

"You don't gotta insult me," Desiree said. "I get what you're saying. But this isn't him getting lost on the way back from the corner store or something. This is him researching, writing out checks, signing contracts, faxing papers, remembering the names of everybody we're gonna see in Zurich, finding hotels. It's a whole operation he executed, the most I've ever even seen him use a computer! And at this point he's allowed to be an expert on his own fucking body, okay? I just thought you should know."

Silence in Cleveland, followed by a big exhale.

"I asked you not to curse at me. I don't know what else to say. Y'all are gonna do what y'all are gonna do. You clearly don't want my honest input."

"That's not true—"

"When he's gone, though, you're going to be the one who has to live with it, Des. You by yourself. Just think about that some more."

"I will. I have."

"Okay. Great."

Danielle hung up.

There was, of course, another way, many other ways to help him. She might vow to take him out more, make him an online dating profile, finally learn to golf, get pregnant. A great-grandbaby on the way might mean something to him. He had been a good father, she knew, doting on Desiree's mother, his only child. He could be a patient teacher, and he didn't mind making fun of himself, which was especially important when raising girls. But even with a great-grandbaby en route, he'd still die soon. He'd already wrapped his mind around it, and after arriving at that kind of certainty, no amount of cajoling would make it worthwhile to leave the where and when and how a mystery again. Nolan never did well with uncertainty. Neither did she, not really, which was partly why she was twenty-two, waist-deep in student loans with no degree or certification to show for it, and waiting tables. Hard to take a step forward when anything could be lurking in the future. She wasn't dating, hadn't been for a year, and she wasn't in school. She didn't have much more to look forward to day by day than Nolan had. If she subscribed to the justifications that she'd given Danielle, that he was old and had no future, well, better to not think what the latter reasoning meant for her.

"Hello? Don't be rude, Desiree."

The waiter loomed above her, a white towel over his bent forearm. He was tall and thin and gray, a look of calculated dispassion on his face.

"Water is fine, thank you," she said.

"No, we're having wine," Nolan said.

He touched the wine menu, ordered without opening it: "Bordeaux, s'il vous plait."

"Now you're just showing out. You never drink."

"Not recently, but historically. And this is a historic trip." He smoothed his napkin open on his lap. "How you think I got diabetes, just off doughnuts?"

The waiter returned with a bottle and poured. Nolan raised his glass.

"Cheers!"

Desiree kept still. Nolan leaned toward her, his eyes narrowed.

"You know I didn't bring you along so you could bring me down." He said this between his teeth.

She had always wanted to get along with him, to not wear out her welcome. While she had not been as impressive as Danielle when it came to grades or extracurriculars, she had been exceedingly well-behaved, and she had learned that good behavior counted for a lot with Nolan, as did making him feel like he was doing a good job raising the two of them. It was a lesson Danielle never learned. She was often indifferent to his awkward overtures, talked back to a man who loved to have the last word. Danielle and Nolan might spend weeks barely speaking to each other, until Desiree could figure out a way to broker peace without hurting anyone's pride.

The tablecloth was scratchy where it touched her hands in her lap. This place, with its vintage romantic feel—black-and-white tiled floors, deep red leather banquettes, gold-accented chandeliers—could not accommodate a scene, or maybe it could, but a steamy lover's quarrel, not a tiff of the kind they'd create. A young woman and her octogenarian companion, very clearly not in romantic love. She raised her glass and sipped her wine. It tasted like wine, which she knew nothing about, having not yet come around to drinking. There was the customary shot of tequila at her restaurant, shared among staff before each dinner shift began. Desiree always gave hers away, usually to her friend Nakia, who'd gotten her the serving job two years ago. Nakia came from money and had been drinking since high school. Back then the two of them would steal the little bottles of liquor that Nakia's father brought back from his work trips, but Desiree never actually drank hers; she stored them under her bed.

They ordered dinner. More steak for Nolan, trout almondine for Desiree. Nolan must have ordered a starter when she wasn't paying attention because the server set down a squat cylinder of raw meat topped with a raw egg. Desiree had enough home training not to make a face or bring her nose down to sniff the food, but she let out a small, childish yelp when Nolan punctured the yolk and dug in. Nolan grinned, his too-white dentures spotted with bloody meat. She buttered her bread and watched him eat in silence.

Aiding and abetting, Danielle had said. Funny, legal language. From time to time over the past few years Desiree had wondered whether her sister and grandfather had colluded in some way to keep her homebound. It wasn't a rational suspicion—she was grown, after all—but why didn't they ever push her to try something else? The three of them had never discussed the convenient set of circumstances, how Desiree's dropping out of culinary school just as Nolan got less able to fend for himself made it possible for her to take care of him. Neither Nolan nor Danielle had encouraged her to move out again, to get back on track, any track at all. They never raised the possibility of some other arrangement. Hire a nurse? Downgrade the two-story house in Leimert Park to one more manageable for an old man? Options never broached. Her own false start, which now felt like a failure to start at all, had been right on time. If anyone had aided and abetted anything, it had been Nolan and Danielle. They ceased pushing her, as they had pushed her in high school when she became uninterested in applying to college, but they should have kept on. She was a mere twenty years old when she moved back home, a young dummy. Much too young to be left to figure things out for herself without a few good nudges. Why hadn't they nudged?

The server returned with their entrees, both of which relaxed in a shallow pool of butter. Nolan gripped his knife until his knuckles shone white and began sawing at his filet, pushing mushrooms to the edges of his plate in the process.

"Say what you wanna say, Desiree. It's now or never."

She ate a forkful of buttery fish. At least this one thing was perfect.

"I'm fine."

"Like hell you are. But fine, I'll say this: I'm surprised your sister didn't ask to say goodbye to me."

She swallowed, refilled her wineglass.

"You walked out the room when I tried to hand you the phone. You're not surprised."

A series of micromovements from Nolan: a shrug, a shake of the head. He coughed for what felt like a whole minute. He wiped his mouth and left a red smear on the napkin. From the meat and the wine, Desiree told herself.

"Did she ask for me again?"

"No."

"Well, there you have it. Only mama, daddy, grand-whatever she got on this planet and she didn't wanna say goodbye."

"She didn't wanna condone what we're about to do."

"Shit. *We* aren't about to do anything. I am." He worked a piece of steak with one side of his mouth. "You know what? If you feel so guilty, you can just put me on the train. In the morning just help me get settled on the train, then go on and stay here. The people from the company will be on the other side anyway. Then it won't be your fault."

Desiree shook her head. He didn't really want that.

"I don't know why you're mad at me and not her," he said.

"Who said I have to choose?"

Nolan's eyes got wide. He laughed. Water squeezed out of the corners of his eyes.

"You can be mad all you want, but helping to kill a granddaddy is a lot more natural than burying your only child, or what you think is your only child, anyway."

She swallowed her food.

"Excuse me, what?"

"Nothing."

Nolan and Danielle had this in common: they'd halfway say something, then leave it to dangle, giving the listener the job of piecing together the hidden information, of drawing out the revelation or confession. It drove Desiree crazy. It was power, this withholding. She always felt obliged to show interest in information that might cause her harm, to be complicit in the telling. But what choice did she have?

"What do you mean, you think she was your only child?"

He said nothing. The waiter cleared their plates and Nolan ordered a booze-soaked cake. It came with its own bottle of cognac, to drizzle more booze on top if desired. Of course Nolan desired.

"I'll tell you this: There was a fella from Charlotte in my army unit, a doctor's son. Black as midnight." He poked at the cake with his spoon. "He got a girl pregnant over here and she tracked him down back home, somehow got a picture of the brown baby to him. Let's just say if it was me, a janitor's son, one who'd probably give you a baby anybody on this side of the world would take for French-French, you might not do much tracking down. You might just say the father is dead, find a new man and get on with your life."

"Are you just saying or are you actually saying, Granddaddy?"

He didn't answer. He sniffed the spout of the cognac bottle then put it back down. He waved for the waiter and wrote a squiggly line in the air for the check.

The sky still held a little light as they got back into the van, the Parisian twilight a periwinkle miracle that Desiree understood to be one she'd likely never see in the exact same fashion again. She wouldn't ever come back to this city, she thought. Nolan had the driver do laps once more. His riddle of a response at dinner explained the extravagance of his choosing to die this way—one last visit to the site of a former life. Did he know he had another child or did he just assume he might? Her own father might one day talk to his new children in such an elliptical way about her and Danielle: "Let's just say I had two daughters back in California . . ." What cruelty.

Would she even want to see Terry Joyner before he died? She didn't know. A foreshock of the guilt and grief she'd endure tomorrow washed over her. They drove on.

Desiree woke when the van stopped. They were at the same corner in Montparnasse where they'd stopped during the day, in front of the same red wooden door. Nolan didn't move. He looked at the door, then away, then back again, then kind of smiled, then ground his teeth. Desiree watched him. Where was he?

"Who lived here?"

"Buncha girls," he whispered.

Desiree unbuckled her seat belt.

"I'm gonna go and see."

"No, no point," he said.

She went anyway. There was no buzzer, nothing to push or ring as far as she could tell, so she banged on the door—a courtyard door judging from the hollow sound her fist made—and waited. No movement, no lights turned on. She returned to the van, buckled her seat belt.

"It wasn't really their house," he said. "I just want to sit here a bit and remember. This ain't about you, Desiree." He didn't sound angry or impatient, which was its own rebuke.

"Alright. We can sit here, then."

The driver stepped out, walked a few paces up, and lit a cigarette. The cell phone in Desiree's purse vibrated. Danielle. She ignored it. She watched Nolan stare at a door.

The train ride from Paris to Zurich is smeared gray. No sun, nonstop rain. This makes the green of fields look greener, the dots of white from sheep's wool a shock. Desiree and Nolan doze, having beat the sun out of town.

She dreams of being in a car with her mother and Danielle, a car she doesn't recognize by looks, but it smells right, like stale french fries and cigarettes. She recognizes the freeway: the 5 headed south, almost to the Grapevine, if the topography can be trusted. They must have been driving to Nolan's from Oakland. Both she and her sister are relegated to the back seat. Despite the fact that Danielle looks like she did when Desiree saw her six months ago—grown, serious, no fun—they must somehow still be young in this dream. Smoke from their mother's cigarette clouds the car because she won't roll down the windows in the rain. Desiree wants to tell her mother something but she can't speak. She opens her mouth and nothing happens. A kaleidoscope of crazy colors outside: turquoise, fuchsia, electric blue.

Her mother speaks: "Whichever one of y'all can figure out this song first wins."

She doesn't specify a prize. She stubs out her cigarette, rifles through a pile of tapes in the passenger seat, and plucks one out. Adult-child Danielle sits up straighter, cradles her Game Boy in her lap, and waits.

The opening chords are obvious; the doo-doo-doos haven't even come in yet when Desiree tries to blurt out the title, but she still can't make a sound. Not even a whisper. Maybe she has laryngitis. So Danielle beats her, yells, "Smokey Robinson, 'Tracks of My Tears'!" and without thinking, Desiree shoves her, hard. Danielle's adult-child head smacks the window and she screams. Guilt rushes in. Desiree feels the car veering to the right, pulling over, and she braces for punishment, whatever form it might take. Her mother grabs her shoulders—how did she get into the back seat with them so quickly?—and shakes her. With so much force that Desiree wakes up.

A man's face is close to hers, his hands on her shoulders. White man in a blue uniform, minty breath. The ticket scanner from hours earlier. His expression, his eyes-wide panic, tells the whole story. She knows what has happened before she turns to look.

They, she, has failed. Nolan's whole body is slack, his head droops too low to the left, his mouth flecked with white dribble. His jaw swings leftward too. He's gone. People are crowding and saying things in French English German and it all means this: they failed. People make her move from where she is sitting, across from him with a little table in between, because these people need the space. She stands on her toes behind the train staff and looks. People touch his neck and wrist and nothing. His hands, bigger and more gnarled than they were mere hours ago, upturn awkwardly in his lap, elbows pinned into his sides, nails clawing the air. Grass-green veins. Above his head, out the window is black-black, which means the train is in a tunnel, underground. Which means they are maybe entering the city, close to where they are supposed to be. Close to the last step of all his planning. But Desiree and Nolan are not there yet. They will never get there now.

2018

Uptown

It was freezing and I had on that leopard-print beanie from Canal Street that you hate. You had a Dramamine patch behind your ear, but it wasn't helping. You kept burping and hiccupping, and saying you were okay. Remember what the tour guide said about the river? It had been filthy from factory pollution and sewage in the early 1900s, and it wasn't until it got really bad that people got together to do something drastic. They reversed the river's stream to clean it up. Imagine people in Chicago doing that a hundred years ago, with technology being where it was. Or today. Seems impossible, and to be honest I haven't looked it up, so maybe it's not true. But I keep thinking about it. If you want to reverse course, you have to do it, literally. Stop going where you're going and go another way. That's how I feel right now.

Faint light crept through January's curtains, the sun not quite ready to rise. If she took a deep breath in and out she might see a cloud of condensation in front of her, but no need to confirm the obvious. Too cold in here.

Her bed had no headboard, so she sat with her back against the wall, head titled forward lest the oil in her hair make a stain. She picked up her phone, put it back down, picked it up, scrolled. So many places not like here. Warm, easy places. The regular offenses didn't prickle today: people she used to know who weren't exceptionally bright or talented or ambitious but owned homes here and there back west, had full adult lives and bank accounts and lawns. That was fine for them. She wasn't them and that was fine. Her thumb landed on a picture of her friends, an image from Nakia's highly curated feed. They were in Martinique without her, spending euros as if the exchange rate favored them, enjoying free and easy travel while one still could. The three of them looked ageless and aspirational, wading in the shallow, glistening shore of a golden beach that appeared to be private or remote. The photo could be used to sell hair products, skin products, water-resistant sanitary products. An image destined to be reposted and re-hashtagged within an inch of salience, its original meaning and intention stretched thin and worn through: #melaninonvacation, #blackgirlsdotravel, #brownandblessed, #afropuffsandpassports, #sisterswithsavingsaccounts. Inanity disguised as ethos, assembled to encourage targeted spending. Even January in her weaker moments might consider buying whatever the photo was capable of selling.

She hadn't planned right. That was nobody's problem but hers. Nobody's fault, but it felt like it should be. How seductive to place the blame elsewhere. The others—Desiree, Monique, Nakia—had been more careful, and she had been what they thought she was: an easily distracted Aquarius, a bit of a mess. They had at least been considerate enough to book their trip so they'd be back for her birthday. January had not yet planned how she wanted to celebrate it. She wanted to be above the desperate need to celebrate, to be celebrated, to have a "special day," but she was not. As she approached thirty-three, she felt the same unreasonable expectation of delight and the fear of possible disappointment that she'd felt at six, when her mother, June, planned a party for her at the Chuck E. Cheese on La Tijera. The possibility of her school friend Angela M. showing up had electrified her. Angela M.—for Mendez or Muñoz, she could no longer recall—was haughty and aloof at age six and a half, with green eyes and long, sleek plaits. She arrived with her mother, and January savored the sunshiny sensation of being the recipient of Angela's smile. Angela and her mother had arrived early enough to hear June and Nelson, January's father, bicker over the cost of pizza, with Nelson even raising his voice at one point, but they pretended not to notice.

She didn't have to do anything about the lack of heat—really, only so much could be done with her landlord—but ethically, she supposed she did have to do something about her own hunger. It just felt so good to lie there, the rumblings of trucks down Frederick Douglass intermittent this early on. She visualized the inside of her fridge: a slimy bag of old spinach, graying ground turkey she'd bought for enchiladas two weeks ago and neglected, a large tub of sour cream likely polka-dotted with mold. Her plan had been to hibernate, to sleep through this day if she could. Awake, her thoughts kept sliding to the unimaginative Worst, fueled by old History Channel–induced fears: jackboots, registries, conscripted military service, books ablaze. "Nigger" back in common parlance, even—why not? These thoughts had advanced and receded at irregular intervals over the past year; they were bound to be more frequent today. Monique would call January hysterical when she expressed these fears out loud, not for thinking the Worst was possible under this president, but for thinking that insidious forms of the Worst had not already been occurring. "Black folks already been to all seven levels of hell in this country," she'd say. "This fool ain't even scratching level one." Why would we want anyone else to go through the hells we've been through? January wondered now.

Just to the corner, then. The fish spot on 130th always seemed to be open. She hadn't combed her hair in over a week—it was a tangled clump of thirsty curls. She patted some oil on her edges and tied a twisted scrap of fabric into a headband, tried to convince herself her afro looked purposeful, not ashy. She picked up her phone and notebook, then put her phone back down. Morris might call, or her mother might. The thought of hearing either of their voices made the roof of her mouth tingle with nausea. But the thought of leaving her phone behind was unbearable. Someone worthwhile might reach out to her, one of the girls, maybe. She slipped it into her coat pocket.

One floor beneath hers, apartment 3C's door was open. Somebody had moved out in a hurry. A heap of plastic hangers in one corner, an old sock, once white, now gray with dust, moldering against the wall. January stepped inside. 3C was a two-bedroom, whereas her apartment was a studio. So much space in here. The unit felt warm, the radiators doing the work hers shirked. Whoever had lived here had been here for a long time. The old kitchen, with its cracking subway tiles and skirted sink, hadn't been updated in at least thirty years. Had she seen them during her month in the building?

January spotted a photo on the refrigerator door. It was an old sepia portrait, affixed to the fridge with an El Barrio Dentist Studio magnet in the shape of a tooth. January's mother had boxes of these kinds of photos, of long-dead relatives, mostly descended from her own mother's white father, January's great-grandfather, a penniless, jazz-loving Okie who came to Los Angeles with not much more than the one box of photos, settled near the clubs on Central Avenue, and fathered two children with a much younger black woman before disappearing. January hadn't looked at those photos since she was a girl. In this photo on the fridge, an older woman in a pillbox hat and floral dress smiled closed-lipped while holding a small, light-colored poodle on her lap. The poodle's fur called to mind the Cowardly Lion. A spaniel mix. Why would anyone leave this photo behind? There were lighter square and rectangular outlines on the fridge where other notes and photos and magnets had been snatched down while packing. This might have been somebody's grandma or auntie, long passed on. Or maybe it was nobody, a vintage photo picked up at a stoop sale. January took the photo down and put it in her pocket. She left the tooth magnet where it was.

A hurricane had hit the curb outside. A jumble of old furniture pieces, disassembled just enough to get them through a doorway. Trash bags bursting with clothes, others overflowing with the kind of detritus a move creates, and a stack of pots and pans. An eviction, then. After so many years in one place, a mad scramble to pack up and get out. Or a death, maybe. It was a wonder they'd left so little upstairs. January tried again to conjure up a face, an elderly body slowly pulling itself up the stairs, maybe, and could not. A month ago, when she signed her lease, January had sensed some sort of exception being made, the landlord's broker likely not expecting someone named January Wells to look like her but lacking the audacity to cancel the meeting on the spot. The broker was suddenly downplaying the merits of the apartment, as if he hadn't written the hyperbolic ad she'd responded to online. He pointed out how loud the housing projects across the way could be, and how a fourth-floor walk-up with no laundry in the building would wear her down over time. This not being her first New York City apartment hunt, she'd brought the completed application, a color-printed credit report, a letter of recommendation from her old landlord, cash for her application fee, a money order for the deposit, and a little extra cash should he come up with another fee on the spot, which he did, despite the apartment having been advertised as "no-fee," for something he called a "key transfer." She could envision apartment 3C's replacements—they would not be old, and if the broker could help it, they would not be black.

The fish spot on 130th was closed, no hours posted on the windows. January's phone said it was 7:25 a.m., which was earlier than she'd thought. The baby might have been conceived on a morning like this. January had always been an early riser, and she'd made Morris one, too. The bed already warm, the world still quiet. If they were going to have sex at all, it usually was between six a.m. and eight a.m. A couple of weeks before Thanksgiving, it had to have been, before their lease was up. She had reached the end of her IUD's three-year lifespan earlier that fall, had it removed, and dithered regarding replacing it. She wasn't the sort of person to take a pill every day. That morning she hadn't told Morris to get a condom, and because she didn't say anything, he never reached toward the dresser, as if engaging prophylactics was her duty alone. There seemed to be a growing list of things that had become her duty alone, ranging in importance from folding the laundry to making sure he called his own mother on her birthday. To an outsider, it still appeared that Morris was the more responsible of the two of them, the general manager of their lives, but it was actually January who had become the overseer of their affairs.

The sex had been fine, as it always was—a hiccup of an orgasm, not even as full-bodied as a sneeze—and he'd gone off to work. When he returned that evening, she told him she wasn't following him to the new place he'd found in a high-rise in Fort Greene; she'd be getting her own place.

"I wanna live close to the girls again," she'd said.

"I need to find a way away from you," she'd meant.

Morris had responded as he always responded to January, as if she were a precocious child making decisions that she hadn't really thought through. "Can you afford to live by yourself?" he wanted to know, and she didn't answer, because they both knew she couldn't, not in any way similar to how the two of them had lived for the past few years. January's list of graphic design clients was growing alongside her online presence, but it wasn't enough to cover an apartment like the one they were planning to move into, with its in-building gym, in-unit laundry, and in-living-room views of the top of One World Trade Center, thick, angular, and boring off in the distance. She'd stared at his back as he loaded the dishwasher, willing him to be angry, to be anything other than concerned for her ability to take care of herself. "I'm not angry," he said, as if reading her thoughts. "We can talk more about this later."

November dragged on and he never brought it up again, confident that she'd change her mind. They didn't have sex that final month, but dry spells sometimes happened and Morris was busy at work. It was possible he hadn't noticed. January searched for and found a new place, probably a 320-square-feet plastered-over crime scene, but in Harlem, close to her friends. When the man with a van arrived to carry her things away a week before Christmas, Morris had seemed confused, as if he'd forgotten the day would eventually arrive. But he had too much pride to try to change her mind. He let her go.

She heard the M10 bus trundling down Frederick Douglass and hustled to catch it at the corner. A typical Saturday-morning crowd hogged the seats: mothers and their children, Seventh-Day Adventists looking Sabbath-sharp, aunties in headscarves running errands, people in OSHA-approved black work sneakers coming home from night shifts, and one potential walk of shame, judging by the slinky dress and off-kilter wig. January grabbed a pole near the back door. The light through the windows shone amber. Frederick Douglass was not as wide as Lenox Avenue, but compared to the cramped thoroughfares of Bed-Stuy it felt like the Champs Elysée. So easy to see what was above you and in front of you. Out front were yellow and green taxis, folks going about their morning business. A group of European tourists in chic athletic wear huddled over a map on the corner. If January focused straight out the front window she could almost ignore the lurching of her stomach.

At 125th Street the bus filled with transfers from the subway. A group of women, younger and whiter than usual at this hour, got on first then crowded up front. The bus driver urged everyone to keep walking back to make room for other passengers. January turned around. Moving to the very back meant she'd feel more of the bus's swinging and bumping.

"There's no fucking way," she muttered. She squeezed her eyes shut.

"You can sit here." A woman behind her stood up. Her hair was cut into a close fade and she wore black jewel stud earrings. She reminded January of Brandyn, the woman Nakia had dated back when she lived in New York—erect posture and high cheekbones, a masculine edge.

"Oh no, I'm alright," January said. "I'm just going to 118th."

The woman gave her an "I insist" smile, lips pressed together. Am I showing? Impossible. It's just a friendly woman on the bus. People are still friendly. She smiled at the woman and sat down. The group of white girls stood in the aisle right next to her now, a few of them clutching rolled-up handmade posters. Glittery teal words from the inside of one roll caught the light for a moment, and January turned her body to the window to avoid reading what it said—something peppy and just barely political, she guessed. It felt like eons since she'd held a poster like that herself, not a mere year. She pulled out her notebook.

Late last night she'd written:

I'd never even thought about the kind of person I'd like to have a child with because the only person I know anything about is you. That would be like having an opinion about water or air. But it turns out it's actually important to have an opinion about both of those things.

She crossed that out. Too cute. She pulled out her phone and texted Desiree:

Planning to tell Morris about baby today, FYI. Writing a letter to drop off at his apt.

By the time Desiree found wi-fi on the island and replied, January hoped to have already mustered the nerve to do it.

Men in headphones held down the three two-tops in the coffee shop, each one sitting by himself. This left the high-top communal table, which was not ideal for writing letters or fighting nausea, but January took off her coat and draped it over a stool before heading to the counter. The theme of the shop seemed to be steampunk-meets-coffee-colonialism. The walls featured framed posters of Victorian-era patent applications for devices—medical or culinary, January could never decide—alongside photos of brown people in coffee fields labeled KENYA, INDONESIA, GUATEMALA, and ETHIOPIA, people who presumably supplied the beans for the shop. Each element of the décor wasn't noteworthy on its own, but slid toward the offensive edge of absurd when put next to the others. An illustrated IMMIGRANTS ARE WELCOME HERE poster was taped onto the lower corner of the front window.

She ordered oatmeal, two croissants, and peppermint tea, then sat back down to wait.

I hope by now it's clear that separating was best for both of us. We probably would never have become fully realized adults if we didn't experience independence. We'd have always been halfway there.

This wasn't bad. Not necessarily where she should start, but it could fit somewhere farther down the letter, after some easing in.

She pulled out her phone, tweeted: "The hardest thing about being a black woman attracted to men is convincing yourself you deserve better than just a 'good guy' with a 'good job.' 'Stable' is not a personality!" Four likes within three minutes. Six likes. She put the phone back in her pocket. She waited three minutes, checked it again. A solid fifteen likes. She deleted the tweet. This was becoming a regular pastime for her: saying something mildly controversial on the internet, then running away from it. She told herself she did this because she only tweeted from the profile she used for business, and J22 Graphic Design wasn't yet profitable enough to be political. But even innocuous tweeting threatened to suck up a significant portion of her day. In the summer she'd made a plan to tweet at least five times a week, mostly links to relevant designs or to articles with advice about creative brand-building that she hoped would attract future clients. She also slipped in a few corny jokes. The platform seemed to reward corny jokes. It worked: she surpassed a thousand followers and earned a couple new gigs. Now she found herself logging on throughout the day, monitoring others' reactions to whatever quip she'd made, as if the likes were a small fire she could stoke through vigilance. Every time she checked a recent tweet, she edited it in her mind. Should have used a contraction to save space, shouldn't have deployed two different hashtags. The rest of the day, while she ate, worked on a website, texted the girls, or talked to her mother, the particular assortment of characters she'd published online would play on a loop in her brain. It was no way to live, she knew. She was here, on this stool in this coffee shop, but always in conversation with a bunch of people elsewhere, some of them very likely not human beings. On top of that were the constant reminders that the Worst was nipping at society's collective heels. Atrocities, natural catastrophes, the dissolution of common decency. Always something new to hate, someone who deserved derision and ostracism. Always somebody murdered, somebody murdered, somebody murdered. Their gone-too-soon faces everywhere, overly familiar. No way to live at all.

The man across from January had red hair that was thinning through the middle, a wiry beard, freckles, and large pudgy hands, though he wasn't pudgy in build. Their eyes met for a moment. His were gray. January smiled tightly then looked back down. The barista called for her to collect her food. She ate two spoonfuls of runny oatmeal, then abandoned it for a croissant, which she finished in three large bites. She ate the second one even faster. Crumbs rained down onto her lap. She jumped off her stool, did a little shimmy, then sat back down. The quick movement threatened to bring her food back up her throat, but she took a big breath, sipped her tea, and the feeling went away.

She never considered cutting back on Instagram. She loved the quick glimpses into others' lives, the opportunity to gawk at and evaluate their aesthetic choices. Why would that veterinarian she knew from college think a somber black-and-white filter suited a photo of him and his French bulldog? Why would her cousin Tyson think the best place for a selfie was the driver's seat of his Honda, with his stained seat belt still buckled and the camera angled up his nose? January reasoned that there was also useful inspiration to be gleaned—interesting color palettes, interior design and fine art trends that could feasibly be applied to a web page layout. Of course, on occasion, the same feeling of inadequate display, of insufficient performance, of missing something found her there, too. Case in point: Martinique.

This was not the first trip the girls had taken without her and it wouldn't be the last. In Thailand, they had cavorted with elephants, and Monique wrote a sanctimonious post on her blog explaining that "actually, riding them is cruel." In Abu Dhabi, a trip for which they'd capitalized on a fare glitch to fly to for cheap, Nakia had uploaded photos of them covered from head to toe—and only slightly costumey—in front of opulent mosques. With the exception of Monique, who had just gotten a cushy librarian job at a university down South, which meant she could now afford more trips, Desiree and Nakia had always had more money than January. At this rate, they probably always would. Maybe this trip rankled because of how well they'd curated their photos, the travel influencers they all followed having rubbed off on them. They looked lightweight, carefree, and unbothered by the things that were riling up poster-wielding white girls on the bus and making everyone else move wearily through the winter streets.

Desiree had posted a new photo since January had last checked: her zebra print–manicured fingers around a shot glass half full of clear liquid. The caption read: "Tí punch and Zouk. If you know you know." If you know you know? January had no fucking idea. Come to think of it, this trip had been January's idea—how had she ended up sidelined? Back in September, the group had been lamenting the impending one-year inauguration anniversary via chat. How futile standing out in the cold had felt that first time around, side by side with people who had not marched with them those other times for those other worthy reasons. How they had pretended their feelings weren't hurt to see that nearly all the other non-white women marching had also somehow missed the communiqués online about wearing a pink hat and the instructions on how to crochet them.

January had texted: We could just leave. Go someplace warm and not American.

NAKIA: YES! Preferably with Blacks/browns.

MONIQUE: Yesssss to an escape plan.

MONIQUE: But do we feel comfortable calling brown folks browns?

DESIREE: LOL don't change the subject. We goin on vacay!!

Nakia, being Nakia, had volunteered to plan, which was her way of ensuring the food at their destination met her standards. She set up a flight-discount alert and looked into a vacation rental. By early October everyone was committed, time off from work approved for those who had the luxury of paid time off. Everyone except January, who had put off mentioning the trip to Morris, because large purchases made from the joint account had to be jointly approved, and she didn't want to hear him express doubt. He would ultimately support her going, probably, but not before a lot of hand-wringing about whether she really should be going to the Caribbean during the height of the expensive tourist season, and whether she wasn't being irresponsible in some way since she no longer had a nine-to-five. It was bullshit. Large purchases had to be jointly approved, but not his Hugo Boss suits, which he claimed were a business expense, a single one of which easily added up to more than a weekend trip to Martinique. She'd sat on a bench in Central Park in mid-October, her laptop on her knees, the day weirdly warm but the trees still resplendent in their customary jewel tones, and realized that she couldn't bring herself to ask him. Outside of general financial frivolity, she understood that her true offense would be spending what he considered his money in pursuit of enjoyment that did not involve him. The realization had made her feel lonely.

By December everyone else had booked their flights. By the end of December, Desiree was the only other soul who knew that January was pregnant. The Saturday morning that she shared this news with her, January stood at Desiree's stove, whisking butter into grits with one hand and shaking a hot pan of shrimp with the other, while Desiree scrolled on her phone. Morris was at the gym. "I mean, our eggs are old, technically," Desiree had said. "We'll figure it out." She'd climbed down from her barstool, hugged January from behind. January felt capable, more capable than she had in a very long time.

"Storytelling really does have the power to change lives," someone was saying now. "I think we can all agree on that." It was the man with red hair and chubby hands. He was on a video call on his laptop. When he paused to listen to whoever was speaking on the other end, the tight pull on the corners of his mouth suggested impatience. He sighed. It smelled like he'd drunk Guinness for breakfast: tangy, hoppy, slightly vaginal. January hunched down over her phone.

Oh, wait, Desiree had actually posted two photos, in uncharacteristic rapid succession. The algorithm had buried the second one down January's timeline. Photo two: Desiree beaming in a strappy tangerine two-piece next to a palm tree that was nearly parallel to the ground, its roots holding on thanks to some sort of tropical magic. The twinkling surf stopped centimeters from Desiree's heels. This photo did not make January upset. Who could ever be mad at Desiree while actually looking at her? Somber, grave, responsible-too-early-in-life Desiree. She deserved everything, that body that never aged (though she needed to stop slouching), even that bank account. January had wanted to be near her from the day they'd met at a Fourth of July barbecue in Inglewood. It was January's first trip home since following Morris to New York, and she felt anxious that this many young folks could ever come together, drink booze, and smoke weed without the event ending in violence. She chided herself—must have been her late nineties/early aughts South LA PTSD flaring up—and vowed to make at least one friend. She had been working as a junior analyst for a bank on Wall Street, her workdays spent scrolling through one spreadsheet after another, her coworkers mostly male, mostly interested in working their way up the corporate ladder by putting in more hours than necessary, or even healthy, in January's opinion. That Fourth of July she had not been ready to admit that corporate life wasn't for her, but she knew she needed to find friends outside of work, friends without that particular kind of professional tunnel vision, even if they lived on the wrong coast.

Desiree had been standing by the taco man but not in line for tacos. She clutched a red cup and watched the tortillas being laid out on the grill, flipped once, then sprinkled with the perfect amount of pastor.

"It's lowkey mesmerizing, right?" January had said.

"I'd buy a video of this happening on a loop and watch it every night before bed," Desiree had said.

"Mmm, like ambient ocean sounds but better."

Desiree had smiled at her for a half second, then her face corrected itself, settling back into a shy frown. A sad girl, January could tell. Being a sad girl herself, but better at hiding it back then, she was drawn to this sort. They were braver for wearing their sadness so openly, unworried about whom it might repel. January bubbled on the surface, smiled a lot and joked a lot, but underneath it all she felt how Desiree looked back then: wary and weary. Standing at the side of the grill, she drew Desiree out by parsing the virtue of King Taco over Tito's Tacos, French dips over pastrami, Dulan's over Chef Marilyn's. Then they partnered up for a game of spades, and January discovered that Desiree was as decisive and cutthroat as she considered herself to be at the table. They beat everyone. That was almost ten years ago now.

"Right, I get that," the man across the table said. "But we need to be honest in our assessment of how big this can get. Without scalability, I don't see the value, and right now the plans for scaling don't seem feasible."

So he was talking about money. She'd suspected earlier that he was using "storytelling" in that near-obscene way people did to sell things these days. Her clients, tech entrepreneurs and "creatives" alike, did this. As in, "here's a story about a widowed woman in Bangladesh who weaves shawls, and we can use her presumably sad story to 'scale' her business and make a profit while 'helping' people." No thank you, January thought. This wasn't storytelling; this was sales pitching by co-opted narrative. It was inventing some kind of fable about hard work, "regular people," and grit to inspire rich people to back you. It was walking around a stage in jeans and an expensive T-shirt in front of millionaires, saying the right thing to make them feel something for a moment and pull out their wallets. It was money-centered doublespeak, and it regularly assailed January on conference calls, which some of her clients insisted on referring to as "syncs." People who were full of seed money (and stories!) but had no actual skills. They contracted out all the real labor—they couldn't code, draw, design, sew, write, cook, or anything. But they knew how to seduce the money people, the venture capitalists and angel investors who needed "storytelling" to buy in. So they spoke in buzzwords, raked in cash, and 1099'd the people who actually built whatever product the stories were about. Once, sensing that this was the only way to not feel taken advantage of by a company building an app that made it easier for people to find mobile pet groomers, January had asked for shares of the company in lieu of money. Shares were worth nothing at the time but could maybe be worth something someday (people are lazy and dogs do get dirty, she figured), and she'd already put in so many unanticipated hours that the flat fee they'd offered her wasn't going to break minimum wage. One guy had actually laughed out loud at her request during the sync. They ended up paying her out for her preliminary work and going with another designer for the rest.

"I'm sorry, can you be quiet?" January said now.

The man on the call ignored her.

"Kiran, I think you're right," he said to his laptop. "It's gotta feel hyperlocal at the same time that it feels kind of ubiquitous."

January looked around the coffee shop for other black people she might embarrass. There was just her and a guy with short, free-form locs having coffee with an Asian woman in denim overalls in the far right corner. Oh well. She cleared her throat.

"Excuse me?"

The man's eyes rounded. He pulled out one earbud.

"Is everything okay?" he said.

"No. You're being really loud," January said. "And there are like, co-working spaces all over the city for having conference calls?"

Had the whole coffee shop just gone quiet? It was hard to say for sure. January felt hot. And dumb.

"I don't think I was being that loud, but—"

"You were. Plus, it's Saturday?" She picked up a little plastic sign that had an illustration of a laptop with a red X drawn over it. "You're not even supposed to be on your computer in here on weekends?"

He furrowed his brows at her.

She hated that her voice kept lilting up at the end of her sentences. She hated herself for being the rule enforcer when she truly didn't care about the rules. The man didn't respond. Instead he looked toward the barista at the front counter. She stood with her back to the room, sorting teabags into airtight containers. The treble clef tattoo at the nape of her neck elongated as she bent her head forward. The man put his earbuds back in and rejoined his call, a half decibel quieter. The noise in the rest of the room amplified once more, and bile rose up in January's throat.

She pushed off her stool and darted to the bathroom. A woman was in line, but the door opened right as January reached it and she squeezed by as another woman exited, slamming the door in the waiting woman's face before she could protest. Bile mostly, plus croissant and clumps of last night's lentil soup. Morning sickness. The first real instance of it. She rinsed her mouth with handfuls of water, avoided meeting her own eyes in the mirror. She knew what she'd find there—a crusty, raggedy shell of herself in a cute headband. The walls were papered with old-timey ephemera, late-nineteenth-century newsprint advertisements for domestic goods, tonics, and cure-alls. The illustrated models, in their Victorian bustles and high collars, were all white. As if these ladies ever cleaned their own floors, she thought. The gall of this place. On Frederick Douglass Boulevard! A stone's throw from legendary Strivers' Row. It was as if the entire world conspired to provoke her.

By the time January had gotten back to her table, the redheaded man had left his backpack on a stool and was sitting on the little bench outside the coffee shop's front window with his computer, continuing his sync in the cold. Good, January thought. Maybe we're not all doomed.

The issue is we've only slept with each other.

Not the whole truth. Morris had slept with plenty of women before he met her.

The issue is we've been together since before we knew what we wanted in a partner, physically and emotionally. I still don't know and I'd like to find out.

Closer, better. She'd met Morris at eighteen, when he was twenty-two. They were on the practice field before her first halftime show and her trousers were too big; even with suspenders she was constantly hitching them up. Her tuba dug into her shoulders and sweat stuck to her back. She was a tight knot of nerves under a heavy brass horn. A skinny boy with thick lips and a snare drum walked over to her as they lined up to take the field. "They say to only dry-clean those, but if you put 'em in the regular washer and dryer they'll shrink and fit better," he'd said, then weaved his way back to his section. January had no idea then that this would be Morris's favorite romantic mode: having the answers, fixing January's problems unsolicited, then retreating. Back then she'd been grateful for his guidance. She was a first-generation college kid with no clue how to exist on campus, which was not geographically far from where she'd grown up but felt distant in every other respect. Black students took themselves too seriously at the same time that they made a joke out of everything. What was funny and what read as patent disrespect mystified her. Morris gave her an older, more mature social circle, a group who shrugged off her missteps as newbie errors and allowed her to hang back and observe, the better by which to learn how to obscure one's impoverished background or employ it strategically. Morris worked at a local accounting firm until she graduated, then he got into grad school in New York. January followed him.

There are things too indelicate to put into a letter. Too crude, too cruel. Things both parties know but some time long ago agreed without agreeing to never articulate. *Your attraction to me has to do with me growing up poorer than you* was one. *You were with me because you enjoyed feeling superior to me* was another. She struck through both sentences.

I wanted to notify you that I am going to be a mother. I'd like you to relinquish your rights to being a father. I can't imagine you being a father to my child.

She dared not send it. She could not scratch it out. It was the only thing she wanted to say. But what had she done with the past fifteen years of her life if this were true? Lied to herself, and to him. It had been too hard to change things, she told herself now. It had become hard enough to wake up and get out of bed. Morris had not noticed, it seemed. Or was her complacency also part of what he desired? Somehow over the last year a single task, any task, really, had begun to feel insurmountable, futile. Send pitches, follow up, tweet slogany bullshit, invoice misers. Repeat. Try to make a dent in the pile of projects she'd promised herself she'd start. Instead she'd spent most mornings after Morris went to work back in their bed, reading the news and often in tears. One morning he'd returned unannounced around lunchtime and found her there, still in the bed, staring at the wall. She'd felt caught and began to explain herself, but Morris had climbed back in the bed in his fancy work shirt and slacks and gone down on her. She pressed the heels of her palms into her eye sockets and tried to relax. She focused on his wiry beard on the insides of her thighs, tickling, and was able to give in to him. She came, and he left. He never asked her why she was still in bed when she had claimed earlier that morning to have so many meetings scheduled. He didn't seem to care. What was that?

On her own, when she tried to figure out what she had to be so sad about, what was making her so lethargic and lazy, she stumped herself. Some kind of survivor's remorse, maybe? It was true that she spent a lot of time thinking about the random luck that had brought her from the underfunded "gifted" program in her high school to college and beyond, how many people smarter than her at that high school had not moved farther than tiny apartments in the South Bay and going-nowhere municipal jobs, but that wasn't it. Not all of it, anyway. That was part of a newer nightmare: the one where some person or event snatched away everything she had—her humble savings, her burgeoning professional reputation, the gigs she was cobbling together to keep it all going. No, the nebulous, ever-encroaching WORST had hounded her for longer than her current thoughts about money and security. So many dire outcomes. What if she got everything she wanted and it was still no easier to start her day? What if her throat still caught when she introduced herself? The WORST: she might never attain what her mother, long-divorced in Inglewood and refusing to retire until she found a new husband, had yet to grasp: a true sense of grounding, regardless of circumstance.

January had been confident when necessary her whole life. A leader, president of student bodies and BSUs. In her early twenties, the outwardly anxious and sad in her midst, the Desiree types, had perplexed her, even while drawing her in. Yes, there was plenty to be down about, but what about moment-to-moment happiness? Might that get a person through the day? The bald-headed baby on the subway whom you look up to notice is giving you an affectionate stare, the minutes on a park bench when the sky shudders from gold to pink. The cold, sweet slice of watermelon that zaps you back to a happy, chlorine-scented memory from childhood. These small moments used to buoy her for months, through career uncertainty, romantic ennui, all of it. Was she naïve back then or was she blinded now? Dread and anxiety had settled inside her brain in her late twenties and she couldn't shake them loose.

Morris was the problem, or part of it. The WORST seemed to find her more frequently when she was with him. She'd be sitting next to him on the couch, reading on her phone while he watched TV—a true-crime docuseries, or football, maybe—and she would feel like dying. All of a sudden miserable. Maybe he would be passionately talking about something—politics, rap beefs—and she'd only half listen, scrolling through articles, bookmarking them for later. He'd notice her inattention and threaten, "I can stop talking," and she'd say, "No, go on, I'm listening," but she wouldn't even look up from her phone. Then she'd feel guilty, and very, very low. Was she so self-absorbed, so checked out that she couldn't listen to her partner think out loud? Or was it that he was always talking and she was always listening, and she had finally grown tired of being his sounding board? The most common emotion she'd begun to feel in their relationship was guilt. Better to be alone, she'd concluded. Better to crawl into some tight space and be still, like a cockroach.

Where had "cockroach" come from? Somewhere she shouldn't venture. She needed to fix her brain from having thoughts like this before she gave birth. She needed to find the sunny side of the street and stay over there for good. Her phone vibrated.

It was Desiree, video-calling. January hadn't brought headphones with her but she wanted to see her friend's face. It might make her feel less alone. It would. She put the volume down low and answered.

Bright sunshine, loud wind. Light shimmered off the drops of water clinging to Desiree's braids. She had a deeper tan already and wore no makeup, no shirt either, just her orange bikini top, the straps not at all struggling to hold the weight of her tiny breasts. Desiree's natural eyebrows were thin from too much early-aughts plucking, which called attention to her large forehead. She looked exposed, and beautiful.

"You haven't done it, have you? Say no."

"I'm writing the letter right now—why?" January tried to whisper. She hunched over and brought the phone so close that Desiree could likely only see her mouth.

"You can't just handwrite a letter like this and drop it in his mail slot. You lived with this man for a decade!"

"Shh . . . I'm in a coffee shop. I just told a guy to be quiet so I gotta be quiet. I'm dropping it off today, it'll be fine."

"No it won't!"

January shushed her once more. Tinkly music with French lyrics played on Desiree's end. January remembered the picture of the shot glass of "punch" and wondered where the other girls were.

"Y'all were practically married. Morris still thinks you're gonna come back to him, you know he does."

"I don't care what he thinks. He's not my husband. And I don't want him to be the father, like legally."

"What? January . . . legally? You don't mean that."

"I do."

"No you don't, come on."

"I do. I can't be tethered to him for eighteen more years. I won't."

Desiree said nothing for a while, and January stared at her hurt face, her large eyes looking off somewhere behind the phone, her real hair drying and curling up into a halo of frizz atop her extensions.

"I mean it," she said again. "If we're not together, it'll be too fucking hard to deal with him and I don't want to deal with him."

The others, Nakia or Monique, would have asked for a better explanation, but not Desiree. She didn't care about why; she'd grown up with no father against her will, and then suddenly no mother. What a mistake. January shouldn't have answered her call.

"Listen to me," Desiree said. "I think you should sit on this for a few days. At least until we get back in town." Her voice was patient, a caretaker's voice, and January remembered Desiree's grandfather, the framed photo that sat on the mantel in her apartment. A handsome old man in a pale yellow sweater. Gone now, too.

"Can you do that? Just wait a few days."

"I don't know. I just really need this to be settled."

"I know you do. But it's gonna be hard, January. Morris has good health insurance and money, all kinds of resources a baby needs. And you know he won't just sign papers like that. It's gonna be a fight. And you might change your mind."

Why did Desiree think her so fragile? She clearly saw something in her, some frailty that January had worked very hard not to show.

"He might sign. I think he might."

She suddenly believed this deeply, though she couldn't articulate why.

"Are you okay?" Desiree asked. "You don't look good. I think you should maybe go back home and lie down. Have you talked to your mom today?"

"I—you don't know what it's like." She was whimpering. "I'm all by myself. I don't have anybody."

Desiree's eyes got larger, then closed for longer than a blink.

Instant regret. It was too hard to think of other people. Cockroaches again. A tight, quiet space to hide.

"You don't have to have it, you know.

"January? Are you listening? You don't have to have it."

"No, I'm having it. That's not a question. It's now or never. I'm having it."

"Okay, you're having it. I was just saying . . ."

She didn't finish her thought. A new song came on wherever Desiree was, a dancehall track that January had heard before in Brooklyn: "I am blessed, I am ble-essed! / Every day of my life I am blessed." She swiped at her tears with a coarse coffee shop napkin.

"I'm sorry, Des. I'm gonna hang up."

"Hold on! That's not—"

January ended the call, turned her phone off, dropped it into her pocket, and rushed back to the bathroom, making eye contact with no one on the way.

She closed the lid and sat on it, cried for real. Her stomach seized with dry heaves, then relaxed once more. She thought Morris would sign away his rights because she knew what he wanted. A stable family and existence, just like what he'd had growing up. Nobody divorced, no weekend visits. Everything on his terms. He could start over and find someone to give him all of that in no time. He could be married and expecting within the year.

Humid in here. The Victorian women on the walls mocked her. She stood up, ran her hand along the wallpaper. She remembered the sepia portrait from apartment 3C and pulled it out of her pocket. The woman with the poodle on her lap looked self-assured, more so than the nineteenth-century women shilling soaps and tonics on the wall. January found a seam in the wallpaper and used her nail to peel back a corner, wider and wider. Sticky under there; something tacky that adhered the newsprint to the wall. She smoothed the portrait onto the sticky surface until it looked as if the woman with the dog had been underneath the newsprint all along, part of some older wallpaper, maybe. January peered at the photo, then up and around the whole bathroom. No. She peeled the photo back off. Someone knocked on the door.

It was her "storytelling" tablemate, laptop cradled in his arms.

"Everything okay?"

"I'm pregnant," she said. "So, no."

He blinked several times. A reassessment.

"Oh, ohhh. Do you need, like, water or something?"

She shook her head, walked past him, got her coat and notebook, and stepped outside.

The cold air helped with her nausea. Across Frederick Douglass, restaurants were opening up for brunch, which meant it had to be close to eleven a.m. So much time unaccounted for. January headed south, in no particular hurry to get anywhere. The cold bit at her ears. A gaggle of young women walked by holding rolled-up posters. They stopped at the corner of 116th right in front of the stairs for the downtown B/C train and the beer garden that January had been wary of when it first opened—too many flags for European soccer clubs flying—but had come to appreciate as a place to sit outside and watch big sporting events with the neighborhood. The group huddled over their phones. January turned her own phone back on. Desiree had called twice and left voice messages, which January would not find the courage to listen to for several days. She shouldn't have spoken to Desiree without thinking through her plans on her own, she realized. She would regret their conversation for a long time.

She was hungry again, but also in desperate need of a shower, hot water. Her breasts and back ached. The group of girls with posters was still at the corner. January walked up to a light-skinned girl with a puffy nose, chubby cheeks, copper corkscrew curls, and a pink beanie on her head.

"Where's the march happening?"

The girl's nostrils flared, and January remembered her own vomit breath, her tear-crusted face.

"It's on Fifth Ave, but it's probably winding down by now."

"Oh, wow, last year was like an all-day thing."

The girl's friends had started walking south again.

"Yeah, I dunno. People aren't as amped up this year?"

She turned away.

"Yeah, I guess not. Thanks."

January watched her jog to rejoin the group. She wore a long puffer coat, the sleeping-bag kind that old ladies seemed to break out as soon as it dipped below room temperature, and pink high-top Chuck Taylors on which she had written with a black marker. She was already too far away for January to make out the words. Another wave of nausea struck, then passed. January turned onto St. Nicholas. The streets were very photogenic on days like this—sunny, brisk, bustling. Beige stone façades of prewar apartment buildings flanked her. Even the clusters of chained-down metal trash cans seemed to shine in the light. The smell of fabric softener wafted over from the air shafts between buildings, relaxing her.

She'd been so upset in the coffee shop. Out of control, almost. She wanted to blame it on hormones. Crossing the street was a woman carrying a baby in a sling on her chest and pushing a toddler in a stroller. The baby dozed; the toddler kicked the air. All three of them had kinky, sand-colored hair. The woman smiled at January as they made it to her side of the street, and January smiled back. God, how she loved Harlem, even when she hated it.

There used to be a bar over here where she and Morris would go for wings and Hennessy cocktails when they lived uptown. That first summer they'd stayed on an air mattress in his friend's apartment across the street. It was the most wings she'd ever eaten. This was years before she answered a Craigslist ad to redesign a then unknown, now slightly better-known documentary filmmaker's website and realized that she much preferred doing that to her nine-to-five analyst gig downtown. That first summer she and Morris did a lot of furtive fucking on his friend's air mattress late at night, but she couldn't remember what they'd spent so much time talking about. What had they ever really talked about? It now felt as if they'd never moved beyond banalities, not in the whole decade-plus of their relationship. It shouldn't have been so hard to remember. She could remember what she and her girlfriends talked about. Money, food, religion, love, death, vaginas, hair, art, politics, white folks, bowel movements, astrology, anxiety, family, everything.

A shower and a nap would be good. Desiree was right: she had time. There was a little park on St. Nicholas, near the police department. Just a triangle of green to be cut through on the way back to 125th. A handful of people stood in the park now, which was more of a crowd than she'd ever seen there. January stopped walking and scanned the park until she found the source of everyone's interest.

It made no sense. How and when had someone done it? She pulled out her phone, ready for whatever. The highlight of this little park was a statue of Harriet Tubman, forever mid-stride, going toward freedom, or perhaps back to hell like Persephone, but with the goal of delivering more souls out of there. Today the statue wore a bright pink hat on its dignified, albeit crudely rendered bronze head. A knit hat with pointed cat ears like the marchers had worn en white masse the year prior. Someone would've needed a ladder, as the statue was at least three times as tall as January, plus they'd have needed some idea of the size of its head. The fit was loose, but it fit. What was the point of this? It made no sense. A few policemen eyed the statue as if trying to figure out whether they could arrest it for its own defacement, which had occurred so close to their doorstep. They weren't discouraging the crowd from rubbernecking, not yet. January stood in front of the statue and snapped a picture.

She opened Twitter and began to upload it, then stopped. She had nothing smart to say about it. She stepped several paces back. She knew the hat should have offended her, but it was too inane to properly rile. A pink pussy hat on the Moses of the abolitionist movement. Everybody has lost their goddamn minds, she thought, me included. She laughed, loud. A few onlookers turned to look at her but she couldn't stop. Everything was just too dumb.

She would send the photo to the girls. They would no doubt make jokes too. Monique would try to be indignant, insulted on behalf of the ancestors, maybe, but that would only last for a minute and then she would laugh, because things like this left you no other choice. Things like this purported to have something, so much, to do with you, but they didn't, not really, and that's what made them funny. January walked out of the park. She took a minute to catch her breath then kept on toward home.

2012

Three Friends Is an Abundance

Cede the city. Cede its smog and cracked sidewalks, its earthquake weather and skinny, parched palms. Cede its crisscrossed freeways, its candy ladies, eloteros, paleteros, lowriders, chili Fritos, hot dog and tamale men. Leave them behind. Cede two-for-three-dollars beauty supply Kanekalon, bulletproof liquor stores, and bumper-to-bumper forever. Cede éses and Insanes, 60s and Hoovers, swap meets and doughnuts, fried chicken and teriyaki and oldies-loving cholos. All of it points to what you no longer have. People. This is not a city navigable alone. It shrinks in on itself but also becomes impossibly diffuse. It is not a city for wandering, not a city for not having plans. Cede it all. Better to remember what was than to prolong your stay and watch those memories curdle around you and crust over. Better to never witness them degrade.

Flying over Manhattan at night, the lights in Times Square blink and flash like an electric toy, a technicolor music box, a *Dance Dance Revolution* simulation. Colorful, kinetic, tiny and outsize at once, beseeching. A cloud passes over Midtown, and the island becomes a black-and-yellow twinkling geode, which makes more sense. City of outstretched, scaffolded arms, city of two million pulsing lights. A socket for every plug, one would assume.

Desiree turned on her phone just before the plane touched down. She texted:

> Doors open at 10 but get there by 11:30. Give my name. Come cute, but not too cute to dance!!

She felt ridiculous, like a party promoter spamming folks to meet a quota. Then she felt giddy. She had never hosted a party for herself. The number that had been thrown for her, at any age, wouldn't add up to five.

After the train to Zurich, after seventy-two hours of filling out paperwork, speaking with various authorities, and harassing Eternus for assistance (the cremation had been prepaid, she kept reminding them), Desiree had embarked on another train ride. Eight hours through the Alps with a box containing her granddaddy between her feet—heavier than she'd imagined. The Eternus people had suggested the train trip; a man named Florian helped her book her ticket. The mountaintops were blue-white with snow and overwhelming, too beautiful. She had no analog for this; her brain kept sifting through images and proffering the Matterhorn at Disneyland for want of a better reference. She got off at stops just long enough to leave a little of Nolan here and there. He wouldn't have liked the cold but he would have appreciated the views.

Then she returned to Leimert Park, where for some dumb reason she expected Danielle to be waiting for her. No one greeted her at home.

She continued to sleep in the back house, but she watched TV and cooked her meals in the main one. Besides the few mementos that Danielle had snatched up when she'd finally thundered through the place six months after he died, all of Nolan's belongings stayed where he'd left them. Everything except for the plastic sofa covers, which she'd long dreamed of snatching off, stayed put. Fifty years of life tucked into every corner. A thought nagged: he'd planned every detail of his trip—why hadn't he thought about the dismal work he was leaving behind for her? He could have given Desiree directions and she would have carried them out before they went to Paris. This lack of foresight threatened to shake Desiree's confidence. Maybe Danielle had been right and he had been in the early stages of dementia. She would never know now. The cause of death was cardiac arrest, true closure a pipe dream.

The brownstone on 123rd and Lenox had been chopped into six units who knows when. A package blocked Desiree's path to the door: a box from LA addressed to Nakia. Inside the apartment, finding Nakia in the shower, water running and Sade blasting, Desiree used her keys to open the box. She rarely got packages herself and Nakia never seemed to mind when Desiree opened one of hers. Nakia's mother, Juanita, was the kind of person who sent cards for birthdays with carefully considered messages and generous checks in them. She listened when her daughter complained about not having a thing, then the thing often showed up. On top of this, she sent spontaneous care packages. This one: warm fuzzy socks, good corn tortillas, Tony Chachere's Creole seasoning, Mother's sandwich cookies, chocolates from See's Candies, five lemons no doubt picked from her own tree, a bag of dried red chilis, and two jumbo cans of red enchilada sauce. The sight of these treasures—love offerings from the other coast—made Desiree's nose sting.

She and Nakia lived on the top floor in a two-bedroom, two-bathroom unit. The trade-off of not sharing a bathroom was having no real living room, just a wide hallway between them that served as a kitchen and common space. There was no room for a sofa, but they'd bought a tiny secondhand café table and two chairs so that they could eat or chat when one of them cooked, which turned out to be optimistic, because Nakia mostly ate at her restaurant and Desiree hated eating alone in the apartment. She put the package on the table and scanned the counter for mouse droppings. She saw none, which meant that maybe the super's poison had finally worked. Or maybe the mouse had found a new favorite part of the apartment. Or maybe Nakia had wiped down the counter recently. Probably not.

Some of the apartment's walls were thick, and some felt temporary. In

Desiree's bedroom you could hear every laugh and grunt on the other side. Right now she thought she could hear the squeaks of sneakers on hardwood from a basketball game on TV next door, or else a multi-mouse fuckfest within the walls that was better left not visualized. A buzzer sounded, confirming the former. Every bit of furniture she owned had been acquired within three hours thanks to Craigslist: a full-sized bed with wrought-iron bed frame; two rickety IKEA dressers spray-painted green; a wooden three-legged round side table; a floor lamp with a crinkly crepe-paper shade; a small circular gray rug. She liked knowing that all these things could be left behind without much hand-wringing, or tossed into a van and hustled away within minutes. A collapsible life. Finally form mirrored feeling.

The dead leave behind surprises. Nolan had owned not only the house in Leimert, but a lilac quadplex in Inglewood, a rust-red duplex off Budlong down past Gage, a sage-green faux Craftsman in West Adams, and a robin's-egg bungalow way out in the dusty part of Fontana. All with tenants, all in some way raggedy and in need of attention. The Fontana bungalow boasted a blood orange tree in its backyard, so fertile that more than a dozen overripe oranges sunned in the parched grass while flies feasted on their innards. The tree, first of its kind she'd ever seen, felt to Desiree like reason enough to keep the property, but the lengthy list of repairs that the current tenants, an elderly Salvadoran couple, handed her when she visited had made her upper lip sweat. What a shock to discover that Nolan had been some kind of slumlord, holding tight to these properties, which he'd bought out of foreclosure in the seventies and eighties, but doing the bare-minimum maintenance. She didn't see why one person should desire to have that many deeds, that many souls sheltered under one's care. New owners would be better stewards, she figured, even if they raised the rent faster. Desiree found a broker from a bus stop ad on Crenshaw, and together they sold every property except the cream-colored Spanish Colonial in Leimert Park. She wasn't prepared to sell that house, not yet. There was also life insurance money, two policies that eventually paid out, because after all that planning, Nolan had up and died of natural causes.

After taxes, commissions to the broker, and that swift, demoralizing business with Danielle, Desiree had more money than anyone she knew. Nothing can depress you quite like suddenly coming into somebody else's idea of good fortune. What followed were twenty-two months of behavior that she now regarded as textbook self-destructive. The turn from never drinking to constantly drinking was gradual: first preshift tequila shots at the restaurant, then shots during shifts, then a plastic bucket of iced tea like the kind the cooks drank, but hers spiked with whiskey. She dropped things, outright ignored customers who complained, and finally got fired. But she did not want to live off Nolan's money, not any more than what was required to pay the utility bills and property taxes at the house she loathed and loved in turns.

She tried to borrow from Nakia, whose parents lived high up in Baldwin Hills in a mid-century stunner once owned by Diahann Carroll or Dionne Warwick or Della Reese, depending on whom you asked. "This is not a real issue," Nakia had said. "Spend that money when you need it like a normal person." But Nakia did seem to enjoy taking on Desiree as a kind of project, someone to work on. Instead of lending money, she introduced Desiree to a financial planner, a cousin—second cousin, actually—who lived in Dallas but camped out for a week at Nakia's parents' house to help Desiree get her things in order and eat all the tacos and burgers that he was denied on trips with his wife. At their first meeting, Desiree whispered the amount of money she now had, as if saying it aloud would prompt someone to burst through the door and rob her: "It's like, almost a million dollars. Nine hundred, fifty thousand and ninety-three dollars." This cousin, Isaac, had nodded several times and twisted his salt-and-pepper beard.

"That's not as much money as you think," he said. "You're young with no job or a degree, no streams of income. Divide that money up over how long you expect to live."

Desiree said nothing. How long she expected to live was not a question she'd ever considered. Longer than her mother but shorter than Nolan seemed fine. That was nearly a forty-year window.

"This money doesn't make you rich. Smartest thing to do is invest the bulk of it long-term, and only keep liquid what you need to survive while you build up your own life and finances. You can think of it like being a less stressful kind of broke. Broke with a backstop."

Build up her own life—how? How to build a life with no one, rooted to nothing but a house full of an old man's things? Desiree began devoting weekday mornings to scouring the internet for jobs. She learned what she had no interest in—hospitality, teaching, medicine—but what she might apply herself to remained as much a mystery as before Nolan died. Evenings were for wallowing on the sofa with cheap wine and reality television. She preferred the shows that centered on wealthy women meeting up for lunch and arguing with each other. The stakes were consistently low on these shows, no matter how much they yelled and fought. The cast members filmed "confessionals" wherein they explained their reasoning behind any given action, but the more they tried to walk viewers through their thought processes, the less sense their behavior made. This struck Desiree as the most true-to-life aspect of the whole contrived enterprise. Most people had no clue why they did what they did.

There was always a moment early on in a new series when you figured out who the problem woman was; she would do or say something to let you know that she wasn't there "to make friends." These women intrigued Desiree and aroused her pity. Imagine not wanting friends! Desiree clung to the one legitimate friend she had and actively, albeit awkwardly, sought out more. Nakia had joined an intimidating fitness boot camp class run by a bunch of very fit lesbian women out of a tricked-out former sushi shop in Mar Vista. Desiree joined too, though she was not at all interested in physical activity and bad at sweaty small talk. Nakia volunteered to make several hundred sandwiches and pass them out on Skid Row on Mondays. Desiree smeared peanut butter onto several hundred slices of dry white bread. Nakia got into a restaurant management program in New York a few months after Desiree met January at a party in Inglewood. January, a funny, baby-faced girl who to Desiree's delight seemed interested in actually keeping in touch, not just bullshitting like that was the case in person, was already living in New York.

The decision was not difficult. Los Angeles was not hers anymore. The bow-tied Nation of Islam brothers selling bean pies and *Final Calls* off MLK; the train tracks crisscrossing Rodeo near Degnan where she fell off her bike and scraped her chin as a kid. That peculiar smog-plus-nagging-police-helicopter combination that reminded her of every lazy, tense summer of her youth. Each corner held a particular memory with whom she had no one to turn to and remember. If no one else remembered the time that Tommy the Clown shut down their block for an appearance at a party on the corner and Nolan came out into the driveway to dance, did it actually happen, his jangly body mimicking the krumping performers? Did all those rides up and down the 5 from Oakland to LA with their mother, replete with the little rituals the three of them created, not occur? Might as well cede the city to its ghosts. Ghosts who didn't even have the decency to show any sign of themselves to her. Had they shown themselves—a whisper, shifting light, a cold breeze—she might have been able to stay. Her mother, her grandfather, even her grandmother, who had died when Desiree was six. She would have welcomed any glimpse of these people. Instead there was silence. On Dockweiler Beach, where Nolan used to build her and Danielle bonfires. On Venice Beach, where she and Danielle used to watch basketball tournaments and flirt with guys. At the Culver City Stairs, where her mother always talked about working out every time they came down to LA but never got around to it. Silence. At the Creole restaurants, the bougie Black health-food spots, even at the fading, barren malls. In books, characters often felt an estranged or dead person's presence at places where the two of them shared memories, but this never happened for Desiree, not for the dead and not for the living. She never felt presence, only absence. She knew where Danielle was, or thought she knew, but this did not stop Desiree from sensing that the loss of Danielle was almost akin to death. She'd moved with Nakia to New York a year ago.

You wear that dress every fucking weekend," Nakia said now. She leaned in the bathroom doorway in a pair of black wide-legged, high-waisted trousers and a single-buttoned black blazer with no shirt underneath. Her breasts, large C cups, Desiree estimated, were shiny from shea butter.

Desiree continued putting on her bronzer.

"And you let them thangs dangle in the breeze every weekend. So what?"

"Never say 'them thangs' again. Gross." Nakia sat on the toilet seat and rubbed the lotion she'd been cupping in her hand into one foot, then the other. "The deep-décolleté blazer is part of my current club uniform, true, but I switch it up. Sometimes it's pants, sometimes shorts. Sometimes there's a camisole."

"Don't lie. I've never seen no camisole under there."

"On the other hand, you wear this same tube dress every weekend, in the exact same way, like Zara doesn't exist. Like fast fashion isn't out there."

"I switch up the accessories," Desiree said. "Clubs are dark. Nobody cares."

She pulled her flat iron off the top of her medicine cabinet and plugged it in. "Be ready in fifteen."

Nakia squeezed by her out of the bathroom. "Don't burn your hair off again, please."

"Be ready in fifteen!"

Desiree wore the hunter-green tube dress so frequently because she believed it made her look like she had hips. Tonight she accessorized with long black leather fringe earrings. She'd planned to wear a pair of ankle-strap heels with matching black fringe, but they were suede-adjacent and it looked like rain tonight. She'd wear thigh-high fake leather boots instead. She appraised herself in the mirror. Her hair had too much frizz near the temples, and lumps near the roots at the back of her head. She flat-ironed these bits until they laid down. Nakia rarely straightened her hair anymore; neither did January. Desiree's hair was neither curly and fine like Nakia's nor thick and coily like January's. It most resembled cotton candy to Desiree, with no discernible curl pattern or density, such that it became a cloud of fluff when dry. She wore it in a straight bob that fell between her chin and shoulders. Danielle had always had the more straightforward hair of the two of them—tight, springy curls that soaked up product and could go weeks looking good without washing. Danielle had worn her hair natural all the way through medical school, way before it became a trend again. Danielle had. Desiree wasn't sure when she'd started thinking about her sister in past tense.

A woman in black leather booty shorts and a matching bustier lead Desiree and Nakia to their table, which was on the other side of an actual velvet rope, near the DJ booth and in between two huge speakers. Unlike other people, who seemed to need bottle service and the special perch it allotted them above the other clubgoers in order to feel significant or superior, Desiree had no interest in setting herself apart; this was just an unfortunate side effect of enjoying sitting down and being able to pay to do so from time to time.

Even this early, when the DJ was playing new jack swing and shiny-suit-era nineties hip-hop, Desiree could feel the bass in her teeth, in her spine. Not a bad thing.

"Perfect seat," Nakia shouted, and Desiree grinned, began mixing a cranberry and vodka from the carafes on the table in front of them.

There were only men at the four other VIP tables, groups of guys in button-up collared shirts and hard-soled shoes, adhering to the business-casual dress code that these kinds of places enforced. They looked uncomfortable, a little neutered. They would spend the evening either lording over their perches, refusing anyone else access, or recruiting as many women as security would allow to sit with them and drink their booze in exchange for fleeting female attention.

"I asked Brandyn to meet us here," Nakia said. "She hates these kinds of places . . ."

She paused, looked at Desiree as if she wanted a response, but Desiree didn't have one. If she were Nakia's girlfriend, Brandyn, she'd hate these kinds of places too.

"Anyway, she might come later," Nakia said. "Uh-oh! Look, it's everyone's favorite CPA."

Below them, the crowd parted for January's boyfriend, Morris, who lead the way as January and Monique trailed behind him, bopping along to Wiz Khalifa. The group made it to security at the entrance to VIP, and it looked like there was going to be an issue getting in, but, of course, Morris said the right thing to grant them access.

January and Monique squeezed in on Desiree's side of the sofa for hugs. They both wore jumpsuits—January's form-fitting black one accentuated her large bust, while Monique's cream-colored one was the linen-blend, flowy kind whose job it was to accentuate no body part in particular.

"We missed you!" January said. Her hair was slicked back into a bun.

"I'd say we did something fun while you were gone, but why lie?" Monique said. "I hosted an event at work and forced January to come so that it wasn't just me and my regulars in the crowd."

"It was cute," January said. "Monique is a good public speaker."

Monique was a librarian in Brooklyn; her "regulars" were drunk-uncle types who spent all day on the computers. She loved them, and loved complaining about them.

"How was LA?" Monique asked.

"It was fine. Weird, but fine."

"Weird like how? You feeling bad about selling the house?"

How to not dampen the mood?

"I mean . . . at this point I'm indifferent about selling it," Desiree said. Not true, but weren't indifference and ambivalence cousins of a kind? "LA is weird in general. I don't know."

Nakia leaned in, a skinny cocktail straw poking out the side of her mouth.

"Say more."

Desiree looked up to see Morris watching them. She did not want to say more, lest she risk receiving unsolicited financial advice from him, right there in the club. She took a drink of booze, closed her eyes, and opened them again.

Suddenly prerecorded gunshots filled the room, then an air horn. The DJ changed the record and the first sinister, frenzied notes of "Niggas in Paris" played.

"Eyyy!" January shouted.

Everyone stood up and bounced along to the lyrics. Utterly unrelatable boasts and undeniable energy. Morris grabbed January's hand and lead her down to the dance floor.

"They're so cute," Desiree said.

"Cute in like a Peeps marshmallow way," Nakia said. "So sweet you kinda wanna vomit."

Desiree and Monique laughed. It was true—January seemed the most unlike herself when Morris was around. They were the same height, but January seemed to always be looking up at him. How was that possible? January appeared to accept that Morris was smarter than her without taking into consideration whether anyone else who knew the two of them had come to that conclusion. The couple kept dancing through a not very good Swizz Beatz song—something about the bells and whistles and tambourines on this one came together wrong—January's butt backing into Morris's front.

"I'm gonna go put some requests in," Nakia said. She two-stepped toward the DJ booth. Monique followed her.

The song ended, swallowed by yet another Swizz Beatz clanger-banger. Desiree didn't really want to dance; she wanted to drink and laugh and watch other people dance. Three friends felt like an abundance, a surplus, almost enough to fill the hole a sister could leave. If she stopped to think about it, she felt undeserving of her friends—she was not special or charismatic, or particularly interesting. Most times, she succeeded in not stopping to think about this. The feeling of unworthiness crept up on her when she was away, as she had been for the past two weeks, emptying out the Leimert house in a kind of to-do list–fueled fugue state. Other people did not seem to see her, sometimes literally, like when the attendant on her returning flight had offered Desiree's window seat to a couple trying to sit next to each other without even asking her first. This was really why she'd booked bottle service and a table at a party for "Young Black Professionals" upon her return to New York. To celebrate her return to visibility.

January was back at the table, her forehead stippled with sweat.

"Is it cool if a couple of Morris's friends come through?" she asked. "He just went to pull them out of the line. Apparently it's down the block."

"What's down the block?" Nakia wanted to know. She and Monique sat back down, sandwiching Desiree hip to hip.

"Morris has some friends outside that he's tryna get in," Desiree said.

"More CPAs?" Nakia asked.

January laughed, embarrassed.

"One, yeah. And the other one, I don't know what he does. A teacher, maybe?"

"Charter school, public, or private?" Monique wanted to know. "Makes a difference."

"Knowing Morris, he's probably some Obama-type 'community organizer,'" Nakia said.

"Oh my god, stop," Desiree said. She turned to January. "The more the merrier. I think we can have up to eight people."

"Not enough vodka for eight," Nakia said.

"Maybe they'll buy more?" January offered, and Nakia sucked her teeth in response.

Just then the DJ stopped playing whatever he had been playing and a husky voice over the speaker boomed, "BASS DROP!" which was the opening to Fat Man Scoop's remix of "Love Like This Before" by Faith Evans. Nakia's song a decade running. She always requested it despite the fact that this was New York and any DJ who was not a sadist would eventually play it. Now she jumped up from her seat and two-stepped on the couch cushions, gleeful.

"You are such an auntie," Desiree said.

"Everybody loves this song—look!" She waved toward the dance floor, where everyone was indeed dancing.

"I fucking saved this party."

She always said this at some point during the night, unless the DJ was the no-requests-allowed sort, in which case she would scowl at every song transition she found to be subpar, and blame every bored-looking wallflower on the control freak behind the booth. Emboldened by this early indulgence, she would request Mr. Vegas's "Heads High" soon, Desiree knew, and eventually, drunkenly, anything by Rihanna. The room began to fill up with people. Even the raised VIP area turned balmy. The four of them danced around the table, clutching their cups, but it didn't feel right up there, separated from the throng of bodies, Monique said, so they picked their way down to the crowd.

Desiree believed January to be the best dancer; her compact, curvy body reached for nothing, yet every correct gesture found it. Monique, bless her heart, always seemed to be marching in place. Nakia was more performative, arms up in the air longer than they needed to be, hips ranging wide. She sometimes looked like she was hula-hooping, but her confidence made it work. A kind of irony undergirded her dancing, and Desiree believed this to be because Nakia felt little to no sexual pressure here in this aggressively straight, straight person's club, no need to use her dancing to promise or advertise anything to anyone, only, perhaps, to ward off certain ideas and advances. "The club is a joke because of people pretending they don't just want to fuck," she'd said before. "Every club except for the gay club and the strip club." She worked most weekends at her restaurant, so spending this night off here with Desiree instead of with one of her new queer friends, which she was making at a fast clip thanks to Brandyn, was meant to show Desiree how much she cared about her.

"All my ladies pop yo pussy like this," began the next song, and all four women screamed.

"You're welcome!" Nakia shouted.

January bear-hugged Nakia, lifted her off her feet a millimeter, and Nakia beamed at her, grateful to be appreciated. The curling synth of "My Neck, My Back" paired perfectly with its raunchy lyrics, which each woman knew by heart. Most nights like this they danced to songs they knew every word of, despite objecting to eighty percent of them. Desiree, Snoop Dogg fan since elementary school, had known for a long time that it was possible to limn the line between enthusiasm for form and endorsement of content. One did this every day, for various reasons. "It's an essential, tragic part of being a Black woman in America," Monique might have said. Most things were objectionable if you looked at them up close. But not this filthy, lovely song:

First you gotta put yo back into it
Don't stop, nigga, do it, do it.

Poetry.

Desiree put her hands on her knees and arched her back. A man drifted over into her field of vision, presumably to try to dance with her, but he was shooed away, likely by Monique. Good. Desiree could feel her hair curling up at the temples without touching it; the swing of her press had stiffened. The four of them danced as the bodies on the floor packed in tighter and tighter. Finally the DJ returned to the current decade: the overly determined electronic R&B, repetitive hip-hop, and fake girl-power "urban pop" anthems that made Desiree's eyes roll. The group held on through three of these songs until everyone's drinks were empty and it was time to reclaim their expensive seats.

Two men waited with Morris in front of the VIP rope. Both were taller than Morris, one darker and chubbier, one paler and slimmer.

Morris touched Desiree's shoulder and yelled over the music. "This is Chika and this is Dale. I told them you wouldn't mind if they came through."

"Of course!" Nakia said, which could have meant anything. Desiree shook their hands.

Chika looked familiar, but Desiree was learning that this world, in which Black people under thirty who had a meager toehold in the workplace liked to call themselves "professionals," was a small one. Everyone looked familiar. Chika had high cheekbones, small eyes, and a wide jaw. A face that looked like it could take a good punch, Desiree thought. Dale, the paler one, was maybe Guyanese or Trini judging from his very straight black hair, which he had buzzed short.

Chika bought another bottle for the table. Hennessy. In the evil economy of the club, this set him back at least three hundred dollars, Desiree estimated. Air horns again, and the music switched to soca. Dale jumped up, danced in a way that incorporated jogging, and convinced Monique and Nakia to go with him to the dance floor. Morris and January disappeared, then reappeared down on the floor, too. Desiree watched everyone from her seat, her feet burning and the sweat on her shoulders starting to chill.

"So me and you are the suckers tonight, huh?" Chika had slid over into the space next to her. "Whatchu celebrating?"

"Um. I guess that I sold a house."

"Oh, you do real estate?" His eyes brightened, as if he had small talk on this very topic primed to go.

"No, I, um, sold my dead grandfather's house in LA." Impossible to hold eye contact while saying this.

"Oh, damn, I'm sorry."

"It's fine," she said. "He died a couple years ago."

"Ah, got it. So you're celebrating closure. That's cool, very mature. Congrats."

He touched his glass to hers.

Closure wasn't right.

"Mostly I'm just celebrating my friends, New York, whatever," she added. "What about you?"

"Kinda the same. Not the house, but NYC and all that, plus a new job, I guess."

"Congrats. Must be a good job for bottle service." She said this just to be saying something, and instantly regretted it. She didn't care how much money he made, and she tried very hard not to care about anyone's job.

"Ha. Not good enough to justify my student loans, but it is what it is, right?"

He laughed and she nodded. She'd been temping as a front-desk admin for various nonprofits since moving to New York and had just quit the latest one when they wouldn't give her the time off she needed to go back to LA.

Chika was one of those people who had trouble sitting still. His fingertips danced on his knees,, not even to the music. Soca had eased predictably into dancehall. Desiree lifted a hand up to her temple to check her edges, but stopped short and put it back in her lap. After a certain point it was useless to monitor such things. Out on the floor Dale and Monique were still dancing, but she couldn't see Nakia. She scanned the room for her golden braids.

Chika had said something.

"What?"

"I said you look hella familiar," he shouted. "Where'd you go to school?"

An inevitable question, more common than "what do you do?" in this crowd. They traded in potential, not actualization.

"You mean like college? I didn't," she said.

Desiree kept her eyes on the crowd, scanning for Nakia and avoiding whatever was happening on Chika's face. She could have said the truth, that she was slowly getting a degree from an obscure online college for job reasons (and because Nolan would have wanted her to get a degree), but Desiree had already decided that for the foreseeable future, in polite conversation she'd continue to say she didn't have one. Hers wouldn't count when it came in the mail, not on this coast, not with these people. She could lie, refer obliquely to some small liberal arts college in the Midwest or Pacific Northwest that Chika wouldn't have heard of, mumble a name, an Anglo-sounding name like Everton, maybe, and he would buy it, but she wasn't a liar, lies being too tiresome to keep track of and keep up. It was a weird badge of honor to have figured this out, how these people worked, how to work around or subvert their prejudices. She'd crashed their gates enough to know a few things.

"So you're not gonna tell me? Okay," Chika said.

She poured herself Hennessy over two chunks of ice. Then she turned to face him.

"I just told you. I didn't go anywhere."

He pursed his lips at her, which made him look older. His bottom lip was pinker than the top one.

"How old are you?" she asked him.

"Almost thirty. Why?"

"School was a while ago. You feel like you would remember me from there?"

He laughed. "I mean, I went to Dartmouth. There were like thirty-two black people, so yeah. Also, I told you I got hella loans. There's been a bunch of different kinds of school since undergrad where we could've overlapped. But it's fine, don't tell me . . . I'm not bullshitting you, though, you look familiar."

The opening pinging notes of "Heads High" by Mr. Vegas came on.

"Finally!" Nakia shouted right behind Desiree, which made her jump. Nakia put her hands on Desiree's shoulders. The waitress came by and picked up their empty vodka bottle. Nakia followed her with baleful eyes.

"Bottle service girls make me horny."

"That's literally their only job," Desiree said.

Nakia stared down at the people on the dance floor, oblivious to the conversation she'd just broken up. She narrowed her eyes at someone or something, then turned away from the crowd.

"January sometimes sucks, you know that, right?"

"No, I do not know that," Desiree said. "What is she even doing right now besides dancing like everybody else?"

"Exactly, she's dancing exactly like everybody else. She's . . . very into fitting in."

"That's not fair."

"Eh, maybe you're right, I don't know. Maybe she's too conservative for me, or humorless. Something."

"And what am I?"

"You? You are my beautiful, kind, generous, brooding, secretly ballin' friend. You can take a joke."

She yanked her purse onto her shoulder.

"Anyway, I'm bout to meet up with Brandyn downtown. She's right off the one, so it's easy. Love you."

She kissed Desiree's cheek and melded back into the crowd. Desiree watched her lean in and whisper to Monique, who stopped her dutiful winding on Dale long enough to give Nakia a quick hug. Nakia did not say goodbye to January, which was annoying.

Desiree turned to Chika.

"Let's go dance."

They edged out space near Dale and Monique. January and Morris soon drifted over. The women, if they focused, could dance with one another while also nominally dancing with the men. They led. Eye contact between women could switch everyone from winding to two-stepping, from being paired off to a tight, partner-free circle. An Elephant Man song came on, full of instructions that everyone on the dance floor followed. January's areola slid into view. Monique quickly signaled her and it disappeared again. Another instructional song, this one from Atlanta, then "Back That Azz Up," which Desiree could comply with for about forty-five seconds before her knees began to hurt. Chika went to refill his drink. In the idle second when Desiree stood there without a partner, deciding whether she was ready to sit down, Morris whispered in her ear.

"Thought you might be into him," he said. "You like a dude who can fit you into his pocket."

"Don't be weird," she shouted. "Does January know you're over here tryna be matchmaker?"

He put his hand over his heart.

"Not tryna do anything, just saying. He's new in town, just finished his med school residency in Ohio. Now's your moment if you want it."

Desiree didn't respond. She grabbed Monique's hand to fake salsa to "Suavemente." These people always found a way to sneak in what somebody did for a living, she thought. They walked around with their résumés in their mouths.

Blue lights roved just above their heads, then green. Chika returned and she danced with him close, but never for as long as she could tell he desired. He liked to dance front to front, his heavy arms alternately draped on her shoulders or reaching for her waist. His gray V-neck grew dark under the armpits and sweat beads glistened on his beard.

After a very annoying wait in line, Desiree and Monique readjusted and reassessed themselves in the bathroom mirror. They swiped paper towels between their breasts and under their pits. Gave a dollar to the elderly attendant for mints and a pump of spray deodorant. January joined them just as Desiree went into a stall. She wanted to ask January about Chika but couldn't risk seeming too interested. Danielle was in Ohio, but Ohio was a big enough state.

The liquor had finally caught up to her; she felt like she was swaying as she squatted over the toilet bowl. She closed her eyes in a bid to find her balance.

"Didn't you ask him to dance?" January was saying to someone.

"How is that relevant?" She was hearing Nakia's voice outside her stall, but how?

"It probably just came off awkward cause he's tipsy," January said. "I didn't even think he was into you like that."

"Actually, I don't care if he's *into me*," Nakia said. She mimicked January's more nasal tone. "Tell him to stay the fuck away from me."

Desiree opened her stall door. Nakia was rinsing her face with sink water as if she was back home in Harlem instead of in a filthy bathroom with a line of women outside its door. She dabbed at her face with one of the hard brown paper towels.

"You're still here? Thought you left like thirty minutes ago," Desiree said.

"I left an hour and a half ago." Nakia said. "Then I decided to come back."

"Are you okay?" Desiree scanned her body for traces of harm.

"Yeah, I'm fine."

"You seem . . . different."

"Me and Brandyn shared a bump of coke when I got there." She tried for a nonchalant shrug.

"Coke. Okay. And then you left Brandyn and came back here?"

"Coke!" Monique's eyebrows nearly met her hairline. "Since when do you do coke?"

"Yes, I came back here," Nakia said. "And I was looking for y'all and ran into Morris's little friend, whathisname, who just sexually assaulted me."

"What? Who?"

Desiree panicked that she would say Chika, then felt ashamed. She didn't even know him.

"Dale," January and Nakia said in unison.

Desiree hadn't seen Dale, who was Guyanese, it turned out, near Nakia all night, or had she?

"I'm confused," she said. "What did he do? What was the context?"

Nakia looked as if she might cry, her chin crumpled.

"The context is he's a fucking pervert, Desiree. I was asking him where y'all were and outta nowhere he reached out and touched me here." She pointed to the space between her breasts, her "deep décolleté" space.

"Fuck a context,'" she muttered. She put her phone and her wallet, which for some reason were on the sink ledge, back into her little purse.

"That was a dumb thing to say," Desiree said. "I'm sorry."

Nakia waved her away, then swiped at her tears. Desiree wanted to hug her but was afraid to do so, she didn't know why. Her heart was beating too fast all of a sudden. January and Monique stood on the far wall in that triangle of space behind the bathroom door that dictated one of them hold it open for the women filing in. Monique held it. Finally, Desiree took a step forward, closing the gap between herself and Nakia, and hugged her.

"What happened with Brandyn?" she whispered.

"It doesn't matter." Nakia sniffed. "The bottles gotta be done by now. Let's go."

The taxi back to Harlem would cost forty dollars, which felt more exorbitant than the eight hundred dollars she'd just shelled out at the club. A kind of everyday, unnecessary unfairness. Desiree stared at the back of Nakia's head while Nakia looked out the opposite window, or maybe she'd fallen asleep. She was very still. It didn't make sense that Nakia should suddenly be so sleepy after doing cocaine, but what did Desiree know? Desiree scrolled through her phone. She found him on Facebook easily; he was a mutual with Morris. His profile photo was of him in a white coat. She tapped it, enlarged it for a closer look at the embroidered logo on the coat pocket. Of course. Her stomach quivered.

She scrolled through his older profile photos. Chika and what looked to be his two siblings—teenaged girls—in ugly Christmas sweaters. Chika in a tank top, his fleshy shoulders shiny with sweat, hiking somewhere deep, misty green—the Pacific Northwest, she guessed, but it could have been Hawaii or even Maine. Chika in traditional dress, arm in arm with an older woman with his same wide nose, high cheekbones, and dimples. The woman wore a fanlike headdress and a shimmering white patterned shift dress. Desiree scrutinized each photo, as if they held a particular secret, but she knew she was stalling, prolonging the discovery she craved and feared. She no longer felt drunk, just hungry. She sent Chika a friend request, locked her screen, and let out the loud breath she'd been holding. Nakia sobbed, or grunted. Hard to know without seeing her face.

"You awake?"

"I am on cocaine. Of course I'm awake."

Desiree looked up at the rearview window. If their driver heard her, he didn't care. They were on the last stretch of the Henry Hudson Parkway before their exit, New Jersey's darkness on one side and the quiet hulk of Upper West Side apartment buildings on the other.

"I really am sorry," Desiree said. "Fuck Dale. A black man can't have a buzzcut, I don't care how silky his hair is. He can be bald or have a fade or a fro, but not no army buzzcut."

Nakia didn't laugh.

"What happened with Brandyn?"

"Desiree, what if nothing happened with Brandyn?" She finally turned around.

"You know what I'm asking."

"Nothing to tell," Nakia said. "Except that I don't know what I'm doing here."

Desiree suppressed her desire to speak, hoping this would make Nakia say more. They were on 125th now, the storefronts not owned by megacorporations dark at this hour, their security gates rolled down. They traveled to the next avenue in silence.

"Y'all broke up?"

"No. I don't know. It's just, like, I'd spent all night with y'all in that club feeling like I didn't belong there. Morris's corny ass and his friends, all those other dudes in VIP making weird eye contact. I wandered around by myself for a good half hour, trying to figure out if the problem was really the club or if I was just in a shitty mood. And then I went downtown to Brandyn and felt like a kid, like I was cramping her style just by showing up. You know, she wasn't the one who gave me that coke. Some random white baby dyke in the bathroom offered me a bump. And I did it cause at least she was being friendly. But when I got back to the bar, Brandyn was mad at me for taking drugs from a stranger. Like . . . her and her homegirls actually sat me down on a stool and made me drink water. It was embarrassing. So when they went back to talking amongst themselves, I dipped out. She's probably been texting me to break up, but my phone is dead."

"She's not breaking up with you."

"Why not? Brandyn has a whole life without me that I barely even understand. I'm a kitchen nerd. I don't have any business dating a fine-art photographer—I don't even know what makes her shit fine art! I don't wanna pretend to have read the books her and her friends have read. If I move back to LA tomorrow, she wouldn't miss a beat."

"You're thinking about moving back." She wanted to sound neutral. Nakia sighed.

"Come on, Des, don't make this about you."

Desiree cracked her window, squeezed her eyes shut. Never about her.

They'd met at an informational session for the culinary school that

Desiree had heard about from her high school counselor. Nakia had sat in the very front of the multipurpose room. During the Q and A she'd explained in front of the group of seventeen-year-olds with lackluster GPAs and middle-aged people considering a career shift that she had taken college courses since her junior year of high school and wanted to know whether it was feasible to try to get a culinary degree concurrently or if she should wait to finish college first. Desiree, who sat in the back corner of the room, safely out of eyesight of the presenter, had never said the word "concurrently" out loud, and "feasible" probably only a handful of times. There was a Danielle-ness about Nakia, so much resolve at such a young age. Of course she'd gotten the bachelor's degree and the culinary degree concurrently. Now, Desiree feared that this Danielle-ness might also include the ability to leave her.

"You know my program is rotational," Nakia said. "I had planned to try to stay in New York, but I could do the next one back in LA."

"Mmm."

"It's just too hard here. I miss my old friends, I miss being able to ride my bike without feeling like I'm gonna die, I miss the beach. And I miss my mom, a lot."

They passed Adam Clayton Powell Boulevard. Only one avenue to go before home.

"Des. You're not gonna say anything?"

Desiree smashed the heels of her palms into her eyes. "Um. It's three rotations, right?"

"Yeah, a year each."

"You could do one more here?" Desiree's voice cracked. "Then move home for the last one, maybe?"

Nakia touched her arm at the inner elbow crease.

Pity, Jesus.

"Des, you're my sister. I love you. And you love New York. It's gonna be fine."

Were three friends enough to fill the void a sister left if one of them up and left, too?

"Yeah, I'm just drunk," Desiree lied. "Hard to process."

They climbed out of the cab, made it to the top of their stairs in silence.

Over the past two weeks in LA, she had donated the last of Nolan's things—the furniture, the old TVs, the exercise equipment, the fancy silverware—to a Catholic charity he'd liked. A neighbor had helped her disassemble the grandfather clock enough to get it out the front door of the Leimert house, and she let him take it home. Her broker had offered to find movers who could have done all of this for her, but it felt important for her to do it herself, to take apart the last vestiges of her LA life piece by piece. Now she just wanted to drive a screwdriver through her own skull.

In her room, she waited behind the closed door for the sounds of Nakia getting ready for bed to die down, for Nakia's white noise machine to turn on. Then she showered and lotioned. Her phone glowed on her nightstand. A notification. She walked in her underwear to the kitchen sink, put her mouth under the faucet, and drank, as she'd done when no one was looking since she was small. She straightened up, discovered that someone was indeed looking this time: a tiny grey mouse, its greasy flank flush with the toaster. She turned off the kitchen light on her way out, leaving it to do its thing.

Chika had accepted her friend request. She had a new message but wanted to ignore it for as long as willpower allowed. Back to his albums instead. Past ugly sweaters and sweaty hiking and his mama and a photo of him wearing an "I Voted" sticker and a T-shirt with that ubiquitous Obama campaign logo on it, there she was. A group photo, at least eight people. This had to be from earlier in 2008, before that autumn of Paris and Zurich, before the beginning of the end. Pictured: eight young doctors-in-training and six children. Haitian children, Desiree knew. Danielle had gone to Haiti early in 2008, and apparently so had Chika, placed as they were in the same Ohio hospital as residents. They did not stand near each other in the photo, so maybe they were not close then, or now.

His message: You left without saying goodbye ☹. You're uptown, right? Me too. 4789 W. 128th #6C. 404-555-7271.

She paced her room, eventually stopped in front of her closet. She put on jeans, a hoodie with nothing underneath, a bomber jacket on top of that. Grabbed her hair into a tiny bun.

She texted the number, omw, and quietly left the apartment.

2019

Black in the Stacks: A Black Librarian's Musings

by Monique L.

May 22, 2019

So many new faces here, if those are actually your faces, haha. Over 20k in one month! When I started this page, blog, whatever it is, I had no real plan, I just knew I was frustrated with my work and myself (and maybe, a little, occasionally ashamed, if I'm being honest), and I knew I'd feel better once I got the story out, or at least down. I had no expectation of anyone outside of my circle of girlfriends (who I force to read all kinds of things I write) reading it. And now we're here, almost 50k followers and a whole widely shared speech later. I never imagined that anything I wrote or said out loud could garner half a million views in just a few weeks, but here we are. (At some point in the near future I'll dive behind the scenes into the Tru Talk experience, but now is not that time!) I don't know exactly why my story, me just talking about my experiences with those slave quarters, resonated with so many people, but I have more than an inkling why it made so many people online angry at me. That's how life goes, I guess. To those angry people I say fuck off forever, obviously.

Moving on. I've spent time thinking about what I'd like this space to be on the other side of my Talk and stint of virality—I really don't like that word—and I've come to the conclusion that I'm going to keep using this platform (cringe) as I always have: to share a mix of mundane former-librarian musings, my poetry, which is maybe bad but y'all will deal, my thoughts about my friends, observations about New York, this city which I've tried to quit but like a heartsick lover keep crawling back to, the world, and whatever else I feel like writing about, in whatever format feels right to write about it. My promise to you, not that I owe you any promises, is to continue to be as personal as I feel is possible and as private as I feel is necessary. I'm going to talk my shit and dole out kindness and shout folks out and squeal with delight. I'm gonna keep being Monique. You are all welcome to be in this space with me if that sounds like a good time to you, and if it sounds like a great time, consider subscribing. I have always valued transparency, especially in this online space, where it's easy to live behind a façade, so I will be transparent in saying that I hope to gain enough paid subscribers to help support myself financially. Every little bit helps.

I want to thank my parents (names withheld because weirdos) for letting me back into their home after my southern librarian adventure went awry. The privilege of having somewhere to retreat to, to lick my wounds and be still, in New York City of all places (borough withheld because weirdos) has never been lost on me. I did not think I'd need that refuge for as long as I did, but what a blessing it turned out to be.

Speaking of shout-outs, thank you to my friend January Wells, badass single mom and proprietress of J22 Graphic Design for my new logo and "branding." Scare quotes because the very notion of me being a brand is scary! But what isn't scary right now, right?

Finally, because there has been some discussion in the comment sections here and elsewhere online, I thought I'd end this reintroduction with the original text from the blog post that became my Tru Talk presentation, which brought so many of you here. I posted this in 2018, after thinking about writing it for a good while. There were reasons—both legal and personal—why I took so long to get the story down. I eventually decided that while plenty of time had passed, my (very messy) feelings remained as intense as ever, and this intensity might be lessened by sharing my story. Some of you longtime readers might remember that when I first posted this I included no context or introduction. I don't want to color people's perceptions too much this time around either, except in this one important way: I consider what follows to be a kind of confession. I wish I had understood back then that I had nothing to confess to, but life is about learning more and doing better. I refuse to be ashamed for what I did not fully understand. This beginning text, this confession, would evolve into what many people rightfully consider my Tru Talk to be—an indictment. An indictment not only of the university I worked for but of an entire revisionist history movement that has only gained more ground in this country. I will not reveal the name of the university in question for legal reasons, and I've changed the names of buildings and colleagues when I felt it was necessary. As some commenters have pointed out, this sort of thing is happening in so many areas of American life, not just universities. The goal of my Tru Talk was not to absolve myself, but to focus on the structural issues at play versus my personal role and emotions. Here goes.

The Miss April Houses

(originally posted on June 8, 2018)

After a survey of university trustees, experts, faculty and community members, the Committee puts forth the following recommendations:

In literature associated with the property, prior occupants of the "Miss April Houses" should be referred to as "people" or "inhabitants." In special circumstances approved by the Committee they may be referred to as "workers." Under no circumstance should they be referred to in any other fashion.

The committee lacked a librarian, they explained, which is why they enlisted me at the start of my first semester on staff. I was so new to campus that my badge wasn't programmed yet. For the first month, I had to stand out front of the Jefferson Building in the humidity before each meeting (twice weekly, at lunch) and wait for another committee member to swipe me in. It was usually Becca Samuels, from campus counseling, with her enamel pins and cat-eye glasses and shaved side, making me feel like I hadn't moved to a new place at all. I could have still been in Brooklyn, passing the time on lunch breaks with my nerdy, hipster-adjacent colleagues, one of whom was actually named Becca.

For each committee meeting, we'd all sit around a conference table in the Office of the General Counsel of the university. My job at these meetings, as it was explained to me, was to vote when called on but mostly to listen to the proceedings and at the very end consider how the library might set up a web page with links to supplemental information and research suggestions for interested students and visitors. That wasn't the only reason I was there, I suspected, but it was a fancier job than I'd had before, and fancy jobs always have their particular requirements.

Nobody wants to be stuck in meetings during their lunch break after just having moved so far—over 600 miles south—and not even having time to get a lay of the land, or buy a microwave or suss out where to get decent towels, but I figured it could have been worse. We could have used parliamentary procedure, and meetings could have gone on forever. Instead, Dr. Gander, the co-chair, kept the meetings under an hour each, no matter what.

> *The Committee endorses the Board of Trustees' proposal to continue calling the structures in question the Miss April Houses and approves the following language for a commemorative placard at the site:*
>
> *"Miss April Lee-June Walters (1902–1974) was born in House #2 and lived in both houses with her two sons and first husband, John Binker Walters (1897?–1955), then with her second husband, Woodrow Gendry II (1920–1981). Miss April was a cherished part of the University community and a longtime member of the hospitality and dining services staff. During the Great Depression, vegetables generously shared from her small farming plots were sometimes the sole source of fresh produce for students and faculty. Following campus expansion in 1963, when the houses were moved from the southeast to the northwest corner of campus, independent community members replanted Miss April's garden, ensuring that she enjoyed sustainable, locally grown produce for the rest of her life.*

It was right around the time that my badge started working that Nnamdi Watson, PhD, joined the committee. A visiting lecturer in American history with a five-year appointment, which had been renewed once, putting him on year eight. The week prior, Lyle Sanders, the ancient professor of rhetoric and oldest Black tenured faculty member (there were only four of them), had quit the committee, citing health concerns, which was just as well. He mostly slept through the meetings, his head dropping suddenly and freaking everybody out. Nnamdi was there to keep our number on the committee at a respectable two, we both figured. Solid build, neat, shoulder-length locs. Short, but cute. Horn-rimmed glasses, bowties or tweed vests over crisp, long-sleeve oxfords every day. A Kappa, I could tell before he told me so. Friendly enough. He said he liked my twist-out, called it glossy. I laughed, said thank you. He called me "sista" and I did not roll my eyes. By this time I'd also finally bought a microwave.

The following informational display has been approved:

A mounted poster highlighting the furniture and tools in the houses, including one kitchen table, one bed with a quilt similar in style to those sewn by Miss April during her tenure, one washboard, an embroidery hoop and one broom.

Items currently in the houses but hereafter prohibited from display:

> *A hatchet, found hanging near the fireplace of House #1.*
>
> *Seventeen handmade dolls that comprised Miss April's collection (some inherited from her mother), donated to the University by her sons.*
>
> *The 6-inch-by-12-inch wooden box with a cross carved into its top, found buried behind House #2 in 1983.*

All contents of this box.

In consideration of the preservation of the approved objects for display, the Committee recommends that access to the interior of the houses be limited to scholars with written permission from the University's Department of Special Collections, and various special persons as designated by the Board of Trustees. Visitors from the general population should view the interior of the houses from the front and back porches via the double-paned, shatter-proof windows.

I wish I could say that I knew the contents of the box that was not to be displayed, but even the committee wasn't given this information. We were told only that its contents were "inappropriate to put on display given the goal of the restoration project." My best guess is that the box, with its crucifix carved on top, was related to root work in one way or another. A *gris-gris* box, maybe. This is outside of my area of expertise, obviously, but I can't imagine what else might have warranted the box being hidden away like that. My grandmothers—one from South Carolina and one from Barbados—did not agree on everything when they were alive, but they agreed that nothing freaks white people out quite like Black "superstitions."

It was through my questioning about the contents of the box that I came to better understand our committee's true purpose. We were a public-facing cover, a way to make it seem like there had been, if not a democratic process, then at least a legitimate scholarly approach to addressing the history of these houses and the university's relationship to them. In truth there was another committee, a secret one, most likely composed of high-profile donors, trustees, and maybe even politicians, who decided the parameters of our group's discussions. Dr. Gander was their conduit, though I doubt even he was invited to their meetings.

A typical committee meeting went like this: We were all given a proposal for an element to be included in the restoration of the houses, then thirty minutes would be devoted to presentations regarding the merit of the proposal, sometimes made by the proposal authors themselves, but more often by third-party experts. Then we'd deliberate for twenty minutes or so (usually less) and issue our recommendation. Patricia Dwyer, the head of the Office of the General Counsel, would then run the recommendation through whatever sort of legal analysis was necessary (and up the chain to the secret committee, I suspect) and return the next meeting with the proper wording for us to adopt. Pretty efficient, I thought. The catered lunch varied from sandwiches to Italian to Chinese.

> *The Committee acknowledges receipt of a petition presented by community member Shaw Hammers proposing that the site include literature about the transatlantic slave trade, including the amount paid for original inhabitants of the houses as listed in University archives.*
>
> *Finding: Committee finds such literature to be outside the scope of the goals of the restoration project.*

From the outset, Nnamdi had taken issue with the omission of the word "slave" or even "enslaved worker" and the use of "houses" over "quarters" or "cabins," so of course he supported Shaw's petition (it had two hundred signees, but only about eighty from people affiliated with the university, and most of those were classified staff). I was with him at first. I mean, if you don't use the word, that's erasure, right? But then Becca Samuels from campus counseling services—the woman who swiped me in in the early days—finally stopped speaking in slogans and said something that almost made sense. Becca asked: Would the relatively small population of students of color find comfort in these houses, or would they become fodder for ridicule used against them? She presented research about young people and constant proximity to sites of past trauma. "It can feel like stepping on the same land mine day after day just to get from one class to the next," she concluded. This was more flourish than reality because the houses, being tucked up in a far corner of campus like they were, weren't on the way to anyone's class. Perhaps if they'd been kept in their original locations, close to the old faculty-housing buildings (the better for visiting faculty of yore to lodge the slaves they brought with them), students of color would have felt retraumatized by the sight of them.

Predictably, Patricia Dwyer rattled off a bunch of legalese that suggested Shaw's proposal could one day bankrupt the university. I didn't care about Dwyer's point, but Becca's was worth mulling over, her land-mine analogy notwithstanding. I thought it was possible that the knowledge of those houses being on campus, with their true purpose laid bare for all to see, could mess with a young student of color's head. Who am I to say what causes another person trauma? Still, in the end I decided to show solidarity and vote with Nnamdi. We lost 2–6.

In accordance with a recommendation from expert linguists, the following language and accompanying illustrations have been accepted by the Committee:*

- *"Lenny Roberts used the phrase 'lee little' to mean very small. 'Lee' is similar to a WOLOF word that means small."*
- *"One of the inhabitants of this House was named Esther Malink. MALINKE is the name of an ethnic group, also known as the Mandenka, the Mandinko, the Mandingo or the Manding."*
- *"To express amazement, inhabitant Buster Griggs would exclaim, 'Great Da!' The FON people (also known as the Fon nu, the Agadja or the Dahomey) worship a god named Da."*
- *"Miss April referred to peanuts as 'pindas.' 'Pinda' is the KONGO word for peanut. The Kongo people are the largest ethnic group in the Democratic Republic of Congo."*

* *Illustrations should show a map of Africa with corresponding geographic regions of each ethnic group highlighted in either of the University's official colors.*

This linguist (there was only just the one—not plural), Dr. Nichole Valdes-James, made a very compelling argument. Even Nnamdi, who hated the committee by now for not passing Shaw's proposal, had to admit it. Gander, the co-chair, looked charmed in spite of himself. Who can argue with enduring language? Who would see information like that and not be impressed, intrigued? Apparently, Nnamdi had expected plenty of people to be offended. After the meeting, he walked me back to the library. "A decade ago you hardly ever heard the word 'Africa' on this campus, if not in the pejorative," he said. I said, "Well, Africa's pretty trendy up north these days." He looked at me like I was an idiot, muttered, "This isn't up north." But then he invited me to get a drink with him.

The Committee recommends the following permanent information placards be added to the façade of the Miss April Houses wherever the restorers find aesthetically pleasing:

- *A display highlighting the restoration efforts of university researchers, with attending photographs of the process of transporting the cabins to their current location.*

- *A display with the names of members of this Committee.*

I left Brooklyn because I was at the point where just walking to the post office made me want to reach out for the nearest stranger's neck and squeeze it, and I'm not a particularly violent person. All of these forever-children in wrinkled clothes with make-believe jobs and very real bank accounts looking down their noses at me, as if the sight of me made the neighborhood bad? I know, I know. But just because it's happening all over the place doesn't make it any easier to stomach. Plus, I was single again. Plus, most of my friends were having kids and moving away, or just moving away because things had gotten so unbearable in Brooklyn. My remaining close friend in the city lived in Harlem, but there was a new Whole Foods coming there and I suspected Harlem would go the way of Bed-Stuy soon enough. I was sitting at my desk at my branch library one day, with a stack of books to weed, and thought: "You know what? They can have this place." I went online, applied for this job and got it, even though I don't have any university experience.

The Committee acknowledges receipt of a petition presented by community member Shaw Hammers, submitted on behalf of Nnamdi Watson, Visiting Lecturer in American Studies (and member of this same Committee, hereby recused from this vote), proposing an informational placard featuring scholarship speculating on how and against what odds particular words and phrases might have lasted in the inhabitants' lexicon over the generations.

Finding: Committee finds that such a placard would be outside the scope of the goals of the restoration project.

If, as I now have come to suspect, the role of our committee, as handed down by the secret committee, was to simultaneously acknowledge and diminish the role of slavery on the university's campus, then it was stupid of the committee to accept proposals on a rolling basis. This was a policy established before I arrived. Of course Nnamdi would try to take the one thing everyone was enthusiastic about and flip it on them. I told him the night before to just leave it alone, be happy they don't just bulldoze the houses altogether, but he said, "It's the principal of the matter." And I said, "That's usually what someone says before they do something dumb," and he shook his head and threatened to leave my apartment. But he didn't. He didn't leave the committee either. He attended twice a week, ate heartily, and smiled too much at everyone there.

The following permanent placard must be affixed within twenty feet of the entrance of both Miss April Houses:

A display thanking the individual and corporate donors that made the restoration project possible. Language on this display is up to the donor's discretion, granted such language meets the guidelines outlined above.

The semester was nearly over by the time we worked our way through all of the proposals. No, I didn't let them put my name on the official committee placard. I was new and maybe I didn't quite understand the stakes, but I knew better than to put my name on either one of those houses. They didn't even ask me to explain why I abstained. I guess my being Black and having voted with Nnamdi was reason enough. No, I did not join Nnamdi, Shaw Hammers, and the seven others who staged a sit-in for three days on the porch of House #1. That doesn't mean I didn't care. No, I did not speak to the local news outlets when they showed up to cover the protests. I know bad faith when I see it.

For the most part I stayed in my lane as a librarian. Part of me thought it was unfair for people to expect me, someone who had just given up an apartment, a job, all of New York City, for this new place and new job, to stick my neck out. Another part of me wonders whether there was a way I could have done more. I don't know. Many people lumped me in with Nnamdi and Co. anyway. I was shunned in certain campus circles for my "allegiance" to the rabble-rousers. To make matters worse, the rabble-rousers shunned me, too. Nnamdi would hardly look at me by the time the committee concluded.

If you focus on what we did accomplish as a committee, versus what was left out, we communicated two important truths: that past inhabitants made due with what they had. A few pieces of furniture, a humble kitchen. And they found ingenious, albeit small ways to make their language endure. That's not nothing. That's huge, I think.

And maybe a later committee can add more information.

2015

And Then There Were Hands

Unlike many Black Angelenos she knew growing up, Nakia Washington's family could not trace their lineage to Louisiana, Texas, or Mississippi. They had arrived in California by way of New Jersey. They were seaboard people, had been for generations, since an enslaved ancestor on her father Conrad's side—Ann, no last name—traveled from Maryland to Philadelphia in the early 1800s with the people who thought they owned her. She absconded into the city, thereby emancipating herself, family lore went. This intrepid ancestor had found shelter among the Black freedmen of Philadelphia and stayed inside one safe house or another for the better part of a year, not stepping into the sunlight or even venturing near windows. Nakia descended from a founding family of Black Newark, New Jersey. Ann, who eventually married a man named Washington, had the prudence after that first year in hiding to make her home outside of the city of her escape. Hers was a striving family, from washerwomen and day laborers to ministers and teachers to many minor First Blacks. First Black assistant superintendent of schools; First Black nurse administrator at a large urban hospital; First Black president of a local credit union; First Black delegate to the eastern regional convention for the Presbyterian church; First Black woman graduate of Seton Hall's business school, and so on. It was Conrad's family history, yet Nakia's mother Juanita, daughter of an electrician, took special pride in relaying it. Nakia, on the other hand, tended to tell only her closest friends that she came from free people. Not free from jump—who but a handful could claim that on this continent?—but free for a good, long while.

Nakia's parents didn't come to Los Angeles to fulfill a dream of palm trees and swimming pools. They came for a short stint—dental school for her father—and stayed. They had been trying for a child for twelve years and got pregnant with Nakia's older brother, CJ, within a month of living in Los Angeles. That felt like reason enough. Plus, distance from their families helped them realize there was a world outside of the Vineyard and Sag Harbor, outside of social clubs and debutante balls, and that they preferred this new world while still benefitting from access to the old one. Conrad continued the Washingtons of Newark's minor First Black legacy on the other coast: First Black-owned endodontist practice in West LA.

The Washingtons had graduated from kitchens before Nakia's great-great was born, so why had she gravitated to this sweaty, often unglamorous work? Not even the work of poor-pay-but-respectable stages, genteel maître d's, and haughty chefs de cuisine, but regular old kitchen labor. The work of ugly shoes and baggy pants and no-degrees-necessary and stains no matter one's fastidiousness. Why work with one's hands—unless we're talking surgery or sculpture—when one didn't have to? Well, there were hands, and then there were hands. Hands for building houses, tapping trumpet keys, turning lathes, cradling newborns, hands that, with the cooperation of feet keeping time on a pedal below, guided fabric through the percussive needle of a machine, hands with greased fingertips that pulled kinks into cornrows, palmed basketballs, rubbed backs, sanded wood, broke bones. A tactile person, Nakia was destined to work in a field that required literal grasping, and she might have taken to many of these other hands' pursuits but for the adrenaline of cooking, the particular eroticism of shoulder brushing shoulder, language abutting language, hips bumping hips in the kitchen. By the time she graduated from culinary school, she could perform any task in a kitchen with proficiency, but none thrilled like expo.

The first time Nakia was called to expedite was at her summer job at a soul food joint on Crenshaw, before her senior year of high school. She was hired as a hostess, work her mother permitted because the restaurant was less than a five-minute drive from their house. Nakia had chatted up and won over the entire staff within a week. All it took was a no call, no show for her to get to try her hand at serving, and once she was that close to the kitchen, pushing through the swinging doors to retrieve her orders, to refill condiments, to hide from tables, she understood that she was meant to be in close proximity to its energy, if not in it. Hence, expo. That particular job—reading orders, making sure the plates created aligned with them, directing cooks to fire dishes at the appropriate time, thereby keeping the pace of service for everyone—was one she thought she could do forever. One had to be despot and supplicant both while on expo, barking out orders, pleading with testy cooks for substitutions, finagling for special cases. It was more akin to racetrack announcing than traditional public speaking, and her heartbeat revved when the first ticket sputtered out of the machine each shift. She was the youngest on staff, but on expo everyone was obliged to listen to her, to meet her eyes from time to time and catch their meaning. She had never spent time alongside so many dissimilar people, of age, country of origin, and perspective, and not being the type of child who gravitated to sports, she had never experienced the combination of competitiveness and conviviality that kitchen work engendered.

Still, she was Conrad and Juanita's child, so she understood that she needed to nurse the flame of her own desires alongside theirs, which was to see her graduate from college. She did this with ease, as she did most things. Somehow the two of them had already known and accepted by the time she told them during her sophomore year at UCLA that their other desire—marriage and domesticity as they knew it—was never going to come to pass for her. This acceptance was a relief, and made nursing the twin flames even easier. Time hustled by.

The road to becoming the twenty-eight-year-old proprietress of the kind of breakfast, brunch, and lunch spot that people loved to put on internet best-of lists began with the bump of coke shared by a strange white girl three years earlier in that lesbian bar in New York City. Cocaine wasn't the end of the world, but Brandyn, her girlfriend at the time, had been right—it wasn't her. In New York she'd found herself reaching for pastimes and postures that had nothing to do with who she actually was. Untethered, was how Juanita put it when Nakia had called her that night from Twelfth Street, her heart racing. "You are an independent girl, Nakia, and you can thrive anywhere, but there's no need to force yourself into an untethered life," she'd said. "You have people, you have family. You can come home and accomplish what you want to accomplish."

Left unsaid was that Juanita and Conrad would help her achieve her goals if she let them. Also left unsaid was who might truly be untethered in Nakia's world. Juanita sometimes acted as if what Desiree had endured was the kind of misfortune that could catch: orphaned, rudderless, "without purpose," as she put it, this last affliction being the gravest. She never discouraged their friendship, but she also never stopped discussing Desiree's life with pity, with derision. Nakia had hung up after that conversation on the street a little less high and determined to take herself a little more seriously. That began with being honest with herself. She wanted to go home. She didn't aspire to be the boss, but she hated being bossed. She did not hold the concept of working one's way up in high esteem, as she'd already seen in her short restaurant career that the kitchen was no meritocracy. Juanita was right. There was little reason to be on the other side of the country finding herself when she knew what she wanted: a kitchen of her own. So she returned to LA, moved back home, stayed in her fancy rotational program to get more face time and bare-minimum chummy with a few movers and shakers in the local restaurant scene, then used a "loan" from Juanita and Conrad to open her own place. A twelve-table café on the border of Inglewood and Ladera Heights.

She didn't aspire to be a restaurateur as much as she liked the way the word "proprietress" felt in her mouth. Salty, old-timey, not to be fucked with. Who could look down their nose at the proprietress of an establishment serving wholesome food to her community? And if she failed, no one would care how she'd gotten the capital to open her doors; they'd only focus on their closure. She decided to be wise with the money she'd been given and build something that might last. Her wisest choice turned out to be hiring a man named Miguel. Petite and wiry, in his mid-thirties, with a broad nose and straight black hair that he wore in a low bun, Miguel had run the kitchen at the middling Oaxacan restaurant where Nakia and Desiree worked before moving to New York. When in the swing of service, his favorite word was "shit," as far as Nakia could tell, which he used not as a curse but in place of nouns he seemed to temporarily forget how to say in English, as in: "You need to fire the shit again, get the big shits from the walk-in, table eight needs more shit on that tlayuda." It was easy to decipher his meaning, and he was the smartest, kindest person Nakia had ever met who ran a kitchen. No belittling, no tantrums, no wandering hands or eyes, no masochistic wielding of the schedule or assigning drudgery to punish and reward on a whim. Miguel had been the one to fire Desiree when she started showing up grief-drunk and sluggish, dropping things and dozing off standing up. Even then he'd been firm but not cold, expressing his condolences while seeing her to the door. When she was ready to open her own place, Nakia had offered Miguel forty percent more than the Oaxacan spot paid him, and together they created Safe House Café, so named to honor her ancestor Ann, no last name.

It was ninety minutes before opening and four hours before the lunch rush on the day in early March when Miguel called to say that although he'd already arrived at the restaurant, he needed to leave immediately. Something about needing to get back to Chiapas in a hurry. She was at the farmer's market in Santa Monica, her wagon laden with eggs and herbs. "Maybe I'll be back in two weeks," he said. His voice already had that staticky, far-away quality that plagues international calls, which made Nakia fear he was gone for good. And unlike "shit," "maybe" wasn't a Miguel word—generally a thing could happen or it couldn't. Her nose stung. Odds were low she'd ever see him again.

The prep crew was wrapping up when she walked in, the kitchen awash in the tang of cut onions and the sweet sweat of bell pepper, every surface gleaming. Eerily silent save for the sound of knife hitting board and the odd scrape, because her prep staff—Angel and Delia—disagreed on music so much that they both wore headphones. Nakia checked the schedule pinned on the bulletin board for a moment before realizing that the two of them were eyeing her. Had it really been so long since she'd arrived early? "At ease," she said, hoping to sound self-effacing, hoping they'd hear her over their music, but they didn't. It had been a while, but she still was confident that Delia, mid-forties, sentimental, listened to Juan Gabriel, while Angel, nineteen, angsty and ironic, listened to Morrissey. They were mother and son. She waved, to which they nodded; then she moved to the staff room. The chef's coat in her locker no longer buttoned across her chest, and even if she tried to wear it half-buttoned, the armpits were too tight. Her chambray button-up and an apron, then. She shouldn't have been nervous. The trick and trap of management, of proprietorship: people presumed you possessed an expertise that you rarely had to perform.

One had to spend time observing the rhythm of a kitchen to expo properly, and Nakia had fallen out of the practice of observing hers. Did a cook move too slow on sauté? She didn't know them like that, and thus called for Kevin's sides too early. They were cold by the time he got his shrimp and grits together. Lesson learned. She would not assume anything about anyone, and would make sure plates cohered to her original plans for them. Though she'd worked hard to build her menu, form had always trumped function for Nakia when it came to food. What a meal tasted like was tedious once a recipe had been perfected, but she never tired of making her plates beautiful. Focusing on what orders should look like put her into a groove.

"I need grits curly, grits white, grits extra-red and grits fucked," she said.

"Got it, got it, got it, got it," Reina, an even newer cook, shot back.

Grits with sautéed kale, grits with white cheddar, grits with extra romesco sauce, and one bowl of sugared grits—a personal affront, but such was life—began to appear before Nakia one after the other. At least Miguel was still using her shorthands. Reina wore a short-sleeve black chef's coat. The jaguar tattooed onto the inside of her forearm leaped in and out of Nakia's view each time she slid another bowl under the lamp. Short sleeves were not allowed in Nakia's kitchen, but had anyone ever told Reina as much? Scouring farmer's markets, scheduling deliveries, staying on top of maintenance, running the social media accounts, working the front of house, and trying to have a social life had kept Nakia away. Monique had been the one to convince her to back off some, to trust in Miguel and try to have a life outside of grits bowls, poached eggs, and mimosas, to try to meet someone. Five months and she hadn't met anyone; she'd only found new ways to stay too busy to meet anyone.

After the opening rush, a whole fifteen minutes without the ticket machine spitting out an order. Nakia looked at the kitchen. There were Nestor and Damian, her young dishwashers; Stacey the Man, as everyone called him, a fifty-something uncle type who worked the fry station; Kevin on sauté; and Reina on the grill and, apparently, anywhere else someone needed her. Miguel had brought Reina's résumé to Nakia as one of two finalists, the other finalist being a guy who had done a year at Le Cordon Bleu. Reina had no high school diploma or GED but she had cooked nearly everywhere small and cool from Long Beach to Culver City. She had taste. Yes to Reina was all Nakia had texted back. In the months since, she'd spoken to Reina maybe six times. A slicked-to-the-side short haircut, a snake tattoo on her neck, and three piercings in one ear, none in the other. Sturdy through the torso and legs. Butch. Nakia had somehow known without knowing, just from her résumé. It felt good to be right. She'd seen Reina cracking jokes in both Spanish and English with others enough times to know she wasn't standoffish, but she didn't seem to enjoy making eye contact with her. That happens when you're the boss, Nakia told herself.

The kitchen made it through that first lunch rush with no big mishaps. She might have been imagining it, and who's to say she was even in a deficit, but Nakia felt herself improve in the estimation of her staff as the day went on.

After closing, she had planned to go to her friend Arielle's gym in Mar Vista for a high-intensity interval training class, to which she usually brought about forty percent of the intensity of the other participants, but since she'd already sweat through her shirt, she figured she was justified in going home. Her old gunmetal Jeep Wrangler made her feel like her nineties high school self had triumphed, at least in this one way. Sitting up high while barely five feet tall, no doors in the summertime, bushels of basil and rosemary from the farmer's market wafting up to the front. As cool as she could ever manage. But it was March. The doors were on. Her whole body ached. She had done the thing without Miguel for the first time in her restaurant's seventeen-month history. An accomplishment that warranted some kind of celebration, or at least some gesture of largesse. A proprietress! When she saw Reina fiddling with her bike on the corner of La Brea and Centinela, she honked her horn one good time, bade her toss her bike in the back, and offered to take her home.

"I live far but you can take me halfway," Reina said.

"Halfway in a car when you were gonna go the whole way on a bike? That makes no sense."

"You know, you can put your bike on the bus," Reina said. "They have these hooks for it on the front."

A smart-ass.

"You grilled the snapper perfect today. Great job."

"It was a good fish. I barely did anything," Reina said. Then: "Thank you."

She directed her down La Cienega, told her to turn onto Stocker, but Nakia wasn't able to cut through the traffic and missed the turn. This felt like a sign. It was a maneuver she negotiated every day to get back to Juanita and Conrad's, one she'd made since she learned how to drive. Nobody needed to learn to merge onto the actual freeway when these fast and wide sections of La Brea and La Cienega were freeway enough.

"Do you smoke?"

Reina looked out the window. The snake on her neck looked fresh, as if it had recently healed, which made Nakia think of shedding skins. She knew nothing about snakes, or most animals, so she did not know whether this was a cobra or a python or a boa constrictor, only that it was black and green and had no rattle.

"Me?" Reina said. "No smoking, but I don't mind to be around it."

Nakia took the next exit. They ended up at Kenneth Hahn park, at the very top. So many giggles, even before Nakia lit up. What was funny, the fact that they knew they would have sex soon, or that they understood they probably shouldn't? Later, Reina would say she'd known it from the moment Nakia asked her to toss her bike in the back of the Jeep. Nakia would say it was missing that turn, how she hadn't even realized she was nervous until then, but once she realized, she'd decided to act on those nerves. For now they contented themselves with looking out past the playground at the smog-strangled city, glancing at each other and giggling as the marijuana did its work, directly on one of them and indirectly on the other. It was the happiest—this moment before the moment—that Nakia had been in months.

She was from Guatemala, an actual Mayan, which Nakia got a kick out of, having never, to her knowledge, met one before. Reina got a kick out of Nakia being a descendant of runaway slaves, as if that were as novel as Hollywood made it seem. "Your people got free just like the Garifuna," she'd said once, which meant nothing to Nakia at the time but upon subsequent Googles meant more. The descendants of maroons and those who survived shipwrecks during the Middle Passage. People who made their safe houses among the Indigenous, in jungles, wherever they could.

Reina used to play the trumpet and had strong, nimble fingers to show for it. If you asked her where something was—a zester, say—she would point with her puckered lips, her chin jutting in the right direction, in lieu of a finger. Once, when they were teasing in the walk-in fridge post-makeout, Reina had said "embouchure" was her favorite word in English, and Nakia stopped herself from telling her it was actually French. Reina had never gone through a femme phase, had only worn lipstick when girlfriends applied it in jest; she supposed her rural band-nerd life had helped inoculate her from certain expectations. Nakia finally learned details about the whisper network among Latino kitchen staff in LA about which chefs were crazy but in a good way, which chefs were fair and normal, and which chefs were just steer-clear, not-worth-it evil. "And what's the word on me?" Nakia had wanted to know. "No words," Reina said, her thumb and forefinger lightly gripping Nakia's chin, her mouth poised to kiss her again. "But people say Miguel is good." Another lesson learned.

Three weeks passed with Nakia on expo, with Nakia on Reina whenever she could manage. She came in early to build the schedule and receive deliveries, did every task she and Miguel had split. In the kitchen she did her best to avoid Reina's gaze, to think of nothing when that jaguar tattoo slid into vision alongside a dish, to ignore the small fire in her stomach that Reina's chugging a bucket of water, her neck working and her head thrown back, invariably caused. Mostly she succeeded. She still lived with Conrad and Juanita, who feigned coolness when it came to her bringing someone home, but Nakia knew it would be a whole thing. Reina remained coy about her own place of residence, always asking to be dropped off at Arlington and Washington, where she waited for a bus, which lead Nakia to believe she had many roommates in a rundown place some point farther east, and likely south. They made use of the office, the store room, Nakia's Jeep, and one reckless time the bar after hours, where someone might have seen them had that person pressed a face against the front windows. High school behavior, and thrilling in that way. Nakia had not been touched by a soul in high school.

On the fourth week, on a Monday when Safe House was closed, Nakia brought Reina to Arielle's. She would not verbalize this, not even to herself, but she understood that Juanita and Conrad were the big leagues. Desiree and Monique, too. She needed to see if Reina could make it out of the minors first, which she defined as someone like Arielle, an open-minded lesbian roughly their age (though Reina was only twenty-five) who was not prone to snap judgments of people but still had Nakia's best interest in mind. Nakia would have liked to think she was above requiring approval of her romantic choices. In truth she distrusted how quickly she and Reina had connected, and wondered whether she was losing her mind to lust, or something worse than lust.

Monday mornings at Sweat Finesse, Arielle's gym, were not for working out but for helping Arielle sort, prepare, and pack food for her other endeavor, her true passion, which was feeding people downtown. Reina accompanied Nakia up La Brea and across Melrose as she collected food and supplies from other restaurants. In its former life, the gym had been a Japanese restaurant; a small stainless-steel kitchen remained in the back, which you had to pass through to get to the bathroom. When the occasional need arose, Nakia would use that space to alchemize the donated odds and ends into a coherent meal.

"So you never have a day off," Reina said on their way over.

"This is a day off. I only go downtown with them every once in a while. Lotta times I just help pack up then bounce. And you know I don't usually work that hard at Safe House. Not with Miguel."

It was probably smarter not to admit this to her employee, but she had realized around week two that it was impossible to keep the boss/employee dynamic intact once the employee started making you orgasm.

"And now no Miguel forever," Reina said, teasing. "Pobrecita."

"How do we know he's not coming back?"

"He called you? You heard from him?"

"Even if he doesn't, I'll find someone else to help eventually. Or maybe I'll just keep expoing forever."

"You already got people who can help. I can help."

Even with her eyes on the road, she could feel Reina's gaze.

"What do you usually do on Mondays?" Nakia asked.

"Me? My cousin in Downey needs help to prep for his food truck on Mondays. It's far on the bus, so I only do it sometimes, when I really need money. Other days I get a haircut. Or sleep."

"What kinda food?"

"Fish tacos. Ensenada style." Nakia could hear the smile in her voice.

"You're joking. Guatemalan Ensenada fish tacos."

Reina nodded, laughing. "He makes good money! He watched a lot of videos online. He parks by the beach in Huntington and they love it."

Nakia drove west on Washington, and the street became wider, lined with boxy apartment buildings, their balconies notional and their windows small. Arielle was a Westside girl; she'd played volleyball at Pacific Palisades, then San Diego State, and returned home set on becoming a real estate broker, before getting a lead on an empty storefront and deciding to open a gym. She was six feet tall, with legs that required her to have her pants custom-made, both due to their length and her muscular thighs. She had been feeding people on Skid Row since shortly before Nakia met her in 2009. She also had a sliding-scale program for some of her workout classes. Nakia found both details at turns fascinating and intimidating. How could a person be that kind?

Today Arielle had dozens of donated burritos from a stand on Sepulveda. Nakia and Reina joined the line with two other regulars, Tameka and L., bagging burritos and adding the snacks Nakia had picked up. Black and teal paint covered three walls of the gym, which was half weight room, half studio space. The fourth wall was all mirrors, and in them Nakia noticed how short both she and Reina looked next to Arielle, how they were legible as a pair.

"Reina, how did you end up in LA?" Arielle asked. And Reina, who Nakia had learned was not easily embarrassed by anything or intimidated by anyone, told her.

"I play trumpet, you know? In high school I was in the band. You ever been to the Rose Parade?"

Arielle nodded. Of course she had.

"They sometimes pick a school from my country to come be in the parade. When I was sixteen, senior year, they pick my school."

She paused to trot over to the front door and hold it open for Tameka and L., both on their way to begin loading up the van.

"So they pick my school, my marching band. And we all go to the parade. It was beautiful. A lot of people, and colors, and flowers everywhere. After we march, they told us we get to eat, then we watch the other people in the parade, and then at the end we get to see the floats again. But before that, no bullshitting, I see my cousin! My first cousin, my mother's sister's son. His name is Manu, like Manuel. We were just marching, not playing, and I hear somebody whistle and then somebody shout 'Choc!,' my last name. I look up and I see Manu standing in the crowd with his baby. I can't wave because we start playing again, but I know he knows I see him. After the parade, when we're just sitting there watching the floats, he finds me. He tells me about the kitchen he works at, how he is making more money in one day than my father is making in a whole week back in my country. So, I stay. I had a visa for tourism, but I just stay. I carried my baby cousin and walked with Manu between the floats and we left. I had only my trumpet and my wallet."

Reina pulled a wallet out of her jeans back pocket, faded green nylon, of the Velcro-closure variety. The kind of wallet a masculine teenager would have coveted in the 2000s. Nakia's older brother, CJ, had owned a similar one in camouflage.

This is the singular story, Nakia understands. It is almost as if to not hear it is to not know Reina at all. And yet she'd never asked that simple question: What brought you here? She knew, or forgot she knew, or perhaps only guessed, that Reina didn't have proper papers. The boss in her, the prudent proprietress interested in plausible deniability, hadn't desired to know anything further.

"Weren't your parents worried?" Arielle wanted to know. "You were sixteen, right?"

"Yeah, but my birthday is January fifth, so I turned seventeen with my cousin. Maybe my mom was worried when she didn't know where I was, but after a few days I always call her. I always let her know where I am. And I sent money. And she knew I was with Manu."

Arielle smiled at Reina in a way that looked familiar. It was the way she smiled in those moments when the homeless were sharing their stories as she and Nakia passed out food. As if she was committed to letting them unburden themselves, even if it was unbearable to hear.

"Manu had a wife, has a wife," Reina said. "For papers, I think, but they had a baby, too. Maybe she just wanted a baby. She hates me, still today. Maybe because I dress like this, I look like this, I don't know. She's Mexicana, so I think maybe because I'm from Guatemala, but so is Manu, so I don't know. So, I leave their place and then . . ." She blew air out of her mouth. "I go through a lotta shit, too much shit."

She ran a hand from the back of her neck to her clavicle. Jaguar grazing snake.

"Did you ever live outside?" is how Arielle phrases it. Nonchalant.

"Me? No, never. Once or twice, maybe, for a night, but I always figured something out. I know how to talk to people, to get jobs. I work hard. I know how to take care of myself."

At this she looked at Nakia and pressed her lips together. Not quite smiling.

That Rose Parade was nine years ago. Something about the mundanity of it, just getting ghost on a field trip, was perplexing. A choice made by a teenager on a whim. Nakia told Arielle as much when Reina went to help load up the van.

"What, you wanted her to have rode on top of one of those trains that goes through Mexico? Or, like, swim the Rio Grande?"

"Don't make fun of me. I'm just saying I don't understand why she did it."

"Why does anybody do anything?" Arielle said. "Maybe she didn't have any queer folks down there, or didn't know she had them. Shit was obviously not great. I don't know. Maybe it's like she said: she heard how much money her cousin was making and figured, 'This is my shot.' I never been that broke, you never been that broke, so it's hard to imagine. Sometimes people just jump. You remember that woman Irma from downtown?"

"Irma with the pink Raiders beanie and them little dogs. How is she?"

"Fine, or you know, herself. She once told me that she came up for like a wedding or something and never left. Said she couldn't risk never getting a shot again. Just left her kid with her parents in El Salvador and started cleaning houses up here. Then she met some dude who got her on meth, and that was that."

"Damn." Arielle knew how to make any gripe or concern feel petty, small in the grand scheme of things. But she wasn't doling out guilt; her tone was too even for that.

"But coming alone as a teenager with no plan is something else. Your girl probably was outside for longer than she wants to talk about. Anytime somebody tells me they were living on the street for a night or two, I multiply it by ten or twenty in my head, depending. I bet it was pretty bad before it got better. I wonder if she's ever looked into DACA. She was a minor, technically."

Arielle was thirty-three, five years older than Nakia, but her demeanor was at once much older—no sad story truly surprised her—and permanently childlike. She remained curious about others and open.

"I see the appeal, though," Arielle added. "She's got charisma. Plus those arms. And those tats."

After that Monday, Nakia no longer thought about the major leagues; she questioned the very logic of needing Conrad and Juanita's approval. They'd never met anyone like Reina, she was sure of it. Part of growing up was accepting that your parents were not the arbiters of your desires, that they didn't need to meet a person, give them the once-over, simply because you enjoyed spending time with said person. They had met Brandyn, whom she'd dated during her management rotation years in New York and for a silly six months of long-distance guilt trips after. Brandyn, nearly a decade older, of the mandatory good morning and good night calls. Brandyn, who showed up unannounced at the steakhouse Nakia was assistant-managing in New York and sat at the bar, befriending everyone, enlisting spies. Brandyn, who had somehow convinced Nakia that the problem with their relationship was Nakia's youth and immaturity, not Brandyn's own insecurity. A lie Nakia believed for too long. Conrad and Juanita had loved Brandyn, likely because she was "established," as Conrad put it. Nakia saw no reason to thrust Reina in front of the scrutiny of the Washingtons, well-meaning but damn near pathologically bougie. She was twenty-eight, not eighteen.

They went on their first real date two weeks later. Nakia chose the movie: *Mad Max: Fury Road*. It was loud, aggressively stylized, full of almost comic brutality. She loved it, perhaps the first action movie since *Alien* she could recall admiring, but Reina thought it oddly sexless. "How come nobody fucks in the end of the world? All those horny boys about to die and nobody is getting together. The only one fucking is the old guy." Fair point.

Reina chose the restaurant, a buzzy "eclectic eatery" in Koreatown. Too buzzy, Nakia feared, the sort of place where somebody she knew—from other kitchens, from college or culinary school—might recognize her. But this was LA, where running into someone you knew was never as likely as it seemed, the city too large and true spontaneity curtailed by cars. You had a higher chance of spotting a celebrity than someone from your actual life. Still, she chose the seat that put her back to the door.

Reina sat facing the open kitchen, the kind of operation where the expo counter is a focal point, so diners can get a sense of the energy back of house. The expediter conducted the kitchen like a baton-wielding maestro, his back to the audience. Reina tracked the kitchen with her eyes between bites of caramelized brussels sprouts.

"I could do that," she said. "I could do that easy."

Nakia had been thinking about whether brussels sprouts and grits could get along together.

"Do what? You already cook, baby. Very well." (Yes, "baby." It felt good to say.)

"You know what I mean." Reina pointed with her lips toward the expo station. Nakia understood it wasn't only expo she was interested in. The past couple weeks Reina had made seemingly offhand observations about Stacey the Man needing to get off the fry station and try something new, about menu items that needed reviving, about processes that needed streamlining. Leadership observations that Nakia uh-huhed in the moment, more interested in kissing that snake—a python, turned out—in the cold of the walk-in, or feeling Reina's fleshy earlobe between her teeth, or simply cleaning up, locking up, and going elsewhere.

"We don't need someone else to do that right now. I'm doing it and things are going good, right?"

Reina swallowed her food, blinked. Were they fighting?

"Oh. You don't think things are going good."

"We ran out of towels last week, and Angel and Delia, they said their pay was off."

Administrative oversights, which she'd addressed. Human error. She was only one person, she said.

"So at least you need one more person."

Reina's hands were clasped in front of her on the table, as if she were waiting to say grace. Odd to be together outside of the kitchen and not at all touching, Nakia thought. Then she remembered that they'd never been out in public on a date before.

She acquiesced. It was less of a hassle to get someone new on the grill and move Reina up than to advertise for, interview, hire, and train an assistant manager to help her with all the tasks she'd neglected since Miguel left. But Stacey the Man would stay on the fryer, she insisted. He fried like somebody's uncle; you couldn't train that.

Since they were already off Western and in a good mood, Reina allowed Nakia to drop her off at home. They drove east on Eighth, then surprisingly north, not south. Up Alvarado past MacArthur Park, surrounded by laundry-festooned apartments, into a neighborhood above the park that Nakia didn't know by name. The gray Victorian had likely been bisected into a duplex first, maybe fifty years ago. In the ensuing years, staircases and front doors had been tacked on willy-nilly, such that from the front it was unclear how many units the house held. Reina kissed her on the cheek and opened the Jeep's door.

"Can I come up?"

"Next time," she said. "It's messy in there now."

She looked beyond Nakia into the poorly lit street.

"Oh, come on, I live with my parents. And you never saw where I used to live in New York. It wasn't cute."

It felt important to know how she lived, to get the mystery of it, whether good or bad—and what would even qualify as bad?—behind them. Everyone lived somewhere, if they were lucky.

Reina did not look at her as she considered her request. She looked up the driveway. She pursed and unpursed her lips a few times, let out a big sigh.

"Okay, if you want to see, come on."

She followed Reina as she walked up the driveway past the large house. At ten thirty at night, the building teemed with the sounds of TVs, water running, pots clanging, Spanish-speaking voices of various ages. In back was a small parking lot jam-packed with cars, mostly beaters, and in back of that was a row of three two-car garages, or what used to be garages. Their front openings had been drywalled over, save for the space required for a regular door. Reina's was on the far left.

She unlocked the door and flipped a switch on the wall. A buzzing florescence from overhead: three loud and bright rods of light. A full-size bed covered in a beautiful multicolored woven blanket. Black lacquer headboard, a matching dresser and mirror, a rack for clothes, and a row of sneakers. A small flat-screen TV mounted to the wall. Cold air prickled Nakia's arms. She must have shivered because Reina moved to switch on a space heater by the foot of the bed. There appeared to be only the one power outlet in the whole room, into which Reina had plugged a very large surge protector. An unpermitted unit, never to be permitted. Nakia knew enough about the way things worked in this city to know that.

"I, uh, where's the bathroom?"

Reina used her chin to point over Nakia's shoulder.

"In the main house. You need a key. I can take you."

A crooked smile Nakia couldn't place. Was she ashamed or amused?

"No, I'm good. I was just wondering."

She sat on the bed next to Reina, who was unlacing her sneakers, and looked around. The room was small enough to inspect from one position. On the back of the door was a full-length mirror. On the wall to the left of the door were menus for some of the restaurants where Reina had worked, their phone numbers highlighted, notes in Spanish squeezed in the margins next to dishes. All of them the neatly printed half-sheet menus that had come to suggest a certain genre of unfussy-yet-cool cuisine. She hadn't lied on her résumé.

A large black-and-burgundy checkered rug covered most of the concrete floor. Nakia wondered whether it also covered ancient oil stains from the room's former life. Spray insulation bubbled up in a wobbly line along the floor where a baseboard might have been. Guilt gripped her—she was the person who determined Reina's salary, which in turn determined these conditions. But she remembered that Reina sent the bulk of her money back home to her parents. She would be able to afford a better place otherwise, surely. It was a kind of sacrifice that Nakia never had cause to make. She hoped she would be willing if circumstances called for it. Why was life so hard for some people? A question people called you stupid for asking, yet no one could give you a straightforward explanation.

Reina connected her phone to a portable speaker and turned on Romeo Santos, the artist she played whenever she was at the helm of the kitchen's radio. Bachata made Nakia feel strangely somber. That keening guitar. She could tell it was heartbreak music despite not understanding many words. She took off her shoes, regretting the choice to wear mules with no socks. The rug was as scratchy as it looked. She sat immobile, too many thoughts.

"Here," Reina said. She handed her a pair of pale blue house slippers. Well-worn but clean. They wore the same size shoe—how hadn't she noticed before? She tried to quiet her mind.

The mirror on the dresser had photos stuck to it, and when she went to it she spotted high school Reina immediately. In her turquoise and white marching band finery, hair slicked back into a low ponytail, breasts pushing against sports bra, which strained against her uniform jacket. A scowl on her face, her trumpet hanging loosely from the fingers of her left hand. Where was that trumpet now? Not easily spotted in the room, and Nakia was afraid to ask. Could have been pawned, stolen, who knows.

January had been a band nerd, too, Nakia remembered. She wondered what January and Reina would make of each other if they ever got a chance to meet. January wasn't a bigot, just boring, with her one boyfriend and one sexual partner, whom she deferred to for everything, but she had grown on Nakia during the years since she'd left New York. January was loyal, and neurotic in a way that Nakia had come to find charming. Nakia knew what Monique would say. That she was in over her head, that she didn't understand poverty enough to be sitting on a bed in a not-quite apartment, falling in love with someone she'd only begun to notice less than sex weeks prior. That there were class and power dynamics she wasn't considering. She would tell her to google United Fruit Company and "Henry Kissinger + Guatemala" and the real origin of the phrase "banana republic," all of which Nakia had already stumbled upon and glossed over in her Wikipedia-fueled effort to better understand this woman. Desiree would say nothing critical, only that she should protect her energy, be pragmatic. But what was the point of life if you had to be on guard all the time? And from what? Heartbreak finds people at every income level.

She turned back to the bed, pulled Reina up to standing, said: "Teach me how to dance to this."

It was easy enough to learn. One,, two, one-two-three, with Reina leading and her following. The slippers made it hard to glide on the carpet, so she kicked them off, and they moved together for two songs, Reina's hand on the small of her back, their cheeks nearly touching. Then Nakia was winded and sat down on the bed. Reina stood over her, not winded at all. She took off her own shirt, her sports bra, all of her clothes, and yet stood over her. It was the first time Nakia could recall her undressing first, as if the exposure of her room, where she lived, had prompted a desire to expose herself as well. Even under florescence she was beautiful, solid except for where she wasn't. Nakia undressed. She pulled Reina by the waist until Reina was on top of her, their mouths flush. How sweet to have the time and space, finally.

Two weeks later, on a Wednesday, they arrived to Safe House early. It had become routine for Nakia to pick Reina up from Washington and Arlington, for the two of them to get to work before the prep team, the better for Nakia to show Reina the ropes. Miguel was in the office, his chef's coat on, printing out the week's schedule as if two months hadn't passed. He was skinnier and puffier all at once, new lines of worry in his face. Nakia came into the room first. Miguel hugged her for surely the first time ever, a long, tight squeeze that only slackened when Reina walked in. A step back, a long, searching stare. He wanted to speak to Nakia alone. She did not feel in complete control of her face as she asked Reina to step out of the room.

Why did she feel so embarrassed, exposed? They hadn't even been holding hands, and *he* had been the one already in the room, pretending somebody expected him, that he still had things to take care of. She felt as if Miguel had caught the two of them out, as if he'd walked in on Nakia with Reina's mouth on her. It took great effort to hold eye contact, but the longer she did the more she calmed down. Miguel was the one caught out. She was the boss, she reminded herself. She could simply fire him. She owed him no explanation; he owed her.

"What happened to you?" she asked.

Another hard life, inexplicably so. Miguel's younger brother had been assaulted on the way home from work, before he even got to his truck.

Jumped, robbed, beaten within an inch of his life for no apparent reason. A coworker found him crumpled in the parking lot the following morning, his breath inaudible. Miguel had been in this very office when he found out, and at the time, that inch, the sliver of possibility that contained the entirety of his brother's chances for survival, was shrinking. He now understood that he'd been in shock when he hurried back to Chiapas, when he took off from the restaurant without explaining. It was as if saying the words to Nakia—*my brother is dying*—made it too true. Once home, it felt impossible to extricate himself. Consoling his parents, sitting at his brother's bedside in the hospital, looking after his brother's wife and children, lurking around the police station for answers to no avail, his own sudden and embarrassing paranoia, his nightly despair. His brother had improved enough to be moved to a recovery facility, but he had sustained permanent brain and spinal trauma and could not yet walk, would maybe never walk. Miguel's parents tried to compel him to stay for good, even introduced him to the owner of a banquet hall in Tuxtla who was looking for a manager. The thought of leading a legion of canapé-wielding cater waiters had snapped him out of his stupor. His life was here now, he said. In LA with his girlfriend, who had just agreed to become his fiancée, and in this kitchen with Nakia, his friend.

"If you want, I take a pay cut, ten, twenty percent."

She did not want to cut his pay; he would need that money to send home. She wanted to make his brother—Ruben was his name, she remembered—whole again, to undo the past two months. No, not undo, but keep Ruben intact, the kitchen as it was before, and still have Reina be who she was now to her. Impossible desires.

"I see Reina on the schedule a *lot* a lot, more than before," he said. His eyes grew large as he scanned the paper in his hand. "More than forty hours."

"She's been stepping up while you were out."

"Helping?"

"Yeah, I needed someone to pick up the slack. She's been on expo and, yeah, pitching in wherever."

Miguel swallowed, exhaled through his nose.

"Okay, we figure it out. No problem."

Such a reasonable response. An adult response.

She parked on the corner of Arlington and Adams, a few blocks away from Reina's bus stop, because there were still twelve minutes until the bus was scheduled to arrive and no shade to be found at that stop. Even the bench was strangely rounded, with rigid armrests so close together a person couldn't sit comfortably. Everything made to ensure people moved on. They had survived the workday with Miguel on expo, Reina on the grill, and Nakia in the front of house, giving her waitstaff and customers some much-needed facetime. Reina had not appeared curious about her and Miguel's talk, nor resistant to him being back on expo, nor hurt when the kitchen cheered his return (Stacey the Man was particularly jubilant), but as soon as Nakia put the car in gear she had turned quiet, feigned interest in the goings-on outside her window.

"You need to pay me for all the extra work," she said finally.

"I was always gonna pay you, you know that."

"Okay good." She reached for the door handle.

"So you're quitting? I don't see how that makes sense. I can still train you, and maybe on weekends we can work something out with Miguel—"

"You know, you say, 'oh, I wanna do good things,' 'I wanna help people,' but what are you doing? You're just messing with people."

"Reina."

"I'm sorry, but you're not a good person."

Unfair. It was precisely because Reina had helped her to better understand a world she had been ignorant of that she had to give Miguel his role back—how was this not obvious? She understood that saying as much now would not help.

"There's no reason to mess up your money over this," she said. "Even if you, um, even if you don't wanna see me anymore."

Reina laughed a little, incredulous.

"I don't mess up my money. I never mess up my money. I can get another job in a couple days, maybe. I told you, I know how to work hard."

Why so mean? Nakia wondered. Why so cold?

"Okay, you can get another job. So why were you taking two buses to come all the way to work for me in the first place?"

"I worked for you cause I thought we were the same," Reina said. Finally, a tiny crack in her voice.

Something hard thumped on the hood of the car and bounced away before Nakia spotted it. An acorn, maybe.

"Alright, how bout this?" Nakia said. "Let's just go to your place and take a minute to calm down and we can maybe think of another setup—"

Just then a fire engine lumbered past them, followed by a second engine, then an ambulance. The inevitable squadron of cop cars. Sirens screaming. The kind of sudden amplification of sound that felt like an attack. Reina left the car during the commotion. She did not look back as she crossed the street behind the final cop car and began her uphill march to the bus stop.

2012

Define the Relationship

Certain weeknights past two, but before four, not much moves uptown save for vermin. The sky dips as black as it can and the streetlights peak at piss yellow. These are hours after those who sleep outside have found their niches for bedding down, hours before sanitation workers bring their Sisyphean labor to Harlem. A figure sprints crosstown in a hoodie, sweatpants, and ballcap. Two whole avenues, not stopping for traffic light or city creature. No way to decipher gender; the figure moves too quick. Gangly, something mantis-like in the way they hold their arms, in the way their hooded head juts forward as they move. Near Fifth Avenue the figure slows, pulls out a phone. The phone goes dark, then lights up again. The figure turns toward a door, waits, pulls it open, and disappears.

She is always damp with sweat, always panting when she arrives. And she wants him immediately, before pleasantries, before even a glass of water to slake her crosstown thirst. There will likely be a second coupling before she strolls home after sunrise, and maybe that one will be slow, tender. But the first one will be what he has searched for a better word for and finding none has called feral. A feral, fast fucking sometimes right against his front door, chain not even slid back into place. Or on the floor of the entryway to his studio apartment, his bike hanging perilously overhead. This long-limbed, deep-brown featherweight girl will ride his face and his crotch, will surprise him with her strength, her focus. She will get down on all fours before him but reach back and grip his upper thigh, guiding him, controlling his thrusts.

After, she's talkative for about an hour, and hungry. Then she falls asleep and he does too. A strange, drowned handful of hours, followed by her leisurely walk home. He has tried and tried to meet her halfway if not at her door, to arrange a car for her, but she's not interested. The run must be its own kind of foreplay, the thrill of sprinting through streets that could crush her.

She never stops feeling familiar, though he pushes the thought aside. Big city, small world and all. Her improbably dimpled chin. Her nose coming to that kind of point that seems black-girl improbable, too. Reminds him of somebody. But the two or three nights she comes to him each week feel like a visitation from another realm, from an alien who thinks of time differently, approaches intimacy differently, isn't interested in what she ought to be interested in. Like the times he's on call and has to slip out shortly after she arrives. She never complains. She sleeps her usual amount in his bed then lets the deadbolt click behind her on her way out. Or the times when he's not in a talkative mood because of what's happened at work, somebody dead or surely going to die, or opting out of something life-saving because of money; the times when his brain, his body, refuse to metabolize death, or the way some people are made to live. Her actual words: "You haven't figured out how to metabolize death yet." As if mortality is a piece of tough, chewy steak.

There are the facile readings: She wanted something of Danielle's for her own, even if only briefly. She wanted to "use him" to get Danielle to reach out to her, even if only to confront her. She wanted revenge of a kind, even if only in her own head. Hard to say, hard to say. No reading feels true for her as she makes her way crosstown to him. She is not so self-absorbed as to be confident that Danielle would care what she does with him, especially in the early weeks when she doesn't know the extent of his and Danielle's acquaintance with each other. Nakia, on the other hand, would care if she knew the particulars, perhaps on Danielle's behalf, but more likely on behalf of what she considers basic human decency. Don't fuck the ex of someone you care about, especially if that someone is your own sister. Whatever. Nakia had told her that she'd be moving back to Los Angeles by September, suggested she start looking for a new roommate. Now it was August. Late August.

He still seems a little afraid of her. Good. Most times she wanders his apartment after their first round nude, appraising his belongings, allowing him to appraise her. Modest bookcase with med school textbooks, sci-fi, and fantasy. The same old Samuel R. Delany novel that her grandfather had read at some point, or at least purchased: *Babel-17*. An uncreased copy of *The Lord of The Rings* suggests an aspiration to dig deep into lore if not an actual commitment to do so. Too many sneakers. His apartment doesn't suggest an easily collapsible life like hers does; it appears to be made of more durable materials. The L-shaped studio is on the eighth floor and faces north out of one window, west out of the other. His L-shaped sofa seems new and expensive, but his bedframe, which groans like an old man standing up too quickly when they have sex on it, does not. He has a record player that she is certain he never uses, as well as a dusty silver six-disc-changer boom box that she is sure he's had since middle school. He remains as easily readable, as open as he'd seemed when they met.

As she speeds past Lenox and Fifth to him, she allows only a second's thought about how exhilarating and dumb it is to run alone in the middle of the night. Most of her thoughts drift to other things, life in general. A kind of clarity that eludes her during respectable hours. If you don't really remember things until around four years old, then she'd had between four and five years of actual, authentic memories of her time with her mother. All the rest was reported to her, and most had been reported by another child—Danielle—so what did she really even know? To live in New York was to accept that despite everyone being in consensus about the cause of a problem, people could not be counted on to fix it. Exhibit A: rats, and the giant black bags of trash lining sidewalks. Do something about the latter and maybe decrease the population of the former, but no. The trash stayed on the sidewalk. She fondles these thoughts and puts them back down the moment she reaches his door, poised instead for the rush of affection, attention, and the blissful single-mindedness of fucking him.

His stomach is the ideal man's stomach—not flat and taut like a washboard. A tiny potbelly, a delicious semi-firm dome that she likes to spread her fingers across. Something simultaneously boyish and old-mannish about his body, his stout torso, his thin ankles, his thick fingers, the dimples hidden beneath his beard. She isn't herself with him, not exactly. She is an idea that formed between the moment of meeting him at that club and arriving at his door that first time. A slick-with-sweat, high-shine version of herself who needs less of everything. Less conversation, less attention, less time. The temp agency had offered her two new positions and she picked the one that was from eleven a.m. to seven p.m., because this idea-version of her requires a late morning. She has never instructed him to keep their nights a secret, yet she knows he isn't telling anyone, can feel it, and this feels like power. He wants to be good to her, wants to honor her wishes. Knowing this also feels like power. He refuses to say he wants more from her, but she can tell he does. It's in his eyes when she leaves each morning, as if he's worried she'll never text him again. She doesn't let on that she hasn't had a boyfriend before, that due to inexperience (and, sure, insecurity) she's unlikely to be the person to ask for more. This seems like an ideal arrangement, given the connection between them, given Danielle.

Late August. Last night she'd run over, too. Rare for her to make the trek two nights in a row, but she needs to be out of her apartment. Nakia has started selling furniture, making her exit plans visible. A gilt mirror that Nakia found on the street last fall sold for $80; the wrought-iron café table and chairs that technically the two of them had bought together had sold for $160. It feels right that he should come into her life at this moment, when Nakia is pulling away from her, yanking up her half of the tenuous roots they've sown together in Harlem. She won't, can't, get a new roommate, as Nakia keeps urging. What is she supposed to do, interview people? She should call Nakia's cousin, the finance guy, and let him tell her what to do. At the very least, she would like to go without a roommate for as long as she can. This studio apartment is the kind she probably needs—small enough to afford alone as long as the building isn't too nice, yet large enough to not want to be outside of it all the time. She hadn't found her current apartment; Nakia had. But she could find one. She could do this. Grow up.

He doesn't broach the subject of a daytime, date-time meetup, of dinner or a movie, because their current setup feels fragile. She isn't skittish like a bird, but she does fly through the night to him like one. And he doesn't know if it is worth risking bursting the bubble the two of them have created—does he really even want to date her? Maybe it's just his own desire for respectability telling him that dating her would be the gentlemanly thing to do. Or maybe the decision hinges on seeing her during daytime hours, outside of his apartment, in normal daytime clothes.

The bubble they create holds its shape through the height of summer, through the perfect low-humidity heat of June and into the swamp-hell heat of July. It lists right as August arrives. Suddenly she comes less often. He texts her and she texts pleasantries back, no promises of meeting up again, then no response at all. He begins to think about going on normal dates with other people. But with a week left to spare in the month, she texts him at midnight, runs over, ravages him with that same determined ease. He comes so quickly that he'd be embarrassed about it if she didn't look so triumphant, so happy to have bested him. She returns the very next night, and this time he's able to stay calm, to take his time. Afterward they lay in silence in his bed, damp and giddy. He realizes he is not interested in dates, normal or otherwise, with anyone but her.

It's still the beautiful part of June—no mug, high breeze—when he is called in to work one predawn morning. She stays in his bed, naked and basking in the air-conditioning, unable to get back to sleep. In the dark his open laptop glows. It isn't locked; he must have checked something on it right before leaving. She used to like to play solitaire, maybe she could do that, she thinks. Or wishes she thought. Really, her brain says: Do it. "It" needs no name. She decided early on that it was best to not know how well he knew her sister, whether they were just work colleagues or more. But she never stops thinking about it, about the potential that his body, which has become so familiar to her, has also been so familiar to her sister.

His email isn't logged in, his text messages aren't synced. No useful photos. So, documents. A pdf confirms it: last summer he'd bought tickets from Cleveland to Cancún for himself and one companion: Danielle Nichelle Joyner. She finds herself scanning for Danielle's birth date to verify it's her when she knows damn well it is her. So, the two of them had been close enough to go on a trip together that he paid for. Shared a bed, most likely. She closes the file, climbs back into his bed. Relief, like two heavy, warm hands on her shoulders, steadies her. Everything gets easier once she knows exactly what is at stake.

Another reading: she wanted to do something to stop the one-sidedness of her and Danielle's estrangement. Something to make it permanent, to put her in control, an actual choice. She does not and has never thought of having helped Nolan as a choice she made, no matter what Danielle claimed. You don't choose to be good to the person who raised you, who was good to you. But this, being with this man, is a choice she's made and keeps making, even as the givens change. This is a reason for estrangement.

That first morning when she woke up in his bed after the club, after the cab ride wherein Nakia told her that it "wasn't about her," she'd lain on his slippery satin sheets—who told him they were cool?—and thought, If you're going to be alone, you have the right to secrets. A right not to explain yourself, not even to yourself. She wondered what she often wondered during that time of day: What was Danielle doing? Then she got mad at herself for the thought. Being estranged from someone you loved turned out to be a grief that came in waves. Loss was loss was loss.

A piano had played classical music through the wall behind his headboard. The same chords over and over. The opening of Bach's *Musical*

Offering. The music would have been outrageous so early in the morning except it was beautiful, lilting up and down. Played by an aspiring composer about her age from Prairie View, she'd later learn. When she and Danielle first came to live with him, Nolan had signed them up for piano lessons. Neither of them took to it but both of them, not wanting to appear ungrateful to their new guardian, soldiered through lessons with Teddy, an Ethiopian music major from USC, for four months. At the end of every session they listened to classical music on CDs he'd bring—for inspiration, he said. Teddy had described Bach's *Musical Offering* as a composition that "isn't about anything but itself," not nature, not love, not a myth or legend. At ten years old she hadn't understood how something could be so turned inward. The very idea felt scary. Now the handful of mornings when she can hear snatches of Bach through the walls deepen her understanding.

On the hot, breezy Saturday evening before Labor Day he plans to ask if she wants to go to J'Ouvert, seeing as how the two of them are awake during those inverse hours anyway. A nocturnal, pre-carnival street party that might include people throwing paint or chocolate syrup on them is not quite a normal date, but they'd be outside together, and they'd be dancing. Again and again this summer he has thought about how they met, how they danced together, and is keen to replicate that feeling of uncomplicated chemistry, of being with her amid a moving crowd.

She comes over as usual, is famished as usual. "I'll make us grilled cheese," he says, and she says okay and gets in the shower, as casually as if it were her own. It's too hot for her to close the door in that tiny, windowless space, so she leaves it cracked while he stands mere feet away at the kitchen stove, thinking about how this girl probably thinks his apartment is darker and danker than it is. She doesn't stick around for the best light of the day. Between eleven a.m. and four p.m. is when his studio really shines, the sun hitting both windows just so and the whole place turning golden. He's thinking J'Ouvert might be the perfect way to get her to see these times; the two of them will either end up back uptown by late morning if they skip the actual West Indian Day Parade, or late afternoon if they stay on Eastern Parkway for it. He's thinking he will propose this outing as soon as she gets out of the shower, when she starts singing.

I don't like you, but I love you,
Seems that I'm always thinkin' of you.

She repeats the last line of the verse, about a no-good lover having a hold on the singer, over and over, as if she doesn't know what comes next, and eventually devolves into humming. But he's heard enough to know enough. The bubble pops. He did not grow up listening to Motown; he grew up listening to his father's Fela Kuti and his mother's 1970s Ghanaian highlife. He learned about Smokey, the Miracles, and a host of Motown acts from the woman whose name used to resound in his head like an earworm before this crosstown sprinter came into his life. A woman he has been glad to finally stop thinking about.

Danielle.

In July the streets smell funky. Rats at 125th and Lexington become brazen at dusk, darting onto the subway platform. She takes to wearing her hair in two afro puffs—space buns, Nakia calls them—on either side of her head. It is a look she can pull off only with red lipstick and dark brown, almost black lipliner. Some seriousness to counter the softness.

She sees him two to three times a week. One night they use his boom box to listen to R&B from her high school years while eating ice cream. He sits on the bed in his boxers. She sits on the floor in her sweats, her hair shaken out into a small afro, flipping through his CD binder.

"'Where I Wanna Be' is so fucked up," she says, holding up the Donell Jones album. "Nobody wants to be dumped so their boyfriend can go sleep around and then come back to them."

"I bet you used to be the type to use songs like these on your voicemail away message," he says.

"Never had a personalized message and I never will. I like the robot lady reciting my number."

"My bad, I forgot you're too cool," he jokes. "You were probably super popular in high school, driving around LA in a drop-top like Moesha."

Moesha, who was supposed to live where she grew up. Whose mother had also died, before the show's first episode. Who always wanted to experience the world beyond where she came from. She's never much thought about these correlations before. So much for seeing yourself in fictional characters. She laughs.

Another night they play cards—speed, a game she is not as good at as she'd like. They sit cross-legged on his floor. His big hands prove nimble, flying from his stack of cards to the table, covering whatever card she drops within milliseconds. After losing six times in a row, being subjected to his short, silly victory dances each time, she refuses to play again. She lies on her back on the floor, hands cradling her head. No dust under his couch. When does he have time to keep this place so clean? She can sense him looking at her from above and feels like a cat in a patch of good sunlight. In the past she'd felt guilty for liking her own face. Nobody ever said hers was a particularly good one, but she's always appreciated it, even if she has very short eyelashes and the kind of chin that Nolan used to say made her look too serious as a child. Spending time under his gaze is overdue confirmation: she's been right about herself all along.

Another night he makes ramen while she flips through his old CD binder again.

"Every time I meet someone from Cali out here, and even when I was in Ohio, I don't get it," he says over his shoulder.

"Just say California, please."

"Okay, whatever. Every time I meet someone from California, I don't get it. One day you just got tired of all that good food and weather and was like, I need to live where palm trees won't grow?"

"What's wrong with New York?"

"Snow, for starters. What's wrong with LA?"

She wants to tell him that sometimes sunshine can be cruel. That cloudy days are a reprieve, and the problem with LA, and maybe even the whole Southwest, is that inevitably the light breaks through, makes the day the same as all others, even when it has no right to such uniformity. Some days feel dark and the sky should allow for this, but it rarely does out there. She'd needed more empathetic weather, she wants to say. I love LA but I don't like it very much, she wants to say. But none of that is the kind of thing they talk about. So she says, "Nothing, I guess," and switches out the CD for another.

In late July, on one of those mornings when she lets herself out, she opens his door and a package blocks her way. A bulky manila envelope, wrapped in tape for extra security. Ohio return address. The sender has written in a familiar hand the last name that was almost, should have been hers. Joyner. Might as well be a bag of dogshit, or a dead animal's carcass. None of her business, she tells herself. She steps over it, quick and delicate. She heads for the elevator and manages to get all the way to the ground floor, to the building's front door, before doubling back and pressing the button to go up again. The elevator light lingers on the fifth floor, as if someone is holding it, and she can't bear to wait. She takes the stairs eight flights up. She stuffs the package under her hoodie and hurries home.

In her room, her door shut and her back firmly against it, she rips the package open with her teeth. It's difficult getting through all the tape. Inside is a slub-gray T-shirt that on instinct she sniffs. It smells like coconut oil, drugstore bar soap, and parched summer lawn. Danielle. It is not until she pulls the shirt away from her face to read what it says that she realizes she's crying. Dark splotches on the cotton.

A merch shirt. Cover art from Erykah Badu's album *Mama's Gun* on its front, North American tour dates on the back. Erykah in that green knit brimmed hat, toothpick dangling out the side of her mouth, eyes low like she's focused, high, or midway to blinking. Erykah at her most cool.

On a piece of printer paper folded within:

Moving. Figured you might want this back. -D

So many questions. She shoves the shirt under her pillow.

The facile readings as well as the more complicated readings feel insufficient. There is something she needs from him, but she cannot figure out what. Embarrassing. A word comes to her: tawdry. That's what Nolan would mutter when he saw her reading vampire romance novels in high school. When he walked through the living room while she watched Pacey and Joey from *Dawson's Creek* kiss on the big-screen TV. Tawdry. He never told her to stop reading or watching what she wanted, but he did let her know, in one way or another, when he thought she was consuming something beneath her. She has never looked the word up but knows it must connote cheapness; cheap ideas and cheap sex itself. Tawdry. Not as lowdown as "smutty" but worse in a way because there is something a bit sad about it, something lazy, unimaginative, desperate. An old-fashioned word that has burrowed into her brain given that she was raised by an old-fashioned man. What is this situation if not that word in action?

It is impossible to go to him for weeks. She tries to focus on her friends, goes out on the weekends and even some weeknights with Nakia, Monique, and January. During an event at Monique's library in Brooklyn she sits in the audience and listens to an author read from a book that she knows she will never read—something about the historical importance of the black bourgeoisie in America—and she feels back to normal, in love with the right things once more. The city, her friends, ideas, even those with which she disagrees. She stops sleeping with the T-shirt under her pillow like some kind of lovesick teenager and puts it in the bottom of her dresser drawer. It only smells like herself now anyway.

Perhaps that would be the end of it, but Nakia begins packing up her half of the apartment, starts begging off the group's plans. One night the two of them sit on Nakia's bed watching a reality show. They eat microwaved popcorn, and it feels like how it should feel, like this is home. A car honks from the street and Nakia gets up, quickly pulls her braids into a high ponytail.

"Be back late."

She's out the door before Desiree can figure out the right way to ask for more information. Standing at the window, she can just make out the profile of Brandyn, Nakia's ex-girlfriend, in the back seat of a cab down below. Her narrow jaw, her close, clean fade. Nakia opens the car door and climbs in. Her head turns toward Brandyn in what Desiree surmises is a kiss. Brandyn, as far as she knows, hasn't been in the picture for months. A tiny betrayal, this omission.

She waits a full, excruciating hour before texting him. She is at his doorstep the earliest she's ever been, possibly the fastest. He is so happy to see her, so relieved and hungry for her that it feels like she's done him a kindness by coming back, by starting whatever this is up again.

Maybe it doesn't matter who they share in their past, she thinks; maybe the only thing that matters is what happens next.

He often felt like repenting in Danielle's presence, like confessing and being absolved. Of what, exactly, he was never sure. After a while the transgression itself began to feel beside the point. She was certain of everything: what kind of medicine she wanted to practice, what kind of life she desired—no, deserved—to have. Hard not to feel insufficient around her. She worked harder than every other resident, seemed to require less sleep, sorted out their various late-twenty-something problems with impatient efficiency. Being with Danielle was like being an athlete tasked with holding the torch at the Olympics—an honor, but taxing. When they'd been dating for only a month, a few of his boys from undergrad came to visit him, and by the end of the trip they were referring to Danielle as "Momma" in a half-derisive, half-covetous way behind her back. He had been into that, too.

She never divulged much about her past, had made any sort of nostalgic reverie or sustained interest in where a person came from seem like a childish impulse, nearly a moral failing. He knew her mother had died young and her father was a deadbeat and that her grandfather had raised her. Knew she had a sister and that they weren't close. That was it. If he'd ever known her sister's name, he'd forgotten it, that's how seldom Danielle brought her up. She kept her apartment clean and filled with the kinds of sunny affirmations—"Dance like no one is watching"; "Live! Love! Laugh!"—that to him suggested a hard childhood, one slim on reasons to laugh and perhaps love, too. In the year and a half they dated, she never wanted to go home for holidays, and he suspected it was because home was either too poor or sad or lonely or chaotic. He filled in his own blanks.

After seventeen months of being together, he finally joined her at her cool millennial church in downtown Cleveland. Outside of cousins' christenings and the like, he had not grown up in church—his parents were agnostic mathematicians—but just as he respected his aunties' and uncles' beliefs, he respected Danielle's respect for religion, for her commitment to a Sunday routine that, barring being called to the hospital, always included a few hours of worship. He'd found himself anticipating visiting her church as the date drew near. It would be a kind of anthropological adventure. It was nondenominational but Danielle had told him, approvingly, that there was a slight Baptist lean to it. What are the young black people doing to make fire and brimstone their own? What do they wear? What kind of music are they playing?

The music wasn't as good as he remembered from the few times he'd been to church before, but there was one ballad, sung by a young guy in skinny jeans and a wide-brimmed, vaguely Western hat, that moved him. Danielle had held his hand and raised her free hand up high, swaying ever so slightly. Following praise and worship, there were announcements, which he didn't really pay attention to; then there was an altar call, led by the pastor, a late-forties brown-skinned guy with a goatee and a blue button-down shirt tucked into his creased stone-washed jeans. Designer sneakers on his feet. Before the pastor had properly invited people forward, congregants started making their way down the aisles and to the front. Some of them stood very close to each other, face-to-face and holding hands or hugging. One, a heavily freckled girl in a long flowy sundress, leaned into another girl's ear, shouting what was presumably a prayer but sounded like plain old yelling over the swelling music. The phrases "Father God!" "By the wayside!" "Right now!" "In Jesus' name!" "Only you!" "Armor!" reached him in his pew. So strange to see people dressed in clothes fit for an R&B concert become filled with such all-encompassing fervor.

Danielle still held his hand, but he could feel her restlessness, a strange current of energy in her fingers. She took a step to the left, out of the pew, lightly pulling him in the process. He had no desire to step forward, so he let go of her hand. Their eyes met for the briefest moment, and on her face was that familiar disappointment. He watched her join up with the freckled girl, squeeze her eyes shut, and hike her shoulders up like it was chilly inside. Danielle prayed with her whole body, tensed up and urgent. It was all too much. When she returned to their pew she patted his arm once without making eye contact, then sat down for the sermon to begin, her hands on her bible and never free for him to try to hold. But he didn't want to try. He'd once again failed a test, fallen short of her expectations, only this time he had no desire to be absolved.

When it was over, he ended up with a vinyl he'd bought for her: *Smokey Robinson and the Miracles LIVE!* He held on to it, never playing it, though he knew he'd never give it to her. It was a gift that required them to spend time together. She didn't own a turntable, he did. Danielle had always enjoyed the act of playing records more than he had, so he might have given her his turntable too had he thought she'd ever allow herself to enjoy it. But who knows how she'd changed. He couldn't bear the thought of Danielle saying something dumb and high and mighty about the record now. Could be that now she only listened to the kind of new-aged, droning singer-songwriter religious music that he'd heard at her church. Music that calls itself gospel but even he knows shouldn't be allowed to call itself gospel.

Now, in Harlem with this other woman, the tap in the bathroom turns off. He plates his grilled cheese, then hers. Sets them on the couch and looks through his vinyl collection. He can't find the Smokey record. His mouth goes dry. Why does he feel anxious? And paranoid, as if one of them—Danielle, or the person in the bathroom who he is now positive is her sister—swiped it from him. Maybe this is a sign. He sits down, chews his food. Danielle's whole thing was always denying him pleasure, or delaying it for longer than seemed fair. She is somehow still doing it, he thinks, throwing a funk over this, whatever this new situation is, this situation that has sustained him for nearly a season. Even if Danielle doesn't know anything about this, she's still managed to ruin it from afar. How is that fair?

She showers, letting the hot water pummel her sternum, and looks forward to grilled cheese. When she gets home in the morning she's going to tell Nakia to stop selling the furniture they bought together, though she doesn't actually care. It's just that Nakia doesn't need the money she's been making off these sales, so why is she doing it? To try to force her hand in some way, to get her to act, to make her plan for a future without her. What Nakia doesn't understand, will probably never understand, is that inertia has its draws.

She lotions, steps out of the bathroom in a towel. He sits in the elbow of his sofa chewing his grilled cheese, her plate waiting on the seat next to him. He watches her, like he always watches her, and like always she does her best to pretend she is accustomed to being watched by a man with whom she's just had sex. Her restaurant days made her accustomed to being watched by men in general—customers and colleagues—but this is different. Instead of willing herself to ignore his gaze, she leans into being observed, looks at him with the same dissecting eye as long as she can stand.

Another thing she's learned in these strange weeks of strange hours together is that he has no poker face. His jaw is too muscular, his mouth too busy, to properly hide his feelings. She can tell when he is preoccupied by work, when he hopes she'll stay longer, that up to this point he hasn't ever been in a rush for her to leave. Now his jaw works harder than a grilled cheese requires.

She picks up her plate and sits down.

"What's up?"

The way he scans her face makes her swipe at her mouth for crumbs.

"So, J'Ouvert is tomorrow night," he says.

"Yeah, Monique said something about it a few weeks ago. I don't really understand what it is. Like a nighttime street party?"

"Basically. I was out here for Labor Day last year, so I went with Dale—remember him from the club?"

She nods. The one who groped Nakia's breasts, or between her breasts.

"I figured me and you could maybe go. My boy who I met in Haiti will be out there, and probably Dale, too. So we could either meet up with them or do our own thing."

Finally he's asking for more. Not a real date, but a gesture. She tells herself to breathe. Small world, small world. She can just say no.

"I, uh."

"It's not a big deal either way," he says quickly.

"No, I wanna go, it's just that Nakia is moving out this weekend, so I gotta be around to help her."

"She's gonna be moving at two a.m.?"

"It's not that I don't wanna go."

"It's cool either way. Really."

He stands up too fast. His knees pop, which makes her feel soft for him. For that old-man side of him.

"You know what? Let's go. I'll still have all of Monday to help Nakia. It'll be fun. Let's do our own thing, though."

"Okay, cool."

Is that a smile? He sits back down, puts his hand on her knee, looks down at it. His jaw is still tense, so she waits for him to keep talking.

"You like Motown?" he asks.

"Like, the record label?"

"Yeah, you know, the music. Like Smokey Robinson?"

"I guess so—my mom did."

"'Did'? She doesn't mess with Smokey anymore? What he do?"

"He didn't do anything. My mom, uh, she died when I was nine. I thought I told you that."

He takes his hand back and rubs his beard and closes his eyes for too long, as if he's working out a difficult problem in his head.

"Maybe you did and I forgot? I'm sorry."

"No, it's fine, I probably didn't tell you. It was a long time ago."

"Oh. Well, um, I used to have a live Smokey Robinson and the Miracles album on vinyl," he says. "I guess I do have it still, but I don't know where."

"Hmm," she says. "I only remember a few songs anyway."

She censors. Unbidden memories. How she'd dreamed of Smokey and her mother when Nolan was dying next to her on the train. How when Danielle was a sophomore in high school, she saved up money to go see him at the LA County Fair but couldn't get a ride out there because it conflicted with one of Nolan's parish golf events. How she and Danielle took a bus downtown to the Metrolink, then another bus to the fairgrounds, nearly two hours each way. How hot it was out in Pomona, how Smokey's light skin was splotched red in places, but he never took his shiny silver blazer off. How after the show, on their way to the gates, she'd convinced an artist packing up for the night to draw one last caricature—her and Danielle. How Danielle had stared and stared at the drawing on the long ride home and said, finally, "This doesn't even look like us," in a way that hurt her feelings for some reason. She packs all those thoughts into a little cube, tucks the cube somewhere deep in her brain. Visiting him has been a reprieve from this constant remembering.

"Hmm," she says again. "You know, I didn't think you actually played your vinyl."

He's looking at her strangely, like she's been picking her nose. She kisses his cheek right where the dimple hides under his beard. Puts a hand on his upper thigh, close, close enough for his body to respond, but he shifts his hips a millimeter away from her. She can feel him move more than she can see it. He rubs his beard again.

"I need to, um, get up early for a meeting. It's cool if you stay, but we should probably call it a night."

"What?" She has been thinking about that little hip shift, not listening.

"I said I should probably get some sleep. But you know you can stay for as long as you want in the morning."

She nods. She has never felt as guilty about their time together as she suddenly feels. It's like the ghost of Danielle, a person who isn't even dead, has entered the room, is sitting on the far side of the couch.

In bed he gives her a peck on the forehead, the kind of dry, we've-been-together-forever kiss he'd taken to giving Danielle fairly early in their relationship. He thinks back to how little Danielle shared of her family, how eager she was to live in the future and forget her past. He's almost certain the woman next to him now knows what she's doing, that she's known it the whole time or at least for a long time. It is not terribly hard to imagine her motives. She might have tired of needing Danielle's absolution, too, of always falling short in her eyes. He wishes she would just confess. Then maybe he could absolve her, or she could absolve herself, and they could keep on. Absolve, dissolve and resolve, he thinks. Without that, whatever was hot here is cold and most likely cannot be made hot again. The thought of even trying makes him tired. Still, he pulls her close, puts his hand on her belly, then slides it up between her tiny breasts to her heart. Her heartbeat is fast and he realizes that she's nervous. Perhaps she knows it's over too. He's sorry about that. He pulls his hand back down, past her navel into her sweatpants. She moves with him, so he reaches down and kisses her neck, puts his tongue in her ear. It takes surprisingly little time for her to come. He would think she was pretending except he thinks he knows her well enough by now, at least knows this part of her. In the dark, her breath slows again.

Sleep finds them both.

He makes sure to wake up early and dress, despite not needing to be at work for hours. He looks at her sleeping face, her wild hair and funny chin. They look the most alike when asleep, he realizes. Why hadn't he noticed before? Or maybe he'd noticed their similarities without naming them, and was attracted to her for the same reasons he was to Danielle. A kind of take-it-or-leave-it beauty.

He remembers another clue. Once, back when she told him that he didn't know how to metabolize death, she'd spoken of her own future death like she was certain how it would play out. "I'm pretty sure I'm gonna die by heart attack," she said. "Maybe when I'm young or maybe when I'm old, but unless I get hit by a bus or something, it'll be my heart. That's generally how people in my family die." Her cavalier tone had rattled him—that and the concept of metabolizing death itself. Danielle had said something similar to him once, that she came from a family of faulty hearts.

He picks up her hoodie from where she left it on the floor by the foot of his bed, intending to put it on the sofa, but he changes his mind and drops it back onto the hardwood. Better to make it look like he was in a rush to leave.

In the morning, when she wakes up alone, she hears Bach's *Musical Offering* through the wall behind his headboard again. She gets out of the bed, dresses, and leaves his apartment for the last time, she knows, though it will be some time before she knows that she knows. Outside his door the music is even louder. She stands in the hallway for ten minutes, her eyes closed. She listens.

2009

That Face in the Mirror

She felt grateful for the parrots. Birds who had no right being in Leimert Park, and yet they thrived high up in the skinny palms and in the equally out-of-place shaggy cedars, their grass-green bodies crowned by vibrating terra-cotta heads. This flock had been in the trees above the pool house—a garage with decent insulation, really—for months, since shortly before Desiree and Nolan went to Paris. Other areas, like over in West Adams, had flocks crowned with gold, but the ones above Nolan's house were always red on the heads, always green on the bodies.

The fact that they were still up there, socializing and squabbling when Desiree returned, had been a comfort. Never seen lower than the rooftops but heard everywhere, they'd helped her distinguish day from night after she'd put up blackout curtains to accommodate her late restaurant hours. Now unemployed, and hungover, she lay in bed at ten a.m., eyes closed and ears open to them, wondering after their urgent business and news.

A clatter at human height. Doors opening and slamming shut, silverware clanging. Someone was in the main house. Nolan's house. Why wasn't she afraid? Could have been the hangover, or her own desperate and lonely hope, but Desiree didn't consider the possibility of a burglar. No cautious peek between her curtains. She opened her door, stepped out, and looked. Past the leaf-choked pool and rusted loungers, she saw movement in the kitchen windows: a head covered in jet-black coils ducked in and out of view. Finally, finally. Danielle.

Inside, Danielle stood on the Spanish tile counter and felt along the tops of the cabinets. She glanced down at Desiree when she entered the room but she didn't come down. No "hi" or "hello" or "I've missed you." She had the worked-over, puffed-up, and greasy-faced look of someone fresh off a red-eye flight. Her skinny jeans had loosened in the butt and knees. Desiree waited, didn't try to rush her down. When she finally stopped feeling along the cabinet tops she held a photo in her dust-blackened palms. She hopped down, pivoted to the sink for a hand wash, the photo next to her on the counter.

"What is it?" Desiree asked.

Danielle dried her hands and held out the photo but did not release it, her thumb and forefinger tight on a corner.

It was their mother, standing in grass in a frilly white sundress, a toddler holding her right hand, her left hand resting on her pregnant belly. In the background, to the right of the toddler, was a man in short red running shorts, tall white tube socks, and a white polo shirt. Their father, Terry Joyner, fussing over a barbecue grill. Toddler Danielle held a babydoll by its tuft of curly black hair. One of very few photos of the four of them, this short-lived family, all in one place at one time. The oldest piece of evidence.

Now Danielle was pulling the photo away, smoothing it against her sweatshirt, not looking Desiree in the eye.

"I put it up there in eighth grade so Granddaddy wouldn't make me use it for Mrs. Ranier's family tree project."

"Oh." Because of Terry Joyner, Desiree guessed. She'd forgotten she was supposed to hate him. Hard to remember to hate someone you knew so little about. Desiree had the feeling she would never see this photo again, but asking to look at it longer felt too much like ensuring that outcome. Danielle walked past her and through the door to the living room. Desiree followed.

Seeing as how Desiree avoided most of the house outside of the kitchen, it was hard to tell what proportion of the living room's disarray was due to Danielle and what had preceded her. The plastic covers hastily snatched off the sofas and left in a sticky pile near the fireplace were Desiree's doing. The books and vinyl records heaped on the coffee table next to an open box were not. But the papers—receipts, files, old homework stacked in an armchair—might have been her on the hunt for something post-Paris, or maybe it was Danielle on the hunt for something now. It smelled very Nolan-esque in here, almost unbearable. Cigarettes, those stupid strawberry hard candies, walnut shells, dry dirt.

Danielle added the photo to the open box. She'd been inside the house longer than Desiree realized, which made her panic, not because it suggested that a burglar could have done the same, but because it suggested that Danielle had no intention of coming to find her out back, that she would have swooped in and out without speaking to her. Desiree sat down. The couch felt mushy without its plastic coating.

There seemed no feasible way to begin a conversation. The grandfather clock on the wall struck ten thirty.

"Feel free to take whatever," she finally said. "If you tell me what furniture you want, I can ship it to you."

Danielle made a noise like "tuh."

"I don't want that much." Still no eye contact. So much interest in corners, the floor, the ceiling. "What happened to the funeral?"

"Um. He didn't want a funeral, he told me . . . If he'd wanted a funeral he would have paid for it ahead of time, planned it out."

"You mean you would have planned it out," Danielle said.

"Yeah, if he asked. If he asked me, I would have. So what?"

Danielle left the room again and came back with her college graduation stole and honor cords, which she wrapped around her hand and dropped into the box. Some of the framed photos on the wall were gone, but now Desiree couldn't remember exactly how many had been there and which long-dead people had smiled down on her from the eggshell-painted wood panels.

"You know, a lot of people think that a funeral isn't for the dead person," Danielle said. "It's for those of us who are still here."

"Yeah, well, you weren't here. So."

Something about her diction was too crisp, too formal. An insult.

They knew each other; if they did not, then no one else in the world knew them. If not sisters, then nothing. Just a single face in the mirror. Danielle still wouldn't look at her.

"Also, I didn't want to plan a funeral after all the shit I'd been through with him. I was tired."

"And that's what mattered. How you felt."

His biscuit-dough skin. All those needles. The dead weight of him, yet alive.

"I did what he asked me to. He was going to do it regardless."

"You did what he asked, including not telling me in time for me to stop y'all."

Danielle grabbed a small stack of records and put them in a box so quickly Desiree could only see the beatific, acne-scarred face of Nat King Cole on top. She should have made a pile, or at least a list of things she wanted to keep, she thought. She was the one ultimately responsible for every item in the house, and she hadn't cared to think about them as heirlooms, artifacts, or even archives. She'd avoided thinking about them altogether.

"You know," Danielle said. "There's, like, a certain type of person who jumps at the opportunity to help someone die, and then there's everyone else. Most normal people wouldn't have done it. Most normal people would've talked him out of it. You need to figure out why you were so eager."

Fuck you, she thought, but she could not bring herself to say it. Too scary. She looked down at her lap. She wore the same long, faded black T-shirt she'd slept in and nothing else. Her thighs now felt too exposed, her breasts too loose; she was essentially naked in front of this person determined to treat her like a stranger, a murderer.

She watched Danielle struggle with the flaps of her cardboard box as she tried to tuck them under one another to close. She had probably stuffed every meaningful family photo in there by now. Growing up, Danielle had been the more photogenic of the two of them, as well as the one with the better eye for photos. Sherelle sometimes splurged on disposable cameras for milestones—birthdays, recitals, theme parks—and when it came time to pick up the prints it was never a question whose were whose. Desiree:

thumbs in corners, underlit rooms, and her own feet. Danielle: violet jacaranda blooms from around the neighborhood, their mother's smiling, mole-flecked face, a row of stuffed animals in stately repose. Things Desiree saw daily would suddenly hold new meaning, including herself. It was like not realizing you'd been staring into nothingness, blank space, until someone cupped the sides of your face and shifted your view to what was actually worth looking at. Just to the left and infinitely better, or at least more correct.

Danielle was coming back inside with a second box, already full of things taken from the garage. She stood over Desiree now, close enough for the smell of her sweat to register. The underside of her chin, dotted with acne scars, looked tender, babylike.

"Did he ever tell you about his son?" Desiree asked. "How he thought he had one in France?"

"That story's not true. It's a lie."

"So he told you?"

"He told me all kinds of things he never told you, Desiree. Most of them weren't true."

"Like what?"

"It obviously doesn't matter now," Danielle said. Desiree did not believe this. Such was their relationship: Danielle keeping information from Desiree while also holding Desiree's ignorance against her.

"So he told you we might have family we've never met and you didn't feel like looking into it, or even telling me?"

Danielle closed her eyes, breathed out through her nose. Desiree waited.

"I've been advised to take enough of my share of whatever money there is to pay off my loans. I don't want a penny more. I expect you to be honest."

"Advised. By like a lawyer?" Desiree stood up. "Come on, Dan."

She cautioned a touch of Danielle's arm. They had never been physically affectionate. Danielle's body was always moving away, slipping out of Desiree's spindly hugs, ducking even Nolan's pats on the head. No huddling close under forts, no cuddling on cold nights or during scary movies. The only exception being those early post-mother days, when Danielle had allowed Desiree to cling to her at night, to share the occasional bed.

She assumed this was how it was with everyone, that a sibling's affection was rarely physical, their hugs by nature awkward.

Danielle took a step back, freed her arm to pick up one of her boxes.

"Desiree, you don't really know me. And you didn't know Granddaddy like you think you did. And now, after all of this, it's clear that I don't really know you, so . . ."

The sun had traveled high enough for weak beams to slant across the coffee table. Desiree waited for her to finish, to say the final terrible thing. It would take some days before she realized it had already been said.

She found herself leaning over and picking up the remaining box, following Danielle out to her rental car and putting it in her trunk. What else could she do?

The day was warm, the street empty. It smelled like jasmine.

"Wait," Desiree said. "I have something. Just wait one second."

Back inside to Nolan's room. There was his bed, the military corners still tucked tight. The photos on his dresser of their grandmother and their mother, two photos Danielle would have taken had she dared enter the room. Between the photos lay a gold-leaf cardboard box, the kind that might hold a pair of cheap earrings. It held a tiny plastic bag full of ashes. She grabbed it.

Danielle was backing out of the driveway. She hadn't waited. Desiree knocked on her window. Danielle rolled it down a crack.

"This is the last of him," Desiree said. "I saved it for you."

She held the box forward. Her sister looked at it, gold foil peeling at the corners where Desiree had gripped it too tight. She did not roll down her window and reach for it, but the car idled. Its fan whirred. On the car radio Sheila E. sang about the glamorous life. Without love it ain't much. Danielle stared at the box then squeezed her eyes shut. When she opened them again her chin crumpled, and Desiree knew she would cry. Her sister did not cry often, but when she did it was violent, heartbreaking to behold. Danielle put the car in park halfway in the driveway and half in the street. She sobbed into her hands, her chest heaving, her face cracked open. Desiree watched her. She knew better than to do or say anything.

Danielle muttered to herself, "This is all so stupid."

How embarrassing. To suddenly understand how much of a burden you are to another person, how much someone else might wish to be free of you. Desiree had never considered this before: she did not fit into the life her sister wanted. There was no space for her. There had hardly been space for her, low-achieving and needy as she was, before Nolan died, and now that small space had shrunk down to nothing. Without Nolan, there was no one left to expect or require Danielle to do right by Desiree, to guilt her into shouldering the burden of sisterhood. What was sisterhood but a mutual agreement anyway? Blood didn't have to mean anything. She lowered her hand. Danielle rolled down her window.

"Give it to me."

Desiree handed it over. In the palm trees above, the redheaded parrots, having migrated from the back, squawked and clamored, fighting or playing or both. Sweat trickled down Desiree's spine.

"I loved him," Danielle said. She looked up at the trees, too.

"I know . . . He knew that."

"He didn't even like me."

Danielle loved to say this about Nolan, as if it was important. Where and what would they have been without him?

"He loved us," Desiree said. "He loved you. That's all that matters."

Danielle shook her head fast, like a child.

"No, no it is not."

What else was there to say? There were worse childhoods than the ones they'd had. Another minute or so passed. She heard Danielle's car shift back into gear. Impossible to look at her sister's face. Desiree studied the palms, counted the emerald bodies amid the fronds, and held her own hand. Not until the car reached the corner did it feel safe to watch it go.

PART TWO

We must distinguish our real worlds from dreams, though we live as long in one world as the other.

—Gayl Jones, *The Birdcatcher*

2022

Group of 7

Jay had lived in this El Sereno building with her mother and two brothers back when it was apartments, back when the neighborhood was still considered the barrio. They'd moved on to other complexes farther east as the rents began to rise, long before this one switched to condominiums, but "this always felt like my childhood home," Jay had told Nakia the first time she slept over, "maybe because it was the only place with more than one bedroom." When a unit came up for sale three years ago, she'd bought it. A dingbat—scratchy stucco exterior and wide rectangular profile with impossible, skinny stiletto posts as support—perched on a steep hill. All upper and no lower, like a linebacker in a minidress. Residents parked their cars below the building, careful not to take out one of the posts and send the whole thing crashing down when they reversed. Jay's unit had three bedrooms, two baths, a long wall of windows in the living room, and a low-slung ceiling, which gave the place the feel of a seventies den. She'd "spent some time with it empty to get a feel for its energy," then settled on recycled bamboo floors, deep cognac leather loungers (vintage, scored in Long Beach), fluffy rugs, gold lamps, a seafoam green semicircle couch, Turkish poufs, and tropical plants. The perfect place to stay too long and indulge too much.

"We need to just go ahead and adopt the Israeli method," someone was saying. Must have been Yesenia, the only voice Nakia hadn't heard much before. She had an accent, hard to say from where. Vaguely Canadian, what she did with her *o*'s.

"And what, exactly, is the Israeli method?" Rico asked. He looked ready to pounce, like a cat after a feather teaser.

"Desalination, relax," Yesenia said. "It's expensive and would need a shit-ton of development, but we can't depend on water from elsewhere forever, especially not with the Colorado drying up and Ag taking the lion's share."

Nakia stood with her back to the room, making cocktails next to Jay's sink. She wrestled with a silicone tray until a large sphere of ice crash-landed into a tumbler of bourbon and vermouth. She repeated this four times. She put the drinks on one of Jay's brass trays and faced the dining room. Six people—Jay, Yesenia, Rico, Kyle, Beverly, and Monique—sat around the table. Jay held a glass of wine in one hand and used the other one to register her objection, a sweeping movement like an orchestra conductor.

"Hold up, hold up. De-sal is murderous for the environment. It's not a real solution," Jay said. She looked at Nakia with an eyebrow raised. Her cue.

"Right, it basically sucks water from the most important ecosystems at the deepest level of the ocean," Nakia said. "Which we know the least about. Plus, you need like a ton of energy to make it work. There's a company stationed right off the coast that's been trying to get their de-sal operation approved by the state since forever. It's a mess."

Jay's mouth turned up at the corners for an instant, grateful. She picked up a glass from Nakia's tray, passed it to Yesenia, and moved from the dining table to the sofa. The others followed her, grabbing drinks on the way.

"Could be solar-powered, though, right?" Kyle asked. He and Rico were the kind of physical opposites that Nakia loved in a couple: Rico short and wiry, Kyle tall and wide. Kyle put a fleshy palm on Rico's shoulder.

"Exactly," Yesenia said. "Plus the deep-ocean problem could be fixed. They always act like stuff is impossible when it isn't. We literally created a vaccine *and* antiviral pills for COVID in less than two years. If you put real money behind an issue, you can probably fix it. Nothing's gotta be done the way it's being done right now."

Nakia watched Monique half-heartedly follow the conversation. This was the first time she'd accepted an invitation to one of these dinner parties, the ones Nakia and Jay hosted every month or so. Each time they assembled a different group of people they'd met or wanted to meet to talk about real issues, not politics for politics sake, not "personalities," which was how Jay dismissed celebrities and influencers, never mind that Jay was friends with many such personalities, but actual ideas and actionable items. Of these they'd covered immigration reform, bail reform, health care reform, higher education reform, affordable housing reform—all of the reforms, really—but every conversation inevitably lead to the climate catastrophe. This was part of the grand design. "Every topic ties back into the planet," Jay liked to say. Nakia didn't consider Monique her greenest friend, not by far—nobody needed a car in New York and yet Monique drove one, an old gas-guzzling Explorer—but Monique knew a lot about a raft of real issues, and she knew how to act among interesting strangers.

Nakia sat on the arm of the sofa closest to Jay. She had once jokingly called these parties the Group of 7 during the early days of throwing them, and Jay had said it wasn't funny. Now Jay called them that too, except in earnest. Seven people, they'd agreed, was a good number to encourage actual listening, and to root out and dismantle spurious ideas. Nakia's role at these dinners was to think up the menu, to help think up the guest list, and to help think up conversational pivots should they be needed. It wasn't direct social outreach like the kind she still did with Arielle on Skid Row, but it was important work. People needed a safe space to think about solutions, to feel safe to let go of their own helplessness. She and Jay agreed on that.

"The term NIMBY was literally invented in LA," Rico said. He sat erect, resisting the pull of the low, deep sofa. "That's how stubborn homeowners are here. Folks in LA take it as some kind of a given that we should acknowledge 'homeowners' as a viable subset of society."

"Wait a minute, now. Is that true?" Beverly said. "I always assumed NIMBY was created by a social scientist in Chicago or something."

She had the kind of booming, permanently code-switched voice that intimidated people on conference calls. Her sheer purple scarf had sustained several dribbles of wine.

"But you know what," she went on. "I do remember when the city wanted to put a light-rail in the Valley, back in the eighties. The people out there sure did not-in-my-backyard that project down to the studs."

"And now they're all stuck in traffic," Kyle said.

"And now they're all tryna get outta traffic and into my neighborhood," Nakia muttered. Nakia's mailbox in Inglewood was stuffed with postcards from investors offering to overpay for her house in cash. After her parents retired and decided to move back to New Jersey, her brother, CJ, inherited Conrad's dental practice and she inherited the house in Baldwin Hills. It was too big and showy for her, so she'd sold it and moved a mile south to Hyde Park, still a beautiful neighborhood and nearly forty percent cheaper because it didn't hold a valuable place in the average Angeleno's real estate imagination. She used the profits from the sale to open a second location of Safe House off Pico and La Brea.

"Let's back up to the homeowner thing for a second," Beverly said. "I didn't know that was an issue. Are we the new persona non grata?"

"I mean . . ." Yesenia trailed off, looked away.

"I think that ever since the protests during the pandemic—" Nakia began.

"The Uprisings," Jay corrected.

"The George Floyd Uprisings," Rico added.

"Right, right," Nakia said. They were being annoying. "Since then there's been a push for folks to stop emphasizing property ownership as a way to assert civic status."

"Yeah, just cause you 'own' land doesn't mean you should be calling the shots," Yesenia said. "This ain't feudalism, and really, the bank owns that land until you finish paying them."

"Exactly," Kyle said. "It doesn't make you more of a stakeholder in the future of this place."

"But doesn't it literally do that," Beverly said. "Make you hold a bigger stake?"

"Shit, not at the rate people buy and sell property nowadays," Kyle said. "And don't even get me started on how many homes private equity owns. They're not even people!"

"Think of cities like LA or San Francisco," Rico said. "When you say only homeowners should be worthy of respect you're basically saying that you only have respect for millionaires, cause that's what it takes to afford these house notes."

"That," Kyle said. "Or you're a Boomer who bought when the buying was good and don't understand the current reality. No shade, Ms. Bev."

"Ah, hmm," Beverly said. She took a sip of her wine. Nakia wondered if she should intervene.

"The George Floyd Uprisings," Beverly said. "Hadn't heard it called that before. Interesting."

She was the oldest woman, at sixty-five-ish, to ever be invited to a Group of 7. Nakia and Jay tried to keep it to guests fifty years and younger, on the basis that younger minds were better at "imagining radical change," as Jay put it, but Nakia knew that Monique harbored a fondness for her elders, a holdover from her librarian days, and she'd wanted Monique to feel comfortable at her first dinner. Beverly was one of those old neighbors who had tracked Desiree down with kind words and valuable memories of her grandfather Nolan in the years since he died. Desiree had brought her to Safe House, and she'd become a regular, and something akin to a friend.

Beverly, oblivious to the tension she'd created, finished the wine and got up for a refill, waving Jay off when she tried to reach for the glass. Nobody wanted to argue with a tipsy auntie in a kaftan and fun haircut, not before dessert. But they would, Nakia knew. They'd tear poor Ms. Bev apart.

"But, you know what," Beverly called from the kitchen. "If you can call what happened in Watts way back when a rebellion, which seems to be the consensus these days, you can call a bunch of young folks burning up Fairfax and Rodeo Drive one too."

Palpable relief. Not perfect, but not all the way bad. She returned to her seat and looked around the room as if she was game for whatever rejoinder came her way.

"Right," Rico said, tentative. "And like, it only got violent cause the cops made it violent, like always. I was out there most nights. Kyle stayed home with the baby so I could go support."

Beverly's eyes widened at this.

"Oh, wow, I cannot imagine you out there at night with one of those things on, those bacla, balaclavas, trying not to get tear-gassed. How'd you even get it over your hair?"

Rico's thick locs shot out in every direction like Basquiat's. He tittered in lieu of answering.

"I was out there too," Yesenia said. "You can't work at city hall for seven years, passing by people with kids and stuff sleeping on the sidewalk, and not want to fight back."

"People do it every day," Kyle said. Whereas Rico was playfully shady, Kyle tended toward genuine saltiness, Nakia observed.

"Yeah, well, I guess I'm not people," Yesenia said.

"I was out there on the first day serving food downtown," Nakia said. "But then it got too crazy. I don't do fire."

"Since I guess we're roll calling," Monique said, "I should probably confess that I was in New York, still afraid to go outside and die from COVID, because by that point I had already lost three people—one librarian friend and two former patrons. So yeah, I didn't go to any protests."

"Oh, honey," Beverly offered, hand over her own heart.

"But!" Monique continued. "Somehow my car got 'all cops are bastards' spray-painted on the side of it in hot pink—the full thing, not even the acronym—and I left it like that for several weeks, which I think should count for something, right?"

Of course Monique knew how to make everyone get over themselves, Nakia thought. How to guilt them down then lift them back up with laughter. The conversation turned to people wanting Monique to explain how New York City co-op housing worked, which she did to the best of her ability, using Desiree's co-op purchase as an example. Yesenia seemed galvanized by the concept of shared ownership and building governance, while Beverly was scandalized that each co-op member did not actually own a piece of the land. Nakia moved back to the kitchen. She put the dirty dinner plates on one side of the sink and dumped a carton of tiny farmer's market strawberries into a colander on the other side. She halved and pitted four peaches and took them out onto the balcony to grill.

It was mid-March but hot like late August; an unseasonable "heat dome" had been squatting over the LA basin for two weeks. Prior to that it had been wintry, in the fifties and low sixties since Christmas. With the heat came a predictable brush fire. Nakia wasn't sure where the fire was, but she could smell it in the twilight air as she placed the peaches facedown on the hot grill. Seemed like somewhere on the far side of the arroyos, probably in some patch of wounded wilderness that grew too fast in the rainy season, dried up within a week of heat, and was forever doomed to be set ablaze by man, either via dumb cigarette-butt accident or the electric company's negligence, an ageing transponder on the fritz.

These parties were best enjoyed before they started and as they began to wind down. Nakia mostly cooked for Groups of 7 now, never at home and seldom at her restaurants. Miguel, steadfast for nearly a decade, handled most personnel issues and day-to-day concerns. After years of rehab, his brother Ruben had learned to walk again. He'd visited LA in early 2020 to see a neurologist at UCLA who specialized in injury-induced epilepsy. His brain surgery had been postponed during the early pandemic but happened last summer. So far so good. According to social media, Reina had left the country shortly after the 2017 presidential inauguration. For a couple years her posts had suggested she was fine back in Guatemala, with a dog and a girlfriend, and then one day, around the time Nakia's parents retired, she couldn't find Reina's profile. She assumed she'd been blocked, and eventually understood that she deserved to be blocked. Nakia spent most of her days up and down La Brea, checking on one or the other locations, showing her face, running errands, scheduling shipments, doing paperwork, but not really feeling essential to either place.

She usually timed things so that it took the first half hour after the guests arrived for her to finish preparing the meal. This way people could see that she still possessed some expertise, that she wasn't just an entrepreneur but an actual craftsperson, someone capable of making something. Bit by bit over the past eight months the best of her home kitchen had migrated to Jay's, but she would not move in herself. It was too far from her restaurants, is what she told Jay, but the truth was she had no desire to live this far from Black people, even as their ranks dwindled on her side of town. And Jay wouldn't move to Inglewood because she liked to be close to downtown for her various meetings in and around city hall, and close to the private club in the warehouse district where she held court and worked most days of the week. Theirs was a very strange arrangement in the eyes of Nakia's lesbian friends, and an enviable one in the eyes of many of her straight ones.

Jay had run a two-person human resources department for a tech company since close to its start, a splashy app that didn't have any proprietary technology but had quickly become a household name nonetheless. A middleman service, essentially. When they went public, her early shares meant she suddenly had a load of money, and she quit. Now she ran her own HR consulting business, specializing in workplace morale, which, it turned out, could be boosted by implementing green initiatives. "Everyone wants to feel like they're fighting the demise of the planet, even at a nine to five," she'd said on one of their early dates.

She also was on the board of a handful of startups and "social ventures," a phrase Nakia didn't quite understand, but one of them was a mentorship program for women in clean energy. Another was for people of color in tech. She'd also recently joined the board of Tru Talk, the fancy, alternative speaker series. It was the same speaker series for which Monique had done a talk in 2019, before videos of Tru Talks started to go super viral in the early days of the pandemic. During that brief period of time in 2020 when people dared to hope that the world might come out better on the other side of such a huge shared crisis—the Great Reset, someone had named it—Tru Talks had become a way for those sheltering at home to kill time while gaining insight into what kind of changes for the better were possible, or even needed. Fast-forward two years and no Great Reset appeared to be on the horizon, but new Tru Talk videos received views in the millions, with speakers garnering book deals and huge online followings.

Jay told Nakia that the great thing about Tru Talk was that they did more than just pander to rich folks; they appealed to everyday people who wanted to help worthy causes. It still sounded like pandering to Nakia, but harmless enough.

The screen door squeaked open.

"You know damn well none of these people want dairy," Monique said. She edged out onto the balcony just as the grill's fire kicked up. "That cream you made in the fridge. I can tell an alternative milk crowd when I see one."

"Not even Ms. Bev?"

"Oh, she definitely *wants* some but you better not let her. The elders are the most lactose-intolerant."

"I have a vision," Nakia said. "I'ma put it on the side."

"The greens were great. Not overcooked at all. You got 'em to stay so green. Same recipe?"

"Same old Granddaddy Nolan recipe. Liquid smoke instead of smoked turkey. Plus some other things."

"I still can't believe she never shared it with me," Monique said. "Not that I cook."

When Desiree finally stopped punishing Nakia for leaving New York, after that strange, long summer where she was never in their apartment at night and Nakia feared she was ruining her life in some way for the dumbest reason possible—a man—Desiree had given Nakia a going-away gift, with the caveat that she keep it to herself. Four index cards with cramped handwriting in blue ink, the totality of Nolan's recipe collection. Greens with salt pork, greens with smoked turkey, an all-purpose roux, "easy French 75s" and steak picado, the latter two provenance unknown, the first three presumably deep knowledge. After forgetting about the cards for a few years, and a few more years of tinkering, Nakia now served a collard greens and cheesy egg brioche sandwich at Safe House that people on the internet loved. Those were Nolan's greens.

"Fish was good too, and the parsnip puree."

"So much praise! Is it my birthday? Are we on camera?"

Monique had large, straight teeth that looked perfected by braces but weren't. She flashed them now, plump glossy lips pulled back, then took out her phone and responded to some missive. Her thick eyebrows furrowed and her nostrils softly flared. She had glanced at her phone throughout dinner, more than five times before Nakia forced herself to stop counting.

On the street corner below, a paletero pushed his cart up the hill, the illustrations of bomb pops and ice cream sandwiches barely visible in the fading light. A relic from the neighborhood's past life.

"Is that factory smoke or like, fire smoke?" Monique said, pointing to a funnel of black billowing up from along the eastern edge of downtown.

"It's probably factory smoke, or an encampment burning. Happens sometimes."

Monique kissed her teeth. "This apocalyptic-ass place."

"Home sweet home. What made you finally want to come?"

"Girl, you know I wasn't getting on no plane unless I absolutely had to. And I still wear two masks when I do."

"You been on plenty of planes in the last few months."

Nakia tried to sound observational instead of judgmental. Monique had gone to Barbados twice and Miami once since getting the vaccine. Family trips, but still.

"Well, also, you never officially invited me before," Monique said.

"Bullshit. I have begged all y'all collectively and individually to come if you're in town. January has been—you know she loved it. Desiree has even been, even though she didn't contribute much to the conversation. You just think you're too cool."

Monique smiled again, slid her phone back into the front pocket of her jeans.

"You know I'm not too cool for anything. If anything I'm too awkward. I feel like I'm becoming one of those internet people who don't know how to handle real-life social interactions."

"You been in your phone all night. I wasn't gonna mention it."

"Oh, yeah, that." She looked apologetic for an instant, her mouth slack. Nakia knew this was as close as one could get in the way of an apology from her.

"This activist I follow followed me back out of nowhere and then sent me a bunch of DMs."

"Who?"

"Aisha Miller? You know her?"

"Of course. I mean, I don't *know her* know her, but I read the news. She's famous. Plus she's gorgeous."

"Yes! Suspiciously beautiful, right? Like, no one is that smart and that good-looking. Anyway, I was responding to her."

"What she want?"

"I don't know, to know me?" She seemed irritated at the question. "We're gonna get lunch when I get back to New York."

"Oh. Cool."

"After that I was just scrolling. Stress habit."

"What you got to be stressed for? Aisha Miller is in your DMs."

Monique looked back toward the smoke, which was becoming harder to see as twilight turned to night over downtown.

"Oh, you know. Adult life. Bills, the usual."

She looked on the precipice of saying something else but smiled again instead.

"Nothing in particular," she said.

"You okay? You need money?"

"No. I mean, yeah, I need money, but I don't want your money. I appreciate that you offer it, though. I'll be fine."

Ever since Monique had found a modicum of online fame following that incident with that school down south, she could be prickly if you asked her about her life, her plans, in too-direct terms. Nakia wasn't good at being oblique, so she tried to avoid asking altogether. She knew Monique had gotten a part-time job at the library when she'd first returned to Brooklyn and was living back with her parents, intent on somehow making money off her blog and growing her online following. Her Tru Talk had been too early to ride the later wave of increased audiences, but it had apparently garnered her enough attention to want to seek out more attention. Nakia knew Monique wrote things—essays and poetry published here and there—and that she had quit the part-time library job in early 2020 when she got a contract to "curate social programming" for a private women's-only club. That club had fizzled out in the pandemic and no longer existed. It seemed a fool's errand, trying to turn a one-time blip of attention into some kind of viable business, to put so many years of effort and energy into making yourself a brand, especially when Monique was a very good librarian—they'd met in Monique's Brooklyn library—but what did Nakia know?

"I know you'll be fine," Nakia said. "I'm here if you change your mind."

Monique bumped her on the hip on her way back into the apartment, on purpose.

"Jay is real cool, you know. Maybe too cool for you."

"Nobody is cooler than me!" she said over her shoulder, just to be saying something.

There comes a moment during most LA evenings when the heat gives up; it happens in an instant. You'll be sitting on a patio admiring the sky's golden turn when the large hand of the clock shudders forward and suddenly night taps your shoulders, whispers up the front of your arms. The temperature might drop ten, twenty degrees. Nakia felt the shift just as her peaches needed pulling from the grill, their flesh crosshatched and glistening. It made her giddy, the sudden chill, reminded her of staying out past curfew, of having nowhere to be.

In her absence, the group had become a series of couples: Rico and Beverly on the sofa, Yesenia and Kyle in the armchairs, Monique and Jay on the floor. The latter two laughing like coconspirators, like old friends. Jay sat cross-legged and leaned back on her hands. The muscles of her biceps looked soft from across the room; Nakia knew they were solid. A year ago, her garden and her breakfast counter and her locally sourced produce had piqued Jay's interest, ostensibly, but Nakia knew when someone was courting her. They'd met through mutual friends almost a decade prior, shortly after Nakia moved back to LA, and it wasn't until she cut her hair, dyed the remaining curly halo light brown, and put on about twenty pounds that Jay had asked her out. Having looked up a few of Jay's exes online, she now understood that she'd morphed into her type—soft, full-hipped, with natural hair. Jay looked like an actor off a premium-channel queer drama: neat, smooth, beautiful. The low fade with impeccable lineup, the perfect deep brown complexion that looked like its own "no makeup" makeup look. The expensive slouchy white T-shirts. The svelte body, maintained by something intimidating and performative. Capoeira, Nakia had guessed when she first saw her naked, but she subsequently discovered it was Brazilian jiujitsu. The juxtaposition of her body against Jay's, the way the two of them together made a kind of geometric sense, roundness and sharpness, curves and edges, in harmony, still thrilled her.

Jay walked over and put her arm around Nakia's waist as she arranged the peaches in wide, shallow bowls, encircled them in thin halos of cream. She smelled like cardamom. Nakia leaned into her.

"Thank god for Monique," Jay whispered. "Otherwise we would've been having the same conversation all night. Right?"

Nakia nodded. She'd been gone for almost a full half hour. She could make it through the night now.

"She staying over?"

"She says no," Nakia said. "She's gonna go out to see January tonight. Flying back tomorrow afternoon."

"Wow," Jay said. "She really doesn't like LA, huh? She just got here."

"She claims she has tickets to some show in New York the day after."

Over on the couch, Monique was saying something that made Beverly let out a squealing cackle.

"But no," Nakia added. "She doesn't."

Jay took a strawberry out of the colander and bit it. She leaned against the counter so that she faced out to the larger room, her face in profile.

"I think this is a good mix, baby," she said. Then, sotto: "Especially Yesenia and Kyle. Been a while since we had regular folks in here."

Regular, meaning people whose income fell under the ever-shifting, loose-consensus threshold of what counted as well-off in Los Angeles. Yesenia, being a low-level civil servant, and Kyle, being a public school teacher, fit that bill.

"Just those two? Why not Rico and Monique?"

"Shhh, you know you don't know how to whisper."

"My back's to the room! Nobody can even read my lips."

"My sweet, loud child," Jay said, kissing her on the forehead. "Your voice is resounding off the backsplash."

They were the same age, but Jay enjoyed acting like she was the elder.

"Rico is a lawyer and Monique . . . Monique has a little bit of a profile now. And some money, doesn't she? Wasn't there a settlement? With that college?"

"You're not supposed to know about that."

"She just told me about it herself. I pretended that I didn't already know."

"Oh," Nakia said. "Well, it apparently wasn't a lot of money. Did she tell you that?"

"She did not," Jay said. She smiled. "Anyway, it doesn't matter, what matters is that everyone here is interested in doing the right thing. And I think Monique is really interesting. She knows how to engage people."

She kissed Nakia's cheek and went back to the party.

Doing the right thing. What did that even mean? In terms of doing good, Nakia's friend Arielle was the best person she knew, and what made this tolerable for Nakia was that Arielle didn't talk about her goodness, or the concept of goodness at all; she simply was. When she first got to college, Nakia had fallen in with a few very earnest aspiring poets after taking a freshman writing class. Some of them drank but most of them didn't; some of them had already gotten sober from teenaged addictions. They had a moral code that informed their politics, which would have been admirable except they seemed incapable of not working aspects of this code into every conversation. They used being right and good as a reason to be joy-killers, or worse, they fixated on "joy-seeking" in a way that made it performative, a "praxis." Sapped the fun right out of it. They were so loudly intentional about everything that they struck Nakia as robotic, which would probably surprise a lot of her friends, as Nakia was someone people assumed ordered every step in service of her goals. The difference came down to style, she supposed. Even as a young adult she was wary of people who seemed to not be able to think about the world, messy as it is, outside of their own integrity and "purpose."

Now she sometimes saw them online; they were the sort of people who wrote posts about how they'd been "thinking about how we can all be kinder to one another" or "what we owe one another" in this way that made her want to roll her eyes even more, because she knew that whether or not they meant it without guile, being kind or good had become a brand for them, a way to differentiate themselves. And, of course, being vulnerable about one's transgressions, self-flagellating in front of hundreds or even thousands of followers when one cheated (join the club) or let someone down (join the club) was only worth doing if one came out the other side burnished, more virtuous. "Just be good! Stop meditating on it," she always wanted to comment, but she never would. She didn't believe in yucking people's yums, not even noisome, virtue-signaling yums. One of those kids from college was an actual professional poet now; another spent a lot of time railing against "cancel culture" in long posts and occasional videos. Of course, of course.

Arielle posted about her Skid Row outreach online, sure, but she kept it to lighthearted all-caps logistics: "BRRRRR! WE NEED HANDWARMERS AND BLANKETS"; "IT'S HOT OUT! PLEASE DROP OFF FROZEN WATER BOTTLES TO [THIS ADDRESS] AT [THIS TIME]"; "GOT PROTEIN?? DONATIONS OF PEANUT BUTTER AND/OR LUNCH MEAT AND/OR POWER BARS APPRECIATED." Even before social media, Arielle had put up simple, straightforward requests on the bulletin board of the gym she owned, which is how Nakia had begun volunteering with her way back when. "COME FEED THE HUNGRY DOWNTOWN, EVERY MONDAY, TEXT FOR DETAILS," the flyer had said, with tear-off numbers printed on the bottom.

The gym had closed for good during the early days of the pandemic, as had many smaller gyms. In 2021, Arielle had snapped up an old smog-check shop in Culver City off Washington and reopened Sweat Finesse as CBH Fitness, which officially stood for Cycle, Bench, HIIT, but Arielle and her friends joked that it stood for Combahee. Arielle had also finally gotten nonprofit status for her work downtown, under the name CBH Collective. Nakia was the largest single donor for the nonprofit, having whittled down her charitable giving to this one near and dear cause. The hours still flew by whenever Nakia helped Arielle, and she didn't feel an impulse to post about it, to improve upon it, to do anything other than show up and try to be kind to people while she was there.

Maybe it bothered her when other people talked about goodness because she wasn't sufficiently interested in doing the right thing, or was simply overwhelmed by the charge to be or do good. She felt too small for it, too meager-minded. It was a question that plagued her more and more these days: What am I doing with my life? In the American sense, the bootstrapping, capitalist one, her life as-is seemed a good answer. She was a relatively successful business owner, she employed young people, she brought good, wholesome food to the hood. During the pandemic she had managed to keep her entire full-time staff on payroll, even through the early months when the restaurant was closed and only she and a skeleton crew fulfilled delivery orders. Sure. And yet. So many, too many people had nothing. What was the point of working hard, having something, when one had to live with the knowledge of so much want? Their numbers swelled on the street, not just downtown and not just under overpasses or parked in a long line of beat-down RVs, but everywhere. In the mornings, there were signs of the unhoused in nearly every pocket of Los Angeles if you knew where to look: where they'd slept, where they'd had no choice but to do their various businesses outside, where they'd dared to stop and rest for a brief second and left something—an important document, a leather belt, a wrapped tampon—behind. Even if she seldom actually saw them on her street or slumped behind one of her restaurants' back doors, she knew they were there, just out of sight, their lives wretched in a city full of glamour.

There were chefs, restaurateurs, who stood more firmly in their commitment to public service, or at least more publicly, making grand shows of their beliefs on social media, partnering with charities, extolling their followers to do the same. That wasn't Nakia. She didn't aspire to be known as good—she loved Monique but had no desire to become an Internet Person. She yearned for something else, something that would put an end to that pit-of-her-stomach feeling, that sense that all her scrambling was for nothing. She would know it when she found it.

Beverly's high-pitched laugh brought Nakia back into the room. She passed out the bowls, the cream on the verge of collapsing from the heat of the peaches. Beverly, far into her glasses of Sauvignon Blanc, held forth from the sofa.

"Oh, honey, no. Companies die just like people do," she said to Kyle, to everyone. "We all can't imagine it'll happen, then one day it does and the rest of us move on, just like with people. Bear Stearns, Woolworths, Wanamaker's, Pan Am, uh, Barneys out there by Monique . . . Who am I missing? Pacific Bell, all the baby Bells."

"So you're saying if we killed BP, the global economy wouldn't actually collapse?" Kyle asked. He had unbuttoned his shirt so that the top of a chest tattoo—hard to tell but it looked floral—was visible on his dark brown skin.

Beverly shrugged, belched noiselessly. "Highly unlikely."

"Jay's old company had the biggest opening on the NASDAQ in a year, then filed for bankruptcy five years later," Monique said. "Definitely happens."

"Random," Nakia whispered to her. "How do you know that?"

"I read the news, just like you," she said, and accepted the bowl Nakia held out for her.

"Listen," Beverly said. "Five years, a hundred years, nothing's gonna save 'em from death if it's their time to go. They all fall eventually. That's something you young folks in the workforce got right: never be loyal to any of them."

"Just like empires," Rico said.

"Exactly!" Beverly said. "But thank God the days of empires are over, right?"

No one said anything for a beat. Monique cleared her throat.

"Okay, hard pivot: I have a controversial Los Angeles take for y'all."

"Uh-oh," Yesenia and Kyle said in unison.

"I mean, it's not *that* controversial, but yeah: Octavia Butler was wrong."

"Wow, this is sacrilege," Rico said, leaning in. "Go on."

"Okay, I come here like every three years," Monique said. "So what do I really know, and obviously she was right about damn near everything, but I can tell that she was wrong about this: the homeless people in LA are not gonna rise up and hurt the people with homes and money. It's gonna be the other way around."

"Meaning what exactly?" Beverly asked. Nakia wondered if she'd ever even read Octavia Butler. She decided the odds were fifty-fifty.

"Meaning the people with money, the housed, will be the ones to wreak havoc on the people without it," Kyle offered.

"Exactly," Monique said. "When you think about it, it's very clear that it was always gonna be the other way around. Earlier today I was coming from LAX, and when my driver exited the freeway there was this homeless man who was kinda hopping in and out of traffic, talking to himself. He was an older white guy, one of those ones who looks like he was in Vietnam or something. Why did my driver—who was also white, but young—speed up until he was like an inch away from the guy then slam on the breaks? And when I shouted, 'Hey, what are you doing?' he acted like it was no big deal, talking about 'These people want us to hit them,' 'Some of them are so messed up in the head they wanna die,' and how you shouldn't go to jail for hitting them because they shouldn't be in the street. I was speechless."

"People are really crazy," Kyle offered, though he did not look scandalized.

"Right?" Monique said. "And obviously I didn't want to get too into it with the guy who literally had my life in his hands, but it really drove the point home for me. A lot of people will be fine with straight-up exterminating homeless people if it comes down to it. They're not gonna wanna do it themselves, but if it happens, they'll let it."

"Jesus," Yesenia said.

"I can see that," Rico said. He sat back on the sofa again and appeared to be mulling it over.

"And by 'people' you mean white people?" Beverly asked.

Monique paused to chew and swallow a bite of grilled peach before answering. A dramatic pause for effect, Nakia thought.

"You know," Monique said, "I used to think it would be just white people, but now I feel like all kinds of people would be fine with it."

"You know what? Me too," Rico said. "I hate to be the person who says 'it's not race, it's class,' but sometimes it is."

"Is there even, like, a critical mass of Black people in LA anymore?"

Monique asked this in a way that to Nakia felt accusatory, as if it were Black folks' own fault that they'd been scattered to the desert and back South and into random exurbs. She could not shake the uneasy feeling that Monique's theory unfairly indicted her and her neighbors, even her customers, made them part of the indifferent-to-extermination masses when they were all doing the best they could.

"Depends on what you consider a critical mass," Nakia said. "There's a disproportionate number of Black men living on the streets in LA."

"Well, we all saw how much the government cared about the disproportionate number of Black men dying during the pandemic," Kyle said.

"Women, too," Beverly added. "And don't even get me started on Black women of a certain age."

"Okay, right. So if a lot of the homeless population is Black," Monique said, her gaze on Nakia, "doesn't that make it even worse that Butler predicted they'd start flipping out on drugs, basically becoming zombies and attacking people?"

This style of on-the-spot debate was never Nakia's strong suit. She took debates too personally. She felt her face grow hot.

"I don't know," she said. "Maybe it's just a novel? But the thought that someone—or as you put it, most of us—would be fine with these people just getting killed off . . . it's not right. It may be what the politicians want, but it's not how most people I know in this city feel. And it's kind of offensive."

Monique smiled, which made Nakia want to scream.

"Come on, Ki, be serious. It may not be right as in what *should* happen, but don't kid yourself into thinking that there's no way it *could* happen. Especially in a postpandemic world, which made a whole lotta people think other people's lives are cheap. The reality of it might make you feel uncomfortable, but it's still the reality. And at the rate that homelessness is rising in New York, it'll be the reality there soon, too. The amount of conversations I've had in the past year with people talking about the men who sleep on the subway like they're feral dogs or something, not human beings, is frankly terrifying."

There it was, Monique's high moral ground. She had named it, claimed it, and now sat atop it, looking down at the entire room. And, to Nakia's irritation, the entire room was rapt.

No one else chimed in. A champagne bottle popped.

"Time for a toast!" Jay said. She smiled wider than usual, it seemed to Nakia, and the phrase "cat who ate the canary" popped into her mind. Jay quickly switched out people's glasses for flutes and began to pour champagne.

"Yes, salud!" Yesenia said, thrusting her glass forward. She had also apparently gotten tipsy during the time Nakia was out on the balcony.

The sneaky smile stayed on Jay's lips as she filled glasses. Nakia had seen her be pleased with herself plenty of times before, and this was not that. This was a scheming look.

"Okay, so, Monique, our guest who traveled the farthest, should give the toast." Jay beamed at Monique, who looked startled, then charmed.

"Right, okay," Monique said. She looked around, made eye contact with everyone but Nakia, right there by her side, then settled on Jay. "Here's to new friends, community, and commitment. Commitment to changing things however we're able. I'm personally very excited to see what everyone does with what we've talked about tonight. Cheers!"

Nakia did not have time to decipher the meaning of this toast because the floor began to tremble just as they clinked glasses. At first it felt like the pleasant kind of quake, the ones Nakia sometimes craved when she'd briefly lived on the other coast. Rolling, like a baby swinging in a bassinet. Just enough movement to remind you that you ate, worked, fought, and fucked on an active, volatile hunk of rock. That there was no such thing as solid ground. Jay's vintage chandelier swayed gently on its chain.

"Earthquake," Beverly said. It's never real until someone says it.

Yesenia crawled under the dining table, grabbing its leg and covering the back of her neck, just like they used to teach in school. Jay, Kyle, and Rico followed suit. Monique sat still on the couch, champagne flute clutched to her breast, eyes closed. Beverly and Nakia eyed each other, not so sure what to do. The dining table was heavy marble. It could crack, Nakia thought, bludgeon everyone to death.

Fucking dingbat—they could all die here. Images of collapsed buildings from the Northridge quake, people pancaked in their own homes, rushed into Nakia's mind. Jay's unit was on the first floor, right above the garage.

"We should go outside," she said, but who could hear her over the *grrrn, grrrn, grrrn* of the earthquake? Jay's copper measuring cups shook loose from their hooks in the kitchen and clattered to the floor. Nakia said it again louder, added, "It's not safe in here!"

Nakia went to Monique and yanked her up by the elbow. Beverly grabbed her other hand. Everyone suddenly sober, compliant. The seven of them made their way out the door and into the shared courtyard with its shared pool. The movement switched from rolling to jolting, accompanied by an unbearable noise. Metal things jangling, primordial creaking and groaning—was it the building, the rebar and plywood and stucco rending themselves? The pool water sloshed Nakia's bare feet and made her jump.

After a few seconds it quieted down to faint rumbling. Then, nothing. A nanosecond of startling stillness before the car alarms and barking dogs.

"Everyone alright?" Jay asked. She put her arm around Nakia, then took it off to help Beverly up out of a pool lounger that she must have hurriedly sat down in. Everyone was fine. The building still stood. As is the case after earthquakes, once these assessments have been made, there was nothing to do but go back inside.

Two hours and several cocktails later, the Group of 7 had whittled down to a Group of 3. Kyle and Rico set off for their long metro and bus rides back to Lakewood, a babysitter to relieve. Yesenia, sobered up by the earthquake, volunteered to drive Beverly, still inebriated, and her thirteen-year-old Jaguar back to Leimert Park. At some point during the clearing and cleaning of dishes Jay had convinced Monique to spend the night. The news said it had been a magnitude 4.6, epicenter in Valley Village. Nakia, Monique, and Jay sat on the living room rug, sharing a joint and listening to Sade on vinyl. Nakia had lit a row of candles on the coffee table and switched off the lamps, dimming the room and drawing it close. They talked about who they all needed to stop following online, which grifters were admirable and which were out of line, Monique's short-lived foray into dating women, and what it might take to get January dating at all again—money, they agreed. January needed to feel like she had made enough money by herself post-Morris before she could be with someone else. Nakia was proud of January for finally growing up, for realizing that it didn't matter what other people thought about your life if you didn't actually feel like you were living it.

The record ended. Monique switched it to Alice Coltrane's *Journey in Satchidananda*. As always, the tanpura, high and warbly as a newborn's cry, made Nakia feel like weeping.

"You know," she said, "random companies show up at my shop tryna get me to fire my teens and replace 'em with machines?" She sipped her bourbon, took the half-melted sphere of ice into her mouth like a gumball then dropped it back into the tumbler. "Machines can't crack funny jokes and teach me the latest dance moves."

"Sure they could," Monique said. "They'd aggregate all the popular dance videos and spit the jokes out at random. Could be hilarious."

Monique giggled, stretched out on her back on the floor, short toes and chubby fingers reaching opposite.

"It's not funny. Working somewhere gives these kids purpose. I'm teaching them how to garden, how to eat better, how to be responsible."

"Very, extremely admirable work," Jay said. She was nodding more than necessary, which was the tell for when she was sleepy.

"Yeah, totally admirable," Monique said. "But also, like, work isn't the only way to feel purposeful. Those teens deserve to be taught some other ways, too. They could garden and eat well outside of making money."

"Fucking robots will turn my shit into a McDonald's. I don't wake up at the ass crack of dawn every day to impart knowledge to fucking machines."

"Do you even go in early like that anymore?" Monique said. "Thought you had managers."

"I mean . . . you know what I mean. I didn't get into food to be surrounded by robots."

"Okay, so don't buy the machines. But don't act like the situation isn't funny to imagine. You and a bunch of egg-flipping, order-taking bots."

The record ended, and Jay snored softly, her back slumped against the sofa and her chin reaching toward her chest. Nakia nudged her with her toe and she shot upright, her body lithe and under her control once again. She stood up, stretched.

"That's my time. Got a hike in the morning."

She bent down to kiss Nakia. Monique stood up for a hug—a long one, like old friends, Nakia thought again.

"And you, safe travels. First thing Monday I'ma set up a call."

"Sounds good."

"Better than good, it's going to be amazing, trust me. The world needs your story."

Jay squeezed her shoulder and left the room. Monique put on Aaliyah's

"One in a Million" then walked to the kitchen. She returned with a new bottle of white wine. She sat down, poured herself a glass.

"What? Why are you looking at me like that?" Monique asked.

"What's wrong with being a librarian?"

"What?"

Monique reached for her water glass.

"I'm assuming you've convinced Jay to somehow get your Tru Talk popping again," Nakia said.

"I haven't agreed, but yeah, she proposed a thing, and I'm thinking about it. I'm gonna have a call with the whole team over there and see how I feel."

"I know you stopped working part-time at the library," Nakia said. "I'm sure you could easily get another full-time gig."

"I don't want another library gig."

"So, you just want to make money off this one thing that happened to you one time, forever?"

"Is that a problem?"

"It's not a problem, just kinda sad, I guess."

Monique propped herself up on an elbow, chuckled a little.

"Sad? What difference does it make to you how I make my money?"

"It doesn't, but— I don't want you to take this the wrong way. It's just that some of the people I've met through her, the athletes, the influencers and writers? They all have this same self-righteousness, like this assumption that what they're doing is more valuable than anyone else's work, but they don't do anything if they're not the marquee name, if it doesn't further their brand in some way. They're fucking hollow inside. I don't know, it makes my skin crawl. And it doesn't help that they all happen to be rich."

"Oh, so now you of all people are fetishizing poverty."

"What? I do not fetishize poverty."

"Or maybe you're projecting, I don't know."

"That's not nice, Monique."

"You're not being nice! You host a dinner once a month for people to talk about doing good things for the environment or whatever—literally just to talk—and you're worried about me becoming too self-righteous?

It's ridiculous. But your message is received. You're saying you don't want me to work with Jay cause you don't want me to become too successful."

"Do you want to be successful or do you want to be famous?"

"Why not both? You're in a better position to help people if—"

"If you want to be famous then you want to be famous. Period. It's not altruistic. Don't lie to yourself."

Monique looked as if she might cry. Her cheeks trembled.

"Whatever," she muttered. This was the moment to back off, to apologize, but Nakia couldn't.

"Why were you and Jay sneaking around talking about this without me?"

"Well, shit, look how you're reacting."

"I'm reacting like a person who is trying to figure out what's going on with her friend. Is this why you finally agreed to come to one of these, so you could meet Jay and she could help you get famous?"

Monique shook her head, more in disgust than disagreement.

"Jay does not strike me as a person who you can *make* do a damn thing," she said. "And if you think Jay and her friends are so terrible, if wanting to make a name for yourself or whatever is so bad, then why are you dating her?"

Because she is beautiful, because she is always sunny, because she is easy and confident and uncomplicated and her easiness makes me smile, Nakia thought. Because turns out it is nice to be with a person who respects you but does not fully perceive you. How very shallow. She kept these thoughts to herself.

"You know," Monique said, "there's something very Jack and Jill, something very *bourgeoise* about you trying to gatekeep how I make money, like there's acceptable work and then there's work that's beneath you."

"Oh, please. I wasn't even in Jack and Jill."

"You know what I mean. Like, me wanting to become more public, be an influencer, or whatever you want to call it, is low-rent in your eyes. It's still hard work, though. Everything is hard work."

"It's not about what's hard work or not hard work, and I'm not trying to gatekeep anything, just like how I'm not fetishizing poverty. I'm saying that *you*, Monique LaMorne, are capable of more than just being an internet personality."

Monique's smile was close-lipped and weary.

"I'm going to sleep," she said. She stood up, found her phone between the seat cushions, and pocketed it. "You need to figure out why you even have an opinion about this."

She paused at the hallway.

"That was my first earthquake. I don't know if you noticed, but I was fucking terrified."

"Of course I noticed," Nakia said. "That's why I grabbed you from the couch."

"I couldn't even speak until the ground stopped moving. My body's instinct was to just sit there, to be still. But that wasn't right, was it? Being still coulda got me killed."

She left the room before Nakia could respond.

In the morning, each of them was careful with the other. Jay was already gone, off hiking as promised. It was hazy outside Jay's bedroom window, downtown not as visible as it should have been. A poor-air-quality day. Monique stayed in the guest bedroom, its door shut, until she was nearly ready to leave. She refused Nakia's offer of a ride to January's apartment, said she needed that time in the car to answer emails, but she accepted the breakfast burrito Nakia had made and wrapped in foil for her. Who knows what it would have meant for their friendship had she rejected it. Nakia carried Monique's suitcase down the stairs and opened her arms for a hug.

Monique allowed Nakia to hold her close. Sandalwood and peppermint castile soap.

"You know I'm just trying my best, right? I don't know what the fuck I'm doing."

"I know," Nakia said.

She thought of her younger self—Nakia the Proprietress—with her lofty ideals and reckless decisions. Before she began to doubt that a restaurant, at least one run by human beings as fallible as herself, could really be part of some kind of revolution. Everyone deserved that feeling.

2019

Two Under

What a wedding they'd had. No bridal party, just the two of them up there, and their baby carried down the aisle like a bouquet by the mother of the bride. Chocolate cake and peach cobbler. Two signature cocktails, a local celebrity DJ. And the flowers! So many orchids, bouquets with eucalyptus and monstera smelling expensive and delicious. The bride wore a custom dress by a Ghanaian designer and her hair natural, a spray of baby's breath dotting her still-lush postpartum afro. She would have looked radiant if it weren't for her eyes. They showed her exhaustion. That is what Desiree remembered most—how tired January had looked. Morris triumphant and Ms. June, the mother of the bride, happy too. But January? Those eyes. It was a wonder she stayed awake all the way to the sparkler-lined farewell, was able to climb into their rented Rolls-Royce of her own free will. Her eyes seemed to communicate what the rest of her would not know for several weeks: she was pregnant again. No one else noticed, or at least didn't care to comment on the bride's obvious fatigue. But it was the only thing Desiree wanted to know: Had anyone ever seen such a beautiful, radiant, jubilant, dead-tired, wrung-out bride?

Aren't our nearest and dearest always our business, even when it's not technically our business? Yes, of course, Desiree reasoned. This reasoning had brought her clear across the country. It had been a little over six weeks since the second baby boy had been born and most of what Desiree, Monique, and Nakia had learned about the status of mother and baby both boiled down to a single text, with photo attached:

> Announcing the arrival of Brook Bali Starling. Born on October 12 at 2:17 p.m. 8 lbs, 8 oz, 19 inches long. Mother and baby are doing well. Big brother and dad are over the moon!!

So he'd arrived at thirty-nine weeks. The last time Desiree had spoken to January was the day before she went into labor, or was induced, or had an emergency C-section, or some combination thereof. All these weeks later and Desiree still didn't know. Unusual. She'd tried to video-call immediately after that announcement text, to no avail. She'd tried so many times since then, too. After Bronze was born, January had called Desiree from the uptown hospital that very night, the baby tiny and wrinkled in her arms, his skin pink but his ears darkening. Morris had been snoring in a lounger on the other side of the room. It had been thirty-one hours of labor, during which Morris's halting text updates had been so unbearable that Monique had tracked down Ms. June's number to keep everyone better informed. At hour thirty and a half, January had been headed for a C-section delivery, but Bronze popped out just as they began to ready the operation room.

"I'm scared," January had whispered on the phone that first night. "Happy and scared."

"That seems normal," Desiree reassured her. She didn't ask her to clarify her fears. "I'm so proud of you."

"I keep thinking about our conversation, back when y'all were in Martinique—"

"Don't," Desiree had said. "Don't cry. Look at that beautiful baby in your arms."

"No," January whispered. "I want to. You saved my life. I been meaning to thank you."

Desiree was afraid to ask how. January would not have died had she decided not to have Morris in the baby's life, nor if she'd decided not to have the baby at all, and anyway she hadn't suggested that January full-on reconcile with him, had she? Desiree didn't remember it that way.

"We don't have to talk about it," she said, and on the other end of the video call something in January's face had shrunk. It was cruel, but what else could she have done? Morris had been snoring but could've woken up at any moment.

Now as she drove east on the 10, Desiree thought through knocking on their door. She'd booked the flight forty-eight hours before, having noticed that the second baby's one month birthday came and went without January, Morris, or even Ms. June marking the occasion on social media. Unusual. And not a single actual phone call, video or otherwise, answered or received. Only a handful of texts that were terse or filled with too many all-caps or exclamation points. Unusual. Almost seven whole weeks, or was it seven mere weeks? After Bronze was born, January had talked about how time moved peculiar with a newborn, but it seemed there would have been a moment to talk if everything had been okay. January knew that Desiree was always awake late; she might have called in those dark, quiet hours, breast pump whirring, like she'd done with Bronze. She might have called while walking or driving the baby around and around her cul-de-sac, desperate for him to nap. She might have called. Instead, a bizarre smattering of texts, the last of which spurred Desiree to book a flight:

J: Two things can be true at the same time.

D: Like what?

Two days later and January still hadn't responded, not even after Desiree texted hello? and are you okay? and please call now. She could've reached out to Morris or Ms. June, but a part of her didn't trust them. They were strangely, similarly formal, interested in being normal in a way that struck Desiree as anything but. Better to just show up.

The farther east she drove, the more the air outside her window took on an orange tinge before rising to dusty blue. A fire somewhere—who knew? Desiree hadn't followed LA news closely in years, just as she didn't drive much, outside of occasional visits to Nakia, who drove her Jeep like someone was chasing her, necessitating that Desiree rent a car. When Desiree and Jelani went upstate for the odd weekend away, he always drove and she always slept, happily. Out of her window now the brown-spotted hills of the San Gabriel Valley gave way to the flat, dusty, stucco expanse of the Inland Empire. She passed the Fairplex, site of her first concert, the Smokey Robinson one, passed colleges she probably should've applied to way back when. Houses and semideserted mega-malls gave way to row after row after row of warehouses. Wide, windowless, low-slung. Blind-mute buildings whose silence made Desiree uneasy. There used to be farms here, she was almost certain of it. If not farms, at least citrus groves. She still braced herself for the intermittent sweet stink of cow shit when she came out this way. But that was before. Now this was a place to hold the shit people ordered nonstop and expected on their doorsteps within hours. Desiree pictured the insides of these buildings stuffed to the gills with baby toys, workout gear, cheap electronics, furniture, school supplies, home décor, prefab tree houses, "personal massagers," light bulbs, power drills, water slides, window curtains, and other crap people were employed around the clock to retrieve and process and transport. All so pointless.

Her navigation system told her to exit in the middle of the warehouses, so she did. She saw no human beings for the first several blocks, just those blind-mute buildings, until finally a sole blue-uniformed body sprinted in front of her car at a stop sign, nametag flapping hard against their chest, face obscured by a floppy sun hat. They disappeared into a building so quickly that Desiree felt cheated.

At the end of seven blocks, the warehouses abruptly came to an end, or rather they parted, like the desert making space for an oasis. This particular oasis was a subdivision of desert-colored McMansions, with drought-resistant lawns and gleaming cars parked out front, some attached to charging stations like dogs leashed to a pole. Why was she nervous? Desiree parked her rental in front of the right house, opened her car door, and took a deep breath of rank Inland Empire air.

Two under two. Too under, too. To undertow. A word joke that hadn't gotten old. The shades were drawn; the sun was out, but what was sun when nighttime and daytime made no difference? Number two butted his little forehead against her nipple but didn't wake up. She'd left it out for him because it was easier that way. Didn't he have a name? Yes. Brook Bali, so named because instead of taking the honeymoon they'd planned to that island, they'd saved the money, moved across the country, and waited for his arrival. And Brook because didn't it look right next to Bronze? Bronze and Brook, Brook and Bronze, a Brook of Bronze. Sure. Number two of easy enough pregnancy and terribly quick, terrible birth and miserable thereafter, what had she done wrong? His first latch had made bile rise in her throat and with every latch since the tingle of nausea or the taste of vomit returned. Something to do with her hormones, they'd said. So it was not like riding a bike. More like getting a bike shipped to you, each piece in a different unlabeled box, no instructions and no time before use was required.

Side-lying was the best way to stave off nausea, so she lay on the sofa with him for most of the day, him on the inside and her on the outside, her breast ready for when he needed it. She could pass hours staring at the whorls of hair on the top of his tiny head. If she dozed off in this position there could be trouble, number two could theoretically be crushed, but she didn't think she ever dozed off. Another problem, the insomnia despite the exhaustion. Where was the fear? With Bronze it had nearly choked her, made her energetic with worry. Concern for him, for keeping him alive had been more important than sleeping but she'd also had concern for what would happen if she was ever too tired, so she dutifully rested when she could. June had praised her, a natural, and Morris had become what people on the internet called a Wife Guy, even before she was his wife, boasting about her nurturing superpowers and strength. Her full embodiment of an ideal she hadn't even spent much time mulling over was likely one of the reasons he'd proposed when she was around this same time postpartum after Bronze. It was early fall in Brooklyn and they'd walked to Fort Greene Park. Her longest walk up to that point, with plenty of pauses along the way. He'd gotten down on one knee near the playground—the tiny one on the south side that the white people liked, not one of the larger two closer to the projects—and pulled a ring out of the bottom of the stroller.

"January Wells, aka Mommy, aka Jan-Jan from Inglewood, you are the love of my life," he'd said. Young parents pushing strollers had stopped to clap and a passing group of cyclists tooted their clown horns. "I have been in awe of you since the moment I saw you toting that tuba in band practice. Will you marry me, and make our family complete?"

A slight prickle at that last clause, but otherwise genuine giddiness. She'd said yes and meant it, and Bronze woke up in the stroller just in time for happy tears, a few stranger-snapped photos and breathless video calls to friends and family, filling them in on the good news.

June, of course, had stepped up to be a doting grandma, suddenly plotting the retirement she'd long said only a new man could precipitate. Bronze was apparently love interest enough.

Desiree had said, "Oh my God, this is the best news," and seemed like she meant it, which made January cry, probably too hard in front of Morris. Nakia had only said, "Oh, wow. You know, Morris, you're a good person," which was not the same as saying she believed he was good for January, but for Nakia this was a positive response. Monique had not picked up the phone but eventually responded with an assortment of excited emojis, a request for them to choose a date as soon as possible so she could "lock it in her schedule," and a promise to hook them up with a good videographer, which she had. No one had brought up those months apart, that whole first trimester of her pregnancy spent uptown alone, trying to make a life for herself before giving up and restarting her life with him. People were kind.

She knew she needed to be patient. Patience, and number two would coalesce into a person, a personality. Patience, and maybe her insides would more or less go back to where they'd been; patience, and she'd settle into it all. But she was no longer curious. That was a problem. The curiosity around Bronze, not who he would be but what it would be like to feed him from her body, to hear his tiny cry, to change his diapers, to negotiate his genitals, to leave him and miss him and be giddy with the leaving of him all the same. These things had interested her deeply. Now they did not.

Morris was a good father. The problem was there was no way to avoid at least a little self-obliteration as a mother, some snuffing out of self. Even if they found a baby formula number two could tolerate so that she could stop breastfeeding—and she prayed the German one in the mail to her would do the trick—the damage to her selfhood, and her body, parts of her she couldn't even fully articulate, had been done. It wasn't superficial, it was visceral. Her teeth ached and felt loose in her mouth; she couldn't stand up as straight anymore. But beyond the physical, she simply couldn't see a way out of being the default parent. Morris would complete any task she gave him, but he had not yet figured out how to anticipate what needed to be done such that she did not have to be the task manager, which was its own mental load. Bronzie, bless him, was a daddy's boy, but when he was sick or very upset or just not right, it was her, always her he was up under, still absently reaching his tiny hand in her cleavage though she'd weaned him as soon as she'd learned she was expecting again.

Brook awoke with a tiny fart, followed by a noise that sounded like a piece of paper crumpling, which meant he'd pooped one of his golden newborn poops. January hauled herself upright, scooped him up as gingerly as possible, slid the changing mat onto the sofa cushion, and stripped him. The doorbell rang.

"Shit."

If it was the German baby formula, she'd need to sign for it. Out here, where it was damn near Dubai-hot, delivery people were known to wait milliseconds before marking you as not home and retreating to their air-conditioned vans, plus they were penalized for taking too long at any one stop. January wiped Brook hastily and carried him quickly to the door. Sharp pain lightninged from her groin to her chin and back. She opened the door wincing, unaware that her breast was still out.

Desiree, squinting in the sun. Looking like she'd just stumbled into a gorgon's lair.

So it's worse than I thought."

She'd meant to think it, not say it. Poor January. Desiree reached for the baby and January nearly tossed him to her. He smelled a little rancid on top, but underneath was the sweet baby smell she remembered from Bronze.

"What's worse? What are you doing here?" January reached forward to accept Desiree's one-handed hug, which seemed to sway her breast just enough for her to realize it was exposed. She snapped it back into her maternity bra.

"Thought you were DHL with my formula."

"Thank God I'm not. You mighta gone viral."

She looked bad, crusty in the eyes and mouth and wild in a way Desiree had never seen her before. Best to keep things upbeat, then. She followed January back into the dark foyer, the baby in her arms rooting around her clavicle.

"It's freezing in here, like a cave."

"Helps with my nausea."

"Don't tell me you're pregnant again."

"That is not fucking funny."

There was a weird hitch to her gait, but Desiree couldn't figure out which side she was babying.

"When I feed him I want to vomit. Sometimes I do vomit."

"Jesus. Oh, hence the formula. You got a tracking number?"

January didn't respond. She walked on and Desiree followed, past the comically grand but still chintzy staircase to the sunken living room with its long money-green couch, which she plopped down on, too close to an open diaper full of orange goo. Desiree pinched it up and took it to the trash in the kitchen. On her return, Brook started mewling. He cast about as much as his weak neck would allow, hunting for milk.

"Here," January said, her arms outstretched, a wince at the corners of her lips. She took the baby and lay on the couch with him, her back to the room. Out came the breast, and the baby latched after a few tries. January closed her eyes and breathed deeply, like the ujjayi breaths Desiree had learned to do in yoga. The coffee table held a bottle of ginger ale, a bottle of coconut water, a small, still-sealed bottle of something called gripe water, a giant sports bottle of regular water, baby wipes, a pacifier, a limp, sweating ice pack, nipple cream, and several stray colorful toy magnetic tiles.

"Where's B1?" she asked.

"In Inglewood with June until Friday."

"It's Friday today."

January kept her eyes closed. The sound of suckling, and those ujjayi breaths.

"Today's Friday. What time on Friday?"

"Like bedtime, after traffic."

"Okay, so you still have a full day. Good. Morris?"

"Back around the same time, depends on traffic. This was his first week back."

Her first time alone with the baby. And so soon. After Bronze was born, back when they still lived in Brooklyn, there'd been a steady flow of people in their apartment for months. Not just June but Morris's mom and cousins, even one of June's former sisters-in-law from San Diego. Even Nelson, January's aloof dad, had come to town for an awkward long weekend. Desiree had been struck by how many people January had in her life every time she stopped by. More people in one room than Desiree had in the entire world. Where were all those people now? She must have not been the only person whose texts January had been ignoring.

January rolled herself back up to sitting, gingerly draped Brook over her shoulder to burp him. Something hurt, Desiree could tell. But of course something might still hurt this early on. Desiree picked up the remote and turned up the volume on the real-estate-and-renovation-show on the TV. A young white couple somewhere in the Northeast were looking for a fixer-upper with a large floor plan close to downtown for under a million dollars. Good luck, she thought. It was the kind of mindless television that could suck up a whole day with its simple propositions, its refusal to offer substantial stakes. The episode ended and another show—about landscape architecture in what looked to be Las Vegas, or Phoenix, or some other too-hot-for-most-plants place—began.

"What two things can be true?"

"What?" January must have fallen asleep.

"Your text. You said 'two things can be true at the same time.' I asked what and you never responded."

"Is that why you're here?"

She watched January place the baby on a little blanket the size of two tea towels sewn together. Then, thinking better of that, January put him facedown on the floor on top of a yellow cushioned mat.

"Tummy time," she said. "It's time for him to start."

They watched the baby squirm. He lifted his head before collapsing back down, complaining all the while. In lieu of getting down on the floor next to him, which Desiree had seen January and Morris do with Bronze, January bent from her seat on the couch and waggled her fingers at him, not unlike one might do to get the attention of a dog under the dinner table. Desiree got down on the floor herself, tried to get him to notice her.

"You're not gonna answer? Why are you here?"

"Well, shit, I'm happy to see you too," Desiree said. Joking felt wrong but she had to try. She cleared her throat. "You answer my question and I'll answer yours. What two things?"

January opened her mouth and closed it. When she finally spoke, it was in a whisper.

"The two things were—are—that I love my children and that I don't wanna be here."

No one said anything for three whole minutes, toward the end of which January figured she'd better pick up number two, tummy time being a strenuous activity at his age. Had she meant it? If she'd sent that text when she thought she had, she'd just finished video-calling June and Bronze after bath time, the baby napping and Morris due to come through the garage door any minute, takeout tacos in tow. Bronze had wanted her to sing his customary bedtime song, Selena's "Dreaming of You," so she did, despite June looking at her crazy in the background. As soon as she was done, June had nagged her about not wearing the postpartum corset wrap thing she'd ordered for her, talking over her when she tried to explain that the compression made her pelvic floor feel like it was going to bottom out, and anyway she was too nauseous for girdles; she needed to breathe. She had actually vomited earlier that day while breastfeeding, a few putrid tablespoons hurled into a baby wipe. She'd hung up agitated. She was full up and wrung dry all at once. Tiny hands, tiny, shrill voices, tiny mouths with no teeth but gums that could draw blood. Giant needs, unforgiving eyes everywhere. Yes, she'd meant it. And maybe she'd texted Desiree because Desiree had listened to her other desire, the one she mostly tried not to think about, and never once since had Desiree brought it up again. Not when January had moved back in with Morris, not when she'd gotten pregnant again, not ever.

"Say something," January said.

"I mean, those feelings are normal, right? Like a part of the postpartum process?"

"Yeah, if you don't really mean it, deep down."

The baby fell asleep on his back in the little docking-station-bed thing Morris's mom had sent. Soon his tiny hands would begin startling open and shut in an almost rhythm.

"Okay, so what do you wanna do about it?" Desiree said. "What can we do?"

January laughed a little. Dear, naïve Desiree. She didn't think everything could be fixed with a spreadsheet-supported plan, like Morris, but she seemed to believe January capable of more than January believed herself able to achieve.

"If I was someone else, I'd say I want to leave, like right now."

Desiree nodded slowly.

"But you're you."

January stood up, winced.

"Follow me."

In the downstairs guest bathroom, January stood bottomless, one foot propped up on the toilet seat. She asked Desiree to kneel, to look beneath at whatever was causing her to feel like her insides might fall out, whatever was making those shooting pains travel up and down her torso. "I have my first postpartum visit scheduled for this Wednesday, but, you know, it's best to go in there with a game plan. Otherwise they just rush you out."

"Right," Desiree said. "What am I looking for?"

January didn't answer. Desiree got on her knees, the teal bath rug damp and the space tight.

"Oh."

"What is it? Some kind of bruise? Or is it a tear? They said I didn't tear enough for stitches this time, but maybe I did? I musta been stunned or something at first, but now it all hurts."

How to describe it calmly, neutrally. It couldn't have been extraordinary, this pink flesh bulging, just extraordinary to her, ignorant as she was. Desiree tried to summon the calm, clinical remove she'd cultivated way back when caring for Nolan. *It's just a patch of decay, we'll manage.* But that had been so long ago.

"I think, um."

"Tell me."

She had hardly seen January's nipple before today; now she was pretending to be familiar with the particular undulations of her labia, their soft-looking black hair, her perineum (which was slightly bruised), and this pink, protruding mass. She stood up.

"Uh, I think it's your bladder? Or like, maybe your uterus?"

"My uterus?"

"Probably your bladder, the way things are arranged, I mean, stacked up down there. It would be bladder before uterus, right? So, not likely your uterus.

"Anyway, it's coming out of your— I can see it. On the outside of your vagina."

It felt important to look January in the eyes just then, which Desiree accomplished for five seconds by counting to herself.

"My bladder. Alright." She nodded and nodded and nodded. She pulled her underwear and sweatpants back on, careful. She turned and looked in the mirror.

"So, yeah, I need to get the fuck out of here," she said. "Right now. Let's go."

The warehouses sat in judgment, closed off to the world as before, despite it now being lunchtime. Two minutes into that eerie stretch of streets and Brook started crying in his car seat, loud, needy bawls.

"Pull over," January said. She moved to the back seat. In the rearview mirror Desiree saw her put a hand on the baby's belly. He quieted.

"He hates being in the car. Bronze did too, then he loved it. Now he hates it again."

The place to go was Nakia's, and the thing to do was show up unannounced. Desiree knew this without knowing why. She knew the code to Nakia's front door lock, but wagered her friend would be there, it being Friday and early enough in the afternoon. Through the windshield the brown lower layer of air in the sky seemed a thing a person might be able to scrape clean with the right tool; it didn't seem possible that humans could live beneath filth like that.

How had life lead them here, and how had she known to show up on this day, at this moment? She had stopped believing in a god in any real way in her twenties, around the time Nolan died. But she did believe in her own intuition, and in something else not nameable that could spur a person like herself, generally averse to quick decisions, to know when the moment had arrived to make one. Maybe it was as simple as love. Love had prodded her onto that flight, into this rental car, and down onto that bathroom rug.

The sunshine outside was too bright for January, who hadn't properly been outdoors in weeks. Should've brought her sunglasses, the baby's sun visor for his window, more diapers, more clothes, more of everything. They merged onto the 10 just as her breasts signaled their need to be emptied. Not now, but soon. A tingly, needly sensation that was among the long list of things she hadn't known she'd feel before getting pregnant. The body was its own closed-network communication system, and there were two types of information: what it needed and what it needed relief from. What Desiree confirmed in the bathroom was the latter. A new message. There'd been no pink protrusions, no errant organs, no stabbing, dragging feeling after Bronze. Nobody had told her this was even possible. But now that someone else had seen it she felt calmer; the system was simply communicating a new need for relief. There was too much, much too much pressing down on her in that house, to the point that she couldn't even hold her own body together. Well, she was out of the house now. Step one.

Desiree fiddled with the radio, settled on smooth jazz.

"Real auntie music," January said.

"You have kids," Desire said flatly. "That makes me Auntie."

She nodded even though Desiree wasn't looking in the mirror to see her do it. Desiree had begun referring to January as family a few years into their friendship, and though she agreed with the sentiment, it always made her bashful. Hard to accept that someone could be so up-front about love, so clear about wanting you in their life.

"Let's exit soon. I gotta feed him. And we might as well find food cause right after I'm gonna be starving. I'm already starving."

They were in Pomona, passing underneath the old Pomona Valley Mining Company building, which seemed to be clinging onto its hillside perch by sheer will, its old wooden façade like something out of a Western. It was already at least five degrees cooler outside and they were still over forty miles from the ocean.

"So am I allowed to ask what the problem is?"

Through the oval of the rearview mirror Desiree eyed her. January looked out the window.

"You don't have to answer if you don't want to."

"It's fine," she said.

Too much to explain. The rise and fall of the day according to a toddler's mercurial emotions and a newborn's raw, constant need. The swing from feeling purposeful and competent to small, petty, and inconsequential. The problem of debasement caused by men. Just how they moved through the world, free and presumptuous. Just how the most they thought to do was always not enough, a task completed never as valuable as true foresight, true initiative. Was it men or was it Morris? Most of the time she loved him dearly, but sometimes, not more than once a week, she hated him so deeply and fiercely it made her mouth turn sour. How dare he get to opt in and out, how dare he deign to veto any of her choices, how dare he pretend that paying the bills meant anything. He paid the bills because things were set up so she couldn't. She had a real company now, had people who had inquired about design work right up until her self-funded maternity leave. He paid the bills because it was the least he could do considering that her insides were on the outside and she might never know true peace, a real night of sleep, let alone a complete bowel movement again. And if something should happen to her, he'd replace her. It was like that book she'd read in high school, about the old man who drags his dead wife around in a pine box, her stinking to high heaven, all so he can get some new teeth. New fucking teeth! Morris would do that.

"Do you remember reading a book about a husband who drags his dead wife's body through the countryside in a wagon so he can get some teeth?"

"Huh?"

"I feel like we read it in AP English. It's a family of poor white folks in the South on a road trip to bury this woman. She wasn't embalmed, so after a while the husband and his kids start being followed by vultures, and he keeps telling everyone he has to do this cause it was the wife's final wish or whatever, but really it's cause he wants new teeth. And a new wife."

"I like that you think I was in AP English, or AP anything," Desiree said. "You forget I was the dumb sister. I wasn't even in honors."

"You never been dumb in your life. Maybe lazy, but not dumb."

"Oh, wow. A friend wakes up at the crack of dawn, flies across the country to rescue you, and she's lazy?"

They laughed. Desiree signaled and carefully changed lanes to exit. They were almost past the 605.

"So, what was the point of the book?"

"Oh," January said. "I don't remember if there even was a point, I just remember my teacher saying that the ending, that part with the teeth, was a trick, like we weren't supposed to take it literally, but I don't know . . . Even back in high school I felt like I knew people who'd do that."

The man's children maim themselves, humiliate themselves in the name of burying their mother, but the man emerges unscathed, January remembered. Maybe if she got her act together her boys could be that devoted to her, willing to risk their lives to honor her dying wish. But she couldn't picture Morris doing anything other than getting someone else to be next to him and raise their children. And fast.

In the car, with the windows rolled down, in the burger joint parking lot, while Desiree ordered lunch, January decided to try feeding Brook sitting up. The fresh air helped; she was able to keep her eyes open. Afterward, she showed Desiree how to burp him, and leaned against the car gulping air and feeling lighter. They put him back in his car seat and carried it to a picnic table to eat. Mostly Asian and Latino patrons, both inside and outside the restaurant, more families than she would've expected for Friday lunch.

"We shoulda stayed in New York," January said.

"That's what I tell everyone," Desiree said. "Nakia gets mad when I say it. It's true, though. Look at this air! It's not sustainable."

"What I wouldn't give to be in the park right now, reading a dumb trendy book, waiting for the nutcracker man to walk by."

"Girl, the cops done run the nutcracker men out the park, damn near. Both parks. You got a better chance of finding a weed guy nowadays than an alcoholic beverage. But don't let me ruin the fantasy."

"For some reason back when I was freaking out about being pregnant with Bronze, I'd decided that there were only two options: raise the baby on my own or go back to Morris. But there were a lot of other options. I was stupid."

"Not stupid. You were going off your gut."

"And then when we did move, how the hell did we end up way out in nowhere? Morris just had to own a home and he needed to feel like he was getting his money's worth. So now he has this psychotic commute and me, I have what? Neighbors who barely speak, and more warehouses for neighbors than human beings."

Desiree just looked at her, which was fine because January didn't want a response. She tore into her cheeseburger and fries, gulped down her strawberry shake. She had to hand it to number two, he did love to sleep. His eyelids were lowering, so she rocked his carrier on the tabletop to help him.

"There's no real problem," she tried again. "I just don't feel like myself with him. Like I can't be myself."

"You can't be yourself with the person you've been with half your life."

"That's a long time, right?"

"I don't get it," Desiree said. "Who is it that you feel you have to be in front of him? How's that person different than who you are with me?"

Well, this seemed obvious to January, but perhaps it wasn't the way other people lived.

"It's a feeling. I'm not even sure I dislike who I am with him, I just . . . That person? That person isn't me. It's like I'm squatting inside that person, I don't know. And the feeling has grown with each birth. I have the kid, and Morris sees the baby and he loves him, like truly loves him, but there's something that feels exclusive about it. Like he's even more indifferent to me, cares less about me now that he's got what he wanted, these sons."

"January, that doesn't seem fair—"

"I know! It's not fair, it's crazy, so after I had Bronze I put it out of my mind. I said yes when he proposed, and I meant it. But, Des, I'm telling you, after Brook was born, his face had that exact same look. Like he alone had won the lottery or something. It came back the moment he held him in his arms. And I had the same thought: I am both completely necessary to this family in Morris's eyes and always on the outside of it. The real me is on the outside of it, at least."

"Unh," Desiree said. She opened her half-eaten burger to squeeze more ketchup inside, closed it, and bit. She was trying to look calm, coolly supportive, but even as she ate her food the corners of her mouth remained tight.

"Do you have an issue with what I'm doing, Desiree? You should tell me if so."

Desiree wiped her mouth.

"I came all the way here to support you. Do *you* have an issue with what you're doing? I don't see how what I think matters. I'm here."

"That's bullshit. Of course it matters."

Both of them were essentially good girls, January thought. That wasn't ideal. Good girls didn't leave a perfectly good man's house with a newborn in tow and no notice. As far as she knew, Desiree had never seriously transgressed in her life. January herself had only let the cup of transgression touch her lips that one time, and she hadn't had the guts to drink. At almost thirty-five what was there to show for all that compliance? Her boys, yes, but also a life she did not recognize or want. A real good girl would be satisfied.

"That's a lucky baby you got right there."

Desiree and January jumped—inwardly, they hoped. Standing in front of their table, so tall that his face was bisected by the table's umbrella, was a man. Or maybe a boy, a tall teenager, hard to say. Patchy beard, pouty mouth with lips that looked picked at, skin the brown of a fallen maple leaf. When he stooped down they saw his eyes were deep green and miserable. Just sad, sad, sad, no matter that he grinned at Brook with a kind of longing. One might have thought he was a local hangabout, or maybe a fry cook about to clock in for his shift, except he wore a dark gray hoodie that looked like it had sustained weeks of soil and sweat. Matted reddish curls tufted out from under his hood. His khakis were creased yet threadbare at the knees and fraying at the cuffs. He wasn't wearing shoes, just filthy tube socks, several pairs, it looked like, or else his feet were badly swollen inside the one pair.

January's hand had drifted up to Brook's carrier. When she realized this was a defensive gesture, she felt guilty but did not move her hand. Desiree stood up.

"Hey, what's up? Can we help you with something?"

There was a lilt to her voice, simultaneously light and firm, that reminded January of how Morris spoke to Bronze in the midst of a toddler tantrum.

The man stopped grinning.

"Yeah, uh, my name is Van? And I was hoping for a little help getting something to eat?"

He said this robotically, like he maybe didn't mean it but knew this was the line required of him in this moment. His eyes slid back to the sleeping baby.

"I'm just out here tryna do right, tryna get back on my feet after being away for a while, it's been—"

Desiree cut him off. "Oh yeah, of course." She smiled at the side of his face as if she might will him to look at her instead of the baby. "I don't have any cash, though. You wanna come in with me and order?"

Van nodded, and January watched him shuffle into the restaurant behind Desiree, the bottoms of his socks somehow never visible. She couldn't remember the last time she'd bought a meal for someone living on the street. When she was very little, her father, Nelson, would do it often, or he'd press a five-dollar bill into somebody's palm, skin touching skin like he lived unafraid of germs. June never gave money, not unless a person performed a task for her in some capacity, like hurriedly washing her windshield at the 105 off-ramp or helping her get into a tight parking spot near Venice Beach. It needed to feel like a trade to her mother, January gathered. The memory more at the forefront was of June quickly locking the car doors if they drove around Inglewood at night—or, heaven forbid, near Skid Row on an errand downtown—locks that had a loud finality to them, locks you could hear both inside and outside the car. "If someone tries to pull open my door, he's in for a wild ride," June would say.

When they emerged from the restaurant, Van walked out first and Desiree followed, as if she'd held the door for him. He held a drink carrier with two milkshakes in one hand and two paper bags of food gripped tight in the other, their grease stains spreading. He lifted the drink carrier up when he saw January, a kind of farewell gesture, and January nodded back, relieved. But then he walked toward her again, and January felt glad, almost proud, that she'd never taken her hand off Brook's carrier because she didn't have to return it there now.

"Looks like she hooked you up," she said.

Van nodded fast, his eyes on Brook again, then on her.

"Lucky little man."

"Aw, thank you."

"You doing the right thing, breastfeeding him and all a that. He a lucky little man. So is your man."

He grinned again and turned away. He shuffled to the corner of the building and was soon out of sight. Desiree picked up the baby carrier and headed back to the car. How had he known about her breastfeeding, or even that Brook was a boy? The baby wore a yellow onesie and nothing else in this heat. Every time she'd taken him to the doctor he'd been called a girl by at least one nurse. Maybe he had seen her before they noticed him, back when she fed Brook in the car. But who was to say who was lucky just by looking at them? She felt strange, like she'd seen this kind of thing on TV before, or maybe read about it. A mysterious stranger, a "beggar," walks up to a new baby and says something enigmatic—a curse or a benediction, only time will tell. January hoped to never find out. She felt superstitious about the whole exchange, like maybe she should cross herself, dab Brook on the head with anointed oil or holy water. Instead she muttered, "Let's get the fuck out of here," to herself in the exact same way she'd meant it earlier in the day and climbed into the back seat.

They'd finally run into traffic, which meant that what should have been only another forty minutes or so of travel could double. January turned on her phone for the first time since leaving home. No check-in texts from Morris, but June had sent a photo of Bronze eating peas and carrots, which he would never eat in January's presence.

As they approached the city, small homeless encampments, heralded by bright blue tarps fastened to chain-link fences, trash, and the odd human figure began to pop up here and there along the freeway's embankments and overpasses. They passed the downtown detention center, which Morris always said put the *d* in "dystopia," and he was right. Big old behemoth dangling over the freeway like somebody was supposed to be happy to see it, so much razor wire covering its "skywalks" that there was no way anyone could truly glimpse the sky. It had the nerve to be right next to the train station. Some welcome.

"Do you really not have any cash?"

"I have a little, why?"

"No reason," January said. "But you told that guy you didn't have any."

Their eyes met in the review mirror; then Desiree looked forward again.

"My granddaddy always told me to buy people a meal if you could, so that's what I do."

"But you told him you don't have any cash, and he hadn't even asked for cash yet."

"Yeah, I did. So what? Do you think that makes me less of a cheerful giver or something? His food was twenty dollars."

She had an urge to laugh at that old-timey phrase—"cheerful giver"—but knew that would only irritate Desiree further. Desiree was full of old-timey phrases.

"Never mind," January said. "I was just curious."

They drove on in silence. Desiree tuned the radio to a station that played hip-hop from when they were teenagers; oldies for people who weren't yet ready to label them as such. January felt guilty for trying to make Desiree feel guilty, but also didn't feel like apologizing. Out the window: the sudden rise of downtown skyscrapers, more buildings in the southern part of the skyline since the last time she'd paid attention to it. Nakia lived on the northern edge of Inglewood, but in a city as small as that one, you were always close to anyone else in it. June still lived within spitting distance of Morningside High, maybe fifteen minutes from Nakia by car. June and Bronze would still be at home, at least for the next few hours. She could not picture telling June what she planned to do.

"How'd everything get small?"

"What do you mean?" If Desiree was annoyed by her, her voice didn't betray it.

"I wanted to be a bigger person than I am, you know? Like a better person, more part of the world, but somehow I ended up with this small suburban life."

"We're not that old," Desiree said.

"Kids age you."

"I thought kids keep you young."

"Have you changed your mind? You want any? This probably ain't the day to ask."

"Ha. It's fine. I don't want kids any more or less now than I did at like seventeen or twenty-eight. I'm just not . . . pressed for a bigger life like that."

"But I just told you my life is small."

"Small in some ways but too big for me in others. I don't know how to explain it."

This made January uneasy, and she wondered if it was immaturity, a kind of childishness in her that needed to be constantly expanding, reaching for more. It didn't feel like something she could stop doing. The sun shifted so that it hit number two—Brook—in his face, so she draped her arm over his carrier to intercept the beam. She remembered something—not a real transgression, but the only time she'd been surprised to learn that Desiree could be impulsive, secretive.

"You know what I never told you? I knew about Chika."

Desiree's eyes met hers in the rearview for a half second.

"I mean, I didn't know when it happened, but like five years ago, out of nowhere Morris told me. He said it like it was old news, which I guess it was by then."

"And . . . what did he say?"

"Just that y'all hooked up for a whole summer, and that Chika was sprung over you, was still fucked up about it like months after you broke it off. Speaking of a big life, he has four kids now, did you know that? Outside Boston I think."

"Good for him. I highly doubt he was sprung, but whatever."

"You know, I always thought he was cute. Why didn't you tell me about y'all back then?"

"It wasn't anything. Just a few weeks in the summer."

Desiree flipped her visor down and squinted against the sun. She wasn't interested in talking about Chika. Fine. In the oval of her face highlighted by the rearview mirror, January could see that what she'd long thought were freckles on her friend's temples and under her eyes had bloomed into tiny, touchable moles. Maybe a dozen of them.

"You know what? I think it's bullshit, you wanting to keep your world small or whatever."

Desiree sighed.

"How's it even possible that what I want, how I feel about my own life, is bullshit?"

"It's bullshit because you still want it all! Just like everybody else. Maybe not a baby, but, like, a life."

"I have a life."

"You have a holding pattern," January said. Why was she saying this? "You have a man you keep at arm's length, an apartment you refuse to even renovate. You're waiting. You've been waiting."

"For what? What am I waiting for?"

January had some ideas.

"I don't know," she said. "You tell me."

"Tuh," Desiree said. "This is your theory. I don't have anything to tell."

"See, this is why it's hard to be real with you. You never really want anything. You don't know what it's like to feel like you're supposed to be having a certain kind of life and you're just not doing it."

January sniffed, wiped her nose with the back of her hand. They were all the way across downtown now, to the part of the 10 that would take them to Crenshaw, then on to Nakia's. When had she become such a poor communicator? It might be due to fatigue, she thought, or lack of practice. The last conversation she'd had with an adult had been with Morris the night before, about setting up a savings account for Brook and what they should do for Bronze's second birthday. That hardly counted.

"It's a prolapse," Desiree said after a few minutes. "Probably your bladder, or maybe your rectum, but probably not your uterus. If you go to physical therapy it might get better, or at least feel better. There's also surgery, but it looks intense."

"How do you know?"

"I googled a little at the house, while you were packing a bag."

"At the house? Why didn't you tell me before we left?"

Finally Desiree looked into the rearview again.

"Because maybe you would have stayed."

You can be as happy as you truly hope to be, Desiree believed this. The problem was that January's hope for happiness was nebulous. She'd never set aside time or been forced by life to figure out the shape of her own ideal of happiness. Yes, part of the problem might be chemical—she was no doctor but was beginning to understand that her friend tended toward depression—but what did happiness actually look like for January? It was important to have a clear sense of its shape. Desiree knew the shape it took for her, or rather, its architecture: it was a many-roomed home, a town house. There were areas she may never gain access to, but most doors could be opened. The ground floor, the foundation—food and shelter and security—had been lain with great emotional cost but minimal sweat from her brow. That was privilege in some people's eyes, not hers. The second floor was populated by the people she'd long loved: this desperate mother-child currently in her back seat, and by extension her children; Nakia and Monique. Even the knowledge of the existence of her sister was on this floor, despite Danielle being on the other side of a long-closed door. The third floor was mostly windows, a great room from which she could look out onto the world and feel a part of it but no urgent need to run it or leave any mark on it. The great room would probably be depressing to a person like January, who wanted so much, even more than she would ever admit out loud, but it was comforting for Desiree to think about. The contentment that came from being still and minding her own business. Last winter she and Jelani finally had a serious conversation about marriage and children, one she'd demurred from for the better part of two years. "I kind of just want to disappear when it's over," she'd told him. "I want to have my little fun with you and my friends and see things and try new things until I'm old and ready to go. That's it." She didn't care about a legacy. The idea of "leaving evidence of her existence" made her queasy. Her impulse to want less was born of her own early disappointments, sure, but life would inevitably disappoint everyone, she thought. Better to figure out what exactly was worth getting your arms around and hold tight to that, and anything else good that fell into your lap could be a happy bonus. She and January were very different in this regard.

"I'm sorry you're going through all this," Desiree said. "I really am." But as she looked into the rearview she realized that January was asleep, one arm draped around Brook's car seat, her head thrown back and her mouth ajar.

That guy who she'd bought a burger for, Van. He wouldn't make eye contact with her for most of the time they waited in line to order. Mostly he scanned the room and looked down at his dirty socks. When they arrived at the cashier, he'd had his order ready, spat it out rapid-fire, and bounced expectantly on his toes while they waited for their number to be called. It was a fantasy—Monique would call it a liberal fantasy—to think she could change his life, she reminded herself. But she could give him an opportunity to tell his story. There were three numbers yet to be called before theirs when she finally got up the nerve to ask where he was from.

"Folsom, before that Fresno," he said. "Believe it or not."

"I believe you. I know there's black people in Fresno."

"Cool, cool, cool. So you been around. Cool."

A teenager in a paper hat called their number: 117. Van claimed the food. When he turned back to Desiree he looked her in the eyes. His were green as a glass bottle.

"I just been thinking about that word, you know? *Verbatim*. Verbatim. Like you are what you say you are *verbatim*, right? It's a deep-ass word."

She'd nodded, no idea whatsoever what he meant.

"And it's just not what you say. What you do verbatim is who you are too, right?"

Desiree had sped ahead of him to hold the door open, leaving that question unanswered.

Now she exited on Crenshaw and drove south, past West Angeles Church and several new Metro stops, the forever-imperiled mall and the blighted husk of the Liquor Bank. Here they were on the sidewalks and alongside her in traffic: the last black human beings in Los Angeles, or rather, the last black human beings in the city with roofs over their heads. She dipped down Stocker for a quick look at Nolan's old house. There it stood, nothing on the outside changed in the years since she'd sold it, but inside she knew all of Nolan's carpeting had been pulled up in favor of the wood floors below, and the beautiful mid-century wood paneling in the living room had been removed, as had the deep blue Spanish tile on the kitchen countertops and the pink and avocado tile in the bathrooms. She'd seen a few years ago online when it was up for sale again that the back "pool house" had been made into a proper, permitted granny flat, or a casita, or an Accessory Dwelling Unit, as the city wanted them to be called. She wondered if someone's grandparent was actually living back there, or else a teen, desperate for some space from the rest of their family. Probably just a regular old tenant, rent being as high as it was.

Verbatim. She would not move in with Jelani; nowhere in the architecture of her happiness allowed for that. But if he was willing, she decided that he could move in.

January awoke because the sun was cooking the right side of her face and her breasts stung again. She was in Nakia's driveway, alone in the back seat of Desiree's rental. She must have been so knocked out they thought it best to leave her there, the windows rolled down like she was some sad TV-ad dog. Had to be only in the seventies out here, a whole twenty degrees cooler than out east where she and Morris lived. Nakia's house was single-story and straightforward, with a low mid-century profile and a drought-resistant, succulent-heavy lawn. January had been inside once before, and the gulf between Nakia's success and her own had never been more apparent, never mind Nakia's head start. A grown-up's house, trendy white bouclé furniture mixed in with the kind of passed-down, durable wood pieces that no one in January's family had ever owned. Nakia had offered to host the baby shower for Brook here, but Morris's mother had insisted on renting space in a tired restaurant in the Marina. What a waste.

The front door was cracked, which was nice of them. Off the entryway one could either make a left to go down the hall to the bathroom and bedrooms or a right to go to the living room and kitchen. January hesitated, thinking about cleaning herself up before seeing Nakia. She could hear them talking in the living room.

". . . yeah and they, like, expect me to come in to settle these tiny-ass disputes," Nakia was saying. "That is literally their job as managers. It's annoying."

"That's why I hate managing people," Desiree said. "It always creates a dynamic that makes me feel shitty. Oh! I meant to ask you. There was a homeless man outside of In-N-Out earlier and I bought him a couple meals, but I didn't wanna give him cash. January thinks I should've given him money."

January turned the corner into the room. Nakia sat on her white sofa with her knees tucked under her, holding Brook close. The shades were drawn and a fan whirred, likely because she didn't "believe" in air-conditioning.

"I didn't say that," January said.

"You basically did," Desiree said. She turned to Nakia. "Am I wrong for only wanting to buy him food?"

Nakia handed Brook over and made space on the sofa next to her. January took her son from her friend, raised his bottom to her nose, and sniffed. Seemed fine. She opted to sit next to Desiree.

"Who am I, the pope?" Nakia asked. "How am I supposed to know?"

"You're somebody who helps the homeless more than both of us."

"People should be trusted to spend money in the way they need to," Nakia said.

"Right," January said. "I was mostly just teasing her but that's what I meant."

"But also? You're not the government. You're just a person trying to do something for somebody else."

"Thank you," Desiree said. "That's how I feel."

"But also, I don't know! We could all do more? I'm just a person too."

She was distracted by Brook, who had decided to stare in her direction from his mother's arms.

"Y'all know this is kidnapping, right?" Nakia said this with a smirk on her face.

"How?" Desiree said. "How's it kidnapping for a mother to take her child to see his aunt?"

"It's not kidnapping yet, but say y'all drove farther east instead of back west to me? Wasn't Monique just in Vegas? What if y'all had crossed state lines and went to Vegas?"

"Then we'd be taking a baby and his only food source to Vegas, to his other aunt," Desiree said. "So what? Nobody would put us in jail for that."

It was typical Nakia teasing, trying to needle January's own anxieties. She was glad Desiree was defending her, relieved. Nakia got up and reached out her hands for Brook again. January handed him over, ignored the petulant voice inside that said don't. This was her safe harbor, irritating as the owner of the harbor could be. She watched Nakia lift Brook up to her face and kiss his cheek. January wondered if bright orange newborn excrement could stain Nakia's white couches permanently.

This whole trip was the most she'd sat upright since giving birth. Could she actually feel it, the tiny, tiny bulge when she crossed her legs, when she leaned forward too far, or was she imagining it? Probably imagining. Hopefully. Part of her wanted to take Nakia into the bathroom and show her, as she'd shown Desiree. She'd finally see her as strong. A weak person wouldn't be able to get up every day and be food and comfort both for anybody in her condition. A prolapse, or multiple. And she still wasn't convinced there wasn't some kind of unhealed tear. She'd have to see about it before Morris took her off the insurance, she thought, which is when she realized that she'd already made up her mind.

Black in the Stacks: A Black Librarian's Musings

by Monique L.

September 9, 2023

If you follow me on social media you may have learned that my father passed away a few weeks ago. Dennis LaMorne Jr. was 68 years old, a survivor until he wasn't. It feels strange to speak about him, to write about him in the past tense, and stranger still to try to sum up his life to people on the internet. He was a reserved and pragmatic person. He worked hard for over thirty years as a logistics coordinator for the city's department of parks and recreation. He loved playing cards and dominoes and chess with his friends in our backyard in Queens. He especially loved chess. One downside of me being so close-fisted with information about my family and friends in my writing over the years, and not being a person who keeps a diary, is that I missed out on reflecting on many important relationships as they evolved. I have been working on being more forthcoming, less guarded in my writing (the better to avoid becoming a "persona"), and I hope to have time soon to devote to my memories, to pay as close attention to the people in my real life as I have to world events and people who, if we're being honest, really only exist for us within the confines of our screens.

I will share one bittersweet detail, which Dennis Jr. himself would take comfort in: he died in Barbados, the island of his birth, during the longest period of time he'd spent there since a teenager.

I want to talk about hard times. I was not prepared for how wrecked I'd be upon learning of my father's death, even though I admit I had spent time imagining it (we all imagine the deaths of our parents, if not in our waking hours then certainly in our dreams, our nightmares). I had thought he'd have a long illness, that we'd all have time to get used to the idea of him being gone, but that's not what we got. He had a stroke on a Wednesday and was gone before the next Monday. The items I'd impulse-bought to ease his anticipated transition back home post-hospital arrived two days after he was gone. My mother, my siblings—my older sister and brother—and I went from thinking through plans for what life would look like for him when he was discharged to thinking through a funeral and burial within hours. And now I see that those early busy days of planning were a blessing because there were distractions to keep us from truly sitting with our new reality.

When I finally returned to my own apartment, I discovered that I had a limited store of energy each day, which I would spend checking in on my mother and, alongside my siblings, helping her arrange her affairs. I could do this for about 7 hours but then it was like a hedge sprang up around my brain, or a moat, separating my knowledge of the things that needed doing—feeding myself, walking my dogs—from my ability to see any task to completion. I would suddenly need to lie down, to sit in a chair and stare at nothing. "Grief paralysis" is how I've come to think of it. This is where my friends came in. What friends! These women showed up for me so completely that I often wept when I woke up to find Desiree on my sofa, or Nakia making me breakfast, or a new hilarious video from January's how'd-they-get-so-big sons. Eventually I felt strong enough to be alone again and keep myself (and my chihuahuas) fed and clothed. I still felt somewhat guilty, especially that two of my friends moved their own affairs around to be there physically. I had kept them from their loved ones, from their own very busy and important lives.

In the days since, I've realized that I have not shown up similarly in any person's life when hard times arose, or rather, befell them. This is an essential aspect of growing up, of figuring out how to remain connected to others as we move into middle age. Some of the people who I did not show up for are no longer in my life, and now I understand more fully why. One reason I fell short is related to my own insecurities, my own stinginess with time, especially in my early thirties. Longtime readers have heard me refer to these as my Scared and Stingy years. In my Scared and Stingy years I constantly felt behind my friends in life, who are successful in their own ways and impressive and inspiring. Meanwhile I often felt like I was still scrambling to build a career, to make a "name" for myself and have some kind of financial stability. Opportunities might dry up at any moment, I reasoned, so I prioritized being available for the ones presented to me. Thanks to a series of professional breakthroughs—several of them brought about by those same friends, in one way or another—I have stopped scrambling as much in recent years, but my reasons for being absent before were never justified. Since when did a lack of funds necessitate a lack of care? Another part of the problem is that I thought I had time. Nobody's parents were supposed to be dying in their 50s and 60s. No one was supposed to be getting an acrimonious divorce in their late 20s or early 30s, and absolutely no one was supposed to be diagnosed with a terminal illness at my young age. But they did get divorces, and they might fall sick, because life is full of unforeseeable calamities. It is our job as friends to figure out how to be there for the people we love, come what may.

Whose fault is it? is the question I think about often, not who is to blame in the back-and-forth that lead to a fallout with a friend, but which side, which participant in said friendship should have known better than to even go there. Given the circumstances, who should have fallen back? We don't live in a fallback culture, we live in a ghosting culture, which is different, and much more detrimental. A fallback culture would normalize putting aside your petty bullshit when a friend is in distress, when their world is truly, structurally compromised, because they cannot be expected to be their best selves. A ghosting culture would, at first glance, look like a fallback was in play—giving someone space to feel what they feel, say—but in reality a retreat would be in full swing. In my experience, limited as it is, when two friends quarrel there is generally some exterior force at play. A shitty job situation, an ailing parent. Either the other party is not aware of the toll this exterior element is having on their friend, or they are unable or unwilling to provide their friend with the care needed given the circumstances. And I have refused to give a friend the benefit of the doubt more than once. The guilt of not showing up when I should have has led me to sense offense when none was intended, to assume resentment lingered in them the way shame did in me.

Since the death of Dennis Jr. I have called and texted two people—one close friend, one friend who was on the way to becoming close—to say that I am sorry for handling them so poorly. The close friend responded, the other did not, likely because I had not earned their trust enough to weather such mistreatment. I have to accept that they may never respond, but maybe life will conspire to give us a second chance.

Maybe the only resolution is time.

Black in the Stacks: *A Black Librarian's Musings*

by Monique L.

September 19, 2025

Too Soon
(for everyone)

I wonder if this is middle age.
not loose skin or old eggs or the accumulation of
bad choices
but this—
every year has become
the year I need to get past, through, over:
twenty-nine.
thirty-three.
thirty-nine.
forty-three.
forty-seven.
A year a loved one caught
some plague
some violence
some uncontrollable growth
some self-ending sadness.
All deaths untimely, making me mark time
different
and who will be added, their names stamped in earth, their ages
an affront?
There is no over the hill,
just a series of small hillocks, plotted out before me,
each one I pray
not to die climbing.

2024

14 Hours in the Loop

10:20 A.M.

"What's so funny?"

January was looking down at the water and chuckling to herself as the boat slid between skyscrapers. Having arrived several hours earlier than their East Coast counterparts, she and Nakia had booked an architectural cruise of the Chicago River.

"Nothing," January said, but she brought the heel of her hand to her eye.

"Oh no, not actual tears. You okay?" January's big feelings, which is how January herself described them, still caught Nakia by surprise.

"I'm not crying for real," January said. "Or, I mean, I am, but not because I'm sad. It's fine."

Nakia sat back down on the bench. She had learned over the years that with January, or at least with herself and January, patience led to more revelations than questioning ever would. She took off her jacket and placed it between them. It was warmer and sunnier in Chicago than it had been when they'd left LA, June gloom having grayed the city since Mother's Day. This early tour boat had about a dozen other people on board and a lot of space to spread out. A young albino woman with a long synthetic ponytail and deep dimples was their guide. She sprinkled in bits of broader Chicago history as she gave peppy descriptions of the buildings they passed, which shot up mere feet from their tiny boat so that some structures appeared to be leaning over them.

"Me and Morris went on one of these tours in like '08 or '09," January said.

"Two thousand nine? Oh, man, don't tell me y'all took one of them Obama-inspired Chicago pilgrimages."

January laughed, one final tear still wet on her cheek.

"You know we did. Had to get the grits from that one diner in Hyde Park and everything."

"My god, I forgot about that place. There was a time when I was obsessed with where him and Michelle were eating," Nakia said. "I'm maybe the only person I know who never made it out here. My parents came."

Nakia had come across Conrad and Juanita's box of Obama family memorabilia—novelty plates, buttons, their tickets to the first inauguration—when she helped them pack up to move back to New Jersey. A time capsule of wild hope, almost painful to look back on now.

"We really thought that man was gonna be the Black Messiah or something," she said. "What a time."

"Yeah, turns out he was very much *not*," January said. "And white people ain't been okay since. Look at them."

She lifted her eyes toward a heavyset sunburned grandpa near the rear of the boat wearing a camouflage baseball cap and red T-shirt with TAKE AMERICA BACK emblazoned across its front and a cartoon elephant wearing a blond toupee and sunglasses on its back. Nakia had already clocked this man and vowed to avoid him. Together, she and January could laugh at these grim realities. It was harder when one was out in the world alone.

"Anyway, I was just remembering how once, when I wrote an angry letter to Morris, I'd mentioned what that girl just said about the river being cleaned up by reversing the current. I had forgot all about it. My memory is getting bad."

There was what January said and what January meant. An undulating line separated the two.

"It's hard for me to imagine you sending an angry letter to Morris back when y'all were together."

"I never sent it. Probably should have."

January smiled and Nakia smiled back, though it seemed like January was still trying to quell some big feeling. She had gotten thinner since leaving Morris, which Nakia attributed to her breastfeeding troubles with Brook. When the baby finally got the hang of nursing, he'd turned ravenous, and January still fought nausea after every feeding. Despite everyone—Nakia, June, even Morris—encouraging her to stop if she felt as bad as she had to have felt, January had soldiered on with breastfeeding for a whole year, like some kind of penitent, much of it spent in a calorie deficit. Nakia wasn't sure if it was the weight loss or the stress of single motherhood, but January looked older, more fragile than she'd looked a few years ago. The skin on her face looked thin, and her cheeks, no longer chubby, sagged slightly.

January got up and went to the boat's tiny bar. She maneuvered carefully back to Nakia holding two sparkling wines.

"Okay, I know this is technically a work trip," she said. "We can't have you nonfunctional, but I'm giving myself the job of toasting you at every stage of this process. You don't gotta feel pressured to finish every drink. Cheers!"

Nakia accepted the drink and the toast, though it wasn't even eleven a.m. yet and she should not have let January pay. "Process" felt like the right word for the weekend. The process of somehow, over the years, keeping her restaurants' lights on, somehow becoming well-connected and well-respected enough to even get on the radar of the people who gave out the most prestigious awards in food. The process of rising to the occasion of the increased attention and scrutiny that she and Safe House had faced in the months since she'd made it onto the short list. More business, yes, but also more customers expecting the sun and the stars to somehow manifest in their grits bowls rather than appreciating the food for what it was: dependable, delicious. The process of getting here to Chicago with her three oldest friends. She'd invited Miguel first, but he'd declined, arguing that summer weekends were too busy at the Inglewood location and he had his sons' weekend soccer commitments. Jay would arrive from a conference in Aspen Sunday night, in time to be Nakia's date for the award ceremony on Monday.

When she thought about the award—Best Chef: California—she felt a quickening in her stomach, a genre of anxiety mostly foreign to her. She was almost thirty-eight. Monique had already turned forty, and January was up next in the new year. This is the kind of thing you want to happen, she told herself. But the feeling, like the heartbeat of some tiny animal lodged deep in her belly, remained.

11:00 A.M.

On a very short flight across a handful of eastern states, Desiree and Monique sat in first class. This was standard for Monique but meant something more to Desiree, who hadn't sat in the front of a plane since her final flight with Nolan. This first-class cabin, if you could even call it that when it was only three rows of seats, had nothing special to offer outside of maybe six extra inches of seat width and legroom, but Monique had insisted on using her free upgrades, and Desiree did not object. "The celebration includes making sure we arrive comfortably," Monique said, happy to board ahead of a handful of older white men wearing business casual.

The seat-belt light came on and the pilot announced turbulence, which felt like something that shouldn't exist on an eighty-five-minute flight across a few Great Lakes. Desiree remembered reading somewhere that turbulence, especially the severe kind, would likely become more frequent due to climate change. She turned to Monique to tell her as much and discovered her friend asleep, her head leaning against the window and her hand still clutching her wineglass. She lifted the cup out of Monique's grip, and Monique's hand closed into a fist. Monique had recently gotten her father's initials—DLJ—tattooed into a pyramid shape, with the *D* at the top and the other letters making the bottom points, on that triangle of flesh between her left thumb and forefinger joints. The tattoo was finally healed. He had been the first of their parents to die in the years of their friendship, and Monique had leaned on Desiree for support, as if her old, foundational losses made her better equipped. Maybe they did.

3:15 P.M.

"You can't just wear different versions of chambray all weekend," Monique said. She sat on her side of the bed she was apparently sharing with January, a towel spread under her butt because she still wore her airplane clothes. They waited for Nakia, who was modeling her outfits for the weekend's events, to exit the bathroom. This was Monique's idea. It was early afternoon and there was time yet to shop for better things if Nakia had last-minute packed a bunch of frumpy button-downs and loose pants, as she had done for January's wedding years before. The past several years had made Nakia, once the best dressed of all of them, into the kind of person who couldn't be trusted to dress formal when formal attire was requested. A person who lived in Chuck Taylors. What really annoyed Monique was that Nakia had gotten away with this, her genius chef–entrepreneur status excusing her from polite society's expectations.

"If you keep pressuring her," January whispered, "she's never gonna feel comfortable."

"It's comments like that that have gotten us to this point," Monique whispered back. "She can be comfortable in real clothes! We've all seen her do it."

Both Desiree and January let out a breath and looked away from her.

"I mean, wear whatever you want, obviously," Monique called out. "You look great in everything."

Nakia opened the bathroom door wearing a tailored chambray suit. Wide-legged trousers, a matching blazer, and a white button-down silk shirt unbuttoned enough for ample cleavage.

"This is for tomorrow night," she said. "The fancy dinner."

January clapped.

"See now, that's how you riff on a theme!" Desiree said.

Nakia turned around in front of the closet mirror. Monique wondered if she'd ruin this look with sneakers but thought better of asking.

"Thank you, thank you," Nakia said. "Monique, you of all people should appreciate my consistency. I'm building a visual *brand*."

"I did not think a brand could be built from chambray and denim alone," Monique said. "But you are off to an excellent start."

"Alright, that's the only outfit I'm previewing for y'all," Nakia said. "I know I'm short but that doesn't mean I'm not grown."

She smiled, curtsied, and returned to the bathroom.

"We're here to support her," January said, voice lowered. "Let's all agree to lean on affirmations for the next day and a half."

She looked at both Monique and Desiree, but Monique knew she was talking to her.

"I am very affirmative," Monique said. "I am *professionally* affirmative, in fact."

"No, you are not *professionally* affirmative," Desiree said. "I wouldn't be your friend if you were."

On the other side of the door the toilet flushed. Nakia sneezed twice, then blew her nose with honking effect. The shower turned on.

"I meant to say I emit positive vibes for a living," Monique said.

"And righteous indignation," Desire said.

"Which is often necessary!" Monique said.

"Oh, a hundred percent it is." Desiree put her hands up, innocent.

"A thousand percent," January said. "I'm just saying, let's keep it overtly positive with none of *our*—meaning all of our—customary, good-natured shade in the mix."

The closer Nakia and January got to each other, the more Monique felt the group's dynamic shift in a way that did not seem favorable to her. She tried her best to ignore it.

Some ten years ago, Monique determined that the four of them had known one another long enough to be prone to the kinds of behavioral regressions usually saved for siblings or parents. Desiree became Nakia's acolyte, doing whatever she could to garner a smile from or be in proximity to the friend she'd known longest and—no need to pretend—likely loved most. Nakia became a super Virgo, making lists, strong-arming the itinerary, bossing the group into submitting to her gastronomical inclinations, and casting unsubtle judgment on others' base, touristic tendencies. Usually, January would go along to get along with whomever, reflecting her only-child's desire to avoid being left out, no matter how little fun she was actually having. On this trip, January seemed possessed by a different regression: she was a part-time bodyguard, keeping close to Nakia and initiating one too many whispered tête-à-têtes for Monique's liking.

It was less clear to Monique how her own regressions manifested, but the feeling that being with her friends spurred in her was similar to how she'd most often felt in her childhood home in Jamaica, Queens. She was the youngest child, always paranoid that her older sister and brother were making fun of her. Often so fixated on earning her sibling's admiration that she overlooked the actions that might garner such admiration, which ranged from turning the double-dutch rope properly to remembering to take the meat out of the freezer to thaw for dinner, thereby sparing all of them their parents' ire. Though she still had trouble describing the mechanics of it, she'd been made aware of her singular capacity to annoy the shit out of everyone in familial group settings since those years in Queens. This trip she'd vowed to tuck these tendencies in.

Desiree paired her phone with the hotel speaker. Drake's "Passionfruit" tinkled into the room, underwater marimba first, which reminded Monique of January's wedding, the last time the four of them had been together. Desiree was truly the great convener, January's maid of honor who had sagely advised January that the best bridesmaid duties were no duties at all. The person who had stayed longest with Monique in Bed-Stuy after her father, Dennis, died. Desiree doubled her commute to Midtown for an additional four weeks until Monique's grief paralysis—a term Monique had perhaps coined, according to one of her longtime newsletter readers—subsided. She felt lucky to have such a straightforward and decent person in her life.

They were all in one hotel room despite Monique's offer to splurge for a second. "You know January don't got money like that," Desiree had said when Monique had brought it up on the way to the airport that morning. "Yes," Monique said. "But by some twist of fate I *do* got money like that. Plus, I can probably get a hookup if I post about the hotel online." Desiree had scrunched up her nose at this. Monique wondered if Desiree was projecting her own uneasiness around money onto their friends, but she let the issue go. A big-brand hotel in Chicago's downtown loop, an upscale offshoot of the brand, but a chain hotel just the same. Carpet thick, drapes heavy, too much blue and gray in the décor. The kind of place for conferences and sad extramarital affairs.

Ever since Jay had convinced the rest of the Tru Talk board to rerelease her video, complete with a new introduction from Monique's new activist-influencer friend Aisha Miller, she had not worried about money the way she had for all of her adult life. She wasn't rich, but she could afford an extra hotel room; it would cost far less than her average speaker's fee. She was working on being less anxious about her sources of income drying up, but it was hard to resist the urge to say yes to everything, to spread herself thin in an effort to make as much money as possible as fast as possible, just in case.

Nakia reemerged wearing a hotel bathrobe on her body and a shimmery gold Korean beauty mask on her face. She sat by Monique on the bed. Too close, comically close, a stiff smile on her closed lips lest she jostle the mask, and Monique knew Nakia was going to mess with her. She did not flinch when Nakia put a hand on her head. Simultaneously calming and menacing.

"I just needed to feel this blowout real quick," Nakia said. "It looks so soft and it *feels* so soft. Impressive. This the Dominicans?"

"Funny. Yes it is, actually. You know I have a girl who does it right."

"A girl who does it right," Nakia said. "I bet you do. Monique c'est *chic*."

"Mmm, Monique *magnifique*!" January said.

"Mmm, Monique le *freak*, ooh la la," Desiree added. She tapped on her phone until "Le Freak" by Chic started playing.

"You all are very dumb," Monique said, grinning. "I don't even remember why y'all started doing this."

"This" being over-the-top disco-dancing while replacing the lyrics of the chorus—"Le freak, c'est chic"—with "Monique c'est chic." It made no sense why this was so funny to the three of them, but it had been this way for years. Them body-rolling and hip-thrusting, Monique resisting, arm-crossing at first before joining in. Some regressions were good.

"Okay, I've had enough," Monique said. The song was winding down anyway. "I'm gonna go get ice."

"Good call," Nakia said. She was out of breath, her mask askew. "According to January's toasting timetable we gotta be overdue for a drink."

"I feel like you're trying to clown me," January said. "But it's true."

In the hallway Monique discovered that the ice was not on their floor but two floors down. In the elevator she looked down at her phone, scrolling past social media images warning of famine here and there in the world, fully expecting to see kids with skeletal faces and kwashiorkor bellies like it was the seventies or something. Or worse, another murdered infant, a tender body broken for no reason that would ever make sense because there existed no good reason to kill a child. The unvarnished horrors of modern warfare were on everyone's social media feeds now, had been for months, and the truly bleak thing was that there seemed to be just as many people outraged by the carnage as onlookers cheering it on. The more powerful a person was—a politician, a celebrity, or even just a person who made a good living online—the more they seemed fine with or were determined to be silent about the preventable misery of others, whether they be Palestinian, Sudanese, Congolese, or Haitian.

What was all of this connectivity for, then? Money, of course. Monique knew this intimately, but she was not so jaded as to have lost all hope that it could be harnessed for some higher good as well. She had written as much in a post just two days ago. It had gone semiviral, reaching almost ten percent of her 114,000 social media followers and almost as many nonfollowers. A less controversial post of just her face and a short poem would do better numbers, of course. Last week she'd posted:

Things I'm Scared Of
(which ain't the same as being afraid)

men in camouflage
July weather in most places now
book bans, but also the way people talk about book bans
men who walk close behind you on the street at night and when you
turn around and look them in the eye refuse to say anything
blond ponytails,
swinging

The tiny poem, dashed off during a subway ride, had corralled three thousand new followers, but it also made her queasy as the days went by. It was too easy to anticipate what people wanted from her, to give them the kind of pinky-toe-deep bon mot that was no skin off anyone's back to reshare, to make mean whatever they wanted it to mean on their own feeds. It felt like tithing to balance these posts with ones about US-funded genocide or corrupt politicians, especially if she lost followers as a result. She had to let some money go so that her soul might fare better in the long term.

Not until the door opened, a man entered, and the elevator began to go down did Monique realize that she'd been going up.

"I'm sorry," the man said, which prompted Monique to look up from her phone. He was about her age, maybe on the far side of midforties, trim, light-skinned, with a very faint mustache and full lips that were very pink. He wore a black baseball cap that had the phrase "Kitchen. Culture." embroidered on it in white, punctuation and all.

"This is random," he said. "But I think we follow each other online?"

7:25 P.M.

A mixer. Years ago, January would have professed deep hatred for the very concept—the networking, the awkward juggling of cups and handshakes and business cards (RIP to those) while standing—but she was a single mother now; she didn't get out much. This mixer, which featured cocktails created by past award-nominee bartenders and small plates created by past award-nominee chefs, felt like a rager to her. The best part was that January did not care if she met anyone, as it wasn't her field, which was likely why people kept introducing themselves. In the past twenty minutes she had met and exchanged information with the head chef at one of the two Mexico City–inspired rooftop restaurants in downtown LA, who claimed to be interested in revamping his menu designs, and a hilarious, down-home sister duo who ran a new and popular barbecue spot in Raleigh. In her conversation with the latter she'd ended up following them to the area of the party where the servers brought the food from the kitchen, the better to finally snag a crawfish deviled egg, and, egg devoured, she was now alone, watching the party and feeling good. She was also six weeks into a new antidepressant, which, mood considered, seemed like a keeper.

Across the way, closer to the bar, Nakia, who was wearing a dark denim Canadian tuxedo with red patent-leather hi-top Chucks, and Desiree, who was wearing a drop-waist black dress, laughed with an older white man with a speckled pate and a silver sequin bowtie. Or Nakia laughed, anyway. Hard to tell if Desiree was interested at all. The older they all got, the more Desiree seemed intent on spending time with people she loved, and otherwise intent on being left alone. She reveled in doing things by herself—the theater, dinner at fancy restaurants, at least one vacation a year—more than anyone else January knew who was happily partnered. Perhaps because her life of late had made it impossible to indulge in such solitude, January had not gauged her own interest in it.

There would be dinner after this mixer, as Nakia had suggested they skip the afterparty she'd been invited to in order to eat at a Mexican-Vietnamese fusion restaurant she'd had on her Chicago list for years. January supported this plan, despite having already eaten too much. Her feet were angry with her. Sitting down for dinner, just the four of them, would be nice.

"When is the last time you had sex, January?"

It was Monique, a tiny deviled egg plate in each hand. What a wild question, January thought. But also, how fun.

"Almost four years—why?"

"Four years? Jesus Christ."

"Thanks."

"My bad. I didn't mean it like that. It's just, four years!"

"Well, it took like a year for my pelvic floor situation to get better."

"Oh, yeah, I forgot about that. I'm glad you're better. Sorry."

"It's fine. But, yeah, there was that, and then, I live with my mother? And I share a room with my kids? And LA is a terrible city for dating."

"Every city is a terrible city for dating," Monique said.

"I tried the apps but too many guys asked me if my natural hair was a political statement. Grown Black men! I had to delete."

"Oh my god, and you have quote-unquote good hair."

"I told you LA is bad."

Monique slid one egg over so that both wobbled uneasily on a single saucer. Then she ate them, one at a time, her eyes closed in rapture for the chewing duration.

"Alright, so, four years," she said. "Damn. And here I thought I was going through it with my little ten months. How do you survive?"

January watched a lot of porn online. It felt Pavlovian at this point, her body primed to sprint up the hill and slide down the other side as soon as she opened her private browser. Sometimes, if she was alone, on the way to pick up Bronze from soccer, say, she could just play a video over her car speakers, with her windows rolled up, not actually watching anything but just hearing the slapping and the moaning, and that would be enough. She could start and be done within the span of one 405 freeway exit and the next, one hand driving and the other not even inside her pants but out, applying bare-minimum pressure. It was usually two women and one man. She preferred watching Black people—"Ebony," they called it in porn world, which was silly—if she remembered to tinker with the categories. Often there wasn't even time to toggle around, and as a result she had consumed too much of whatever was on the homepage of America's leading pornography website. Fake-busty blond white women, mostly, and how did everyone's skin get so tight? Just smooth back and butt after smooth back and butt, even though she made it a point to never, ever click on a video with the word "teen" in the title. The word "teen" was in many, many titles, alas. She did not like how much her body responded to close-ups of orifices, which America's leading porn site was keen on showing her. She would have preferred to see more faces and hands. She loved men's hands. Nakia had explained that there was better porn out there, stuff made by and for Black women and queer women, and even though January wasn't queer, it would be more ethical, she'd said. But January couldn't imagine that level of porn commitment, a whole subscription, what would it say about her? Monique probably had too fulfilling a life for porn—all that online adulation had to spur its own kind of arousal—or else she consumed porn like an actual adult.

It seemed that Monique had lost interest in her own question, perhaps due to the amount of time it had taken January to consider it. She was now trying to spear a Luxardo cherry out of the bottom of her inky drink, squinting into her glass while baring her teeth like a pirate.

"Why do you ask?" January tried again.

"No reason. Or, yes, a reason. I'm thinking of breaking my own streak."

"With who? Someone here?"

"No. I mean, yeah, maybe someone here, like here in this city. But I don't know. There's not really time for that, right?"

"Hey, you're grown," January said. "You do you."

She hoped she sounded just the right amount of reproachful. Monique had gotten better after a few years of being shamelessly self-motivated, but she still put her own interests first to a degree that grated on January's nerves. This was Nakia's weekend.

"Never mind," Monique said. "Forget I said anything. Blame these fucking activated-charcoal cocktails."

January had avoided those because she feared they would somehow make her teeth turn black. She'd gone for the first time ever to a teeth-whitening place in West Hollywood two days earlier in an effort to turn back the clock on the past four years of entirely too much coffee. No one had remarked on the difference, but to January it seemed her teeth glowed. The favored actors on America's leading porn site all had very white teeth.

"Do you still watch porn?"

"Sometimes, yeah," Monique said. "But it kinda depresses me. And, oh my god! I don't think I ever told y'all about how I came across a travel-influencer friend of mine butt-booty naked! This was in the pandemic when no one was traveling, so I guess she needed the money? But, *girl.* It was a lot."

Something or someone across the room had caught Monique's gaze. She gulped down the last of her drink.

"A story for another time, though," she said.

"Wait—"

But Monique walked away, without even looking back, directly toward a light-skinned man with beautiful lips who stood by the front door.

8:00 P.M.

Donnie Gleeson was sweating. Nakia could see the moisture on his head multiplying like bubbles in boiling water, and wondered why he wouldn't take off his blazer. Probably too late, she guessed; the back of his white shirt had to be soaked through. He could at least loosen his spangly bow tie.

"The key to surviving this weekend is, one: hydration," he said. "And two: don't work the room. If you come to these parties with a goal, you wanna meet all the Food Network bigwigs or what have you, you're bound to be disappointed. Just be nice, talk to everybody who wants to talk to you. That's how the magic happens."

"That makes sense," Nakia said. She wasn't sure why he was telling her this. She wasn't seeking any magic. She hadn't come to Chicago with her heart set on meeting anybody in particular, though it was always nice to meet other Black chefs.

"I'm gonna get some water," Desiree said. "I'll bring back some for everyone."

"Here, take this," Nakia said.

Having tried and failed to figure out a polite way to ditch the plate of too-chewy miso-glazed pork belly she'd been holding for twenty minutes—you never knew if the chef lingered in the room—Nakia handed it to Desiree, who carried it away from her toward the trash. Donnie was the only food person in the room who Nakia knew from real life. They were in Chicago, but the room felt tilted toward New York City in the way that certain rooms, no matter where in the country you find yourself, can tilt toward New York City. In fact, Donnie was from New York, a figure from way back in her restaurant management program days, a program he'd facilitated. Now he ran a "foodways think tank" in DC.

"So you made a girls' trip out of this," Donnie said. "That's smart."

"Yeah. Maybe not a great idea considering all of the egos."

"Tell me about it. Food people are not as bad as art people, which in my experience are the *very* worst people, but they can still be plenty obnoxious."

"No, I mean the egos of my friends. We're just . . . four very different women, with a lot of opinions and only two queen beds to sleep on, ha-ha."

"Oh, well, that a girls' trip for you. But I'm sure your lovely friends are nothing compared to the egos in this room. Just look around at all the angling going on in here. It's why I keep a stiff gin and tonic in my hand at all times. It's my protective shield."

The room was full of people taking selfies, mostly. Every introduction and reunion seemed a pretense to take a photo with a food person someone on the internet might be impressed that you knew. No, that was ungenerous. It was just a room full of people grateful to be in each other's company, Nakia thought. Grateful to find people who shared so many overlapping interests. Across the room she saw that Desiree, water bottles tucked under her arm, was huddling with January. Where was Monique?

"So," Donnie said. "You know I know one of the judges in your category."

"Oh, Donnie, don't stress me out even more than I already am."

The word "category" made her stomach tremor return.

"Don't be stressed! You've already won by being here. Remember that."

"So, I'm not winning, is what you're trying to say."

Donnie mimed zipping his own lips.

"I didn't say anything. Mum's the word from me."

That tiny belly heartbeat, doing double-time.

"I didn't expect to win anyway." She hoped her voice was even, neutral.

"You definitely *deserve* to win. And I'm not saying you're not, for the record. But closer to 2020 and our, air-quote, moment of racial reckoning? You would have had it in the bag, easy. You make food people like, plus you do a little activism. Judges love that."

Nakia was not sure how anyone outside of her friends and a few of her staff knew about her work with Arielle, but apparently people in this world had heard. In two different interviews since becoming a finalist she'd been asked about it, and she'd made sure to give Arielle proper credit. It wasn't Nakia's project; that was part of what made it so special.

"But you know these fickle people," Donnie went on. "They've moved on from diversity, or at least certain kinds of diversity. They're over it. They wanna go back to awarding chefs for making haute cuisine for crazy-expensive prices, or taking them on exotic journeys that don't recall the darker parts of American history."

"So you know for sure I lost? Just tell me."

Perhaps the tiny belly animal would die if Nakia knew outright.

Donnie pulled Nakia in for a hug. She remembered that about him. He was one of those older gay white men who liked hugging. His sweat had dampened the back of his blazer.

"These people don't know you," he whispered in her ear. "I know you. Your girlfriends know you. You're a fucking rock star and we're proud of you."

He gave her shoulder a squeeze as he walked away. Under these circumstances, Nakia appreciated that Donnie was the hugging kind.

January and Desiree came back with three green cocktails and four water bottles between them.

"Cheers!" January said.

"Everything good?" Desiree asked.

The tiny belly animal somersaulted. Was the solution to call it an early night and sleep away this feeling or to get blackout drunk? Nakia couldn't decide. She wanted to call Jay. She wanted to scream. And to laugh. She used to be so proud of how early in life she'd known herself, known what she wanted to do with her life. Known what her hands were for. Nights like this were never her aspiration.

"Cheers?" January tried again. They clinked glasses.

"Where's Monique?" Nakia scanned the room.

"She left with some guy," January said. "We already texted her to figure out what the deal is. Waiting for a response."

"Oh? What guy?"

"Light-skinned, beautiful lips? He kind of looked familiar, actually."

"Oh my god," Nakia said. "It better not have been Niles Dickerson."

"That is exactly who it was," January said. "I *knew* I'd seen his ass before."

"Who is Niles Dickerson?" Desiree asked.

"You know him," January said. "He has that show where he talks to people on the street about what they'd want as their last meals."

"And a podcast where he just talks a lot in general," Nakia said. "He's in LA pretty often but I've never met him. He seems extremely mixxy."

"Wait, Monique just texted back," Desiree said. "She's outside."

The tiny belly animal seemed to be responding favorably to the margarita. Its heartbeat slowed.

10:15 P.M.

Leave it to Monique to get the four of them onto a party bus full of caviar and champagne and some of the hottest Black names in food. It was a bewildering and mostly delightful part of her life now, being recognized by the right person and having a door open to some other world. When she'd followed Niles outside, she had intended to make out with him, maybe right there in the parking lot, then return to her girls' trip, no harm, no foul, but Niles had told her that he was waiting on a bus, a party bus chartered by a very famous older Chicago chef who, no longer spry enough to party like he used to, still made it his business to facilitate a good time for the young guns he'd mentored over the years.

As the bus navigated traffic to them, Monique and Niles had gone on a little stroll during which they'd kissed, yes, but more of interest to Monique, Niles had expressed an interest in her archival research acumen. "I'm trying to find all of the best Black restaurant menus over the past fifty years and put them in a book, maybe even do a show about it," he said. She could help with something like that. She was born to help with something like that. She'd told him as much. This was how things were done in her new life—people spoke their dreams out loud, and if you could contribute, you claimed a piece of that dream, followed through on your part, and more often than not the thing got done. Could a librarian actually become a TV star? Unlikely, Monique figured, but a librarian like herself, once she shook off the cobwebs, could certainly contribute to a research project that helped birth a TV show or, even better, a book.

She'd been high off the prospect of this collaboration when she cajoled the girls out of the mixer and onto the bus. At first it was just them and Niles, who was a very gracious host, congratulating Nakia and pouring them all champagne. The bus was lined with two white leather banquettes on either side. There was, thankfully, no stripper pole in sight, but the purple tube lighting on the floor and ceiling still brought exotic dancing to mind. The rear of the bus had been customized to accommodate a deep ice chest for bottles on one side and a raw bar on the other. Jumbo shrimp cocktail, cracked stone crab claws, and tins of caviar rested on pebbled ice.

"A moveable feast!" Desiree shouted upon entering. "I'm sorry but someone had to say it."

January took a very detailed 360-degree video and sent it to her mother to show to little Brook, who loved unusual vehicles and the color purple. Nakia, who still seemed a little funky with Monique at first for derailing their dinner plans, brightened with a champagne flute in one hand and a crab claw in the other. When Nakia offered to play music from her phone—all of the classic Nakia-at-a-party DJ requests, naturally—Monique felt sure she'd saved the night, and maybe even made her friends proud of her.

Twenty minutes passed with the four of them content while Niles texted and called and coordinated. Monique, Nakia, January, and Desiree mostly looked at one another and giggled, their eyes all saying, *Who would've thought we'd end up here?* Then the bus stopped for more passengers. Three men—younger than Niles, and two of them more food-world famous, according to Nakia—boarded the bus, followed by six women. Younger women, mid-twenties, seemed like. Short dresses with low necks, high heels.

Monique and her friends were not snobs, or prudes. This is what she kept reminding herself as she contemplated the number of bundles of weave now on board, as she witnessed one of the men—a guy named Eugene who had once cooked for Obama—instruct the women on how to eat "bumps" of caviar off his fist as if it were cocaine, as she overheard one woman tell another: "LA has the best Botox in the country. But not in Beverly Hills. You gotta go to Koreatown, trust me."

More important, all three men had properly acknowledged Nakia as a colleague once Niles introduced her. Eugene had even stopped bumping caviar long enough to toast her. But Monique was self-conscious that Nakia would begin to chafe under the new and not-ideal gender dynamics at play. A bunch of men their age and older carting around eight women nearly two decades their juniors, women who maybe were sex workers—no judgment—but were more likely just fans, invited for adulation. Who wouldn't chafe under that dynamic, honestly? Desiree and January engaged the girls gamely, out of a kind of anthropologic interest, Monique suspected. But Nakia retreated into herself again, as she had when they first boarded the bus. To make matters worse, one of the food-famous men commandeered the music selection, abandoning Nakia's playlist.

Monique, Nakia, January, and Desiree exited the party bus just as Niles was gearing up to saber a magnum of champagne.

Midnight

They walked along a street that traced the river. Nakia's phone said they were less than a quarter of a mile to their hotel, too close to bother with waiting for a car. The temperature had dropped. Dewdrops tickled Nakia's cheeks. January tried to walk barefoot, but Desiree, lifelong germaphobe, shamed her back into her shoes. Now January hobbled along, taking breaks every few yards. They progressed in silence for several minutes.

"Where are all the homeless people?" Desiree asked. The street was quiet, as was the nearby river.

"It probably gets too cold for homeless people," January said. "I mean, they have them, yeah, but they can't just live outside all the time."

"This is America," Nakia said. "There's always unhoused people. If we looked harder we'd see 'em."

"Where are the cops?" Desiree said. "I thought all downtowns were supposed to be crawling with cops."

"Probably busting heads on the South Side," January said. "Isn't that what they do here?"

"Never doooo, what they do what they do what they doooo," Nakia sang.

She was ready for Jay to get there. She'd decided on the bus that she wouldn't tell Jay that she knew she wasn't going to win the award. There was no reason to tell anyone. They could still have their fun together, get dressed up, and the rest of them could have their hope.

"Alright, I apologize," Monique said. "To all of you. I tried to do too much, as always. We shoulda just gone to dinner. Lesson learned."

The first genuine Monique apology Nakia could remember receiving.

"Apology accepted," she said. She meant it. The spectacle of the bus had made her forget about herself for a moment, which she appreciated.

"You know what would really drive home the lesson is if you gave me a piggyback ride for the rest of the way home," January said.

"I don't know what to tell you," Monique said. "I am a forty-year-old woman with bad knees."

But she crouched down in front of January all the same.

2027

Her Entire Life

It took Danielle Joyner Johnson over a decade to act on an impulse. Her temples grayed, her hips spread, the moles on her neck grew tactile, and finally she was ready to meet her father. "Meet" because who can know a man at four, or at fourteen, which was the last time she'd seen him. "Meet" because he knew nothing about her, couldn't possibly. The old impulse had waxed and waned with the highs and lows of her own life, which was a dynamic she distrusted. She had vowed long ago, back in the mortifying years of teenage mood swings, to never be a slave to emotions that felt too mercurial, too ready to burn her up or freeze her solid. Terry Joyner had grown in her mind to a giant opaque unknown, as constant as a cloud in winter and just as inscrutable. Hard to believe this day had come at all.

The Acela from Washington to New York was supposed to shave over an hour off her trip, but the train had gotten delayed somewhere between Baltimore and Delaware and was now just twenty minutes ahead of the regular. She'd paid for less time on the train so that she would have less time to worry about New York, a place she'd managed to avoid since moving to DC in 2013. But Terry Joyner was taking his grandchild—he probably called him "grandbaby"—to see *Fortnite* on Broadway and Danielle thought neutral turf—not DC, definitely not Durham—a smart choice. She was lying to herself. New York was not neutral. Desiree was here, presumably still uptown and still employed somewhere nine to five, which meant she probably used the train to commute, which meant that anything could happen. This was a giant city where nevertheless you might run into someone you knew. The train doors open, you step aside for exiting passengers, and one of them is someone you used to know, used to love. It had happened to her before, when she lived in Ohio but dated a New Yorker; twice when they'd visited the city the train had fostered chance run-ins, a reunion with someone from his past. She had six hours before the Amtrak would take her back home. She prayed to remain undetected until then.

She'd told her husband, Warren, that the decision to finally act on this impulse was the outcropping of prayerfulness and deep thinking, which had spurred in her a desire for connection to someone, somewhere linked to her past. That was only part of it. The other half was base, too petty to share.

Years before she met Warren, when she'd just arrived in DC, a package forwarded from her old Cleveland address arrived. Hastily taped up, her name written in a sloping, sloppy hand that made her stomach jump. It was penmanship she'd tried to correct when she was a teen, no, a tween. She carefully opened the package on her rooftop, in a corner—what she did fear, anthrax?—and said a prayer to God for protection as she pulled out its contents. Maybe, maybe it was an apology, an offering. No. A very familiar Erykah Badu merch shirt, which she sniffed on impulse and regretted. It smelled like the wrong kind of home. The note was her note verbatim from four months prior, in that childish, barely legible handwriting:

Moving. Figured you might want this back. -D

What?

Oh.

Oh oh oh oh.

Nobody ever used that rooftop, thank God, because the noise she made was not normal, not human. She bleated, confused and hurt then not confused at all and furious. How could she how dare he how embarrassing how didn't he remember she told him too many times how it's not like you forget so how'd he do this why how dare he. What was the word? Tawdry. How fucking tawdry. Cheap and low. She had a wild desire to eat the note, just to have something to gnash on, but she settled on using two hands to crumple it up small and pitch it over the side of the building, where it drifted down and became one more speck of Northeast DC trash, the flotsam and jetsam of a halfway-gentrified block.

She felt explosive for days, full of rage and physically ill. She'd been a virgin—had Chika forgotten that? If Desiree wasn't so busy being self-absorbed she might have used her bony fingers and toes to count, to come to the same realization. Danielle had known that they were both in the same city, but it was a large city, and didn't people talk before they fucked? She must have, they must have at some point, otherwise this wouldn't have happened. The shirt she'd sent to him in hopes he'd remember what goodness they'd had between them and reach out to her. What a stupid, bewildering violation.

Thank the Lord for work, interesting enough and never-ending. She leapt into it as she always had, and the bleat within, the slaughtered thing crying out, the fear of things wet and warm and dirty up against her, of being out of control, receded. When she felt more in control, she called her sister, but the number was disconnected. Better to call Nakia anyway, so that she might deliver some kind of message, a warning, without Desiree's unnecessary replies, her pathetic interruptions. Nakia, a person who'd known what she wanted for herself so early. They might have been friends in a different life. But Nakia had stopped her almost immediately when she called, before she could even lay out her full complaint.

"Look," Nakia said. "I really wish you and her could figure out how to be in each other's lives, but that doesn't sound like what you're calling about. So I'm going to do y'all both a favor and act like you never called me. If you're in the mood to come correct and actually, you know, try one day, you're welcome to reach out."

"It's not me who needs to come correct" was the only response she could muster.

Nothing to do but move forward. She joined a church in Alexandria, not as youthful as her church in Cleveland, but she signed up for the young adult choir (she was just at the cutoff at thirty-two) and met Warren there. Warren Johnson, middle name Divine, a senior water researcher with the Environmental Protection Agency. Having grown up a Five Percenter and defected, he also had an interest in looking forward, not behind. But. An impulse, a desire, had been born on that rooftop, since putting so much effort into forgetting. She needed to reach out to Terry Joyner. To snatch back a strand of her history since that other strand had frayed to nothing. She had briefly entertained a fantasy of finding Nolan's lost French son, but if he'd ever existed and was still alive today he would be elderly, a man who had probably lived as white for his whole life. Too complicated. So, Terry of the original abandonment. Terence Lynn Joyner, betrayer and possible woman-beater.

There existed a memory she shouldn't have been able to remember, as she was on the cusp of too young at four years old, but she could never stop recalling it. A green-green East Oakland kitchen, a giant Sherelle and a looming Terry, him in 1985 short-shorts and tall athletic socks. The shorts blue. Shouting, shouting, and a shove in the back that sends Sherelle across the green expanse. That's all. Did she fall down? Memory doesn't say, but the look on Terry's face, an expression never seen before and never sought out since: hatred. It was that expression, clearly recalled, that had guaranteed her distance from him once he left. Nobody's daddy made that face and didn't say sorry, didn't try his best to make things right.

Parts of Penn Station looked the same as they had over a decade ago, a dark maze filled with confusing hallways and rushing bodies, commuters moving at top speed with their heads down, eyes locked on their phones. She managed to get to the A/C/E without colliding with anyone and stood on the platform heaving, her tote bag slipping off her shoulder. She'd held her breath as she moved through the crowd—why? Big city anxiety, she guessed. Overhead, grime and peeled paint and something gray and bubbly but rigid, a filthy subway stalactite that dangled too close for comfort. Down the platform, near the turnstile, a large robot had appeared. It looked like a fat, sentient traffic cone on wheels. In NYPD blue and white it swiveled its head from side to side in search of fare evaders, she guessed, a contraption both juvenile and menacing. Expensive and stupid—who could forget when two of these robots blocked the emergency exit during a shooting at the Union Square station, helping the gunman slaughter more passengers? But these things were everywhere now, doing more harm than protecting. In DC she'd only seen the robot dog variety, mostly stalking the National Mall. She remembered that she'd read somewhere that some of them had tasers now, and inched farther down the platform to be safe.

Countdown clocks, those were also new. Used to be you had to just stand on the platform, stare at the tunnel up ahead, and pray that a tiny light might grow large and a train with your number or letter on its forehead would stop where it was supposed to stop, in front of you. This was way back when she and Chika had visited his childhood friends in the Bronx, his frat brothers in Bushwick. Odds were low she'd run into him this trip because he'd moved to Boston, or to one of those suburbs outside of Boston where they let Black people live. She'd never blocked him online. At one point or another he'd met a woman who convinced him to get saved, to leave New York. Good for him, but why hadn't Danielle been good enough? It didn't matter now, but sometimes she wondered. Sometimes she yearned for an explanation for all of it, still. She'd drafted and deleted at least five emails a year to him for those first few years, but she never unfollowed, unfriended him. It felt both like admitting defeat to do so and impractical. A periodic reminder of one's lowest moments was useful to have around. One's moments of poor judgment. She took care to never interact with anything he posted.

How people were still allowed to hire horse-drawn carriages at Columbus Circle baffled her; it must have had something to do with the city's penchant for idiotic mayors. She spotted a particularly miserable-looking horse, mane matted into pink-ribbon ponytails (is this what one called them on a pony?), neck sloping low, its flanks decked out in a pink fake-flower garland, the poop-catch under its ass laden and steaming. The mother and daughter in the carriage were Black, the driver white. What were they playing at, burdening that sad beast on such a beautiful afternoon for walking? Something to keep the day light and a little bit silly, she guessed, with an easy-to-share photo to accompany it. The mother trying to create a "core memory" for her daughter, like the mom influencers she likely followed online advised her. One of those still images the mind conjures when a certain period of time is called up, as if one day in the future the daughter would think about being twelve and remember this frivolous fun ride, and not some other image that her mother couldn't control, didn't want remembered. Poor mother, Danielle thought, that's not how memory works.

Before having Nina and Naima, she never did like photos, even though Sherelle used to tell her she was good at capturing them. The trick of them bothered her, the lack of context. Take the photo she'd rescued from the top of Nolan's kitchen cabinet. It was, had to have been, taken around the time of that push, that green-green kitchen push, when her mother yet carried Desiree. But you wouldn't know or suspect as much from the still, from Sherelle's genuine smile or Terry's posture in the background, the way he leans over the grill with one hip jutting out like maybe he'd been dancing, two-stepping to Parliament, say, while flipping burgers, not plotting on leaving his wife, abandoning his family. Even Danielle's own four-year-old face, not quite smiling, looks content. The photo is a lie, or if not an outright lie then certainly not the whole truth. She felt compelled to take photos of the girls now, for herself as much as for them, but she retained a deep suspicion of other photos, even more so now that you really couldn't tell an artificially created photo from a real one, or a video for that matter. Everything nowadays was too easily manipulated, too open to interpretation.

She walked straight across Central Park South to Fifth Avenue. She entered the park now and sat on a bench by the pond. A few trees still clung to the last of their russet leaves, which should not have been the case this far into November, but it was always warmer than it should have been. A few quick, strong gusts would fell the last of those leaves easy. She had begun to wonder whether noticing the way weather had become so violent or winters so warm was a sign of entering old age. Expressing unease about a seventy-degree New York City Thanksgiving might be akin to yammering on about the steep price of owning a home—for a whole generation, things had always been this bad.

Terry Joyner would stroll in here soon, his fourteen-year-old grandbaby hopefully deposited at the Apple store or someplace. Her whole life people had told her to stop dwelling. First Sherelle, when she refused her father's phone calls, or as good as refused them by not having much to say, then Nolan, who couldn't care less about Terry Joyner but was tired, as he put it, of "walking around my own house like I'm on parole" any time they had a disagreement. Now Warren complained of the same. But was it a grudge if the other person had earned it, or when she simply needed some time to warm up to them again? She could forgive easily enough, but it took time for her to forget. Motherhood had required her to let all kinds of slights and minor humiliations roll off her back—when it came to the girls. Adults were different. Adults liked to knowingly treat you any kind of way and only get contrite about it when you said enough is enough. Still, she said a prayer for strength to keep her Terry Joyner gripes under wraps, to show the genuine curiosity about his life and interest in connection that had brought her here. This curiosity had so often been buried under rage, and ancient shame. Not today. She looked in her tote bag for her earphones, queued up her daily devotional—today's was on Ruth and Naomi, loyalty and sacrifice—and tried to channel patience.

Often Danielle wondered if she loved the rituals of church—the songs, the fellowship, the lecture-hall studiousness of fellow congregants during the sermon—more than she loved the Word itself. She had always been a sucker for process. It was why she'd wanted to be an orthopedic surgeon in medical school—so many steps to follow, such high stakes—before discovering that she did not do well during long stretches in the operating room. She now felt that anesthesiology required sufficient high-stakes adherence to process. The only break from process at church, a delicious deviation from the norm, came during altar call, where anything might happen. The urge to come forward during altar call was not far from the urge she'd felt the time Sherelle had taken her and Desiree to the Grand Canyon: an almost-magnetic pull to the edge of the railing, to step over into oblivion. A desire to be consumed, her mind overcome, wiped clean. She had only been twelve but understood that there was ecstasy in releasing yourself to an unknown, to letting your body fall where and how it may, to not resisting rapture.

Terry's face and hers had more in common than anyone's she knew. Nolan had looked near-white but Desiree still had his nose, and Desiree's face had Sherelle's angularity. Here, walking up the trail from Fifth Avenue, a true mirror, finally. The same cool-undertone brown skin, the same chubby cheeks, flat nose, and low hairline, the same the same the same. Except for the eyes: his were too ready to laugh. Distrust rose up from her stomach as he strode toward her. Sixty-eight but looking fifty-four. Trim, moving like no part of his body ached. How the message "beware the face that mirrors your own" came into her mind she couldn't say, but the message grew louder as he hugged her and she stiffly received him, accepted the presumptuous real-milk hot chocolate he'd brought her, which had the nerve to be delicious.

"You look just like your mother," he said. "Wow."

So, he was going blind.

"It's been a long time since you seen a picture of her, I bet."

"That's true," Terry said.

Awkward already, dead-ended. Her train was at six. The girls would be asleep, but Warren might be awake at eleven, eleven thirty, watching a doomsday doc about mass extinction or microplastics.

Terry was one of those men who couldn't keep his leg from jumping. Probably blood pressure related. She wondered after his health, not because she'd decided to care if he lived or died but because of what it might mean for her own health, the health of her girls.

Why was it quiet? Why wasn't he explaining himself? She supposed he thought the ball was in her court because she was the one who had reached out.

"Um," she started. "How many kids and grandchildren do you have?"

"Three grandkids." Not grandbabies. "A pair of girl twins who are about to be two and Terry the Second, who I brought here. His dad had him young. And I got three kids: two boys, also twins, and one girl. Or three girls, I guess, including you and your sister."

So, twins ran on his side of the family.

"And like I said, Terry the Second, his parents had him young, so me and Retta, my wife, we helped out a lot. Took care of him."

"Ah, that's admirable," Danielle said. If he picked up on her facetiousness he didn't let on.

They had sat down too quickly. Was she taller than him? She couldn't tell from the height of his torso or the whole of his body in repose. He didn't sit upright on the bench; he leaned back as if the two of them had earned the use of lax postures with each other.

"What's your sister up to these days? Where she living?"

"Here, actually. I don't know for sure, but I think she's still here."

"You don't know?"

She looked him straight in his eyes. A dare.

"I do not."

"Oh, so y'all don't speak."

"We do not." She picked her coat where lint ought to have been and braced for admonishment.

"Wow."

"Wow what?"

"Isn't that kinda lonely?" He asked this without guile.

Danielle tittered. Had she ever tittered before?

"Lonely? No worse than growing up without a father, or a mother for that matter."

He nodded quickly to himself as if she'd just given him a needed confirmation.

"Your mother—rest her soul—she didn't want me in y'all's life once I got remarried, and by the time she passed, she'd turned y'all all the way against me."

"We were kids!" she might have said. "We needed a father!" she might have said. Instead she said a true and insufficient thing: "We had Granddaddy Nolan to look after us."

Terry nodded some more, adjusted his hat on his head. He wore a teal golf polo underneath a hunter-green parka despite the mild weather. Dark, creased jeans and brown duck boots. Black Titleist cap concealed whether his hair was receding or all the way gray or whether he had one of those patchy bald heads covered in thick wrinkles. No mustache, though he had the kind of upper lip area that would be greatly improved by one. Danielle suddenly felt compelled to catalogue as much about this person's appearance as possible, as actually talking to him was proving a mistake. She was forty-six years old. He could do nothing to ease her loneliness, that kernel of isolation that had been part of her so long it was like a prosthetic fused to her body. She'd grown a life around it, and at this point maybe it was naïve to spend time imagining a life without it. She drained the last of her hot chocolate—too thick and sweet at the bottom. It made her thirsty.

"Listen, I've thought about how this would go for decades," Terry said. "And I know it's on me to say sorry, and I don't got no problem saying it. But I gotta be clear on what I'm apologizing for."

"You really don't have to—"

"No, I do," he said. He looked down at his open, deeply creased palms as if notes were there. "I'm not sorry I left Sherelle. Sometimes leaving somebody, putting as much distance as you can between you and them is the best thing you can do for them, for yourself, the only way to keep everyone alive. If I had stayed even in the same state with Sherelle one of us wouldn't have made it. She knew how to make me become a person I didn't want to be."

"Nobody can make you be—"

"Please, let me keep talking," he said. She did not know why she relented.

"So, I'm not sorry about leaving. I am sorry that leaving meant I was so far away from y'all. I'm sorry that the two of us, me and Sherelle, got to the point where she wouldn't even give Desiree my last name. That must have been confusing for her, for y'all. But I'm not sorry I met Retta so soon after and started a new family—I didn't plan it, but I don't know who or where I'd be if it didn't happen."

"Please stop," she said. Whimpered.

"I'm not saying any of this to hurt you, Desi— Danielle. I just have to say it is all. Could I have tried harder to be in y'all's life? Yes. But I didn't know how to be in your mother's life even a tiny bit, and by the time I matured enough to even try, she had died and it was too late."

"It wasn't too late!" Her jumping up startled a squirrel; it scampered up a nearby tree. "It wasn't too late when we were right there at Nolan's, dependent on him for every scrap of food, every fucking stitch of clothing, getting his little handouts of attention and affection. I didn't even know how to contact you for *years*, you know, so I figured the best thing to do was to hate you like you obviously hated us. I made Desiree hate you too because it seemed easier for her, less *confusing*, like you say. But you knew where we lived and you never even tried. You had a new life! Just admit it. You had a new wife, new kids, and you didn't fucking care, for thirty whole years."

She sat back down, spent. She had gone full nineties sitcom abandoned child on him when she'd sworn to herself and Warren that she wouldn't. Oh well. A cliché is a cliché because it is common.

He unclasped his hands again and looked down at them.

"I paid child support until y'all were twenty-two, four years longer than I had to. I tried—".

"I never got a dime from you."

"You did too. Four hundred dollars a month, then it went up to six hundred because Nolan made a cost-of-living appeal. Why do you think your granddaddy never told you that?"

In fact, one of Nolan's favorite refrains, of the several he seemed to save just for her, was "I'm all the momma, daddy, or anybody you got in this world," which suggested a financial as well as an emotional singularity to what he provided. It drove her away from him, drove her away from the bulk of the money he left behind. Better to be fully orphaned. People were so strange.

The sun was beginning to set, which meant it was after four. She had planned things so that if they hit it off—imagine!—they'd be able to grab a quick early dinner before she needed to get on her train. She'd even made a reservation. Now she stood up, wiped her wet face with her hand.

"I, uh, gotta go. My train home is soon."

Terry stood up as well. They were the exact same height. She looked past him, toward Fifth Avenue and Central Park South. Waiting to cross the intersection on the far side was a teenaged boy holding a shopping tote from the Apple store. Could have been anyone but there was something about his carriage, confident and a little old-fashioned. Terry the Second. No way she could meet him. Her daughters had no grandparents, doting or otherwise. The boy hesitated after crossing the street, as if he didn't know where he should enter the park.

"I appreciate you reaching out to me," Terry said. "You sure you don't have more time? I figured this was gonna be real emotional at first but then we could move on to getting to know each other."

He couldn't hurt her. She was already back home, on the couch with Warren, telling him everything, with the confidence that it would only be this one time and he'd never bring it up again.

"Hey, if you hold on for a second you can meet Little Terry. I told him to come back at four."

"Train's at five, I really gotta go."

"Okay, real quick, would you mind giving me your sister's information? Figure I might as well reach out since I'm in town. It's crazy, she's not on Facebook or Instagram or nothing."

He did not seem to have an inkling of the obscenity of this request.

"Like I said, we don't speak, so I don't have it."

She lifted a hand, not a wave, more of a warding off, and turned back west. The trees were bare now. A strong wind must have blown by and claimed the last of the leaves.

With an hour and a half to spare, she ate sushi at a place off Columbus Circle, too worried about getting punished for no-showing to cancel her reservation. She sat at a two-top by the window where she could see the edge of the park and the cars creeping through the roundabout. It wasn't a sports bar but there was, inexplicably, one TV in the far corner of the bar, on which she could see a news story about protests and police clashes in LA. There were always protests and police clashes these days, especially in LA—at what point would they stop being news? Happy hour meant two-for-one cocktails, and because she'd explained her train situation to the server, she had two lychee martinis sitting in front of her. She rarely drank outside a glass of wine with dinner at home. It made her too sleepy, as did marijuana, never mind the offers from seemingly everyone these days to find her the right cannabis strain. She sipped one of the drinks and focused on its sweetness, followed by the chemical-adjacent taste of vodka.

She texted Warren: Went worse than expected, can't wait to get home.

He would be in the middle of post–school pickup dinner-making, hopefully encouraging the girls to do something constructive like their language workbooks. But he'd respond eventually. He would tell her he was proud of her.

She couldn't point to what had made everything go so wrong so quickly. Maybe she just wasn't ready, or perhaps the moment for reconciliation had passed. When the girls were born, she'd missed Sherelle with a ferocity she hadn't felt since the early years. What had breastfeeding been like for her? No doubt easier with just one infant versus two. How had she managed Danielle's tantrums while being stressed about making ends meet and the collapse of her marriage, not to mention caring for infant Desiree? Terry, so calm and normal and not strung out or fucked up in any discernible way—how dare he. To think she'd imagined things could go so well that Terry and Little Terry would have been eating spider rolls with her. Terry's country ass probably didn't even eat sushi. It wasn't Terry who had been missing her whole life. It was always only Sherelle. Even when Sherelle was alive, Danielle couldn't get enough of her, Sherelle always working and splitting her affections between Danielle and Desiree. Sherelle her best friend. Only Danielle knew that Sherelle liked her drinking water so cold it was almost frozen, that she liked her Oreos a tiny bit on the stale side, that the two of them, best friends, would gladly eat crispy-edged turkey kielbasa and white rice most nights.

Only three stops until Penn Station. She should call Nakia, she thought. She hadn't been ready for Terry Joyner, but maybe she was ready for Nakia, and eventually Desiree. She had tried one additional time to reach Desiree via her friend. It had been in 2019, in the cartoonish, sleep-deprived final weeks of her pregnancy, when she was so large, the girls squeezed into every part of her torso, one under her ribs, one pushing down on her bladder, that she could only manage forty-five minutes of uncomfortable sleep at a time. A kick from one or both of them or the need to pee would rouse her. She had called Nakia at ten p.m. LA time.

"You know, I always assumed you two would end up together," she said when Nakia picked up the phone.

"Are you drunk? I'm at an event."

"Drunk? How can I be drunk if I'm pregnant with twins?" she'd said, then realized this was the kind of thing a drunk person might say. "I just called to see if Desiree had kids yet, then I realized that the only person I could imagine her trying to raise a kid with was you. She was always in some kind of unrequited love with you, seemed like."

A long pause on Nakia's end.

"The only unrequited relationship Desiree has ever had has been with you. And no, I'm not telling her you called."

The audacity of Nakia to think Danielle owed Desiree something, anything at all. Desiree, like the guilty often do, had avoided Danielle after Nolan died. She didn't check in on her, not even once, for months after. And by the time she did, it wasn't even to ask for forgiveness, just to start "settling up affairs." Danielle had wanted no part in Nolan's affairs. Nolan had made her feel like a burden and a disappointment, too independent, too smart of mouth. His put-downs, his lording over her just how alone she was in the world. He had, for some reason, spared Desiree most of this meanness. A dropout, directionless, but still appreciated by their grandfather in a way he never appreciated her. She had spent so much time—years—trying to figure out why. Why was Desiree worthy of unconditional, no-strings-attached love and she wasn't? She hadn't just deserved an apology from Desiree for trying to help Nolan kill himself; she deserved an apology from Desiree for the secrecy of it. It was one final intimacy between the two of them, one last thing from which Danielle had been excluded.

Maybe it had to do with how old she was when Sherelle died, already a teenager with opinions and keen observations, not easily impressed by Nolan's stingy displays of affection but hungering for them all the same. She was a teenager! Hadn't she deserved grace? Her entire life, every day of it, no matter how easy or hard, she'd had her back propped up against their mother's bedroom door, bearing the unbearable while Desiree banged on the other side, too stupid to know that inside with her, seeing what she saw, was nowhere anyone wanted to be. She was only now beginning to understand how much Sherelle's death had left her feeling exposed. She had been thrust into the wilderness of adult life, frog-marched into a deep, hard-to-navigate forest of decisions and failure and hurt, sheltered by Nolan in name only. Even now, with her job, with her girls, with Warren and the church to bolster her, there were nights she felt like every edifice she'd propped up to separate her from the elements, the wind-blasted outside of aloneness, could crumble, and she'd have nothing but her own uncovered self to brace against it. It might not take much for her to end up in the wilderness once again.

About a year after moving in with Nolan, she'd finally grown out of her training bras but was too embarrassed to tell him so, so instead she asked for money for clothes in general. "You ain't growing that fast at fifteen," Nolan had said. "Unless it's outward." He'd meant it as some kind of old-man joke, had chuckled to himself, but she refused to laugh. She'd stared hard at him, furious that he'd make her beg. He left her in the living room, walked out muttering: "Just like your mother, always coming around with your hand out." She couldn't recall her mother ever talking about getting money from Nolan but suddenly realized she must have. There were all the bills that she and Terry used to split for her to manage alone. The ridiculous part, the part that she could not help but take personally, was that Nolan had money. Plenty of it. But it had never really been about money, of course.

Her subway stopped at Penn Station again. This time no robots in sight. On the Amtrak she found an aisle seat facing backward in the hope that no one would want to squeeze in next to her. It worked. The train pulled out of the station. When it surfaced in the New Jersey evening and her cell phone service returned, she saw that Warren had sent her two text messages:

1. bandaged heart emoji

2. photo of the girls asleep in their beds with the caption: I'm proud of you. Come back home where you are loved.

The farther away from New York, the closer to Warren and the comfort of their sofa, the safer it felt to think about her sister kindly. She wondered whether Desiree was happy. It was blessedly too late now to give in and visit her. But Nakia. Yes, maybe she could check in that way, keep her temper in check and actually request Desiree's number this time. Terry Joyner had proved a paltry substitute for real family, for someone who actually knew her. She would not apologize for anything, but she could offer the olive branch of Terry's contact information, should Desiree want to avail herself of it.

The train stopped in Wilmington. A rush of passengers. Danielle put her tote on the seat next to her and stared straight ahead, willing people to leave her be. No luck. A pink-flushed grandma type with a white bob squeezed in, nearly squashed her bag. She smelled minty at least, and after a terse smile she pulled out a romance novel, intent on minding her own business.

Danielle dialed Nakia. It rang and rang and rang, and just as she pulled the phone away from her face to hang up someone got on the line.

"Hello?" Not Nakia's voice at all. A sniffling yet dulcet-toned woman. Voices. Too many voices in the background.

"Uh, hi? Maybe I have the wrong number, or an old number. I'm looking for Nakia."

"This is her phone. This is her partner, Jay. Who is this?"

"This is, this is Danielle Joyner? Her friend Desiree's sister." She felt guilty feigning closeness. What if Desiree was in that very room? A noise that sounded like a baby's cry or an adult's anguished shrieking in the background. It was hard to hear anything else. Not a baby's cry. Something strange was happening.

"I'm sorry, what did you say?" the voice on the phone said. "You know Desiree? Where is she? We've been trying to get a hold of her."

Danielle clutched her bag as if she might need to flee. This person's voice sounded wrong.

"Looking for Desiree for what? Did something happen? What's going on?"

Danielle Joyner walked out of Union Station into heavy rain, enough to turn her tan suede boots dark in an instant, enough to ruin them, but she would not notice this for several days. Her phone battery was dead. She cut in front of a family of four for a taxi and directed the driver to Petworth, home. Up Georgia Avenue her mind tumbled, teemed. The only place she wanted to be was home, yet leaving New York now felt like an ominous mistake. Cosmic. She could have turned back, even in Delaware she could have turned back. But now it was done. She pushed the code to open her front door. No lights save the glow of the TV in the living room, before which Warren dozed. An old documentary about cobalt extraction in Congo. Small children beating up rocks, forced to ruin their bodies in their hunt for blue. She dropped her keys into the bowl on the counter. Warren roused.

"My baby's back from slaying those parental dragons," he said. He opened his arms. "Come here."

Danielle sat next to him, stiff.

"What happened? Do I need to have words with this man?"

"This man" being Terry Joyner. It was now hard to believe she had thought him important at all.

"No," she said. "I'm okay, but my sister—my sister's best friend—more like her sister, really. Nakia. Something happened . . . I called her and somebody else answered. Nakia's dead."

PART THREE

There was something just to the right of her, in the air, just out of view. She could not see it, but she knew exactly what it looked like.

—Toni Morrison, *Sula*

PART THREE

[illegible]

—[illegible]

Get the music right she'll come. The mood right my candles the good candles my soap the one she wanted she might be just at the counter chillin, leanin on her tiptoes, judging me for scorching a pan not using enough butter being me. Come and be a gentle scolding and a story and nothing nobody saying anything just be here in this apartment that I didn't want but needed her to think I was okay here without her I could grow up and be a person without her and I did, didn't I and for what? How long before things start to go she just needs to come. Her voice. Come sit by me in the dark and be alive and funny and my friend I am not too old to need a friend a friend is not a man a man is not a sister but a friend might be, you need them more is what I think. I know it. I need her more. If I scorched a pot played Sade created a vibe burned some sage okay she might find me here she knows I'm here, waiting. Come. Hatch a plan for improvement you know damn well I'm not gone do but please plan it make it seem simple and doable like everything for you because you are you how can you not undo what they've done this time? Find a way. Hours and hours in the white-white mountains, banging on a closed-closed door, none of that like this you chose me. We chose we. You are the one not the one my mama made you are the one I sheer-willed and held tight and prayed not to God but to my mama I think I asked her to protect you way back there, over there in that place I was too scared to be in anymore. Twenty and four years how about five more minutes of flesh and blood I don't want spirit I need warm hands I will hold out my hand and you can grab it here in the dark and we don't have to say anything nothing just come.

Not the best of us, who is best? Just one of us, my sister, how gone, how gone, how did this happen, no. I loved her, she was my sister, I loved her more than her woman, I think, I loved her. Why was I ever away, lonely on purpose stubborn and she knew herself and me better than I know me I pined wrong, wished wrong. Forgive me. Just there, I want her to be just there there on the bed the sofa the counter smiling at me teasing me haunting me, whatever. I'm sorry. What does ash smell like when it rains she smells like that, like nothing I know it's not right never. The longer I sit, the longer I don't move don't go there don't fly there don't eat don't text the more she'll know I am serious. She can come. Not in my dreams but in this room right now. Tell me how to undo it tell me who will love me make me a project make me anything who might bother with me now. Who?

The sun comes up the snow melts and falls loud I wait for her. She's not too far yet to come, clear across the country to me. Come back.

Blind Date, or Where I Was When I Found Out My Friend Was Dead

With a man whose face is blank
The food tastes blank
The music, blank
My phone facedown on the table, see it, next to fork and knife and glass and
in this way I steal seventeen minutes
Seventeen blissful-ignorant minutes she lives for me longer than she should
It is an impulse, a bad habit says my mother,
to reach for my phone when I feel unease
so I am trying
It makes the tabletop vibrate and still I ignore it, focus on the blank-faced date's
nonsense words,
the sawdust food
fix my posture, sit up in my seat, mind my manners, am what they call "present"
for seventeen whole minutes.
What does he say to make me reach for it?
I want to curse him for being dull or too forward or not forward enough, whatever made me waver
curse him for not being more compelling than reality
she might have lived on, if only for me, for 18, 19 minutes, maybe,
for the whole evening, into the quiet
of strange-bed sunrise
instead I turn the phone face-up and die then, too, some part of me that I can't name but know
one day I will try to call it forth and find it missing

The body is a mere vessel, but still. I couldn't stop thinking, which lead to me imagining, what exactly it meant for her to be dead. For her body, her physical presence to be gone forever, just gone. Poor, poor Nakia. How Juanita described it, first on the phone, which I only understood after the call was over, then in person when I picked Juanita and Conrad up from the hospital, took them to their hotel because they couldn't bear to stay at Nakia's and they didn't want to upset CJ's kids, was that her body, the body itself had sustained real damage. Conrad and Juanita, the two of them aged exponentially, and me, awkward, bouncing between being solemn and telling dumb jokes. Nightmare language. "Sustained." "Ruined" was better, but then again a dead body was already ruined, already done being purposeful, right? Poor Nakia. Forty-one years old. What a theft.

She would not like any part of the chyron that scrolled past again and again every twelve or so minutes on the news: "Local Restaurateur Found Dead." Nightmare language. She would not have wanted to be called that; she would have wanted to be called something closer to ordinary, or something that suggested she was trying to make things easier for others. And was she actually "found dead," and if so, by whom? Those who killed her? Is it finding when you did the hiding yourself? She would not have wanted to be made history, to collide with it, like this. The only thing worse than seeing her mentioned on the news will be the moment when the news stops mentioning her.

She who held me at arm's length for so long, until I was ready to grow up. She who came around to me, we who came around to each other. Brought my boys treats and flowers and plant wisdom. Brought my boys something I didn't have enough of—something steady, sure. Look how they did her. Her! They could do that to anybody. Poor, poor, poor Nakia. It will never make sense.

Twenty bushels of collard greens on Nakia Ann Washington's kitchen counter, intended destination unknown. Unwashed, presumably from her garden. Within the leaves nestled eight insects; two fat black slugs clung to stalks. In the first week the leaves turned ochre, then mustard, then mottled brown. The wavy edges went limp, followed by the interior of each leaf. They spread flat, like discarded skins. A withered forest on quartz.

When dill dies, its texture is akin to heat-damaged hair. Brittle, like something to be crumbled, not combed. Its scent—celery and pine trees married—reduced to a whisper, only heard by drawing in close. The dill crowded the kitchen sink, rinsed and drained but never refrigerated.

The laurel of fresh bay leaves dried out without incident. It retained its scent well and would eventually be stored in muslin, to be brought to the nose when her partner wanted to remember.

The white onions sprouted green stalks that, high and arcing, begged to be planted, to begin again.

The nightshades were more dramatic.

Dark, frowsy mold pocked the small heap of tomatoes, six of them piled and festering in her grandmother's wooden bowl. First, tiny bruises, only slightly darker than the whole. Their skin tightened, split open here and there, juice running, pooling. One tomato rushed the others to communal demise, bursting then beckoning an insect to dine on what was left of it, of them. White cottony growths spread from their tops and ends. The bowl would have to be thrown out, a black permanence marring its crosshatched wood.

The sole eggplant resisted change the longest. No visible signs of decline within the first week, and in the second week only slight creases to the skin, like a well-cared-for leather sofa. But temperatures outside and in the kitchen rose. The eggplant sustained tiny dimples. No one was there to mark the moment when deep purple bleached to yellow, which marked the beginning of the end.

Potatoes, their eyes grown to spiky green cactus arms, reaching,

reaching, on the far end of the countertop, puffing up before crumpling inward like expired stars.

All peppers, from bell to Anaheim to serrano, a kaleidoscope. Colors twisting and bursting vibrant and shiny and often red before fading, before dulling, before wrinkling and diminishing in size.

We often argued, my friend and I. She did not agree with me making my life, my thoughts, as public as I have made them over the past decade and change, was wary of what might be lost as I gained followers, gained a real-time awareness of others' expectations. I always suspected she was being more than overprotective—I told myself, I needed to believe, that she was jealous. It was an assessment that fed my own ego while allowing me to feel like the bigger person. I could ignore her concern for me and forgive her by telling myself it stemmed from envy, not earnest misgivings about the way that scrutiny from strangers can corrode one's sense of self. She knew a thing or two about scrutiny, being a young Black chef, being a woman who loved women. She knew how other people's real-time reaction to your work can alienate you from the work itself. The young, queer Black woman chef, providing food, jobs, and in the end a convenient narrative, one that wasn't about who she really was. I understand now what she tried to tell me in so many ways over so many years: be careful. Had I ever once told her the same?

How do you prosecute a machine? And I mean that a machine killed her, no matter how she died. In this country justice itself is a machine programmed to make logical the illogical. A five-foot chef is a threat, could be a terrorist with the right coding. Of course her death could be deemed justified in a million different ways. And of course the civil suit would be successful. This country has little issue with using our money to pay for the silence of those of us whose lives it ruins. If only money had the power to resurrect. My friend is still dead, and money isn't even real. A gesture signaling nothing.

This is what truly saddens me, and maddens me: in her death she has become a public symbol, a tool for hand-wringing and clever rebuttal. The story of her death serves to alienate us from the story of her life. She is not simply Nakia Ann Washington but part of a processional of names, one more meaning-laden symbol in a grim pantheon of the same. But the truth is her life does not have to represent anything. She just was. Somebody's daughter, somebody's sister, somebody's boss, somebody's lover.

And even these things I have read before, have even said before about so many others.

Her death has taught me nothing. I always knew the wages of this place—this life—were deadly, as did she. I suppose the both of us thought we could find ways to keep getting over, to keep living, for a little while longer.

She came to me in my dreams again and again that first year. I welcomed her, even though I still wanted her to bless me with a flesh-and-blood visitation. I would have accepted, relished, a haunting. But I was thankful for the scraps of dreams that my brain could manage to remember each morning. Sometimes she wore the smokey-eye, cleavagey club look from our youth, sometimes the no-nonsense overalls or loose dresses from our thirties; sometimes it was not as a figure at all, but a feeling, or a voice. She never offered words of comfort, never told me I would be okay without her, which was good. That would have made me wary she was a manifestation of my own psyche, my desperate need for somebody to tell me I could survive this. No, she would be talking about plans I didn't really know about, like a dinner party, and could I go with her to find some good seafood. In the mornings I would type out whatever I could remember into a note on my phone, try to make it make as much sense as it had the night before, but when I looked back on those notes there wasn't really anything there to decipher. The year, the years, smeared together. I told Jelani that I had never felt this alone in my whole life, which was really saying something. He was supportive, but there's only so many times you can tell your partner that you're lonely before they start taking it personal, so I stopped telling him. I tell January and she's stoic, I tell Monique and she's too angry, too ready to fight somebody. She accuses me of giving in to despair. I didn't give in to despair. I looked up and despair had already entered the room, made itself at home.

I was on the A train shuttle bus uptown, because after several weeks the rain hadn't stopped and the subway was flooded. The bus was packed and it was still cold inside. People's breath making tiny clouds. I didn't see a woman reach up toward the strap I was holding and grab my wrist. "Mami, a friend is trying to contact you," she said, and I swear my whole body warmed up. I should have been worried but I wasn't. I was calm. I had been on my way to meet Jelani for dinner off 116th but followed her uptown instead. Sonia. She was short, with one of those tiny waists and large backsides girls are still paying good money for, but hers was just how she was built. She looked younger than me, maybe early thirties, but her low bun was full of gray. Her shop—studio, whatever you call it—was in the back of a botanica off Amsterdam. Sitting back there, surrounded by herbs and candles, the faces of saints and orishas I didn't recognize aglow, I realized she'd oversold what she had to offer. Nakia had no actual words for me, no verbatim message to be delivered, never mind I would have paid too much to hear it. For her actual voice, or even the cadence of her speech, I would have paid half my soul. Turns out deleting voicemails is a terrible, terrible habit. She sang me happy birthday so many times—now they're all gone. Sonia simply said Nakia's soul was at peace. She got the first letter of her name right, which made me think she was legit, but I refused to believe that was the message she'd grabbed my wrist to share. How could Nakia be at peace? She loved life too much. And anyway, Nakia, she knows me. She would know I didn't want to know that; I wanted her to tell me something real. Like, "Des, you need to get over yourself," "Des, you need to stop pressing your hair with that old flat iron before you end up baldheaded," "Des, I was so afraid at the end—where were you?"

Anything but this generic status update. So, she's at peace, but what about the rest of us? The Nakia I know, the one I will miss until the day I die, would have had a joke to crack, some shit to talk. If she was in that botanica with me, she would have said more than a benediction. She would remark on how I go to church sometimes now, or how I started cooking again for the first time since culinary school. How I've up and forgot how to make my own granddaddy's greens. How I have finally, deep into midlife, managed to grow a little booty. She would say something about my sister, who has reached out a couple of times. She would say it's worth a shot but to watch my back. It's funny how things and people that used to mean so much can slip down the ladder of importance the instant someone you truly love dies. If I try at all now with Danielle, it'll be for Nakia.

She still would have been mad at me for missing the funeral, even after her parents pushed it back a full week for me to be able to make it, for me to get myself together and come. She'd be pissed at me for that, for convincing myself that if I just stayed in New York maybe none of it was real. I did make it out there, just a week or so late. And I hugged her mama and daddy and brother, I did. I cleaned out Nakia's fridge, her whole kitchen. That was something nobody else but me could bear. I didn't dare look in her bedroom, though, and I didn't dare look out into her garden. I accepted the bit of ashes they gave me despite my whole body saying no no no no no. Jelani got the ashes made into a necklace for me, which I will never, ever put on. There's no substitute for flesh and blood. It hangs on a hook on the wall over my nightstand, the ashes packed into a charm shaped like a pyramid..

I left the botanica disappointed, disgusted with myself, with my own foolish hope. Sonia gave me a pack of matches with her phone number on it and a tall red Chango Macho candle. I've been Black and in New York for over twenty years now; I'd seen Chango before. The candle was another misread—I didn't want anybody's luck. What I want is resurrection.

I am leaving New York, I am leaving the United States. I have decided this today and will be gone by the end of the month. It feels important for me to remember every part of the day that brought me here.

I was in Bryant Park on a call that I'd almost forgotten about. A video call with subscribers who'd paid for small-group access. To me. They'd paid for access to me. It was the orientation call for my subscriber-only "Heartwork: How to Live a More Socially Conscious Life, Online and Off" workshop. It is not like me to forget such a huge thing, as workshops are how I make a significant portion of my income, but for whatever reason I had woken up that morning positive the call was on Tuesday and not Monday—why was that? My morning had been a strange one. Construction on the street outside my bedroom window began at seven a.m., which is against city regulation, so I spent a fruitless half hour on the line with 311 trying to report them and get it to stop. I decided to go to the library building and work in the Rose Main Reading Room for a few hours to get away from the noise, and to recenter myself. The library still does this for me. When I exited my building, I discovered that one of the giant holes the workers had dug precluded me from stepping more than two feet from my stoop. I was stuck, trapped, yelling on the steps over the noise of the machines, staring at a gaping hole the size of a grave. I looked down into it. Dirt and pipes and old roots and who knows what else. A grave. I looked away. I felt nauseous. I retched my morning matcha into one of the planters my landlady keeps on our stoop. It was so loud on the street, and warmer out than it had any right to be this time of year. I peeled off my jacket, sat down on a step, and put my head between my knees. I cried.

Finally someone noticed me—two workers, Yusef and Jon—and laid down boards to bisect the hole, the grave, so that I might walk across. The boards were regular old planks of plywood, and I worried that they wouldn't hold my weight, or that I would, now being hungry and disoriented, slip and fall into the grave. Maybe Yusef and Jon could sense this because they each offered me assistance. With Yusef holding one of my hands in front and Jon holding the other behind me, we carefully traversed the grave to get to the intact portion of the sidewalk. Thank you, sincerely, to them both.

So, the library. I was on the side of the building along Forty-Second Street when my phone alerted me that the orientation call, the one I'd forgotten about, was in fifteen minutes, so I grabbed a table and a chair closer to Fifth Avenue and sat down, hoping to make the best of being outdoors. I opened the online room on my computer and waited for people to arrive. I had planned to begin with a talk about . . . I now can't even remember what I was planning to talk about. Book bans, probably, how the attempts to ban everything had finally made it in full force to New York, where one list, for a school district in Scarsdale, included half of the Bible itself. The Old Testament! I'm sure I planned to use the phrase "now more than ever." I sat with my eyes closed and visualized the words I'd say, which is a trick I'd learned back in the day from the Tru Talk people to combat public-speaking nerves. But every time I closed my eyes I saw that deep, dark hole in the sidewalk, that grave. The roots, the crumbling soil. I did a quick breathing exercise and felt calm enough to push through the call. People started to file into the waiting room. Twenty people had signed up for the class but three had already let me know they'd be missing this orientation, so I was waiting for seventeen people total. It felt like a typical warmish day outside the library, a mix of locals on their lunch breaks and tourists ambling around Bryant Park.

This is the part everyone thinks they know. A Black woman dozed on the sidewalk in front of a bootleg Mister Softee truck—a Mr. Soft-Serve—on Fifth Avenue. The truck appeared closed, its window shut, with a handwritten sign on it that said *back soon*. The woman and the truck were near me, in my line of sight from where I sat at a table, maybe thirty feet away. She slept in a fetal position on top of a rectangle of cardboard long enough to protect all but her shins and feet from the bare concrete. She wore just an orange T-shirt and jeans, and while it was unseasonably warm, it wasn't warm enough for her to only be wearing that, especially not while lying on the ground. I watched her shoulders closely for a few seconds, verified that she was indeed breathing.

Seventeen sign-ons, as expected. I granted everyone access to the call. I put my headset on and started speaking just as the ice cream truck driver returned.

First he dumped a paper cone's worth of water on the sleeping woman, and she stirred but did not wake. Then he banged on the side of the truck and screamed at her, called her a junkie and a bitch. Said he had a business to run and she was nothing, useless, she needed to get out of the way. He called her so many bitches; he doused her again. The way he sneered, I thought it was only a matter of seconds before he spat on her. I was out of my seat and over to the truck before I even registered my body moving. I never ended my call, never turned off my headset. I squeezed my body onto the thin curb between the woman and the truck, told him to leave her alone, that there was a lot more sidewalk he could use. He told me to shut up, to get away from his truck before he called the police. I told him this was typical, threatening a Black woman with police violence. His defense was that he wasn't white, he was Puerto Rican, and that nobody was falling for "that" anymore. "That" meaning . . . I don't know. I told him being Puerto Rican made it worse. The truck had three CASH ONLY printed paper signs on it. Was he paying his taxes? I wanted to know. People have subsequently seized on this question. I simply meant to highlight that all of us are trying to get by, that he was no better than anyone else. At this he called me a bitch, too. And other names my brain refused to absorb in the moment. I ripped down two signs and balled them in my fist. It felt as impotent as it looked.

Around this time, the woman—Octavia, I kid you not—got up and began gathering her things (a backpack she was using as a pillow, the cardboard itself) to leave. I went with her, across Forty-Second and up a few blocks. She was lethargic, did not seem to fully comprehend what had just happened, or maybe just didn't find it all that noteworthy. I asked her her name, what she needed, and she said money, which is when I realized that I'd left all my stuff save for my phone in the park. I asked her to wait for me and sprinted back to my table. My computer was gone but my bag was there, my wallet intact. There were two cops talking to the ice cream guy now; I'm assuming he flagged them down. I jogged past them back to where Octavia should have been waiting for me, but she was gone.

In the long history of altercations that I've personally witnessed on the streets of New York, this one would not rank in the top ten, or even top fifteen. But I understand that things are different now, people expect the worst of everyone, and when something out of the ordinary happens, everyone's impulse is to record and share. It is an impulse that has trumped our more human impulses to either retreat or intervene. And in my case, not only did several people in the park film this, but I myself had broadcast every word, even those muttered under my breath, to my workshop participants, one of whom thought it worth recording, editing, and sharing. I will survive being called out by name by the mayor on social media. I will survive this moment ending up on local news, and eventually I'll laugh at finally making it into a ridiculous headline in the *Post,* even though "I Scream" was low-hanging fruit. But I have to leave all the same. Few of the videos I've seen being shared pan down to show Octavia, and none of them tell the full story, that there were two of us being called bitches, that the entire altercation began because this man wanted to treat another human being like she was not human at all. From the angle of most of these videos it's as if Octavia doesn't exist until she stands up at the very end and walks away, and many of the clips stop before even this moment.

I have been thinking for some time, since the pandemic and all of its messy tailwinds, that I do not want to live in a wealthy city, in the wealthiest country, where people are so violently cast aside. I have also been thinking, audaciously, that I would like to live for a long time, and that some time very soon I would like to have a child. I do not want to raise a child in a country where people are chomping at the bit to "catch" one another at their worst, to expose human beings as fallible. I had thought I could find a comfortable place within this and, I admit, maybe even profit off it, but the mental gymnastics, the soul death required to feel comfortable, to accept these terms as the cost of doing business, is too high a price to pay.

Don't ask me where I'm going.

If you live where June lives—where I live, though it sometimes still feels strange saying so—in Inglewood, you can't avoid La Brea and Centinela without a little bit of work. I became an expert at it, familiar with side streets, back streets, short and long detours. I skipped certain invites altogether to never have to drive by if I could help it. Because every time, without fail, Bronze and Brook would spot it out the window and sing, "Momma, that's Auntie Nakia's restaurant." It was a cheerful singsong voice, and they were—are—innocent children, but it drove me crazy. I had to say, "Oh yeah, it sure is," and push down the sob that rose in my throat. They understood that she was gone, but not at first that she was gone-gone, even though I'd tried my best to help them understand. And then by the time they got a little older and definitely understood, it had become a kind of game, or a habit, to say it when we drove past, with no more thought put into it than holding their breath in a tunnel or making *beep-boop* sounds every time they spotted a robotic meter maid or buzzing like bees when they saw a drone overhead.

The other day I was listening to one of Monique's podcast episodes. I listened to her brag about the virtues of abandoning America for the umpteenth time, mostly just to hear her voice and the snippet of a giggle from Ann, her baby, which is in the intro music, and I forgot to take one of the other ways to get to La Cienega. This is never a problem on the other side of town, because that second restaurant location never reopened.

It was Tuesday at eight thirty a.m., and there was already a line of people waiting outside the door. I immediately saw it: Miguel had finally changed the restaurant's name to Nakia, like he always promised he would. A sexy neon purple sign. She would have liked that. Okay, she would have gone back and forth about whether it should have been with an apostrophe *s* on the end, because Black folks are just gonna make it possessive anyway, but she would've smiled.

Juanita and Conrad stopped coming to LA as much as they used to. They finally convinced CJ to sell the practice and move his family closer to them in New Jersey. A few months back, Jay, Conrad, and Juanita called me on three-way, offering me Nakia's house. Rent to own, they said, but the rent they quoted me was so low I knew they were only charging me the property tax. I said yes. I thought of what Nakia would say about Brook and Bronze scuffing up her hardwood floors. As soon as I got off the phone, I called Desiree on video and told her and we wept together, face-to-face.

Before Morris brings the boys back some Sundays, they stop at the restaurant for brunch. I know because the leftovers cram up my fridge. A whole extra meal sometimes, which I know is for me, but since he and the boys never say anything I tell June it must be for her. I know more or less what's on the menu because I still have that design account, still tinker with the website and collateral when needed. I'll have to do a big revamp for the new name.

I know that her picture, a portrait commissioned by Juanita and Conrad and done by an artist whom Jay knows, hangs on the wall opposite the front door. Jay texted me a photo. It's big, almost half the wall, like she was an eighteenth-century aristocrat or maybe one of those Waspy ladies John Singer Sargent painted. She stands in front of her Jeep, her chef's coat half unbuttoned, face crowned by that curly golden fro. There are crates of vegetables by her feet—she's in Chuck Taylors, of course—and the sky is one of those LA sunset stunners. Washed-out clouds, pink and purple stripes.

Two middle-aged women sit on a bench in a park. For decades, many locals called it Malcolm X Park, but new arrivals to the District seem intent on leaving Brother Malcolm out of it, on reverting its name to Meridian Hill. The two women sit at odd angles, neither in a posture of ease. But they sit, and they talk. They do not look like sisters from afar. Up close, they have twin sets of hands. Long fingers, delicate joints. Age has handled them similarly, evident in the eyes and the edges of their hair, which curl up gray. The weather is fine for sitting outside, the sun not yet a menace.

To the left of these women, closer to the staircase and cascading waterfall, a pair of teenaged sisters—actual twins—observe them, curious. It is like witnessing a birth, the miracle of arrival when before there had been nothing, except today the newborn is their auntie, nearly fifty years old but brand-new to them all the same. They wait, these younger sisters, for their moment of introduction.

PART FOUR

I am about to teach myself
to fly slip slide flip run
fast as I need to
on one leg

—June Jordan, "I guess it was my destiny to live so long"

2027

The New Old Bridge

She was dressed stupidly, that much was clear early on. Leggings with fat reflective stripes up the side of them would make it impossible to blend in for long. The sun would not set for hours, but it was already dark as dusk, the city covered by a smog-fog combination that the weather apps were simply calling a "lid," having run out of buzzy ways to describe worse-than-usual air. A small crossbody bag held her phone, wallet, and keys. The only pocket on her person the loose tunnel of her hoodie, into which she jammed her hands, because it was colder out than she'd understood at home. At home she'd woken up like most everyone else in the city, the county. Her phone screaming at 7:07 a.m. with a compulsory notification:

EMERGENCY ALERT

THE LA COUNTY SHERIFF'S DEPARTMENT WILL BE ENFORCING
THE COUNTY CURFEW FROM 12 P.M. TODAY
TO 5 A.M. TOMORROW FOR ALL LOS ANGELES COUNTY

Which meant that everything downtown must still be happening. Which meant that in certain pockets of the Westside, of Mid City, everything must still be happening, too. Before yesterday she had not received this kind of alert, the curfew kind, since the summer of 2020, when the alerts—which areas were off-limits between what hours—had possessed her phone so frequently and nonsensically that she'd turned the thing off, depended on her car radio and TV news to tell her where protests had sprung up and in what brutal ways they were being shut down. She had gone out back then, too, despite what her phone commanded, and for the same reason: people needed to eat. Back then she'd helped Miguel and Delia and Stacey the Man fulfill delivery orders, and if a cop had questioned her, tried to "enforce the curfew," Nakia would have said she was essential, would have reminded them that food delivery was deemed a necessary part of locked-down life. But no one had asked. This time, this morning, as soon as her phone quieted down, she called Delia, her Juan Gabriel–loving onetime prep lead who now managed the North La Brea location, and Miguel. They agreed with her that it was best to close both restaurants for the day, not for fear of something happening to the restaurants, but for fear of something happening to an employee as they made their way in.

Still, people needed to eat, and there were plenty of hours before curfew, if it would even be enforced. So here she was, dressed stupidly, worrying about feeling cold. Today, Arielle and one of the other regular volunteers, L., had set up a food and supply station about a ten minutes' walk from the Little Tokyo Metro station, out of the way of Skid Row. The four of them were not attempting to hand out food there or on Bunker Hill, or at Pershing Square, precisely because everyone else was, or wasn't. They all had heard about and seen videos of even regular staffers of the Mission being harassed by police these past few days, not to mention getting caught up in the fray of demonstrations turned into confrontations. But if volunteers were being scared off, and businesses were closed downtown, including the major grocery stores, what would people eat? It was no good sitting at home, feeling helpless, Arielle had texted them.

Water, sandwiches, protein bars, beanies, hand warmers. They did this all the time, Arielle pointed out, so why not now? No one would see three middle-aged Black women handing out food and think trouble.

Nakia hadn't been to—been through, rather—this particular part of downtown in months, and never on foot. The closest she'd been was to the

Arts District with Jay last month for the opening of a group show featuring a few artist friends. That there were large encampments so close to that fancy gallery and restaurant wasn't surprising, but she wondered how she'd never known it before.

"Way more tents over here than usual," L. said, as if she knew what Nakia was thinking. "Folks musta been trying to find someplace more quiet."

It was the third day of protests, unrest that social media had already dubbed the Bunker Hill Uprisings, no matter that it had come to include pockets as far west as Venice. The spark was the same as most sparks, historically: the police. And like most contemporary sparks, it spread via video shares. An unhoused, one-legged woman in a wheelchair filmed the police standing by as her tent and all of her belongings burned. They told her to stop filming, and when she refused, one cop knocked the phone out of her hand and another knocked her body out of her wheelchair, onto the ground. She had been going Live, and somehow the recording continued after her fall. Her name was Nancy Hurtado.

Perhaps because the world was now one where unspeakable violence had been made consumable, where carnage had been caught on camera ad nauseum, in 4K even, the relatively analog experience of seeing nothing but an overhead streetlight and hearing off-screen horrors jolted something in viewers.

HURTADO: [*panting*] Gimme my phone back.

OFFICER 1: Move against the wall with your hands up.

HURTADO: I can't *move* without using my hands, pendejo.

[a muffled thud]

OFFICER 2: Hey, hands up!

[a sound like metal hitting concrete, the whirring spin of a wheel going nowhere, shoes scuffling]

HURTADO: Wait! Wait! Please.

> *[Her voice gets smaller. A large gust of wind, or the whoosh of a fire roaring. Glass breaking, more shoes scuffling.]*

The video ends.

Hours later a body was found in the charred rubble of a tent, someone's home. A little over five feet tall, female. The body lacked a left tibia, fibula, and foot. And so it began.

The media reported that groups of mostly young, rowdy unhoused men were not only destroying their own encampments, setting tents ablaze, but destroying and looting nearby stores, too. Depending on one's algorithms, social media told a different story. Local vigilantes and groups of people who called themselves DM, for "digital militia," had driven north from Orange County, south from Bakersfield, or just a few miles from Beverly Hills, and were confronting the unhoused and their allies—who, to Nakia's relief and pride, were numerous—wherever they found them. Leftist activists on social media, including a few friendly with Monique, insisted that some of these vigilantes were cops themselves, or agitators—mercenaries, some called them—hired to make the unhoused population look out of control, to make those with homes feel threatened. There seemed to be some truth to this.

The day before yesterday, a so-called militia member had laughed gleefully in front of a row of RVs ablaze along the 110 North while streaming to his followers online. The tower of fire could be seen from the balcony of Jay's condo, where Nakia slept about half the days of every week. The fire was close enough that they heard the occasional explosion, which they'd then heard again on the livestream a few seconds later. A neighbor had sent the link to Jay. Nakia had an uncanny feeling watching the livestream and the real thing side by side. Instead of real life helping to contextualize and make tactile the virtual, the reverse had happened, so much so that the next morning, upon waking, when Nakia saw posts of people alleging the footage had been faked, she had asked Jay if the fire actually happened. To which Jay responded, "Feels too crazy to be true, but what doesn't these days?" A day and a half later and they still had not heard whether anyone had been inside the RVs.

The police did not seem to care about any of this vigilante mayhem—no surprise to Nakia—but it didn't matter what the police thought. It mattered what the public thought, and trying to track which way the blame was being volleyed in the court of public opinion was like watching very good tennis.

Still, people needed to eat.

"Supposed to drop to thirty-nine degrees tonight," Arielle said now. "Thirty-nine here and only a low of forty-two in Chicago. Fucking crazy. It's this 'lid' or whatever they're calling it."

She opened a jumbo package of hand warmers with her teeth, heaped them into a basket. In recent years the number of people found dead outdoors per winter night in LA had ballooned to forty. Nakia followed the city controller online, and the frequently updated map of who was found where let her know that save for tiny pockets of the Palisades, the Hollywood Hills, and Brentwood, people died of hypothermia everywhere in the county, at a higher rate than anywhere else in the country. Nakia opened a box of gloves and beanies and stacked those on the table, too.

It was quiet on this side of downtown. Too quiet, Nakia thought. All these tents but no commotion, no radios, no shit-talking, no spats. Nobody spilling out onto the sidewalk, either, everyone's belongings tucked away tight inside.

"Who's even over here right now?" she asked. "Feeling crowded and empty at the same time."

L., closest to her, looked up from where she stooped to open a box.

"They're either laying low here or getting active somewhere else," she said. She was older than Arielle, closer to fifty, and she'd driven a Big Blue Bus for the city of Santa Monica for over twenty years. The kind of quiet person who people read as standoffish when in reality she was extremely shy. She wore an oversize camo-print puffer coat over her stocky, muscular body, jeans, and sensible, thick-soled walking shoes. She had a large port-wine stain on her neck and chin that looked like a tattoo until closer inspection. Over the years that they'd known each other, they'd only really interacted while volunteering. Nakia often caught herself trying to get L. to laugh, a challenge which time had not made easier.

"People are here," Arielle said. "We'll go knock on doors in a few, when folks feel warmed up."

By "folks" Nakia knew Arielle meant only her. All these years later and Nakia could still be awkward when she had to knock on "doors": tent flaps, cardboard, the odd actual door, salvaged or purchased and fitted to sheet metal or plywood or corrugated plastic for added security. It used to make her feel guilty, unfit for the work of helping others, the way she instantly morphed into some weird imitation of a city agent. Her voice suddenly higher, overly polite and inquisitive, her eyes not knowing where to look. Then, after a few efforts at canvassing for candidates she supported, she'd realized that it wasn't interfacing with the poor that was the problem; it was the inherent vulnerability of stopping by a stranger's home unannounced.

"I'll start whenever," she offered.

Around nine thirty, the sun came out for about ten minutes but did nothing to warm up the day. In an hour they'd gone from convincing folks to come out to having to be careful they didn't run out of food. People had started showing up from wherever they'd been lying low, and some had walked several blocks. There were more teens on this side of town compared to where CBH usually set up shop. Shy, flighty teens presumably flying solo who refused to make eye contact; brazen, ironic pairs of teens who couldn't be bothered to say thank you—and who could blame them? They were children. More than anyone they shouldn't have had to live outside. Nakia wanted to impart a specific, hopeful message to them but she didn't know exactly what she should say. She settled for giving them extra snacks. One guy, maybe twenty years old, with an ancient Bluetooth hooked onto his ear, had lunged quickly toward where an older man was standing in front of the table. The younger man took three extra sandwiches from the stack behind the older. Arielle, muscles visible even under her track suit, stepped in. "That's a good idea, bro," she said. "You never know what you'll need when things start popping off like this." She smiled, turned back to the table and gave an extra sandwich to the older man, too.

Just before the food ran out, Irma arrived like a favorite character on a sitcom. Nakia hadn't seen her in an almost a decade, not since shortly after Miguel came back from Chiapas. She still wore her signature pink Raiders hat—now bedazzled with rhinestones—and a velour track suit to match. She carried only one elderly black Dachshund now, Hielo, if Nakia recalled correctly, and had no front teeth, but with her mouth closed, with her eyes smiling, she looked unchanged. Skinny as all get out and constantly in motion. She walked right to the front of the line and no one protested.

"Oh, it's my friends! My lesbian frieeeends," she sang with her head thrown back, which made the three of them laugh. "You girls are so brave, I love you."

"Where you been, Irma?" Nakia asked.

She realized, by her own giddy relief, that some part of her must have presumed Irma to be dead.

"Where *you* been?"

"In Inglewood. I still got a restaurant there. And one near La Brea and Pico."

"Okay, boss lady, I see you." Irma spoke English like someone's Black auntie, which always tickled Nakia.

"For real, though," Arielle said. "Where you been?

"Girl, you know them fools from ICE tried to deport me? They had me locked up for two months, but this program hooked me up with a good lawyer, and shoot, he made *them* look dumb. I got me a room off Spring now," she said. "Mostly been in there since the pandemic. I got me a job cleaning up a store, too. But it's too crazy on Spring right now, me and Hielo had to get outta there. I'm over here with my girlfriend until everything calms down."

She waved to her left but no one was there. Must have been someone in a tent. Irma grabbed a beanie and a pair of gloves.

"Y'all promise me not to be out here after it gets dark. Oh, I guess it's already dark, ha-ha. You know what I mean. I know y'all are some tough ladies, but these people? These people done lost they minds."

They packed up, moving faster than usual, speaking only when necessary. They had not discussed it, but it was nonetheless agreed that if they could not make it all the way home before curfew, then they should at least not be in the vicinity of downtown. Nakia helped L. fold up the long table and shove it into the back of Arielle's van. All three had driven separately.

In order to go west, in the direction they all lived, they had to go east a little, over to Santa Fe then to Washington, which they'd traverse together for several miles before going their separate ways. The police detours on the freeway were plentiful and swiftly changing, so it made more sense to try the streets. Unless, as Arielle had heard from a woman in the line, they'd cordoned off some kind of buffer zone around USC.

L. said that was just a rumor.

"They might lock down the campus, but you can always drive past. They haven't done more than that since '92."

L. was old enough to really remember those uprisings. Nakia thought she remembered being sequestered in the house and smelling the smoke from the nearby Fedco store, on fire, waft through the window of her bedroom. But who could trust that a memory was really your own when certain stories are repeated so much within a family that everyone takes ownership of them? She of course remembered 2020. Early during that week, the three of them plus Arielle's wife, Tameka, had stood on a corner on Skid Row and distributed food without incident. Tameka had been five months pregnant and triple-masked. Now she and Arielle had a seven-year-old and a two-year-old, and uprisings were no longer once-in-a-generation events.

Van packed, Nakia walked back to her Jeep. When she unlocked her door, she noticed tendrils of pale orange bougainvillea had snaked their way from the side of an abandoned building all the way up a telephone pole. They were the same color as the bougainvillea encroaching on her garden at home, via the back wall she shared with her neighbors, the Freemans. She'd had plans for that wall, to vine up some blackberries and maybe put in a few birds of paradise, but Jay had encouraged her to make peace with the foreign flowers. "That is a top-five bougainvillea color," she said. "I've only seen it like a handful of times." Leave it to Jay to make the case for natural beauty via statistics. She was right, Nakia thought now. Still, she could squeeze some jasmine in the mix easily enough.

The front of the truck reflected light in such a way that it was impossible to know if a human manned it. And "tank" was a more accurate word.

"Exit the vehicle," a voice boomed. "Do not bring your belongings."

Nakia felt like fleeing, but she tucked her phone and keys into her hoodie and exited.

Arielle had led them to Santa Fe as planned. They had not gone two full blocks before encountering this vehicle. The color of stainless steel, a lane and a half wide and as tall as two pickups, with something slanted on its roof that might have been a solar panel, or maybe a satellite. No way to see inside. Out on the street, Arielle grabbed Nakia's right hand, and L., shy no longer, grabbed her left. It was instinct, but they should have known better.

"Hands up. Keep your hands up and walk."

The vehicle crept toward them, and they understood they were to turn around and walk back up Santa Fe. It stayed close behind, setting a brisk pace. Nakia, shorter than Arielle and L., had to trot occasionally to keep up. They walked this way for around twenty minutes, over a mile, Nakia guessed. If only she could access a human being, she could explain herself, they could explain themselves. People needed to eat! She wanted to text Jay but did not dare reach into her pocket. If they were indeed being arrested, she'd get a phone call. She was not as well known as some of her peers in the restaurant space, despite her award nomination, but Black cops, and a good number of Latino cops, knew Safe House. Early on, first Conrad then Miguel had helped her understand that a strange but necessary part of her work entailed making sure cops knew who she was, that they cared about her business. So many free meals over the years, and for what? There was currently no human present to even put a name to her face.

They arrived at the car on-ramp for the Sixth Street Bridge and paused. Santa Fe was blocked up ahead by yet another of these giant vehicles. Nakia, Arielle, and L. looked at one another instead of in front of them, instead of behind.

"Keep walking," one of the vehicles said, or both of them, it was hard to tell.

So, they walked, right up the ramp. Nakia had seen online that protestors had briefly sieged the First Street Bridge the night before last. They'd sung songs and locked arms and brought tents along. They announced their plans to bed down for the night on the bridge, but a swarm of cops on foot and bicycle had overwhelmed them, split them right down the middle and pushed, dragged, and kicked them off the bridge. The cops didn't want people on bridges except for when they wanted them on bridges.

"They're probably kettling us with a larger group of people," Arielle said. "They're gonna make us walk all the way to Boyle Heights, get our info, then let us go." The tone of her voice almost sounded like she believed this.

"Yeah, and then they're gonna tow all our cars for parking bad," L. chimed in.

Nakia couldn't come up with any way to make light of things. She was sweating, panting. Her feet hurt from the walk, and the ramp up to the bridge was steeper than it appeared in a car.

The bridge was almost seven years old, which meant it was and wasn't new, depending on the Angeleno. To Nakia it was still the new Sixth Street Bridge, which had opened to much fanfare and feigned civic frustration. Those first few days, it seemed all of the Eastside had turned out to claim the bridge as theirs. Lowriders hit switches on it; a barber set up a chair and shaped fades on it. Somebody got married on it, and a folclórico group staged a thirty-person costumed dance recital on it. Now, newness worn off, it was just a bridge again, no water underneath unless it rained to flooding in the city. Most times, like today, down below was barren concrete, part of the giant storm channel called the LA River. An image of them being pushed over the side the way James Baldwin had written about French police shoving Algerians into the Seine crossed her mind. She let it pass. People needed to eat. They had done nothing wrong.

Nakia tripped on nothing. Nerves, she thought. She looked down and noticed her shoe was untied. How ill-equipped she was to be under police orders. Assuming these vehicles did indeed contain police; her brain wouldn't process any alternatives. She stooped to tuck her laces in, thinking that would be quicker than tying them, and the voice from the vehicles boomed,

"KEEP MOVING." Her mouth, suddenly dry and tingling. She had not been properly afraid until then. Until then she had not been singled out.

As they arrived at the top of the bridge, they joined a small group of people who had been rounded up just as they had. Nakia recognized the young guy with the old Bluetooth in his ear. She was glad no teens had been caught, nor Irma and Hielo. There were eight in this group, all men, all Black save for one heavyset guy with a "Hecho en Mexico" T-shirt and a long beard.

"Oh damn," the man with the Bluetooth said. "They grabbing folks for passing out food, too? We're fucked."

"Shut up, Jacques," the man with the long beard said. "They didn't even grab us, fool, we walked here."

Before Jacques could respond, the robotic voice from the vehicles commanded: "SIT DOWN." Everyone quickly dropped to the concrete. It seemed to Nakia that whoever was in the vehicles had turned the volume up on the PA, or else the acoustics on the bridge were very different than on the street. She tried kneeling, then squatting, finally settling onto her butt, each leg stretched out in front of her. Her thin leggings allowed the cold of the concrete to reach her thighs, which burned from the walking and climbing. The vehicles remained close by, inscrutable. Nothing to do but wait to see what was what.

Two things happened. First, those of them on the bridge with cell phones received a compulsory alert. The same loud, siren-adjacent tone as the one that morning.

EMERGENCY ALERT

DUE TO A DEVELOPING SITUATION THE
LAPD WILL BE ENFORCING THE FOLLOWING CITY CURFEW FROM
11:30 A.M. TODAY TO 5 A.M. TOMORROW.
AREAS UNDER CURFEW INCLUDE ALL PUBLIC STREETS BETWEEN THE
110, 101, 10, 60, AND 5 FREEWAY INTERCHANGES (CLICK HERE FOR
DETAILED MAP).
INDIVIDUALS FOUND IN VIOLATION OF CURFEW
MAY BE SUBJECT TO ARREST.

It was now 12:17 p.m.

"Motherfuckers," Arielle muttered.

A wave of grumbling passed through the small group. "They're kettling us," someone, a skinny brown-skinned man with a unibrow, said. How was everyone but Nakia familiar with this term? When the man didn't get a sufficient reaction he said, "They're gonna corral us on this bridge then exterminate us like bugs."

This got people going. Another Black man, late fifties, maybe, with freckled skin and one fat, waist-length, sun-bleached dreadlock, shouted, "They'll have to kill me first!" Which in a different context would have made Nakia laugh. He tried to stand up, but the person next to him pulled him back into a crouch by the hem of his jacket. The vehicles remained still.

When faced with a situation over which she had little control, Nakia reached for facts, facts related to the situation at hand, preferably, but any solid, indisputable, top-quality fact would suffice. It was a trick Jay had learned in therapy and shared with her. Jay, who probably wasn't even worried about where she was yet, early as it was. Unless she'd gotten the same insane LAPD notification, in which case Nakia hoped Jay was in the process of tracking her down. Facts. Her mind would run over and over a fact like a thumb on a small, smooth pebble, noting contours but disinterested in improving upon anything, changing anything. No need to improve upon facts, and no need to obsess over that which you could not prove.

The Sixth Street Bridge was actually a viaduct, and it was 3,500 feet long, 45 feet wide. Nakia repeated these facts to herself as her body temperature regulated from the walk and climb, as she began to register the chill in the air again. After a few minutes, it felt easier to breathe.

"You know," L. said to her, "they're probably just trying to separate everyone seeing as how—"

She was interrupted by the second thing that happened. The bridge began to bounce, not high up and down like a basketball dribble, but low and short like the way a good smack can make a drumskin vibrate. Nakia sat up on her knees and placed both palms on the concrete. The bouncing, now accompanied by rumbling, was increasing. Nakia was comforted by the fact that from afar the bridge would not have appeared to be bouncing at all.

Voices on top of voices, some yelling curse words, but most making wordless noises of fear. And footfalls, hundreds it seemed. A stampede's worth of feet. Everyone in her group shot up to standing; it made no sense to be trampled sitting down. Over the crest of the bridge came a mass of people, somewhere between fifty and seventy, Nakia guessed. More women this time, one who carried a baby in a sling across her chest. It was not immediately clear who lived outside and who lived indoors. Filthy cargo pants, pristine pullovers, Nikes, bare feet, limping and sprinting they came toward Nakia and her tiny contingency of the trapped, who had shuffled over to the northern edge of the bridge to make way. An outrageous proportion of these new people were Black, but everyone else was represented, too.

"STOP," the vehicles said.

And like a game of freeze tag, everyone stopped. A woman, Blasian, with a big, bushy ponytail and an overstuffed pink mini backpack, stopped a few inches from Nakia, her chest heaving. Those behind her stopped too. She scanned the opposite end of the bridge from whence she'd come, spotted the vehicles.

"There's trucks on this side, too," she yelled. Her voice was clear and strong; it echoed off the bottom of the river. Panicked murmurs spread back behind her. Who knows why she chose to lock eyes with Nakia, but she did, and Nakia saw that she had a shiner, right under her left eye socket, as if she'd taken a recent hit.

"They're kettling us!" she shouted. To which Nakia mouthed, "I know," but no sound came out.

"SIT DOWN," the vehicles said. This time the command came in surround sound, as whatever number of vehicles that had chased the newcomers onto the bridge joined in. Everyone complied.

The new crowd turned out to be around forty people, which brought their total to just over fifty. There was a slight wind, and the added weight on the bridge was helping it to sway slightly, a sensation Nakia's stomach disliked. The woman with the pink backpack, Lisa, wanted to know how the smaller group had ended up on the bridge, and Arielle told her, with Jacques chiming in where he could.

"Wait, so you guys weren't even part of a direct action?" she asked Arielle. "What the fuck."

"I mean, apparently now even passing out food qualifies as a direct action, right?"

"Yeah, I guess so," Lisa said. "Still, that's so awesome. Y'all are brave."

Anytime someone called Nakia brave—for speaking out against double standards in the restaurant business, for considering a third restaurant location, maybe in Compton, she interpreted that as them calling her stupid. If not stupid then naïve. Bravery implied a full assessment of the risks and a decision to act anyway, and Nakia rarely considered her decisions to be risky. "Brave," to her, suggested she'd missed something, failed to fully grasp the stakes. It was the easiest way to make her feel unsure.

"How were y'all in the action?" Nakia felt embarrassed by how stiff the words sounded in her mouth. She had only a slight idea what she was asking.

Lisa took her phone out of her backpack and turned it on, looked at it, then put it back. No signal, like everyone else.

"There's more protest sites today than yesterday, and yesterday was more than the day before. Do you guys remember when the LAPD put out a study after the George Floyd Uprisings talking about how they weren't prepared to respond to multiple actions at the same time if they were spread across the city?"

L. nodded yes. Nakia and Arielle said no.

"Well, we figured it was time to test out if that was true. There's a huge encampment at Hollenbeck Park right under the 5, so a big group of us went over there this morning. I brought my RV. Seemed like we were going under the radar, just playing music and having a teach-in, until around eleven."

"Then a bunch of pigs on bikes rolled up and started fucking with us," a younger Asian guy with a yellow bandana over his nose and mouth chimed in. "They started pushing us out the park and moving us north."

"Yeah," Lisa said. "And next thing we know the ones on bikes are gone and four of these robo-trucks bear down on us like steamrollers, pushing us toward the bridge. Some people in the rear got a little fucked up trying to avoid getting run over. Luckily somebody had a first aid kit with them."

"Jesus Christ," Arielle said.

"Is anybody actually inside the trucks?" Nakia asked. She had begun to suspect they were unmanned, or remote-controlled, like drones.

"There's families in that camp," Lisa said. "Kids, old people, lotta wheelchairs. Who knows what they did with everyone else."

Nakia noticed that Lisa's breath had become visible. Little puffs of condensation accentuated each word. Lisa seemed unfazed. She turned back to her group, where people were complaining and despairing and full of righteous anger. After about a minute of looking them over, she began to sing:

Which side are you on,
oh, which side are you on?

It was easy enough to catch onto, one of those call-and-response patterns recognizable to anyone who'd spent time in a certain kind of church. Arielle joined in, as did Jacques, who had a beautiful alto, and finally Nakia herself. L. did not sing; she sat staring forward, tears rolling down her cheeks. Nakia put a hand on her shoulder. Who could blame her for despairing? Nakia herself had only wanted to help Arielle do this thing that she understood to be of central importance to her friend. Her mind had not fully caught up to the rest of what was happening. Of being a protestor, somehow an agitator, of being at the whim of giant anonymous robo-trucks, of being trapped a fatal distance above hard, unforgiving concrete. She had never thought it practical to put her body on the line for someone else's. Maybe if she had children, and sure, she had come to really care about January's children, her brother CJ's children. She could see herself stepping in between them and harm's way if needed. But imperiling herself for an idea, or for people she did not know personally? Conrad and Juanita had never stressed that as a goal. Only that Jesus himself had been required to make that kind of sacrifice precisely so no one else would have to. Plus, Nakia's ancestor Ann, no last name, had already put her body on the line.

Okay, yes, she would also put her body on the line for Jay. She would give her a kidney, a nice healthy chunk of her liver, or as many juicy sluices of bone marrow necessary, if ever necessary. Nakia was not sure when she'd been disabused of her assumption that Jay did not fully perceive her, but it had been several years since she'd let go of that belief. Jay perceived her perfectly well; she just did not pass the kind of judgment based on her perceptions that Nakia had come to expect from other partners. An important distinction.

For the most part, people remained seated, or only stood up to stretch for seconds. An hour passed uneventfully. Twice, the urge to pee had tried to assert itself, and twice Nakia banished it to the back of her mind. Her heart had not stopped racing; impossible to self-regulate given the circumstances.

"Wait, I just remembered something," Jacques said. He was just a goofy kid, Nakia surmised; he'd told two actual knock-knock jokes within the past hour. She'd also determined that the Bluetooth speaker in his ear was some kind of prop. Jacques claimed to not own a phone.

"Where are the choppers and shit?" he wanted to know. "Like, where are the news stations? We should be on KTLA right now. They should be zooming in on Jorge's bald spot and butt crack right about now."

Jorge, the man with the long beard, flipped him off.

"The news is probably covering one of the other actions," Lisa said. "I guess that's the downside of having so many at one time."

"What the fuck is that smell?" Joon, the man in the yellow bandana, asked.

A loaded question, Nakia thought, considering so many among them had been deprived of regular access to water for so long, considering there were no bathrooms on this bridge. A moment later the smell in question caught up to her. Something burning.

"It's a fire from downtown," Arielle said.

"The fuck it is," Nakia said. "Look!"

To the east of the bridge and a little south, a huge black column of smoke rose.

"That's Hollenbeck!" someone yelled. "Our fucking park!"

Lisa jumped up, shouted, "We need to get loud!" She crouched down and fished around in her backpack. A small bullhorn! It seemed a miracle. Maybe they could grab the attention of someone, somewhere.

"It's time to get loud," Lisa said again. "They're burning down our community, one of the places we made home when we had no place to call home. Make some noise, let them know we're not going anywhere!"

The people shouted with her, chanted. Clouds of condensation like dialogue bubbles in the twilight. The position of the bridge, with the concrete river below and the mountains to one side, high-rises to the other, caused a great echo, something Nakia thought could surely be heard for over a mile. They stamped their feet, which made the bridge bounce and Nakia's legs feel alive again.

From behind the sierras a helicopter appeared, as if they had indeed conjured it. "Helicopter" seemed insufficient for the size of it. Huge, big-bellied, and loud, it seemed to have trouble moving quickly, and instead coasted through the air like an eagle. Hunter green and cream, not police colors.

"The national guard!" Jorge shouted.

"National guard?" Jacques said. "Are they cops or not cops?" He squinted at the helicopter with his hand shading his eyes as if there was sun out.

"Depends on their orders," Lisa muttered. She craned her neck toward it as it lumbered through the sky. It cast a long, dark shadow as it passed the bridge on its way east.

All fifty-something heads—save for the sleeping baby—tracked the helicopter as it circled the area where the smoke billowed up from the park. It retreated northbound, then doubled back and dumped a stream of water from its belly. Cheers from her neighbors on the bridge. Nakia had seen planes and helicopters like these drop water over wildfires on TV, but it had always seemed so pointless, the fire raging for acres on end and the water a literal drop in the infernal bucket. This was different; the smoke turned from black to white instantly. There was something almost soothing about witnessing it. Technology working as it should.

Joon was the only person not elated.

"Everybody's shit gonna be soaked now," he said.

"Better soaked than scorched," Lisa said. Nakia wondered if Lisa's RV had also gone up in flames, and how much an RV cost these days.

The overall consensus on her side of the bridge was that this was a triumph, a rare mercy, and as soon as they got off the bridge everyone—including Nakia, Arielle, and L.—promised to pitch in to figure out what could be salvaged.

The helicopter made another wide turn, almost graceful now with some of its weight expelled, then at double speed it headed west again, toward the bridge. When it was nearly over them it opened its hatch once more and unloaded the remainder of its cargo.

Later reports, the ones that took the Guard's word for it, would say that this second discharge was due to computer error, that the aircraft unintentionally dropped thousands of gallons on fifty souls without so much as a single umbrella to protect them.

A fact: There are several huge self-filling water tanks on top of various peaks in the Santa Monica Mountains. Water-carrying aircraft can use these to refill when fighting wildfires. On average they hold around fifty thousand gallons each. Nakia remembered this fact from an old NPR episode she'd heard, and tried to hold on to it as the water pummeled her. She had never felt a bullet, but this felt like bullets, like something hot piercing her skin, not something cold. There didn't seem to be individual drops of water but a solid mass of it, hard enough to bruise or worse. People surely screamed but she didn't hear them. She only heard the sound of the water slapping people's skin then crashing to the ground. Perhaps foolishly, she looked up. The aircraft was already on its way back to the mountains. Three minutes after that it was gone.

"Nakia, sit down," Arielle said.

She hadn't realized she was standing. Must have been on reflex as the water fell. She wasn't the only one. About twenty people stood now, wringing out clothes, cursing the sky. What was the point of sitting down now, anyway? They'd already been attacked. She lifted one knee to her chest and held it, then dropped it and picked up the other knee.

"SIT DOWN," the trucks warned, but Nakia and a few others—three others now—ignored them. Maybe she was in shock. She was strangely giddy and her whole body felt like it was vibrating. She looked south to where a cluster of mid-rise lofts and warehouses stood. She'd been to the members-only club over there with Jay before, though in large doses that crowd—"creatives"—still rubbed her the wrong way. Too bad the club and its rooftop would have to have been closed today given the curfew; some well-heeled member might have spotted them and come to their rescue.

"SIT DOWN. THERE WILL BE NO FURTHER WARNINGS." Somewhere deep in her heart there did beat a warning as urgent as the one the trucks intoned, but she couldn't access it. Now it was just her and the man with the single thick loc standing, a man Nakia felt she had now spent enough time in close proximity with to determine was mentally ill. Still, she and him were kindred in their indignation.

She felt a tug on the hem of her squelching hoodie—Arielle yanking her down. Okay, fine. She was being reckless. Too afraid to even be afraid of the right things. She turned to look beneath her before sitting. A ridiculous sound, like foam being shot out of a Nerf gun. A pain in the space between her left clavicle and shoulder like the quick jab of a needle, then a deeper, more complex pain radiating out from that. Screams from those close enough to witness it. Nakia, on the floor now, looked down at her body expecting to see blood, but her sweatshirt was still only soaked with water.

"Oh my God," L. said.

Nakia saw the fear in her eyes and felt sorry for being the cause of it.

"Are you okay?" Arielle said. "They fucking shot you, oh god."

Arielle picked up a solid rubber cylinder from the ground. It was the size of a tall shot glass and black. She handed it to Nakia.

"I don't want it," she said, and since Lisa reached out for it, Arielle handed it to her. Lisa closed her palm around it.

Pain shuttled up and down her arm, middle finger to shoulder, again and again and again. The pain seemed to need her fingers to dance, so she opened and closed her left hand, wiggled her fingers, tried to help the pain get to where it wanted to go.

"Are you bleeding?" Arielle asked. Her temporary panic had vanished; she was herself once again. "Let's take your hoodie off for a second."

This sounded like a bad idea to Nakia, so she shook her head. The only good ideas were to let her fingers dance and to stay seated no matter what. She had learned her lesson on that one. But Arielle and L. tugged on her hoodie, tried to coax her into lifting her arms. The left arm, the one with the dancing fingers, would not move. Even trying felt like attempting to bend one's forearm in the middle: a bone-rigid impossibility.

"I don't want this," she said, louder than she intended. L. and Arielle backed off.

"Leave her," Lisa said. She still held the rubber bullet in her closed hand. "If she's bleeding we'll find out one way or another."

Nakia closed her eyes and tried to still her heart. Her teeth chattered. She heard other people around her complaining of pain, of cold. In the grand scheme of police attacks she knew this one would rate relatively low—she was alive, after all—but she felt that this situation's particular cruelty was in the small scale of it. How much did a water drop from the National Guard cost, anyway? Too much to justify it being wasted on fifty people, she bet. And why were their cell phone signals blocked? The inability to call Jay or Juanita and report this violation to them was an added violation.

"There is no good and evil, only healed and broken," Conrad liked to say when Nakia was growing up. It was his way of priming her to forgive, to build instead of burn bridges. But this generosity, this grace, could it be extended to machines?

The sun had fully set, the cloud cover preventing all but the lowest sliver of pale pink to peek through before it was gone for good. Nakia had fallen asleep, for how long she wasn't sure. Now awake, her body shook with cold once more. No person currently on the Sixth Street Bridge was dry, except for the infant whose mother had, thankfully, a change of clothes with her that had not gotten soaked. Not a single person on the bridge was equipped to spend the night.

More people die of hypothermia in LA than in any other city, Nakia remembered. Not me, not me. The left hand still danced. Now the right one, freezing, did too.

"We won't survive the night out here," Lisa was saying to herself again and again. It was if they all possessed a single, desperate mind. Lisa's ponytail was still limp against her back. Nothing would dry off quickly at forty degrees.

Nakia could feel drowsiness pulling at her again and tried her best to fight it—didn't hypothermia entail the body slowing down, getting sluggish? If they could only stand up, if they could only run in place. From off the bridge, down back the way she'd come, she could hear sirens. In fact, sirens had been the only constant noise on an otherwise eerily quiet downtown day. She hoped no one was being put through what they were being put through. She had almost given up hope they would be rescued.

"You know what?" Jacques said. "They're just some souped-up police vans. They can't fucking kill us all."

His Bluetooth earpiece had been lost during the deluge, and without it Nakia noticed that a good portion of that earlobe was missing, almost as if someone had bitten it off.

"Shit," L. said, "maybe they could. You don't know what kinda machine gun they got rigged to pop out the top of those things like Obama's old car."

This was the most L. had said in some time. Since the water came down she had been methodically wringing out her puffer, bit by bit, in silence.

"I don't think anyone is in there, high key," Jacques said. "Like y'all were saying earlier, they can't be everywhere at once, so they sent these robo-trucks to babysit us."

"Yeah," Joon said. "but if there's nobody in there then they could be using any kind of algorithm they want to figure out how much force is appropriate."

"Shit," Jacques said, "I'd rather take my chances against the computer, then."

A debate ensued but it was too hard for Nakia to focus on it. An hour ago it had not seemed possible that they could die simply by sitting there, even drenched, but the human body was more fragile than was easily appreciated. Once her second hand had started dancing from the cold it seemed likely that more of her body would resist her control moving forward. But the human body was also strong, resilient. And there were so many human bodies huddled on that bridge.

A jostle to her right side. Arielle, her mascara running down her face so that she looked like she'd been crying. Maybe she had. Arielle, always so kind.

"Are you good?" Arielle asked. "Are you gonna be okay to run?"

So, they had decided. Okay. It was either this or death by standstill. Dancing hands be damned, she could still use her legs.

Lisa, leader Lisa with her water-ruined bullhorn and iron resolve, wolf-whistled three times in a row. Everyone, Nakia included, raised to their feet. There were so many of them—why had they been afraid?

"SIT DOWN," the trucks chirped. No use. The crowd jogged forward, the bridge lightly bouncing with them. Making up the front as they were, Nakia could see that beyond the two trucks the street appeared empty, no bike cops, no squad cars, no foot patrols. They simply had to get past the trucks to the end of the bridge, then cut left or right to scatter, ideally back to their cars or at least somewhere to hide. Others on the bridge must have realized this, too, because they picked up speed in unison. Hard to run fast with one arm straight, its fingers dancing, but Nakia managed.

"YOU HAVE BEEN WARNED. PREPARE TO RECEIVE FIRE."

A different command than before. Whatever. The people yelled, defiant. Rubber bullets and something harder—an assortment of newly acquired "less-lethal" projectiles, they would discover later—shot forth from the trucks in a sweeping, horizontal arc, hitting people in the legs, the stomach, the groin. The older man with the long loc fell to the ground, but Jacques came up behind him, scooped him up under the armpits, and pulled him along. Nakia kept running, fast as she could until she reached the trucks, then—blessedly—past the trucks.

Just get to the bottom now. Arielle, still to her right, began running in a zigzag pattern when it became clear that the trucks could shoot from their rear as well. Nakia tried her best to do the same. Without eyes in the backs of their heads they couldn't anticipate the shots, but they could juke them as best they could. It seemed very important to Nakia not to look back. Had she deigned to turn around, she would have seen the trucks from the far side of the bridge bearing down on them, pelting the rear of the crowd at random, including the mother of that baby. Two stragglers, those who'd dropped to their knees for a second too long, would be crushed by Truck 17, as it would be identified upon decommission.

Just get to the bottom. Jacques and the older man had made it, were no longer in sight at the bottom of the bridge. Something whizzed by Nakia's ear, close enough to jostle her water-shrunken afro.

To the bottom. A rubber bullet in the small of her back. The trucks no longer shouted commands, they were too busy acting. She saw L. reach the bottom, deliberate for a half second, then go left, back toward their cars.

To the bottom. The problem was she was limping. Since when? Arielle was still at her side, and Nakia understood that she was holding her back. She swung her arm in an attempt to move faster. Soon they would be too far down the hill for the bullets to reach.

To the bottom. Shorter than a block. She could feel her heartbeat. Her own heart doing its one job. She must have slowed down because Arielle slowed, too. "Keep going," she told Arielle. Arielle, who had two kids waiting for her at home and would still probably be back out here feeding people within a week. Another projectile glanced off the bony protrusion behind Nakia's ear. The force of it made her jaw click, her eyes squeeze shut,but she shook her head and felt okay. A few blessed steps later, they reached the street.

They had done it. All of them. They had fought back, run past. They had been beaten but they prevailed. Together.

In Nakia's garden, what were once beds for fruits and vegetables became graves, festooned with weeds and rusted wire netting. The sweet purple basil was doomed, first too cold and then too hot. The mint lasted longer than it ought to have, but in a flash it gave up and went back to the earth. Clover covered all. The melon and squash spawned prodigiously, freakishly, and Arielle came to gather them, to distribute the food to the hungry before night things claimed them. No human set foot in the garden for many months after that.

The night things. Possums, raccoons, skunks, coyotes. Never all at once but in turns. Even a rat twice, when the berries came in, when the apricots came down. The night things ambled around and clambered through the garden, with no care for the care that had once been put into its design. They ate the easy pickings, trampled what disinterested them, came back night after night to make love, to fight, to see what was new.

The rosemary bush burst into flowers, powder blue and almost as fragrant as its lavender neighbor. Despite the strange, here-to-stay humidity in Inglewood, both of these herbs prevailed, grew shaggy, grew fat. The pale peach bougainvillea, boisterous throughout. Hummingbirds investigated each bloom. Off the back roof, in a rain gutter, mourning doves nested and cooed over the scene.

The cornstalks intended to thrive. On the southern end of the backyard they withered and bent and fell to the earth, and some of them, a miraculous handful of them, came back the next year, and the one after that. They competed with the sunflowers for height and won. They remembered that they were descended from wild grass and spread out some, grew multiple ears to a stalk.

This resurrected corn would be waiting for Desiree, who would be joined by Monique and January, when she returned. When she finally decided she was ready to come see about Nakia's garden. January and her children planned to make a home there, and a garden good for only night things would not be good for boys. Until then, the cornstalks bided their time. Their silks slipped from blonde to brunette, their sheaves the green of young limes. They waited. They bristled in the wind.

Acknowledgments

This novel of friendship, and my belief in the power of true friendship, was first inspired by the 51-year, soul-deep connection between my late mother, Francine Harper, and her best friend, Leisha Williams. The sisterhood of Charlene, Valerie, Francine, and Sharon made me who I am today, as did the love of my own siblings, Candice Coffey, Jordan Harmon, and Joy Flournoy. Thank you to my father, Marvin Flournoy, for being my most enthusiastic hype-man, and to my stepfather Bob Harper for being so steady.

A decade is a long time to work on a book, or no time at all, depending on whom you ask. I am grateful to the organizations that helped me take the time I needed, including the National Endowment for the Arts, the Dorothy and Lewis B. Cullman Center for Scholars and Writers at the New York Public Library, and the Mary Ellen Von Der Heyden fellowship in fiction at the American Academy in Berlin.

My agent, the brilliant, legendary Ellen Levine, never rushed me to write a word, and never had a doubt that what I eventually wrote would be worth the wait. Thank you, Ellen, and thank you to her assistants over the years: Alexa Stark, Martha Wydysh, Audrey Crooks, Lauren Champlin, and Miles Temel. Thank you to my editor, Rakia Clark, and to the entire Mariner team: Tavia Kowalchuk, Eliza Rosenberry, Ivy Givens, Kathleen Cook, Mumtaz Mustafa, Lisa Glover, and Jen Overstreet.

Thank you to the generous friends who read all manner of manuscripts in various stages of completion and coherence, for offering the feedback I needed to hear—Emma Borges-Scott, Justin Torres, Brit Bennett, and my other brother, Vinson Cunningham. Thank you to Yahdon Israel for being Yahdon Israel. Thank you to Roberto Suro, my fellow Berlin Prize fellow, for talking to me about Bach.

Lan Samantha Chang and Alexander Chee are the teachers who still teach me, grown as I am. David Haynes and Diana Napier enriched my life by letting me be a part of their Black writer community, Kimbilio Fiction.

If it wasn't for my LA pomodoro cult holding me accountable, I may have never finished this book: Jade Chang, Aja Gabel, Jean Chen Ho, and Xuan Juliana Wang. And this would be an impoverished novel without decades of growth and laughter and love with my OG girlfriends, Sophia Williams Kapten, Vallery Lomas, and Zoé Zeigler; and my line sisters, Stephanie Parker, Kiana Butler, and Martinque Williams. Thank God for my framily, Roderick and Madia Scott, Bentley Kapten, and Aman Habtezghi. Robert Valadéz remains my king of sage advice and chisme sabroso.

To Ian, daily source of serenity and co-collaborator on my only perfect creation, "thank you" is insufficient, but it is the least I can say.